CUPID'S QUEST
SEASON ONE

CUPID'S QUEST SEASON ONE

NOT YOUR TYPICAL ROMANTIC COMEDY

PRU WARREN

Qui
Legit
Regit
Press
She who reads, rules

Copyright © 2023 by Pru Warren

All rights reserved.

No part of this book may be reproduced in any form or by any electronic or mechanical means, including information storage and retrieval systems, without written permission from the author, except for the use of brief quotations in a book review.

This is a work of fiction. Any references to historical events, real people, or real locales are used fictitiously. Other names, characters, places, and incidents are products of the author's imagination, and any resemblance to actual events or locales or persons, living or dead, is entirely coincidental.

Cover design by The Killion Group

Published by Qui Legit Regit Press
Alexandria, Virginia

ISBN 979-8-9883359-1-7

Discover other titles by Pru Warren at https://www.pruwarren.com/

070323wch

❦ Created with Vellum

To Julie Moore, whose warmth and charm inspired the character of Julie. I took a few liberties, but she became one of my favorite characters ever—and she gets her own Happily Ever After in season three!

And to Bunny, who backed my Kickstarter with a whopping ton o' cash and who I am proud to immortalize in this series as a behind-the-scenes mastermind...which definitely fits the inspiration.

CONTENTS

1.	Wink, Wink, Nudge, Nudge	1
2.	Refusing the Call	9
3.	Now Boarding	15
4.	What's Going On Here?	21
5.	Lights, Camera, Action	29
6.	A Mite Airish	38
7.	Zephyr, God of the West Winds	46
8.	The Bliss of Heat	54
9.	You Want Me to Wear What?	62
10.	On Thick Ice	70
11.	Water Sports	80
12.	The Scoop	91
13.	Out of the Frying Pan	96
14.	And into the Fire	105
15.	Lost in Translation	114
16.	Make It an Event	121
17.	Pharaohs in Black Tie	127
18.	Heart of the Arrow	134
19.	The Land Down Under	142
20.	Solar Radiation	150
21.	Down Under's Down Under	159
22.	In the Sandbox	170
23.	My, How Puzzling	179
24.	Living with Disappointment	188
25.	Bonjour à Paris	199
26.	In the Court of the Sun King	207
27.	May I Have This Dance?	219
28.	Rules and Reveals	230
29.	A Pull to the East	237
30.	Off-Camera	248
31.	The Proposal	260
32.	Japanese Anime	270
33.	Tokyo Page by Page	278

34. Put a Ring on It	287
35. Messing with My Head	294
36. Sky-High Hijinx	300
37. Breath of Life	311
38. Temple of the Moon	320
39. The Family Car Trip	330
40. Straight Talk	339
41. Meet the Fam	351
42. No Matter What	359
Epilogue	367
Tempting Note	372
Bliss & Giggles	373
Acknowledgments	375
About the Author	377
Also by Pru Warren	379

1

WINK, WINK, NUDGE, NUDGE

The woman at the *Cupid's Quest* registration table knew who I was before I said my name. That was unnerving.

"Jocelyn Markey O'Neil! Come right on in!"

Jeez. How did she even know my middle name? "Um, call me Joss. Please."

"Oh, I know it!" She had short, dyed-green hair and wore a casual outfit of jeans and a plaid shirt that didn't mix with her high-octane energy. "See? It says Joss right here on your name tag. You'll want to put that on right now. And here's your contract, and you can give me your luggage and put your phone in this baggie and I'll hold it for you and I'm Julie and I'm Shout's PA. If you have any questions, you can just ask me, okay?"

This bewildering flood of information swamped me. I had a million questions, like *Are you sure you want me as a contestant?* and, *Who's Shout?* and, *What does PA stand for in this particular universe?* but she was moving efficiently through a process, and I wasn't going to stand in her way.

"I have to give you my phone?" I asked the question even as

I surrendered my lifeline. There went my schedule, my calendar, my contacts. My usually-abundant confidence, She zipped up the bag and wrote my name in large black letters.

"Oh, just for now—you'll get it back. No social media in the auditorium, okay? Until you sign that NDA, we need to keep our secrets!" She consigned my life to a box with other baggies. I looked doubtfully at the collection of phones. Julie went on. "Okay, now, there's a pen in your envelope, but don't sign the papers until after Wink's little talk, right? You'll sign in front of someone from the legal department, and that will be a little intense, right—I mean, like, lawyers? But it's in your interest, too, you know? Go on in now, honey—take any seat on the floor. The balcony's for alternates, and you don't want to be up there with them. You made it! You're going to be on *Cupid's Quest!*"

Julie was more excited than I was. Even after the six-month selection process, which had been shockingly thorough, I found it hard to believe I'd been chosen for what they were billing as "America's newest reality adventure show."

Three feet into the auditorium, the frigid air conditioning hit me, and I turned back for the sweater in my backpack. But Julie had moved on to the next contestant, a buff Black woman named Val who looked a great deal more like an adventure-show contestant than I did.

I could wait. Julie didn't need to be interrupted.

I slid into a chair near the door and spent the following ten minutes eyeing the people around me, all of whom were more beautiful or more fit (or both) than I was. What the hell was I doing here?

At exactly three o'clock, studio lights blazed on and men wheeled huge television cameras across the stage, most of them pointed into the audience. I jumped at the white-hot glare and nervously smoothed my hand along my boring, brown hair.

Had it escaped its ponytail? Did I have parsley in my teeth? Should I have had my teeth whitened before coming?

Too late now. Maybe the lights would raise the temperature in the theater. My blue sundress had seemed so perfect for the dress-code directions ("No logos. Solid colors. Early November in Los Angeles is often quite warm. Dress accordingly."), but now I regretted my lack of sleeves.

Julie, now armed with a clipboard and a headset, stood to the side of the stage and counted audience members. Then she scanned the balcony above us and was apparently satisfied with what she saw. She nodded to someone offstage, and a hearty man in khakis and a blue work shirt bounded out. He looked vaguely familiar in an "anchorman on the local news" kind of way. Handsome, if impersonal.

"Welcome!" he shouted. He was mic'd up; his voice boomed through the auditorium. "Welcome, fortunate contestants! Welcome to *Cupid's Quest!*" He paused as if waiting for applause. I took my cue and started clapping; others slowly joined in. "Thank you! Thank you! I'm your host, Wink Tannhauser!"

He paused again. Were we supposed to know that name?

I looked around nervously and caught the eye of a petite blonde who had dyed her hair pink. She shrugged back at me with a smile. Oh, good—a potential friend. I clapped again, and she followed. Soon, we inspired enough applause for the host to graciously raise a hand to stop us.

"No one is named Wink," a loud voice said from the back. I turned and saw a large man with one leg thrown over the seat in front of him. He was bald but had the scruff of a five o'clock shadow and didn't need a microphone to make himself heard. "Wink is not a real name, cupcake."

An itchy flash of adrenaline burned through me as my anxiety rose. I wasn't a fan of conflict.

"Ah, our resident rebel." Wink was not at all disturbed by being heckled from the crowd. "Theo, right?"

The bald man nodded. "What's it say on your birth certificate, *Wink*?" He emphasized the host's name with scorn, but Wink was more than up to the task.

"As it happens, my given name is Van Winkler Kenniworth Tannhausen. Does that satisfy you, Theophilus?" Wink landed on Theo's full name with the same measure of scorn.

I breathed out a little tension. Wink could handle Baldy. Good.

Wink dismissed Theo from his attentions and went on. "Did any of you wonder why an adventure-based reality show would be called *Cupid's Quest*?"

I wasn't the only one in the audience nodding. We all checked our neighbors to see if someone knew something we didn't.

"Sure you did—you're all intelligent men and women! Well, I can tell you now that our show's tag line isn't just 'Searching the World for Treasure,' as we told you. It's actually 'Searching the World for *Love* and Treasure.' Doesn't that sound more fun?"

I tensed and looked around me in confusion. I was on a dating show?

Was that a good or a bad thing?

Did I *want* to be on a dating show?

No wonder they'd been so interested in who I was dating at the moment (no one) and why they'd insisted on testing for STIs (clean).

Well...shit.

The audience was awkwardly silent. None of us had friends to whisper to. No one to consult. No one to advise. Stay? Or go?

I looked at the pink-haired blonde and wondered if anyone would notice if I snuck over to sit with her. What did she think of this?

"You've each taken exhaustive personality tests and, as a result, we're prepared to match each of you with a partner—someone you'll work with on challenges throughout the show. You're all single. You're all heterosexual. You're all free of communicable diseases. And you've all been matched with someone in this audience." He drew his finger coyly across the theater, taking us all in. "We think you're compatible. Maybe you'll think so too!"

Omigawd. I had taken eleven separate personality tests over the course of the six-month selection process. What had they found out about me that I didn't know? Had they really found a man for me? Now I eyed the male contestants with a heady blend of alarm and curiosity.

"So, let's talk about the bad part. Ready?"

I was definitely not ready. I shook my head. Wink ignored me. He ignored all of us.

"A month ago, you were all sent a copy of the contract you'll be asked to sign today. You were advised to look it over with your lawyer and any trusted advisers. Today, if you sign the contract in your envelopes and complete the nondisclosure agreement, then you are agreeing to be filmed and recorded at our discretion, twenty-four hours a day, for eight weeks." He eyed us sternly.

Of course that's what they wanted. I'd known it would be so in my head, even if I hadn't quite gotten a grasp of the concept in my heart.

"And yes, that includes in the bathroom."

Gasps of outrage. I froze. How . . . tawdry. Humiliating.

Wink held up a hand. "Now, now. Hang on. We have the *option* to film you. I'm not saying we *will*. Remember, the Watch Now Network is launching its live broadcasts as family programming. From nine thirty to ten thirty every night for the next eight weeks, the *Cupid's Quest* audience will include kids.

Kissing is allowed. So is a little skin. But think of this as a PG show."

"So why do you need to record me in the bathroom?" That was a beautiful Black woman with her hair in intricate braids.

"*Because*, Euphoria." He knew everyone's names. She was Euphoria. I'd remember that. "We've learned over the years of reality programs that contestants like to sneak off to the bathroom to plan or plot or discuss. Or make out. And we want to ensure the rights to film that part of your adventure too. You need to know that up front."

I was going to plan or plot?

I was going to make out?

With one of these guys?

Some of them were alarmingly attractive. All of them were cute at minimum. They made me nervous.

"Plus, the Watch Now Network is scheduling a late-night program at midnight after forty-five minutes of dead air as a deliberate, child-boring buffer. That program is intended for adults only." Wink was stern. An angry father. No giggles or nervous titters would be tolerated. "And *that* program will include R-rated content. You understand?"

"So, you *do* want to film us naked." That was the buff warrior who'd gotten to Julie after me. Her voice was strong.

"Yes, Val, we want to film you naked. We won't show anything you can't see in an R-rated movie, and frankly, if you're naked by yourself, we're less interested. But if you wind up in the shower with a friend, remember you're probably on camera." He eyed us. "Any questions?"

My question was—how long before I could sneak out without making a scene? One of the alternates in the balcony was about to get a ticket down to the main floor.

But there were no out-loud protests. A curvy blonde near the front preened. Did she just wink at Wink?

He grinned. "Okay. That's the bad part. Let me tell you the good part."

"What, public nudity isn't the good part?" That was Theo again. His contempt broke the tension. I found I'd uttered an unwilling chuckle.

"Oh, I think I can sweeten the pot. Remember, my friends—the winning couple will split the prize. Which will be . . . Ten. Million. Dollars." I gulped through a suddenly tight throat. That kind of money would completely change my world. Wink was relentless. "That's five million dollars for each winner. Not a bad benefit, huh, Theo?"

Even Theo was brought to silence. Now I tried to do a quick count of the contestants. Were there twenty of us here on the auditorium floor? Thirty? Was there a prayer in hell I could win this thing?

My determination to leave as soon as possible was weakening.

"While you're thinking about what you'd do with that kind of money and what it would mean to you, consider this." Wink let the tension build. *Cupid's Quest* is not an elimination game. If you sign the contract, you're in it for all eight weeks. You don't have to fear getting voted out or handed a rose. Once we set our contestants, our contestants are with us for the run of the show. Got it?" He looked at each of us one by one with a focused gaze that demanded acknowledgment. It took a while. I nodded when he caught my eye. "Good. Because the Watch Now Network knows what you're giving up. That's why they're going to pay each contestant while they're taking you all around the world. Ten thousand dollars."

Despair. My "I'm leaving" balloon deflated a little at the realization that I had to make a choice. I wanted to hide . . . but I could use the money that would result from manning up.

But Wink wasn't done. "Each week."

He grinned at the shiver that ran through the contestants. To my side, Pink Hair faintly whispered. "Oh my."

Ten thousand a week. For eight weeks. All I had to do was agree to be filmed constantly, and I'd make eighty thousand dollars.

My mother, so abused by life, and my sister, sickly from the day she was born, would have at least another year in the house. Another year for me to figure something out.

Even if I didn't win the big prize.

Well, *now* what was I going to do?

2

REFUSING THE CALL

It turned out that sitting so close to the door was a blessing, because I was the first one the guy pulled over for an on-camera interview after Wink gave us an hour for deliberations. I didn't have to wait before I could escape.

An interview. Now. Of course, now. This was how reality shows worked. It was naïve of me to forget that.

The line of contestants trying to get out of the auditorium mounted behind me while I stammered stupidly about my surprise (huge), my confusion (massive), and my decision (I didn't know whether I would sign or not). I was so fumble-footed, in fact, that the guy shrugged and let me go.

Pink Hair stepped up into the circle of blinding light. I headed for the lobby doors.

Outside, the hot, humid air was delicious on my chilled skin. I'd left my sunglasses in my backpack. Wink had told us we could have everything back the minute we decided to leave the show (and he pointed to the alternates in the balcony, who were praying we'd bail), and I'd almost asked for my stuff as I left.

But a guaranteed eighty thousand dollars ... could I afford to pass that up?

Regardless of the indignity?

And the potential lifelong mate?

So, I'd suffer through wincing in bright daylight, my sunglasses still locked away under Julie's highly efficient and possibly temporary care.

I stopped on the sidewalk, not sure what to do. A voice called from behind me. "*Cupid's Quest*, right? You're Joss?" A woman was sitting on the retaining wall a bit away from the door, smoking a cigarette.

"Yeah." She was utterly normal—a little older, a little overweight. She looked like someone's mother, and I was drawn to her. "How'd you know?"

She smiled and held one hand out to me as she reached with the other so the cigarette smoke wouldn't get to me. "I'm Bunny Stanhope," she said. "I'm the casting director."

"Oh." I shook her hand. "So you—you know all of us?"

She nodded. "I picked through thousands of candidates and eliminated hundreds of potentials. Every test you took, every interview you filmed, you can blame me." She gestured for me to sit next to her, and I did, glad for the warmth of the wall soaking through my sundress.

"Thanks for that," I said with what I hoped was a touch of humor.

"Think nothing of it." She laughed back at me. "This is the most magnificent cast any show has ever assembled." She looked both proud and bored. I liked her.

In fact, I liked her enough to risk the question that had been grinding away at me since I'd gotten the final acceptance. "So, Bunny, you can probably tell me."

She blew a lungful of smoke away from me and eyed me with a smile. "Go ahead. You can ask."

I nodded and took a breath. "Why would anyone cast me in

an adventure show? Every single person in that auditorium is beautiful. They're all fit. They're all strong. What am *I* doing here?"

Her smile became a grin. "You're my everyman. Well," she corrected herself, "my everywoman." Something about that seemed strangely familiar, but before I could track down the thought, she went on. "I'm the proudest of casting you, Joss."

"Me?" Astonishment froze me, and I blurted out the unspeakable truth. "I don't think I'm going to stay."

Her eyebrows went up, and to my confusion, she barked out a laugh. "Refusal of the call," she said. "I love it."

Something was definitely not making sense. "Refusal of the call?" If I tipped my head more or wrinkled my forehead a little more tightly, would logic be clear? "Are you talking about the hero's journey?"

This time, she was the one who was astonished. Her mouth fell into an *O*, and then she barked with laughter again. "There's that master's in English you thought would be so useless! Good for you. You know Joseph Campbell?"

Of course this utter stranger knew I feared my master's degree was useless; she'd been interviewing me from afar for half a year. "Yes, I know Joseph Campbell. Step two on the typical hero's journey is the refusal of the quest, which tells the reader the hero is reluctant—that he's leaving his real world behind. Or he is once he gets to step three, when he's persuaded to accept the quest by the wise older female—Jesus! Did you set this conversation up?"

Bunny was now howling with laughter. "Oh, God, I love it! No, I didn't set this up. Although now I wish I had."

I was being manipulated . . . wasn't I? One of my favorite sayings was, "If you can't see the sucker in a deal, it's probably you." I stood. "I'm out of here."

"No, wait." She held out a hand to stop me. "Did Wink explain how this competition eventually spits out a winner?"

I shook my head. Had he explained that? "I don't think so."

"Okay, sit again for a minute. Come on, you can leave anytime. Let me tell you why you should *not* leave."

I exhaled my frustration, but I sat beside her again. "Okay. Go ahead."

"The Watch Now Network is an experiment. The executives insist it's so we can all return to some happy time when families gathered on the couch to watch TV. Families together, making time for each other, some wholesome fun that'll inspire connection and discussion and closer bonds. Yadda, yadda, yadda."

"I've read the news stories."

"Right. Well, really it's to sell more ad time to advertisers. Watch for plenty of product placement in your quests. Never mind—that's neither here nor there. The point is every show they're launching has an audience participation component. The HonorBucks betting for the sports program. The "what happens next" vote for the sitcom. They're going to make *Cupid's Quest* into a must-watch experience by leaving the winning decisions up to America."

"What, like *American Idol*? People phone in to vote for a winner?"

"A little more sophisticated than that. The internet has changed things a lot. But basically, yeah. This show is going to end up being a popularity contest."

I shook my head. "I'm definitely out. I've never been popular."

"You are going to be popular, and I've got the science to prove it." I looked my disagreement to her, but she waved me off. "You're the perfect everyman. You're two inches taller than the average American woman. You're ten pounds lighter. You've got brown hair. Your eyes are neither brown nor green but somewhere in between. Your features are normal, except you have what is statistically a highly symmetrical face."

"Um . . . thanks?" What could be more awkward than hearing oneself discussed so clinically?

"Hang on. My point is that you won't intimidate the voters of America."

"And that's a good thing?"

"Millions of Americans are going to look at you and see themselves. They're going to want you to succeed because *they* want to succeed. Add on to that your quiet intelligence and your astonishingly high scores in empathy, and you're a shoo-in. The other candidates should be scared of you winning. But they won't be." She spoke with satisfaction. "I know they won't."

All kinds of negatives warred for supremacy as they rose in me. I settled for, "America likes beautiful people. That's been proven. Every woman in there is prettier than me."

"That's not true and you know it. Plus, America likes pretty women in two varieties. They love a pretty evildoer who they can hate and despair of and delight in. And they like pretty women who are kind and lovely and who they want to have as best friends. Guess which category you fall into?"

No, no, no. That couldn't be true. "I don't have best friends," I admitted. "You're not talking about me."

"Too much time with that mother and sister of yours. Oh yes, I've looked into them too. You're going to learn about yourself once you're away from them." This "I know all your secrets" attitude was tough to take. She was wounding me. Her words—her implications—stung. She knew it too. She rolled her hand in a "wrap it up" gesture. "Plus, I've found someone for you to be with who I think might change your life. A guy. Maybe *the* guy."

I inhaled to speak and found I had nothing to say. "Really?" I squeaked.

"Joss, don't back out. Trust to fate. Let the wise old crone help you commit to your own personal hero's journey. I'm pretty sure you won't regret it."

After a moment, I realized my mouth was hanging open. I closed it and stood. "I'll think about it. I'm going to walk around the block for a bit."

"Walking in LA," she said. "How retro. You'll probably cause traffic accidents." She grinned, and I found I was grinning back.

I hadn't made it more than a few feet down the sidewalk when I realized where her comment had come from. I turned back. "You said I was the everyman. Would you also perhaps refer to me as the orphan?"

She chuckled. "Who said that master's degree wasn't worth anything?"

Now it was clear to me: she'd stocked her TV show with all twelve of the classic Jungian archetypes. I'd have to be on the lookout for the magician, the hero, the innocent, the lover. Bald Theo was a classic outlaw.

I took my walk, but when the time was up, I was back in the auditorium, at the legal desk in front of a Watch Now lawyer, signing up with all the other contestants. Sorry, alternates. No luck for you today.

I had a secret handle on why the contestants had been chosen.

I would make eighty thousand dollars.

And the casting director thought I could win the five million.

Okay, then.

Time to meet my future enemies—and my one true love.

3

NOW BOARDING

I attached myself to Pink Hair on the bus ride to LAX; her name turned out to be Rosemary. That pleased me. Rose is a kind of pink, and she'd dyed her hair to make her identification easier.

"I can't believe we're doing this!" she whispered.

"Me either!" We were sudden sisters in our uncertainty, even though the bus had been outfitted with large microphones hanging between every pair of seats, and a cameraman at the front of the bus somehow remained upright and filming through every stop and start in the rush-hour traffic. He was an older guy with gray hair but it didn't seem to slow him down at all. "It feels weird to talk when I know we're being recorded," I confessed to her.

"I know. Think we'll ever get used to it?" Rose was breathless in her excitement. She was about half a foot shorter than me and probably weighed about fifty pounds less. She was everything I longed to be. "How long will it take to get to the airport? Where do you think we're going?"

We'd been assured our belongings would be waiting for us upon our arrival. My sunglasses, my sweater, my phone—all denied. I would have looked up the route to LAX on my phone, but without it, I was a Pennsylvania girl in a strange labyrinth of highways. I shrugged. "Don't know." It answered both of Rose's questions, and she laughed.

Some of the contestants had found friends. More sat alone. The only boy-girl pair I saw was the hot blonde from the front row who had winked at Wink. She'd glued herself to the side of a tall Asian guy with hair so lustrously black, it was almost blue.

Already working the "love" angle.

I took my time and counted the passengers. "Looks like there are twenty-four contestants," I reported to Rose. "There are more than that on the bus, but the others are all wearing headsets. I'm guessing that's crew."

Rose giggled nervously. "Twenty-four of us. Must be a dozen guys and a dozen girls."

That fit the Jungian archetypes perfectly. There were twelve classic personality types, according to Carl Jung. I'd probably have to figure out who on the male side was the "everyman." He was possibly my perfect match.

Rose saw I was still looking at the people around us, and she stood to peer over the top of the seat too. "Do you think we'll really find someone to love on this adventure?"

Sudden movement at the front of the bus caught my eye. Someone with a headset nudged the cameraman and pointed at us. Oh—got it. The eavesdropping had begun.

The headset nodded at me. *Go ahead.*

Okay. In for a penny, in for a pound. I grinned bravely at Rose. "I don't know. I hope so. It would be something to find a true partner here. It doesn't seem possible."

Rose didn't appear to have caught on to the fact that we were the focus of the camera. Should I warn her?

"Oh, I know. I just got out of a bad marriage. I don't even know if I'm ready to meet someone new."

This was getting personal. Did Rose want all of America to hear about her failed marriage? Headset Guy turned around in his seat and nodded to me again. *Keep going.*

I shook my head and nudged Rose. When she looked at me, I pointed to the cameraman. "Oh!" she said. "They're listening, huh? I guess this is how it starts."

"I guess. I thought you ought to know."

"You're sweet. Thank you!" Impulsively, she leaned up and kissed my cheek, which startled me into a laugh. "But they interviewed me about a million times about my breakup. I guess if America wants to know why I'm here, they're going to find out."

Her smile was blinding. It reassured me. "I got interviewed a million times too. It was weird, right?"

"So weird! And all those medical tests!"

The Watch Now Network was really, really dedicated to rooting out any diseases. "They were thorough, all right." The camera was still on us. There were too few couples; we were among the only ones talking. I took pity on Headset Guy. "At least we know everyone else here is as free from disease as we are, though. That's good, right?"

"You mean if we end up . . . ?!" She couldn't finish her sentence for giggling, and that dragged me into snickering too. Headset Guy held up one thumb where I could see it; he was liking the discussion.

"Yes, if we—exactly. I'm not sure I could, though. I mean, how long do you have to know a guy before . . ." Now it was my turn to not be able to finish a sentence.

"Well, with Robby, it was the first date, but look at how that turned out. Now I'm divorced and trying hard not to be bitter about it. So, do you figure, what, third date? That classic?"

It had been four years since I'd made it to the third date with a guy, so to speak, and I felt like a Victorian lady offering advice on dating in the digital age. "I guess. You don't want to be slutty, you know?"

"Oh, for sure. Not slutty. But not frigid either. Women constantly walk that tightrope, don't we?"

I nodded. I knew. "No one ever accuses guys of being slutty if they sleep with someone on the first date."

"God. Can you imagine? What do you think dates will be like on this show? If we get to choose, will you room with me, Joss?"

It was dawn in the arctic landscape of my chest; warmth flooded me. "I'd love that! Maybe we can request it."

"Okay!"

I looked to Headset Guy, but he was no longer sending me silent signals across the bus. The camera had swung to the curvy blonde with her hot Asian. His hair was exactly what I had longed for since childhood—silky, straight, shining in the evening gloom. I'd be filming him, too, given a choice.

As we entered the roadway madness of LA's overwhelming airport, Wink stood at the front of the bus (but not blocking the camera) and got the microphone from the driver. "Welcome to LAX, girls and boys. If you haven't flown charter before, get ready to enjoy how little time it takes to get through here!"

"Where are we going?" a curly-haired redhead called out. He had a nice voice.

"Not telling, Knox!" Wink seemed pleased with the question. "Each week, you won't know your destination until you arrive. I can promise you'll be circling the globe and visiting places that will astonish and amaze you!"

A few hardy souls cheered at that. Most remained silent. Perhaps they, like me, were unnerved by the utter lack of control over their lives.

Take a deep breath, Joss, and relax those shoulders. This will be okay.

And if it wasn't, there wasn't much I could do about it now.

Wink was right. The time it took to board the plane was far shorter than expected. Security opened a lane just for *Cupid's Quest*, and even our lone cameraman passed through with a minimum of fuss. Efficient Julie had all our passports and documentation; it was the easiest transition I'd ever been through. This was luxury.

The plane, however—there was no disguising that it was a repurposed cargo plane.

"No windows!" Rose cried once we'd boarded through a rear door.

It would be like flying in a metal tube. The sense of helplessness got worse. Lack of control.

Julie had given us each our boarding passes. "What's your seat assignment?" I asked Rose.

"I'm in six-A. You?"

"Four-B. Maybe we can switch with someone."

Julie, who was standing behind us in the galley, chirped up. "No switching, please. Sit in your assigned seats, thanks. Do this quickly and quietly. We need to keep to our schedule, so find your place and take your seat. No luggage for the overhead compartments—isn't that nice? Come on now!"

"We'll talk later," I promised Rose. I squeezed her hand as we parted.

And oh, look at that. Seated in the window seat (if there'd been a window) was a handsome, dark-haired man.

"Hello," he said as I sat. "I'm Luke."

"Joss," I replied, flustered. I wished I had some luggage to put away or anything at all to make the moment less awkward. Was this the man Bunny thought was The One?

Luke was trim. He looked like he'd have long, lean muscles under his plain, black, long-sleeved T-shirt.

And his hair. Oh, I wanted his hair. It was as thick—if not thicker—than the Asian hottie's. Luke wore his hair shorter, and it stood on top of his head like a stuffed animal. I wanted to pet him immediately.

It took a moment for me to realize I was staring at the crest of his head, and he was laughing about it. "Sorry. I'm admiring your hair."

"Oh." He ran a casual hand through it, and it bent beneath his fingers and then sprang up again. "Yeah. It's kind of thick."

I had thick hair—thick, wavy hair. It didn't look anything as wonderful as Luke's. "It's good," I said lamely.

He grinned. I realized he had the look of an islander, like a Polynesian. Tanned skin, dark eyes, excellent smile. "Thanks. What's with this rig, do you think?"

He gestured to the seat ahead of him. I realized I'd been ignoring what I'd assumed was an entertainment console in the headrest. "Oh, shit," I said stupidly. "That's a camera, isn't it?"

4

WHAT'S GOING ON HERE?

Luke's handsome face twisted in a frown. "I was hoping I'd misunderstood something. It is a camera. And I bet that's a microphone. Boy, they weren't kidding about twenty-four-hour filming, huh?"

"I guess if we're all supposed to be meeting The One, they want it on tape, huh?" I blushed to imply that maybe Luke was my The One, and he ducked his head too. We sat in embarrassed silence for a moment until we were rescued by Wink at the front of the cabin.

"Okay!" he said through the PA system. "Looks like everyone's accounted for. We're going to take off now, and I'll be back to give you some more information. Seat belts on, everyone. What?" Julie had appeared at his elbow and was whispering to him. "Oh. Right. There are safety cards in the seat pouches. Please review them thoroughly. Let me know if you have any questions. Up, up, and away!"

He disappeared through a door into what I assumed was a crew cabin as the plane taxied down the runway. "That's so fast," I said as I reviewed the safety card.

"I know, right? Some days, I've spent months at LAX waiting for a plane to get off the ground." Luke and I chuckled together.

This was going okay. My shoulders relaxed—at least, until I looked across the aisle.

Theo, the bald rebel, was in seat four-C, next to a pretty Latina. He had his long legs stretched blatantly into the aisle and his seat belt dangled below him.

"Your seat belt's not done," I said helpfully.

He rolled his bald head on the seat until he regarded me. "Big Eyes, if this plane crashes, one nylon belt across the belly isn't going to save any of us. I'll take my chances."

Annoying. And also irritatingly delicious to have been accorded a nickname like "Big Eyes." Made me sound . . . attractive. But where was the flight attendant? Shouldn't someone have *made* him buckle up?

He turned, dismissing me. I looked away, dismissing him too. Big Eyes, indeed. I was glad I was with Luke.

Once the plane was successfully up in the air and no longer required my concentration and willpower to get airborne, I turned to my seatmate, determined to help our future romance progress. "Where are you from, Luke? I can hear a little Kiwi in your accent. Are you from New Zealand?"

"Good ear on you!" He beamed at me. "Most people think Australian, which is farther from my home than New York City is from Los Angeles."

"So, you're from New Zealand?"

"Close. Well, sort of. I'm from the Cook Islands."

"How interesting. I don't know a thing about them."

He chuckled. "There are all of eighty people on my island since I left. There's no reason why you should've heard of it. Where are you from, Joss?"

I let him draw my background out of me (in the interest of advancing our love story, of course), and in a surprisingly short time, he'd learned about my mother and sister.

"So, neither of them have jobs?" He was politely incredulous.

I shook my head. "It's for the best. My mother hasn't worked since she married my father. When they divorced, she got a good settlement plus child support, but the settlement ran out eight years ago, and my sister's child support will run out this year."

I caught myself. Why was I sharing such intimate details? And in front of a camera, no less? Luke was easy to talk to.

"And my sister," I finished quickly, "has severe asthma. They're both better off at home."

Luke cocked his head. "Who takes care of them if your dad is gone? Is it just you?"

I was spared the indignity of my answer (which would have included waitressing by day, being a teaching assistant in the evenings, and scaring up freelance writing jobs whenever I could fit them into my schedule—none of which I was particularly proud of) because Wink appeared again at the front of the cabin.

"Hello, *Cupid's Quest*! Welcome to the Arrow. That's what we call our plane. An arrow—get it? Like what Cupid would shoot?" He seemed so pleased with his joke that I couldn't help but smile in response, and he caught my eye and nodded delightedly. "Joss gets it! Attagirl, Joss!"

Wink had proven he knew everyone's names, and yet I felt absurdly pleased to be recognized. I blushed and bit back my smile.

"And now I want to introduce you to some important people. First up is our showrunner and director, Jeremy Shouderberg."

He held his hand up and Headset Guy stepped forward. The showrunner himself had been egging me on in my girl talk with Rose?

Wink pushed the microphone into Headset Guy's hand.

Forced to speak, he came up with, "Be yourselves. We'll be fine," then handed the mic back to Wink, who laughed.

"The guy doesn't talk much, but he's the best in the business. You'll be amused, I think, to know his nickname is Shout." We huffed our little chuckles at the thought. "And everyone's met Shout's production assistant, Julie. Come on over, Julie. Say something."

Ah, mystery solved. Julie had introduced herself to me at the registration table as "Shout's PA." That meant she was the production assistant to the showrunner.

Julie's green hair still bristled with abundant energy. "I think I've met everyone! And you can ask me questions if you have any, and I don't mind talking when Shout doesn't want to, so you can just assume I'm talking for him." (Shout, in the background, nodded.) "And I know you'll all listen carefully now, but tell me if you blank on something because if I don't know the answer, I'll find out, and if I can't find out, I'll make it up, and this show is going to be incredible and you're all so beautiful and we're going to have so much fun!" She finished with such a giddy smile that the contestants broke out into the first spontaneous cheers of the day.

"I think I love her," Luke confessed quietly to me.

"Who doesn't? She's great!" He and I exchanged grins. I got a buzz from the secretive sense of connection between us. Luke and me. Okay.

Wink introduced us to a bewildering array of additional crew members. There was a line producer, a production manager, a story producer, everyone had PAs—I lost track quickly. The head of the camera team was named Quincy. He was the older man who had filmed us in the bus. Wink explained who handled travel arrangements, who oversaw financials, who dealt with tech, but none of it stuck. My eyes glazed over.

"You know the one thing we're missing?" Luke whispered to me.

"Um, chef? Pilot?" I was casting about, trying to think of what you'd call the person who took the green M&M's out of the bag for rock stars with bratty brattish demands.

"Cameramen," Luke said. "Who's on the other end of these?" He gestured to the headrests, where the staring eye had faded from my conscience. (That quickly? Wow.)

"They must be on the other side of that wall, focusing on us. Headsets on."

"Must be," he said. He waved at his lens. "Hiya."

I waved at mine. "Hope we can be friends. Don't film me if I have parsley in my teeth, please!"

Luke sniggered. "Me either."

We were chortling together, promising to always tell the other if we saw something embarrassing, when Wink walked his microphone up the aisle and put his hand on my shoulder. "Now that we're done with introductions, let's get to the game."

He looked at me with a smile and I nodded back, chastened. I'd be good.

Luke nudged me, and from the side of my eye, I saw his eyes were bright with mischief. I smothered my giggle.

Wink returned to the front of the cabin. He was alone again; all the others had faded back through the door to the crew kingdom.

"Here's the game format, which we'll repeat each week. Every Monday, you'll take part in what we're calling 'True Love or Double Dud.' This is the first of two weekly challenges. The Monday challenge is short and fun. The winners will get luxury accommodations for the rest of the week, and the losers will be housed in a place you'll want to move out of. The others will end up in average rooms. Sound fun?"

I was uneasy about the losers' rooms, but we'd see how bad those turned out to be. I nodded obediently with everyone else.

"Now, the second challenge is the big one. These are far more complicated and will test your skills, your patience, your endurance, and your creativity."

I had none of those things. I found I'd grabbed Luke's hand. At least it was below the level of the camera, so I had the brief illusion of privacy. And he wasn't letting go.

"You'll have four days to accomplish your task. And every Friday, America will decide which couple wins."

Wink held up a cartoonish toy—a small gold dollar sign—and waved it at us. "This is what you win. We're calling it 'Cupid Cash,' and you can redeem it during the final challenge for five thousand dollars. Two will be awarded after the vote—one to a woman, and one to a man. And I promise, you're going to want to have that money!"

Wink was twinkly with delight over this revelation. I didn't need any help being excited about an extra five thou. It took a lot of hours as a waitress to make that much money.

"What if we don't use it for the final? Can we turn it into actual cash?" I looked around to see who'd voiced my question. It was Knox of the curly red hair, in the second row, next to a trim, blonde woman.

"Yes, you can," Wink said. "If you don't need it for the last challenge, then this will add to the total you get for being in the show. But don't spend it yet. Wait until you hear what we have planned for the finale!"

"Sure," Theo muttered sarcastically from across the aisle. "That doesn't sound alarming at all."

"All right, then!" Wink consulted his wrist. "It's almost time for the inaugural broadcast of the Watch Now Network. We're going to air it here so you can watch. *Cupid's Quest* airs at nine thirty, and I know you'll want to see that. The introductions will take two nights, so some of you won't see your intro tonight, but you'll all find you've got some camera time. Our editors are finishing the final details right now. And they deserve special praise for the last-minute job they're going to have to do every single day."

There was an uneasy silence, broken by Theo. "I'll applaud them once I see how they're presenting us. Or I won't applaud."

His comment was brusque, but I found I was nodding along with him. I'd seen reality shows where it was clear the editing was selective and biased. Who knew what this team wanted from us and what they'd show?

"Fair enough," Wink said. "You show us what you've got, and we'll show you what we've got. And we'll make *Cupid's Quest* a massive hit from coast to coast. Hell, the network already has millions of subscribers. We're going to be a hit all the way around the world!"

Applause started at the back of the plane and rolled forward, and I found I was clapping too. Even though the thought of seeing myself on TV (splatted out there in all my parsley-toothed glory to millions of subscribers) terrified me.

"After that, I suggest you try to get some sleep, if you can. We've got a long day tomorrow." So, we'd be flying all night? "Questions?"

The Asian-looking hottie commanded attention. "Where are the stewardesses? When will dinner be served?"

Wink grinned. "We have no *flight attendants*, Alaric" He hit the more PC term for stewardess with pointed effect. "You'll find box dinners in the galley, and the bar will always be open. Make yourselves at home. If you use the call button, one of the PAs will have to come see what you need and they've all had a very long day, so I advise you to do your best at solving your own issues."

Wink fielded a few more questions in which he essentially said nothing, and then he disappeared into the crew cabin.

"Probably have actual beds up there," Luke grumbled.

"Do you think?"

"Hang on—the show is starting."

The cabin lights dimmed, and the screen at the front of the cabin came alive. We cheered again when the Watch Now logo came up.

"Here we go," Luke breathed. "I hope to hell this works."

5

LIGHTS, CAMERA, ACTION

Like everyone else in America, I'd been blasted by the prelaunch Watch Now Network's publicity campaign. For three weeks, you couldn't turn on the TV, listen to the radio, scan social media, or even see a bus driving by without being made aware that "watching as a family" was back in a big way.

It was gutsy. In a time when people binged entire shows in a weekend and most parents were as buried in their phones or tablets or laptops as their kids, the Watch Now bigwigs refused to use the on-demand format that would have let a viewer choose when to watch. If you wanted to watch one of the four scheduled shows, you had to watch it live. Watch *now*.

The first show was a half-hour-long sitcom, which the entire United States knew was designed to delight kids as well as their parents. *School Daisy* was about a boarding school where both students and teachers were all beautiful. Even the "ugly ducklings" were beautiful; I could tell that if the homely teacher took off her glasses, it would be all, "Miss Perkins! You're beautiful!"

But there's a reason candy is so addictive. The TV show

they presented was sugary and funny and sweet. I was sucked into it by the first commercial break. I loved it, even though I knew "Daisy" and her friends were professional actors skilled in the kind of improv necessary to sustain an ever-changing story line for eight long weeks.

"How much extra do I have to pay in my subscription," Theo asked from across the aisle, "to get the Watch Now Network's all-adult after-midnight program? Because I'd pay extra to see the gym teacher get it on with the school principal."

Ugh. I turned away from his crudeness (even if the idea was ... well, titillating). This was a family show.

I turned to my adorable seatmate, determined to ignore Theo. "Well? How do you like it?"

"I love the counter at the bottom of the screen." He gestured with his chin.

I hadn't noticed the strip across the bottom, where a series of numbers was growing and shrinking. "What is that?"

"That's the number of registered viewers. Didn't you see the network is going to broadcast viewership during all its shows? It's supposed to make viewers feel like part of a community. You know—we all watch together, I guess."

"Huh." I squinted at the numbers. "I mean—wait. Are half a million people watching this?" The thought made me sort of breathless, but Luke grinned.

"That's not so many. I did the research before I came. I wish I had my phone. I'd check the numbers, but I think it's something like the biggest networks average over five million viewers." I blanched. I thought Wink had been kidding when he said we would reach millions. "And this is just the first fifteen minutes. Who knows how many people are kicking themselves for forgetting to tune in?"

More than half a million? It seemed ... impossible.

"Wait for the sports betting show. I'm thinking we'll see a boost there."

Luke was right. At the end of *School Daisy*, any registered viewer could vote on what would happen the next night (I would have voted for option C—Daisy does her history homework—but I was pretty sure America would go for option A—the midnight switch with the boys' dorm).

The second program was an hour-long sports show called *Watch Now Sports*, which focused on a very broad definition of "sports." There was a tiddlywinks competition, the prequalifying round for the Danish Olympic show-jumping team (the horses were gorgeous), a drunken quartet of man-boys working to climb the competitive bar darts ladder, and an intercity trivia tournament that inspired all of us to uselessly shout out answers.

"I was right. See? Almost a million viewers." Luke's comment caught me by surprise again; I'd gotten caught up in the show. "A lot of guys are going to watch this because Watch Now has figured out how to make betting legal across the nation."

"I heard about that," I admitted, "but I didn't pay attention. What's the draw?"

Luke shrugged. "No money involved. You bet for honor, and winners are listed by zip code, state, and nation. Top winners get a badge on their network profile, and that's it. Without any cash exchanging hands, it's legal everywhere—and there are lots of people who would bet on anything. Even tiddlywinks. See?"

There weren't as many bets being placed as there were viewers, but the number wasn't much smaller. And why not? It would be fun to bet on which of the gleaming, powerful horses would make the Olympics team.

In fact, the sports program (which I thought I wouldn't be even slightly interested in) had me so diverted and entertained that when it ended and the *Cupid's Quest* logo popped up, it felt like I was being ambushed.

Oh god. Here we go.

Wink appeared on the screen, his artfully long hair blowing in the late afternoon light as a huge jet took off over his head. When had they shot that? We hadn't gotten to LAX until after sunset.

"Welcome to *Cupid's Quest!*" he called heartily once the overwhelming crescendo of sound had roared away. "Young singles from across the nation are going to spend the next eight weeks circling the globe in search of love and treasure—and the winner will be decided by you, the Watch Now Network subscribers." Wink walked casually off the runway and headed for safety, the camera coming with him. "As you watch this, the contestants have boarded our special plane—the *Cupid's Quest* Arrow—and are flying to their first destination. I can't tell you where they're going, because they're watching this program right now, too, and this adventure will be as much of a surprise to them as it is for you!" He pulled open a door and invited the camera into the bowels of LAX. At least he was inside. "I can tell you they have no idea what they're getting into! For now, come on along with me as we meet some of our contestants."

I had an overwhelming longing to be at home, watching this in my pajamas. Mama and Claire could be beside me on the sofa. I wouldn't object to us spending family time together. Or not. Anything as long as I wasn't actually on the Mystery Plane To Nowhere.

The camera cut to a scene from earlier that day—of the auditorium. Mostly empty, A scattering of strangers dotted through the seats. That's us, I realized. That's me. Clips of Wink's introductory speech were laced with shots of our faces (I looked alarmed) as he explained the "bad" and the "good" parts. We'd always be filmed. We'd earn money—maybe a lot of money.

I couldn't look away, even though I'd lived it hours before.

(How could it only be hours before? Surely this was months in the past?)

"Look at the viewers." Luke nudged me. "The women of America are showing up for this."

The sudden constriction in my chest forced a gasp out of my mouth. "Over a million!"

Luke nodded, his handsome face set and serious. "Those are Hallmark Channel numbers. Not bad for a first night. If we don't screw this up, those numbers are going to go up."

I blinked and then had to close my eyes. "I can't watch. You mean, the Network's success is going to depend on . . . us?" My voice was squeaky. Why was I such a child about these things?

Luke's response was preceded by a little huff through his nose. I didn't have to peek at his face to know he wore a frown. "Yeah. I guess, mostly."

A hot roll of nausea broke across my belly. "I don't think I can do this," I admitted in a whisper.

His sudden movement startled me, and my eyes flew open, despite my desire to hide from the whole mess. "Hey, you're white as a sheet. Take it easy. Have you eaten? I'm going to get you one of those dinners. Hang on."

Before I could offer to stand, he climbed neatly over me and was up the aisle to the galley. Some shouted for him to bring them food, too, while others called for silence so they could watch the show.

Me? I was frozen. Pretty sure food wasn't going to help.

By the time Luke put a box lunch in front of me, I'd been drawn in by the vignettes of my fellow contestants. Asian hottie Alaric was actually Hawaiian. He was a successful businessman whose friends had egged him on to apply for *Cupid's Quest*.

Val, the beautiful Black woman who had checked in at the registration desk after me, really was a warrior—she was an Army veteran who had been on a championship bomb-loading team.

"Sounds like a competition they'd show on *Watch Now Sports*," Luke commented as he opened a bottle of water and put it in my hand.

"Shh," I said distractedly. He nudged my hand. I took a sip.

The sexy blonde who'd been all over Alaric in the bus was Jane-Alice. She said she was a sportswear buyer, but her list of places she'd been and extreme sports she'd mastered made it feel like her profession should have been listed as "adventurer."

By the time they got to me, I had sunk into my seat, embarrassed by how boring I was. Kindly, I was listed as a travel writer, with no clarification that I'd never been anywhere and wrote clickbait by lurking on Reddit and royalty-free photo sites for content. My two-minute bio even made me look sort of saintly, with my asthmatic sister and my fragile mother looking up at me with affection.

It could have been worse.

"Now you can eat," Luke said, pointing to the sandwich on my tray table.

I found I could nibble on the grapes and felt better.

By the end of the program, I was overwhelmed by meeting my fellow contestants and wished I'd had something to take notes with. Luke rose in his seat and scanned the cabin. He sat and gave me his assessment.

"Every pair of contestants here has one person who was profiled tonight. The rest of us must be getting our two minutes tomorrow night."

I looked too. Yes, I'd learned Theo was a software engineer and Knox was a stand-up comic, but I knew nothing about their seatmates. "Is the hour up already?"

Luke leaned over to bump his shoulder companionably with mine. "Not so bad, right?"

"Ha," I said inarticulately. "I don't want to eat this."

"Eat the turkey out of the sandwich. You'll need it. You have to take care of yourself, Joss."

Luke was my hero. I could love him. I could spend the rest of my life having him tell me to eat the turkey.

Obediently, I did as I was told, and he smiled. "Take the cookie. Save it for later."

Then he climbed over me again and cleared my place.

The final half hour of programming was a bloodfest called *PANIC!* that I knew I wouldn't like. And I was right. Between visits to emergency rooms across the nation, holding cells in police stations, and massive fires fought by the nation's firefighters, it was sensational and terrifying at the same time. When America was invited to vote for that day's hero, I was grateful that programming ended at eleven. I was exhausted.

"Wait! What about the adults-only show?!" Surprisingly, this came from a woman, not a man. I scrambled for her name. She was . . . Olivia. We were supposed to call her O. She was a stir-crazy farmer who looked like she had too much energy.

Theo and others cheered, but there were no answers from the authorities. In fact, there were no authorities.

I spoke without meaning to draw anyone's attention. "Wasn't there a buffer of dead air so the kids would go to bed before things got R-rated?"

"Shit," Theo said. "I have to wait?"

"What kind of after-hours shenanigans do you think anyone's gotten up to already?" Knox the comic turned around in his seat with a laugh.

"I dunno," Theo replied with a grin that displayed an alarming number of teeth. "I thought maybe Jane-Alice and Alaric might have put on a show for the cameras."

Alaric turned up his nose at the thought, and from behind me, I heard Jane-Alice. "I'm willing. I didn't know it was an option."

Saucy. That's what she was. And I was unnerved by saucy.

"I'll see you in the galley," Theo suggested, but Jane-Alice just laughed.

Luke returned. This time, I stood so he could get to his seat without the nimble-monkey act, and he thanked me. We settled.

"Can you sleep?" he asked me. "It would be better tomorrow if you could sleep now."

He was so sweet. "Absolutely," I said stoutly, even though I was pretty sure I was a million miles away from the utter vulnerability of sleep. "You too."

"You're right. Ignore them. Let's get some shut-eye."

I closed my eyes and concentrated on relaxing. It may have worked, because when I opened them again, the cabin lights had dimmed. The contestants around me were dozing. What else was there to do? No one had a book to read, a puzzle to solve, a teeth-whitening kit on hand. It was sleep or stare at the camera staring back at us.

I tried again and dozed unhappily.

The next time I opened my eyes, I was trapped in the miserable state of Too Awake To Sleep, Too Sleepy To Wake Up. I unclipped my belt and heaved myself to my feet. If I could do nothing else, at least I could stretch and tour as much of the Arrow as was available to me.

The walk was short. There were only six rows of seats for the twenty-four of us, with bathrooms and the tiny galley behind the seating area. And the galley was full. Jane-Alice and Val, both on the short side, were grouped around Theo, who towered over them.

Ew. Had I interrupted some Watch Now adults-only fodder? But Val saw me and waved me over. "Come look at this," she said. Friendly. Another potential friend! I blinked, trying to clear my thinking, and joined them.

Theo was working his hand back and forth on the frame of an open cabinet. "I don't like not knowing where I'm going," he said, as if that explained everything.

It's the middle of an endless night, Theo. Don't ask me to be intelligent. "What are you doing?" I asked.

"Magnetizing a paper clip. See?" He held out a straightened clip to me and went back to his motions. "There's a pretty strong magnet to keep the cupboard door shut. I should almost have it by now. You've got the cork, Army Girl?"

Val held out a cork disk, and Jane-Alice took a swig from an opened bottle of wine. The galley was apparently well-stocked with all kinds of booze.

"Thanks," Theo said absently. He pushed the paper clip through the cork and then laid it down gently to float in a pan of water that vibrated faintly on the counter. "Here we go."

We all leaned in to see what he saw.

"Will you look at that," Theo said in satisfaction.

I raised an eyebrow. I could look at that all day and still not see what he was seeing. "Look at what?"

He turned and grinned at me. "Plain as day, Big Eyes. See how the paper clip is pointing directly toward the cockpit?"

"Well, toward the cockpit or toward the tail," I offered.

His face took on a comical expression of surprise. "Head of the class for you, my little mink!" I had a new nickname, possibly from the boring brownness of my hair. "You're exactly right. We are either flying due north or due south. And given that we've been in the air for some eight hours now, I'd wager a guess we're heading to the bottom of South America. Maybe even farther."

"Farther?" I gasped.

"Antarctica!" Jane-Alice crowed. "Antarctica!"

Oh my god. Not really?

"I'm wearing a sundress," I said stupidly. "I can't go to Antarctica."

Theo's grin managed to get even bigger.

Oh, damn.

6

A MITE AIRISH

If Dante Alighieri had known about intercontinental travel, it surely would have defined his fourth circle of hell at least.

I spent the remainder of the plane ride alternately frowning over the thought of Antarctica in a sundress and finally, at last, falling asleep.

When I woke, pleased to have gotten actual rest (surely I'd slept for at least four hours?) my wristwatch, the traitor, told me I'd been asleep for twelve minutes.

Aghhh.

At last, just after seven in the morning (assuming we were still in the same time zone), green-haired Julie appeared and unlocked what turned out to be the breakfast cabinet in the galley. To those of us who admitted to being awake (because surely the others couldn't possibly be sleeping, could they?), Julie whispered rapidly and amply without, somehow, telling us anything.

She looked fresh and happy and had a different plaid shirt on. I sniffed her as she went past; she definitely smelled clean. There was a shower somewhere on this plane.

Now, *that* would be a prize worth winning.

Not even a comb. No toothbrush. Nothing to do when I stared at myself balefully in the tiny bathroom but run my fingers through my hair and pull it back again into a messy ponytail. I sighed. Nobody would want to look at this on their TV screen. Sooner or later, they'd have to return our luggage... right?

Finally, an impersonal captain's voice told us to strap in for landing. After almost fourteen hours in the air. Let me out of here, I thought.

It had never occurred to me how useful it is to be able to see out a window when a plane lands. Without anything to let us brace for the bounce, we all gasped when the plane touched down. No more flying in planes that have no windows, please.

Wink appeared while we were still taxiing to somewhere. Didn't he know not to unbuckle until the plane had come to a complete halt?

"Welcome!" he called heartily. He, too, looked suspiciously clean and well-rested. "Welcome to Tierra del Fuego!"

"Told you," Theo muttered from across the aisle. He seemed to be addressing the universe in general.

"We've just landed in Ushuaia, at the largest southernmost airport in the Americas. Bienvenidos a Argentina!"

How bad could that be? Would a sundress be a good choice here?

"We're going to be met by minibuses to take us to our accommodations. Take a look at your name tag. There's a sticker on the back. See it?"

Like everyone else, I flipped my name tag over. Sure enough, I had a 2 sticker. I looked at Luke and found he was looking at me.

"Did you get number one?" he asked.

"I got number two. We're being separated?"

"It'll be fine, I'm sure. They have to bring us back together at some point, right?"

The movement of the plane stopped, and Wink called for the bus-one riders. Luke rested his hand on my shoulder and gave me a smile. "See you soon," he said.

There went my True Love. Maybe.

We were all standing in the aisles now, the bus-two people clogging up the path for the bus-one people. Rose ended up at my side. "Are you a two?"

"I am! You too?" Her presence immediately reassured me. "Maybe it's all the girls on bus two?"

The wall of T-shirt in front of me turned. I was right next to Theo. "Sorry, sweetness. I'm bus two too." He grinned at both of us. "Come on, Big Eyes. Surely you can figure out why we were separated this way."

A fizz of panic brightened my senses. Was there something I was supposed to have realized?

I scanned the group still left on the plane. Knox, the red-haired comic. Val, the veteran bomb loader. Alaric, with his lush, black hair (although not as lush as my Luke's fine head). Twelve of us.

Twelve people whose faces I now more or less recognized. I could put names to people I hadn't spoken to yet.

"Bus two is all the contestants who were profiled last night on the show," I realized.

"Attagirl," Theo said smugly. "The other dozen of us are probably going to face a phalanx of cameras. We're done being introduced to America. It's their turn now."

Rose was wide-eyed. "How'd you figure that out?"

Theo scoffed. "Pattern recognition. I'm a coder. This is what I do, Little Pink."

I turned away to hide my dislike for his patronizing air—and his dismissive nicknames. I'd figured it out, too . . . once he'd pointed me at it.

Wink reappeared. "Bus two, c'mon up! And if you're near someone on the small side, make sure you hold on to them. The wind out there is a little zippy this morning!" He said it with a huge grin, so I thought he was kidding.

Until I stepped out the door and into a staggering wind tunnel.

A minibus waited below on the tarmac, rocking on its chassis. A cameraman inside the van's door focused on us. Between me and the van was a staircase and a blast of wild, fresh air like a vengeful wind god.

"Jeezum!" I said as I grabbed my skirt with one hand and the stair rail with the other. With a little aerodynamic angling, I could have probably become airborne. At least it wasn't freezing cold.

I followed Theo down the stairs and then heard Rose behind me utter a scream. When I turned, she'd been forced into the stair railing by the wind. Through the wild lashings of my hair, torn loose from what turned out to be a very ineffective ponytail, I saw her panic.

I had a split second to question my decision—there was a camera conveniently placed below me, after all—and then let go of my skirt to reach a hand out to her.

She grabbed my arm in a panic, and my skirt flew up and got caught on what I rapidly realized was Theo's head.

"Thanks," he called, and I cringed at the humiliating arrogance in his voice.

"Knock it off!" I shouted. "Help me with her!"

"I've got her." The next person out the plane door was the nurse—Milton? Michael? Mason? He had enough bulk to resist the tornado and wrapped an arm around Rose, who glommed on to him. She filled her hands with his shirt, and with my freed hand, I tugged my skirt off the bald, grinning head below me.

"We must do this again sometime," he shouted above the wind.

"Get going, please!"

Once in the van, I watched nervously as the other contestants clawed their way down the staircase, but Rose was the smallest of us, and she was safely in her seat, still clutching Mason. (It *was* Mason. She'd remembered his name, even if I didn't. I knew she did because she thanked him repeatedly. He was kind in response.)

Instead of sending us into the airport, a cluster of customs officials came to us to match our faces to the passports Julie handed them. We were frowned at, questioned about what we were importing, and then dismissed. The formalities had been observed.

Wink was the last one on our bus. He'd managed to scare up a fetching knit cap that kept his impressive anchorman mane of hair tidy in the wind, and he sported a Watch Now Network windbreaker. Could I get one of those?

"Here we go!" he called cheerfully, and there we went. Past the airport, down a bare and windswept road, through a colorful town filled with intriguing public art between our road and the thin fringe of beach, and finally . . .

. . . onto a long pier.

No hotel, then, I thought, as we pulled up to a smallish cruise ship.

"Don't be surprised if the wind is a little stronger here," Wink announced. Great. "Hold on to your hats! Up the gangway, inside, and we're going to meet in the lounge. Just follow Julie!"

Julie, herself a little small for the wind, waved happily from the ship. Rose took a deep breath and a death grip on Mason, and we left the van.

The wind was so powerful that I couldn't help but laugh at the buffeting. This was definitely outside my normal morning.

Who knew wind this strong was blowing around, and everyone here thought it was life as usual?

Once inside (oh, the relief of still air!), Julie led us like ducklings up the stairs and into a pretty lounge. Where was Luke?

We sat in clusters. I'd now been drawn into the Rose-Mason dyad, and Mason and I shook hands formally. He had a pleasant if unremarkable appearance—sandy hair and a soothing smile. Cute but not terrifying. He was probably a comforting nurse, and he was caring for Rose with kind professionalism.

We sat there long enough for me to wish I had a comb. The knots in my hair from that wind were staggering. Getting them out of my hair would leave me as bald as Theo.

Knox, at the dockside window, announced when the luggage truck arrived. I wasn't the only one relieved to hear my suitcase had made it to the bottom of the planet with me. I had a comb. A toothbrush. A sweater. A perfectly respectable pair of jeans that wouldn't expose my nether regions in a stiff wind. Could I have those things now, please?

We sat and sat and sat. People got restless. We all took turns at the dockside windows (where not much was going on) and the oceanside window (where mesmerizing cat's-paws of sea spray were lifted in the air by the wind), and three different people checked to see if the bar had any booze in it. It didn't.

Finally, the low rumble of the engines under our feet changed pitch. "We're leaving!" Knox shouted. "We're underway!"

I didn't understand the compulsion that made us all rush to the windows to see this amazing feat, because there wasn't anything to see except a guy in a yellow rain slicker on the dock, braced against the wind, who waved at the ship.

"Bye, Ushuaia," Theo said. (He'd refused to get up and still sat in a rude sprawl, his legs blocking anyone who wanted to go past.) "Hello, Antarctica."

This sparked a vigorous conversation about where we were going and what we would be doing (and if anyone had a comb, and it wasn't just the six women who wondered. That made Theo laugh).

Ushuaia disappeared with startling rapidity. We were still within sight of land, but all signs of civilization had vanished by the time Wink bounded into the lounge, his hair neatly combed.

"Hello, *Cupid's Quest!*"

Mason nudged me and nodded to the closed-up bar. Somehow, a cameraman had appeared without anyone noticing. I sat up straighter and regretted my hair once again.

Wink went on. "Welcome to your first day of competition! As you know," (we didn't) "we are sailing across Drake's Passage, the most notorious waters in the world!"

I looked at my fellow contestants. We all wore the same, *Say what now?* face of confusion. Wink did not satisfy our curiosity.

"And in thirty-six hours—well, thirty-five now—we'll be making landfall in Antarctica! Exotic enough for you?" He beamed, and the camera panned the room. I felt uncombed and disreputable. "I'm sure you remember that each week begins with our fun little competition, True Love or Double Dud. This challenge will determine who will be staying in the owner's suite and who will get a bunk in the crew's quarters, so you're going to want to win this one!"

"Where's Nessa?" Of course it was Theo shouting the question. (Who was Nessa? What would Theo's "The One" be like? And where was Luke?)

Wink ignored him. "Let's get you all situated so we can start the challenge. Gentlemen, you first. Down that hallway, you'll find your name on a door. Go inside and follow the directions you find there. Well? Get going!"

The six men stood, eyebrows raised, and looked uncertain.

Alaric, Theo, Knox, Mason, and two others—why couldn't I remember their names?

"This way!" Julie called from the doorway. "Come this way! Here we go! You've got it! Come on, come this way! It's your first competition. Are you excited? I know—me too. Yep, just down here. See your name on the door? There you go."

We could hear Julie like a sheepdog, cajoling and nudging the guys farther from us until there were just us six women, Wink, and the silent camera at the bar. We'd been carved into successively smaller and smaller groups.

Julie appeared in the doorway and nodded at Wink.

"Ladies! Let's get you to your first competition!"

7
ZEPHYR, GOD OF THE WEST WINDS

Wink was showing all his blindingly white teeth. "Ladies, same drill! Down that hallway, you'll find your name on a door. Go in and follow the instructions you find there."

I'd done better with the women's names. Rose and I were already good friends (she clutched my hand as we walked the hallway, and I clutched back), and I'd met warrior Val and curvy vixen Jane-Alice at Theo's I'll Make A Compass Out Of Household Items demonstration the night before.

The final two women were less well-known, but at least I knew their names. Olivia was supposed to be referred to as O, and the artist was Euphoria. Great name; it sounded made-up.

"Look!" Rose's grip on my hand tightened. She'd found her name on the door label . . . with a second name. "There I am. Cabin six—and I'm with Mason!" She squealed. "Oh, thank god!"

She paused at the door, and all five contestants and Julie turned to look at the first of us to disappear into the unknown. She heaved a sigh and pushed through the door.

"Look, Joss," Val called to me. "You're in five, right here. With Knox."

Knox? Not Luke? I hoped America was understanding this better than I was. I ducked my head to hide my confusion and pushed through the door. It closed behind me with a *click*, and I was alone.

I was in a typical cruise-ship cabin. One double bed. A wall of glass led onto a balcony.

On the balcony—three people.

Two were covered in flare-orange arctic parkas. They carried large cameras.

The third was Knox, his curly, red hair blown almost straight in the wind. He looked at me through the sliding-glass door. His long, boxy shorts rippled against his legs. He shrugged at me and then gestured. *C'mere.*

Wait. Out there? In my sundress? I didn't understand.

Then one of the cameras turned to focus on me, and I saw the face behind the lens.

It was Luke.

My brain screeched, *What? I don't understand.*

Luke reached out a mittened hand and slid the door open. "First competition starts in two minutes. Come out now. You don't want to be disqualified."

"Luke?"

His big, dark eyes looked abashed. "Sorry, Joss. I'm not actually a contestant. Come on out."

What?!

I stepped through the door, and he closed it behind me. The wind was—incredibly—worse. How could this not be considered a hurricane? I wadded my skirt up and pushed the extra fabric between my legs, clutching my thighs together to avoid treating everyone to an up-close view of yesterday's underwear. "What is going on?"

Knox shrugged again and then thought to hold out his hand. "We haven't met yet. I'm Knox."

The cameras zoomed in on his outstretched hand, and I took his in mine. He was warmer than me, even though he'd been out here longer.

"I'm Joss," I said. "Any clue what's going on?"

He shook his head, trying to hold his hair back from stinging at his eyes. "Nope. But we're all out here." He nodded left and right, and I stepped into the wind far enough to see that six balconies held people. Mason and Rose were next to us on one side, with their own pair of cameramen (or rather, one cameraman and one camerawoman). Mason had an arm around Rose's shoulder, and she was tucked into his side, her eyes wide and frightened.

On the other side, Euphoria the artist was grouped with one of the guys whose name I couldn't remember and their camera people. Three more balconies past them stretched along the side of the ship.

"Here we go," Luke said, who was looking over the side.

'Here we go?' What did he mean? Was he a traitor or what? He was supposed to be my Guy! Come on!

A black inflatable boat appeared off the side of the ship. I took one quick look over and down the side of the ship, where the wind was horrible, and saw a marine door below us. That was where the Zodiac had come from.

Wink was crouched in the bow of the Zodiac, Julie on one side and the gray-haired cameraman from the bus on the other. All three were dressed in massive orange parkas. Damn it. Where was *my* parka?

Wink held up a microphone. When he spoke, I could hear him from behind me. Luke and the camerawoman each had radios wired into their safety harnesses.

"*Cupid's Quest*! This is the first True Love or Double Dud! If you can hear me, raise your right hand! Very good—that's all twelve of you. Now, as you have probably guessed, the twenty-four of you who traveled in the contestants' cabin of the Arrow were actually twelve contestants and twelve field producers who are doubling as cameramen and women. We're sorry to deceive you, but we got great footage of you from last night!"

My outrage heated me up, which was nice. Even though the air wasn't very cold, the wind was stripping heat from my body with powerful efficiency. I turned to glare at Luke. He shrugged.

It's a job, he mouthed. Didn't want his words to be picked up by the microphones. Deceiver.

"Our first competition," Wink called from the Zodiac bouncing along beside our ship, "is simple. First couple to go back inside gets crew's quarters for the week. Last couple on their balcony will stay in the owner's suite. You'll want to know the owner's suite has a sauna that is already heated up and ready for you. Sound good?"

Jesus. The wind was pounding at me, and I was losing heat. A sauna sounded like heaven. I looked at Knox, and he nodded at me.

"We can do this," he said stoutly.

I nodded back. I wasn't going to give up.

"If everyone understands, then here we go!" Wink fired off a starter pistol, its sound all but lost in the wind.

"Clearly, we've already started," Knox said.

"Let's get against the door," I said, but Luke and the woman with the other camera shook their heads and blocked us. They wanted us away from the enclosure around the door. We were to stand fully in the wind, the five-rail fences between each balcony and the outside doing nothing to offer some kind of wind block.

I glared at Luke and then did an assessment. What were my options here?

All these cameras. All these people with unbrushed teeth

and hopelessly tangled hair and our clothes being closely molded by the wind to our bodies—right. They wanted ratings.

"Knox," I sighed. "I'll warm your front if you warm my back."

I moved so he stood behind me. Knox reached tentative arms around my waist. I took his hands in mine and pulled him close up against me. Might as well—and he was a warm bulwark against the strength of the wind.

Luke murmured into the walkie-talkie on his shoulder and the cameraman on the Zodiac zoomed in on Knox and me, utter strangers who were now clinging together.

The other pairs on their balconies noticed, and the ripple effect down the line would have been amusing, if a smile in this wind wouldn't have dried my teeth.

"Look at them," Knox murmured in my ear. He turned me bodily to look down the line of balconies. The only two people who weren't now clinging together for warmth were Jane-Alice and Theo. Of course—not Theo. He was the most rebellious of rebels.

"What is she doing?" I asked.

As we watched, Jane-Alice did the unthinkable: she took off a layer.

Every camera with a sight line was now focused on the balcony of cabin two. It was hard for me to see from the balcony of cabin five, but she was definitely busy doing something, with Theo leaning down to watch.

Her hand came into sight, holding something dark. Theo uttered a bark of a laugh that carried even over the wind. He took it from her and pulled a knit cap onto his bald head. The activity went on, until the people in cabin three (Alaric and O) took pity and turned to explain to the guy and Euphoria in cabin four.

Euphoria turned to us. "She's zipping sleeves onto her vest."

"Where did she get sleeves?" Knox asked.

"Pockets, I guess. Her vest is covered in pockets." Euphoria's braids looked like they hurt against her face and neck in the wind.

I left the warmth of Knox's embrace long enough to explain to Rose and Mason. She was shivering, but her determined little chin said she was going to tough it out.

It seemed like hours in the shivering wind but was probably only a few minutes until Jane-Alice finished turning her simple canvas vest into an effective windbreaker. She then proved her brilliance by putting it on Theo and having him zip her up into it with him.

He stood with his arms around her, only the top of her blonde head poking out under his chin, and he lowered his head into the wind. Then they stood still. Like statues.

Indifferent to the tempest.

"We're going to lose," Knox murmured.

"No, we're not," I said loyally, even though it was pretty obvious we sure weren't going to win.

The cameras caught all of it.

I closed my eyes and thought about sun-drenched beaches. The dry, baking heat next to a roaring fire. The bone-deep heat of the sauna, already blazing away in the owner's suite. "Mind over matter," I said to Knox. "We can last."

"You'd better turn around and face me," he said. "Protect your core. I swear I'm not trying to cop a feel."

I found I could still laugh. My back resented being turned into the wind, but my front cheered when pressed up against Knox's chest. The clot of skirt fabric between my shivering thighs channeled a chill straight into my core.

"Man," he gasped when I first laid my front against him. "You're cold."

"Sorry."

"No, it's fine. You're okay?"

I nodded against his neck. "You?"

"Yeah. I'm good."

We stood that way, trying to emulate the statues in cabin two. The wind fell briefly, and I heard Mason trying to talk Rose into giving up.

"We'll be fine in the crew's quarters. You're too small to stay out here—you're freezing."

The wind rose again and I lost the thread of their discussion, but I opened my eyes and turned my head to look.

Mason had his back to the ocean, with Rose tucked into him. Her eyes were open, and she saw me looking. She gave me a brave smile through her shivering.

"Knox," I said. "Come on."

He was confused but let me shuffle us sideways to the railing that separated our balcony from Rose and Mason's. I reached out an arm and gestured to them. "Come here," I said. "All four together. We can warm her up."

Mason simply picked Rose up and came to meet us. I reached an arm around Mason, and Knox pulled Rose against him. We made a knot of humanity with a hard, cold railing between us, but the four of us created enough of a wind block that our faces were protected from the worst of the wind.

"Good!" Mason shouted. The four cameras were clustered around us, trying to get a good image of two pairs becoming one larger unit.

Parts of me were colder than before. Parts of me were warmer. And Rose, nestled at the intersection of the three larger bodies around her, stood more of a chance.

Mason raised his head and looked past me. "The next two pairs are doing this too," he said. Well, it only made sense. The four of us were more likely to give the statues in cabin two a run for their money.

"How about cabin one?" I asked. "Are they sharing heat with Theo and Jane-Alice?" My lips were numb. My words were thick, but Mason understood.

"Nope. Nick and Val are on their own. Theo and Jane-Alice aren't moving."

Figured. Why help someone else?

Now my job was to endure.

"In summers, where I come from," I said into the pocket of stillness at the center of us, "it gets really hot. And kind of sweaty. The air doesn't move, and the heat bakes into your bones. Can you imagine that, Rose?"

"Wh-where?" She shivered.

"Pennsylvania. Reading, Pennsylvania. You?" She didn't answer, so I asked more urgently, "Where are you from, Rose?"

"Naples," she said. "Naples, Florida." Her pink hair tickled my chin.

"I bet it's hot there. Is it hot there, Rose?"

"Hot," she agreed faintly.

"Tell me. How hot? Rose? How hot?"

Rose didn't answer. Mason looked at Knox. "Can you feel her shivering?"

Knox shook his head. "Not anymore."

Mason pulled away from me. "That's it. I'm taking her in. She's got hypothermia."

"No!" Rose protested, but her face was white.

"Good luck, you guys," Mason said. He picked up Rose again—the cameras loved that—and fumbled with the sliding door. Then they were gone.

"And there it is!" Wink, in his Zodiac, was gleeful. "Mason and Rosemary will be sharing a bunk in the crew's quarters! Now, who's going to win that sauna? Any bets, America?"

Knox and I shuffled back from the cold railing and clung to each other. Just us against the wind once again.

I gritted my teeth and closed my eyes.

I wasn't cold. I wasn't cold. Knox felt good. I wasn't cold.

8

THE BLISS OF HEAT

I was pressed so close to Knox on our wind-blasted balcony that I felt his words in his chest as much as heard them.

"We're not going to beat Theo and Jane-Alice, you know."

I couldn't control my hair, which was now beating against Knox's face as much as mine. I turned to look past the final remaining quartet from cabins three and four, to where I could see tall Theo's bent head. They hadn't moved.

They weren't human.

"I know." Despair filled my frozen heart.

"So let's go in. What do you say?"

"What?" His words so surprised me that I lifted my head from his chest and looked at him. Knox was cute, with thick, dark lashes framing warm amber eyes. Anything warm was good. "Give up?"

"Yeah." The cameras had discovered our faces were now visible; they moved in to get close-ups and not miss a word in the shrieking wind. "Why not? The crew's quarters are taken now, and we're not going to get the sauna. Unless you think we are."

My brain was frozen in the wind, but his words broke the ice dam. "We're not going to. Not now." I meant we didn't even have the benefit of four bodies anymore, but my mouth was too stiff to form the words.

Knox didn't need my explanation. "We can no longer lose, and we know we can't win. What are we doing out here?"

It took me a few seconds, and then I had to figure out how to unlock my arms from around his back. "Y-yep," I said. I stumbled for the door, not caring that Wink was now announcing our withdrawal.

Together, Knox and I tugged open the door and fell into the warmth and stillness of the cabin in front of us. Luke and the woman came in behind us, and thankfully, one of them closed the door because my hands were too stiff.

The four of us stood in silence. I was trying to think of how to gather the warmth into me when I realized introductions would be appropriate.

"Knox, this is Luke," I said in a gasp. "Luke used to be my One True Love, but now he's a cameraman. Luke, this is Knox."

Luke—damn him—was laughing as he reached for Knox's unresisting hand and shook it. "Nice to meet you. You already know Danika."

She was the cute Nordic blonde who'd been sitting with Knox in the first row on the plane. Of course she was. We'd all apparently been sitting next to the man or woman who would film us for eight straight weeks.

"How do you do," I said politely to Danika. She blinked but shook my hand while still filming. "Wow. You're dedicated."

"Your luggage is outside the door," Luke said.

"I'll get it." Knox stumbled around, dragging in bags and my backpack.

Comb! Sweater! Why hadn't I packed a snowsuit and an electric blanket? I grabbed my phone. "Is there a Wi-Fi password?" I asked.

Luke pointed me to a card on the desk. No texts awaited me. How could they not have tried to reach me? Never mind. No news was good news; Mom and Claire were probably still okay. I sent my first message of a long twenty-four hours to my family. I shivered as I waited for a reply, but the three "I'm texting back" dots didn't show up.

Knox must have seen me shivering as I hunched over my phone. "You can shower first," he said gallantly.

"My hero," I said, overwhelmed with love and adoration for a red-headed comic who I already knew far more closely than anyone else in at least three years. I set the phone down. But as I tugged my suitcase behind me toward the bathroom, I remembered.

Cameras.

In the bathroom.

The thought of a hot shower—of baking away my shivers—was the only thing keeping me from hopeless despair. But there I would be: naked. And wet. And on tape for the late-night program. Disgusting.

"Does this mean you're supposed to come into the bathroom with me?" I asked Luke.

He shook his head. "Camera's hidden in the bathroom. Don't worry about it. With that contest going on outside? This is probably your best bet for privacy. There's too much going on out there to pay attention to what's going on in here. Plus, soon there will be twelve naked bodies in those showers. Go now. Don't think about it. Just warm up."

Behind the serious, professional camera with the lidless, staring lens, it was still kind, friendly Luke. The guy who made me save my cookie in case I got hungry later.

I knew—I *knew*—he was misleading me. It didn't matter what went on outside this room; the camera in my bathroom would still record my nude, wet body and my girlishly small bust, and the Watch Now Network had my written permission to use that footage whenever they wanted.

But I was so cold.

"I won't be long," I said to Knox.

He'd grabbed a blanket off the foot of the bed and wrapped it around himself. He nodded. "I'm good. Go ahead."

The heat was almost painful on my chilled skin—at least, at first. After the initial shock of warmth, the water was a baptism. Go ahead, I thought. Film this. Watch all you want as I stand with my face turned up to the stream, letting hot water wash down me. Wing bones. Small of the back. Behind my knees. Ankles. Ohhh.

As soon as I could force myself to, I shut off the water and stepped out, mindful that Knox was still waiting for his turn. My hair was still hopeless and now wet too. Combing it out would take far too long. I needed to turn the bathroom over to him.

I emerged, clean and warm and dressed in more appropriate clothes, but with a mat of wet, snarled hair like a bird's nest woven onto my scalp. "Go ahead," I said.

Luke and Danika had made themselves comfortable in the two armchairs. "Three couples still left out there," Danika reported to me.

"You're kidding!" I'd been in the shower for at least ten minutes. No one could survive out there that long in shorts and T-shirts.

"Not kidding," Danika said. "Wink's getting annoyed. It's cold out there!"

I looked at her, wondering if she thought she was telling me something I didn't know. "Theo and Jane-Alice," I guessed, "and then the quartet next door?"

Luke shook his head. "Paul and Euphoria lasted about two minutes after you guys bailed. Now Alaric and O are fighting about going in or not, and that's keeping them warm. Nick and Val are staying firm in cabin one. And the odds-on favorite of Jane-Alice and her magical vest are still standing like they're made of stone."

"And all three couples are standing alone?" I clarified.

He nodded. "Now it's down to willpower. Danika and I would like to thank you guys for giving up when you did. That was the smart move."

"Are you supposed to be talking to me like we're friends?" I asked.

He shrugged. "I'll still tell you when you have parsley in your teeth, Joss." So cute. So annoying. "No one in America is going to want to look at you with your hair like that. Comb it out and I'll interview you."

I turned in a huff and plopped down on the bed to take a long time to untangle my hair.

The snarls were incredible and absorbed all my attention. When I realized I was sitting on the only bed in the room, I shook my head. I'd been so naïve. Of course there was only one bed.

"This is my cabin with Knox, right?"

Luke's camera was up and filming. Apparently, my hair was now suitable for American families. Danika answered. "That's right."

"And based on that space you're sitting in, Danika, I'd bet there used to be a sofa there, but it's been taken out."

She grinned, smug. "What would be the fun of giving you two separate places to sleep?"

Luke was filming my face. I was sure I looked like I'd bitten into a lemon. "Did Knox realize this while I was in the shower?"

She smiled. Then—the sound I was dying to hear: the text message signal on my phone.

Claire was typing for Mom. They were excited by the show and wanted details.

"Remember your nondisclosure agreement," Luke said as I started to type back.

Damn. He was right.

I contented myself with telling them I was fine and wasn't allowed to say anything. Claire pouted, but we agreed they'd watch the show that evening and keep up with me that way. I reminded her about her doctor's appointment and told her where her asthma inhaler refill was.

Then Danika swung her camera up to her shoulder. Here came Knox out of the shower, clean and cute in jeans and a sweater. I set down the phone and shifted so I could face him. "Did you realize you and I are going to be sleeping together?" My face flamed through the heat of a blush, and I rushed to correct myself. "I mean, you and I are going to be sleeping in the same bed. Like, side by side. Not *sleeping together*—I mean, sleeping together."

He laughed and held up a hand. "I know. I can count beds too. It'll be fine."

I swallowed my anxiety, and he saw my expression. He sat at the foot of the bed—same mattress, decent distance between us. "No matter what they're hoping for, Joss, I promise to be a gentleman. Scout's honor." He held his fingers in the scout's salute.

His expression was so earnest, I had to laugh. "Were you a scout?"

"For almost three weeks," he said. "Once I realized they wanted me to do community service, I joined the marching band instead."

Knox was adorable. "And how long did that last?"

"Oh, almost three days. Did you know they have to march at the same time as they play?" I uttered an unladylike snort and covered my mouth in surprised shame, which made him laugh too. "So, we'll sleep together—we just won't sleep together. Deal?"

He held out a warm, freckled hand and I shook it gladly. "Thanks, Knox. I'll be a gentleman too."

"I hope not." He waggled his eyebrows at me in a parody of lust, and my mood brightened more. Knox was fun.

"That's it," Luke interrupted, his hand on an earpiece. "Alaric broke first, and then Nick dragged Val inside. Theo and Jane-Alice get the owner's suite. Good. Okay." He stood, as did Danika. "You guys have about two hours until dinner. Take a nap, have hot sex, whatever you want. Just be in the dining room at six."

Time change—I forgot. In my mind, it was lunchtime, but here in Drake's Passage, it was after four in the afternoon. "You're leaving?" We weren't getting some actual alone time to get to know each other, were we?

"We're leaving. Production staff meeting in fifteen minutes. But don't worry, you're still on film." Luke gestured broadly across the room.

Hidden cameras. Of course.

"Well, don't be a stranger," Knox said, hurrying to open the door and usher Luke and Danika out.

The cabin seemed awkwardly large once our population was halved. "I can't believe," Knox said as he came back and sat in one of the armchairs, "that she was going to be the future Mrs. Knox Dobiecki."

I knew what he meant. Luke was undoubtedly a nice guy, but I still felt betrayed by the fake-contestant falsehood. I'd thought I was cozy in the intimacy of a long plane flight with my future true love, not the field producer who was pumping me for information to share with America.

Still, there were fresher topics of discussion to consider. "Your last name is Dobiecki? Don't you want to be a stand-up comedian?"

He put his hand to his chest in feigned outrage. "Want to be? Ma'am, I *am* a stand-up comedian."

I laughed. "It's just—Knox Dobiecki doesn't sound like a comic's name."

"Really? Okay. Then how about Johnston Dobiecki? That's my middle name."

The twinkle in his eyes betrayed his air of innocence, and I chuckled. "So... what do we do now, Johnston?"

He stretched, lacing his fingers together far overhead. "I'm sure we should be plotting against our brother-and-sister contestants, trying to figure out how to win. Or exploring the dark recesses of each other's souls in order to further the Great Passion We Will Share." I laughed again. I could hear the capital letters in his voice. "But after that flight? I'm in favor of a nap."

"I second that motion. Together, though? On the bed?" I looked doubtfully at the bed I was sitting on. It seemed very small.

"Together." He was firm. "Side by side. I'll bump my foot against yours deliberately so we don't have to be jumpy about the first touch. We'll pull up the blankets and look at the gray, windswept ocean out there and go to sleep. What do you think?"

I was already pulling back the covers. "Yes. Yes, please. Right now."

The sleep I'd been chasing for the entire plane ride was waiting right behind my eyelids. I lay down next to Knox, who smelled of shampoo and clean clothes and warmth, and I went to sleep.

Paradise.

Until the loudspeaker jerked us awake, pulses pounding.

9

YOU WANT ME TO WEAR WHAT?

"Dinner in fifteen minutes!" It was Julie's voice—the director's assistant—coming from a loudspeaker in the ceiling. "Wake up! You have a quarter hour to get to the dining room, and that's on deck four, and you just have to go down one staircase and then go toward the back of the boat—I mean, ship—and it won't take you very long, so you've got time to wash your face and brush your hair and things like that because you've got time, but you can't go back to sleep, so don't think you can because it's dinner in fifteen—what? Okay. This is your wake-up call. Dinner in the dining room in fifteen minutes. That's all."

Knox was on his side, facing me. "If we killed her, could we sleep some more?" His eyes didn't even open as he spoke.

I stretched. "I don't think she's killable. No one with that much energy can be distracted so easily."

We lay there for a moment, and my eyes closed again.

"I can see you!" Julie shouted through the loudspeakers. "I can see all twelve of you! Get up!"

I jerked awake again and rolled out of bed. Being vertical would help me wake up, surely.

Knox followed more slowly. "Coffee would help," he groaned.

My stomach was already filled with acid. "Yuck."

He stopped. "You don't like coffee? How can you be the future Mrs. Knox Dobiecki if you don't like coffee?"

"I thought I was going to be the future Mrs. Johnston Dobiecki. Can you hand me my comb?"

My phone showed no emergencies I needed to solve. Knox and I stumbled out of our cabin with almost three minutes to spare.

The dining room was designed to hold more than the cast of *Cupid's Quest*. They must have bought out the whole boat for a week. Someone was spending some money.

Because they did, most of the dining room was empty. A single oval table was set up for the contestants (which was obvious, since the table centerpieces were short tripods bristling with cameras), and smaller tables were scattered around for the crew and the camera team. Luke waved from his table with Danika and two others. I grimaced at him, and he laughed.

"Welcome to dinner! Please sit. You'll see place cards with your name." Wink was annoyingly awake and unwrinkled. "Thank you for being on time!"

A waiter put down a bowl of soup before us as soon as we sat, not waiting for the whole table to arrive. When Knox grabbed his spoon and growled in pleasure at the taste, I realized I was hungry. Starving. Ravenous.

The soup occupied my attention. It was almost too hot, which was the perfect temperature. I blocked out everything else while consuming it, scraping my spoon hopefully against the china when I'd finished.

"Roll," Knox said helpfully, handing me the basket.

Yes. Yes, roll. And butter. Ahhh.

Green-haired Julie appeared at last, shepherding the final two contestants (Euphoria, the artist, and the guy whose name I couldn't remember, who was blushing at being the last to arrive). Then she and Wink took their places at the head of the table, our *Cupid's Quest* mommy and daddy.

Well, sort of. Julie wore a headset, as did Shout the director, who sat in the corner, staring at a screen. Ah. Shout wanted to give us directions, but he wouldn't speak out loud. Julie was a cheerful, bright-eyed spokesman.

"Please," Wink said. "Go ahead and eat. I know you're all hungry, and the food is great on this ship. But while you're eating, I'm going to give you some information so we can keep things moving along."

"Fish, steak, or pasta?" the waiter at my elbow murmured quietly.

We were served our meals and dug in as Wink went on. "The network execs are pleased with the ratings from last night, and we know tonight's will be good too—because this will be the night they see your shock when you realize you've been sitting with a field producer on the plane."

"Of course," Alaric said dryly. "Why wouldn't America want to see the faces of a dozen people who have been betrayed?"

Wink offered his best anchorman smile. "No one told you your seatmate was your ideal partner, did they? You assumed it."

"Assumptions make an ass out of you and me," Rose said brightly.

Alaric glared at her. "How are the crew's quarters, loser?"

Rose was startled by Alaric's venom. "Just fine!" she said staunchly. "At least Mason and I are both slim enough to fit in a single bunk!"

Rose seemed to think she'd landed a blow there, but Alaric had no fat on his body. He rolled his eyes at her.

"Let's get back to the ratings," Wink said firmly.

A red light came on atop the camera pointing at his handsome face. Wink was now being recorded.

"The Watch Now Network is adding a potential prize for all of you. Interested?"

For the first time, the collective focus shifted from the food. "Yes, I am," Theo said. We all nodded.

"As you know, we've done extensive psychological testing on all of you and have selected your ideal partner. We hope you find love on this quest, along with treasure. We hope Cupid's dart will strike you!" He beamed at us. It was Val the warrior who snorted, but Wink went on. "That's why we're now offering a five-million-dollar prize to the first couple who gets married."

All the camera lights were now on. Shout was watching our reactions from his corner, and soon America would be watching too.

"I'm guessing you mean we have to marry our partner here—not someone else?" Knox linked his fingers with mine and waved our united hands over the glasses of wine.

"Thank you for that clarification, Knox. That is what I mean. The first *Cupid's Quest* couple to marry will win five million dollars!"

My hand felt clammy in Knox's. Was I supposed to get married? Did I *want* to get married? Knox was adorable—but did I want to tie the knot with him? He hadn't even met my family yet.

"Yes," Wink said happily. "I can see I have your attention. After dinner, your field producers will interview you to get your reactions. Let's get to some legalities." He waved his hand toward the corner where Shout lurked. The red lights on all the cameras went off. I wasn't the only one who sighed in relief. "Julie, the contracts?" Julie opened a folder and passed around a fan of paper. "Everyone take one. Talk to your lawyer or trusted adviser before you sign this," Wink said robotically. "As you'll see, you'll get the five mil on your wedding day. If you divorce before the first year ends, you'll be on the hook to repay that money, so either bank it or don't pretend. Right? Let's get to the details."

He walked us through the document. Not one of us asked to consult with our lawyers. When Julie passed around pens, everyone signed.

Julie gathered the papers into her efficient folder and nodded to Shout. The cameras came back on again, and Wink's personal wattage went back to full-on. "Tomorrow, our first big challenge begins! Want to hear about it?"

I was dazed by the double whammy of a potential marriage and a potential fortune, but Wink's words refocused my attention. "Yes," I chorused with the others.

"We'll reach the peninsula of Antarctica tomorrow. Maybe you didn't know, but this crossing of Drake's Passage is unusually balmy. Aren't you happy about that?"

I thought about the bitter, heat-shredding wind we'd endured on our balconies and decided I didn't need to fake a smile at how pleasant our passage was.

"The captain tells me we're expecting unusually stable weather tomorrow, which is a sign that the Watch Now Network has good karma!" Wink beamed. "When we get to Paradise Cove, you're going to be dazzled by the icebergs, the mountains, the mirrorlike water—but you'll also see something sad." His voice dropped, and we all leaned forward.

"Sad?" Mason said uncertainly.

Wink nodded, wrapping himself into a somber attitude. "You see, for most of the year, Paradise Cove is at the end of a global wind pattern. Garbage blows into the inlet almost year-round. You're going to see it tomorrow. Blue plastic bags and red gas cans and yellow tape. It turns this pristine Antarctic landscape into a dump!" His voice rose in outrage, and we were carried along in frowns.

"That's terrible." That was O, short for Olivia, the farmer.

"It is. The Watch Now Network thinks so too." Wink stared

us down and then grinned. "Which is why we're going to clean up Paradise Cove! Or rather—you twelve are."

Yeah, I guess I should have seen that coming. Wink and the cameras took a moment to enjoy our confusion.

"Each couple will fill garbage bags. Tomorrow, you'll do it on the beach. If you meet your quota on Tuesday, you'll be given a kayak on Wednesday so you can get to places you can't from the beach. And if you meet that quota, you'll get a rigid inflatable on Thursday—a Zodiac—with an outboard motor, so you can move around the cove more easily. With six teams of two, we think we can clean up a lot of the trash in three days. Great, huh?"

"What do you mean about quotas?" I looked for who'd spoken; it was Nick the carpenter who'd lasted almost as long as Theo and Jane-Alice on the balconies.

"Yes," Wink answered with a grandfatherly smile. "You'll need the quotas. And the rewards. On the first day, when you're on the beach, each pair will need to fill ten garbage bags, and I do mean *fill*. Once you have the kayak, your quota is twenty bags. And with the Zodiac, you're expected to fill forty bags total. Oh—except for you two." He turned to Rose and Mason.

"Us?" Rose squeaked.

Wink nodded gravely, a physician with bad news. "I'm afraid the losing couple has a higher quota. The two of you will need to fill an extra ten bags on the first day."

"Ten?" Mason's eyebrows met over his nose. "We have to get twenty bags when everyone else has to get ten?"

"These are the costs of losing the True Love or Double Dud contest," Wink intoned.

"But—but—we're living in a closet under the waterline," Rose protested. "Isn't that enough?"

Wink winked. How coy. "Don't you want to know about the rewards?" He addressed the table, most of whom were suddenly even more grateful they hadn't lost the balcony wind shredder.

We nodded.

"Once you fill your ten bags, you'll get a pair of waterproof pants."

"That's confusing," I murmured, but Wink heard me anyway.

"Oh." He looked so innocent that I braced for what was to come. "Didn't I mention? On the first day, you'll be cleaning up the trash in your bathing suits."

Shocked silence grabbed the entire table.

Euphoria broke first. "In Antarctica? Are you insane? I won't do it!"

Wink allowed the buzz of excited chatter to bubble for a moment. Ratings, I thought. It's surprising they haven't gotten us to show skin before this.

"I'll do it." Jane-Alice's voice broke through the shouts of confusion and outrage. "I don't care. I'll do it." She telegraphed fierce determination to all of us with a look. Of course she would. She had a perfect body. *She* wouldn't look like a child in *her* bathing suit.

"Thank you, Jane-Alice. You'll have to leave that remarkable vest onboard, though." Wink regarded her genially.

I hadn't noticed, but he was right. Jane-Alice was wearing the vest (stripped once again of its zip-on sleeves) over jeans and a sweater.

"Won't bother me at all," she assured him.

He turned to the rest of us. "No one has to participate, of course. But America will be deciding who the winner is based on this challenge. And remember: if you decline, you'll be dooming your partner to working alone."

"He could refuse too," Euphoria said grumpily, but her protest was automatic. We all knew she'd do it.

We all knew we'd all do it.

"Well!" Wink stood. "Time zones being what they are, the Watch Now Network will be on the air starting at ten o'clock local time, and the second episode of *Cupid's Quest*, starring you"—he eyed us gleefully—"will be at eleven thirty. Join us in the lounge to watch, or consider getting to sleep before then. Tomorrow's going to be a long day!"

"I'll say," Rose said faintly.

"But if you want a nightcap, it's happy hour in the lounge. I hope you'll all join me!"

Of course. Skin and alcohol. Best way to boost ratings.

Knox turned to me. "Come on. I need a beer!"

Sure, that's what we needed—to get a little drunk and let the filters drop. Oh dear.

10

ON THICK ICE

"It's forty-three degrees out there. Brilliant sun. Still as a millpond. You'll be fine." Wink, who wore a parka despite his assurances, gestured out the open marine door, where the ship's crew waited to load us into the Zodiacs. "It's high summer in Antarctica. You're not going to freeze!"

Easy for him to say. We'd been told to wear our bathing suits under our clothes (they wanted to film us stripping down in the snow), and I was shivering in my sweater. Sunlight was pouring down on the mirrorlike water, but no amount of sun could disguise the fact that icebergs floated not twenty feet away.

"No, thank you," Jane-Alice said dismissively. I turned.

The Argentinian crewman was unimpressed. He held out the bulky orange life vest, ignoring her protests. Jane-Alice was the only one who'd skipped the sweater. Her perfect boobs were barely restrained in a shimmering gold bikini top.

"I don't need that," she said. "I'm a great swimmer."

The Argentinian crewman laughed. "Freezing water. You wear. Has to. Ship rule."

She rolled her eyes but took the life preserver. It covered her chest completely. The poor dear.

I buckled myself into my life jacket and then helped Knox untangle the straps on his. Together, we managed to work the strap that went between the legs. It was bulky and hard, but any layer of insulation was welcome.

"Everyone got their life jackets? Okay! Let's get going!"

Luke and all the camera operators were already onshore. Filming the twelve contestants lined up meekly in a mudroom was too dull, I guessed.

We were loaded into the Zodiacs and pushed off from the ship. It took me a few minutes to figure out where to put my feet, how to hang on, whether the hard rubber side would hold me. But after I finished fussing in my stress, I looked up and took in my world.

We were in a bowl formed by mountains that stretched up to an achingly blue sky. Every chunk of ice in this still cove was perfectly reflected in the flat water it floated in—and the ice, shaped by winds that were no longer blowing, passed before me in ever more fantastical shapes.

"That one looks like a rearing horse," I said to Knox.

"I've seen showgirls in Las Vegas with less impressive headpieces than that fan thing over there. But what's on the tip of that spire?"

We both squinted in the bright sun. Rose, at my side, saw where we were looking, and she looked too.

"It's a plastic bag," she realized.

Ugh. It was an offense. The place was fairyland. Pristine. Nothing but white and silver and deep blue sky . . . and a glaringly yellow plastic bag waving in the air.

"That's ugly," Knox said. Then we came around a large iceberg and saw the beach for the first time.

There was a collective gasp of dismay.

"What are those blue things?" Mason asked.

"Bags. More plastic," I replied. The blue was most obvious, but the entire end of the cove was covered in litter. I stared, shocked by what I saw. "It's gross."

"It really is," Knox agreed.

The ship's crew had set up a platform that made it easy to go from the Zodiac to land, although it wasn't actually a beach. We were standing on thick, generations-old ice. Was there a beach under us? Or were we standing over deep, icy water?

"Welcome to Paradise Cove!" Wink called. The camera operators were arranged in front of six squares laid out on the ground in black tape. Each featured a sign with a pair of names on it. Knox and I were in square five.

To the side, where they might remain out of camera range, Shout and his team of headset people were at a long table. Water bottles were neatly lined up, and a large urn stood next to an army of ceramic coffee cups. They'd avoided anything that might become trash in Antarctica—no paper cups, no plastic bottles. I approved.

"Life vests in a pile over here, please," Julie called. "Water and coffee available anytime you need it, and there are energy bars here if you want them because you don't want to get low blood sugar out here for sure, so stay hydrated and eat something, you know? Right over here—that's right, make a pile, watch your step, I know it's slippery, so you should walk like a penguin, see? Like this."

It was hard to be stressed or unhappy when Julie was around. She was an automatic giggle. They should give her her own show, I thought.

"Okay!" Wink was, as usual, alarmingly happy about what he was about to do to us. "Welcome to the first *Cupid's Quest* challenge, sponsored this week by the amazing people at Hefty, makers of the toughest garbage bags in the South Pole! Hefty cares about the environment, so please dispose of your trash properly, America!" Wink beamed at the camera for what seemed to me like an awkwardly long moment. Then he turned to us. "Contestants, stand in your squares. This is where you'll bring your filled Hefty bags, see? Don't put them in someone else's square. You only get credit for the bags in your space! Each couple gets one of these excellent heavy-duty Hefty bags at a time—you can't separate. You have to stay together. Any questions? Okay—strip it off!"

Guh. The moment I was dreading.

Jane-Alice slithered out of her jeans with a saucy wriggle. Quite a few others simply took off clothes until their bathing suits were revealed. I looked at Rose, who was standing in square six, and made a face at her.

"I know," she said. "Turn your back to the camera? Face them? Which way is worse?"

"All ways are worse," I said. "Sideways? I'll face you and you face me?"

"Deal. You first."

I gulped and peeled off my sweater. Knox kindly tried to get between me and the camera, but this was the problem with the Luke-and-Danika double team: Luke sidestepped around Knox.

Unlike Jane-Alice, I'd packed a simple, forest-green tank suit. At least I didn't have to worry about my lack of abdominal definition.

I was stumped for a minute, since my jeans wouldn't slide off over my shoes, but Knox offered his arm. "Take one shoe off and stand on it," he advised. "Take off that leg, put the shoe back on, and do it again on the other side. I'll hold you up."

This was awkward, but it also made me laugh, which lightened my mood. All too soon, I was standing on an ice shelf in a racing tank, wool socks, and ankle-high hiking boots.

You know. Like you do.

"Sun block!" Julie ran from square to square, a large tube in her hand and three more poking out of the pockets of her fleece hoodie. "You can't imagine how powerful the sun is down here, and the water is so still, it reflects and it'll get you in places you never expected, so you need sun protection—really, don't skip this step, you'll get sick and blister if you don't! Guys, help the ladies, and ladies, make sure you help him get his back, okay? Who needs some? Everyone have some? Make sure. You need more. No, more. Do it. Now—work gloves! Everyone have their work gloves?"

It felt like being oiled up before making a porno as the cameras got shots of near-strangers rubbing each other. But the sun was fiercely brilliant and I hadn't thought to add sunscreen, so I ignored the suggestive nature of the task.

Once we were given our lone garbage bag ("Hefty—America's choice!") and got moving, it actually wasn't horrible. The air was chilly but still, and the sun did an amazing job of keeping me warm. Eventually, we all realized it was useful to turn often, so the nonsunny side of our naked skin could take its turn in the light.

Knox and I picked our way across the ice, collecting the litter that had blown in on an indifferent wind. We learned quickly to stay out of the shade, and sadly, there was enough trash that we didn't have to leave the sun's warmth.

"This isn't so bad," Knox said. His red-gold curls blazed with particular cheer in this monochromatic landscape. Maybe I could come to love those curls.

"It's really not. It feels right to clean this up too." I kicked with my hiking boot to dislodge a yellow bag from the icy snow at my feet. "Like, this trash should not be allowed to be here."

"Someone should be issuing some fines. What careless idiot let that bag get away from him?" Knox had found a white bag iced to a boulder, identifiable mostly because of the crimson target on its side.

"No one, probably. It might have come off a garbage barge somewhere."

"Great," he said with a smile. "I was envisioning a grumpy woman in Teaneck, New Jersey, who bought a dozen eggs and found when she got home that two of them were broken."

Luke and Danika both trailed close alongside, filming. I saw the edge of Luke's grin behind his camera rig. If nothing else more interesting happened, Knox would probably get a little attention tonight on the broadcast.

"There goes Mom's hummingbird cake," I said to encourage him. "Of all the nerve. Now she has to go back to the store."

"Or make a lesser cake. And you know her."

"No doubt. She has to outdo Gretchen from down the street."

"Gretchen from the office," he corrected. "Gretchen has better hair, so Hazel needs to make a better cake."

"Hazel? Her name is Hazel?"

"Hazel or Mildred. Which do you like?"

"Oh, Mildred. That's the name." We entertained ourselves as we moved along a reasonably straight line. It seemed like no time at all before we had a full garbage bag and we turned back to put it in our square and get our next bag.

To our dismay, several of the other squares already had one bag; one had two bags. "Whose square is that?" I asked.

"Who do you think?" Knox said as we set off again. "Check out Indiana Janes over there."

I snorted at the nickname and scanned the broad ice shelf until I found them. Jane-Alice and Theo (whose near-naked body looked to be a good match to Jane-Alice's toned physique; Theo had an actual six-pack) were striding away from the shore, ignoring the trash they passed. Their cameras trailed along behind them, having a hard time keeping up with their pace.

"How are they—oh, wait." I saw their plan. "They go out fast and come back gathering trash. That way, they're at their square when they're done."

"Why is that faster than going out slow and coming back fast?" Knox followed me as I increased our pace and headed toward the rock wall of the mountain in front of us.

"Because you don't have to heave back a full bag," I explained. "Come on! We'll try it."

The plan worked. We began to catch up. A good thing, too, because Mother Nature conspired to make our work harder. As the trash on the sunny ice shelf got more and more scarce, a gentle breeze drifted across my hardworking body. My nearly naked body.

"Damn," Knox said as he wrestled the shreds of a blue tarp out of the ice. "That's too cold on parts of me that have been sweating."

I joined in the tug for the tarp. It was big enough that it would give us our seventh full garbage bag. "Don't look now, but there are clouds coming in," I muttered.

"Shit. Really?" Knox finished stuffing the tarp into our bag and we dragged it back to our square. "Hey, Julie?"

She bounded across the ice in her pants and jacket (Oh, aren't we special?). "Do you need something? How about coffee? Or sun block? Do you need more sun block?"

Knox pointed at the far edge of the mountainous bowl we stood in. "If the weather changes while we're out here in our all-together, we'll be in trouble. Is there a plan for that?"

She turned away and triggered a mic, speaking into her headset. Shout was about fifty feet away, hunched over a screen on a folding table. He could have shouted an answer, but Shout didn't shout.

Julie turned back to us with a beaming smile. "Not to worry! No one is going to die on *Cupid's Quest*. Keep going—we're watching the weather. Ready for your next garbage bag? Here you go!"

"Hmm," Knox said suspiciously, but he took the bag.

We turned back to plot our next tangent across the icy

tundra, and I spotted Rose's small figure trudging along with Mason, their camera team tracking them. She wore an adorable polka-dotted bikini, and her skin was faintly blue.

"Knox." I got his attention and nodded with my chin. "Look at them."

"Yeah," he said. "I see them. Let's go that way."

"Hang on. Let's put one of our bags in their square."

"What? Why?" Knox rounded on me, and Danika moved in to catch his reaction.

"Because we've only got three more to get, and bad weather's coming."

"I know. That's my point."

"They've got to get to *twenty* bags."

"B-but—" Knox sputtered. He wanted to keep moving, to head for the next appealing cluster of trash.

I planted my feet.

"This isn't like who gets the sauna in the owner's suite," I argued. "It doesn't matter how long it takes us to reach ten bags. It matters that Rose and Mason don't half kill themselves getting this task done."

Knox looked doubtfully from our square to the larger square next to us, which was big enough for double the bags. Then his innate kindness won out. "One bag," he said. He dragged one of our bags over the line, and I stepped up to kiss his cheek impulsively.

"Well, that'll warm me up," he said with an unwilling chuckle. "Come on, we've got more work to do now."

By the time we dragged back our tenth bag, Knox had given the situation some thought. Once Julie verified we had our quota and pointed us to the Zodiac waiting to ferry us back to the boat, Knox asked her if we could get the pants right away.

"Absolutely," she replied. "They're already in your cabin."

"So, not here, then?"

"No, not here. Go back and you'll have them for tomorrow,

in the kayaks." She gestured again to the waiting Zodiac, where Val and Nick waited.

"Come on," Val called. "Let's go. This wind is killing me."

I looked at Knox, and he looked at me. Rose and Mason's square had twelve bags in it, and they were trudging out to get their thirteenth.

"You go ahead," Knox called to Val and Nick. "We'll get the next boat. Let me have another garbage bag, Julie." Astonished, she gave him one, and he turned to me. "Where are you going to kiss me *this* time to thank me?"

I shouted in laughter and then shivered in the breeze. "Let's get going."

On our way back with the filled garbage bag, I looked across the ice shelf to see who else was still struggling along. "Look." I nudged Knox. "Val and Nick."

The veteran and the carpenter met us at Rose and Mason's square, dumping their bag next to ours. "Good idea," Nick said.

Mason and Rose arrived, open-mouthed, and watched as our bags added to theirs.

"That's sixteen," Val said. "Only four more. Come on—we've got this."

Rose and Mason both tried to express their gratitude, but there was no time left to exchange pleasantries. The three couples set off in three directions, no doubt dreaming of windbreakers and tropical shores.

I had my head down, focusing on getting one foot in front of the other, when it occurred to me that Luke had to have something stuck in his throat; he kept coughing.

When I looked up, he gave a surreptitious nod to one side.

I looked my question to him, and he nodded again to a boulder covered in ice.

"Huh?" I said stupidly.

He rolled his eyes and nodded again.

Oh. Got it.

"Come on, Knox. Let's look over here."

Knox was too tired and cold to put up any objections. Halfway around the rock, we came across a wind trap filled with tightly compacted trash. Most of it wasn't even trapped in ice.

"Jackpot!" Knox sighed happily. Our bag was filled in record time, and I called for Val and Nick to finish off their bag in this treasure trove of garbage.

For the final bag, all six of us went out together, followed by six separate camerapeople.

"That's it!" Julie cried. "Twenty bags! You're done!"

We had a brief, fatigued moment of celebration and then turned as one for the Zodiacs.

Luke's camera landed gently on the ice. He unbuckled the rig he wore and unzipped his jacket. "Here," he said, holding it out to me. "Nice job."

I reached out, astonished, to take it when Danika stopped me. "Give that to Knox. Mine won't fit him, but it will fit Joss."

Soon, all six camerapeople stood in sweaters, and all six nearly naked contestants were gratefully wrapped in the heat and bliss of actual jackets. My legs were still bare and chilled by the wind, but that was secondary. I teared up at my relief and gratitude.

No time for a nervous breakdown, though. The clouds were thick in the sky as Julie nudged us to the boats. "Let's go. It's going to snow. That's right. No, you have to have the life preservers on here, I'll help you—oh yes, put up the hoods, that's good, the coffee's already gone, but we'll have something warm for you to drink—be careful, those cameras aren't cheap—there you go. Everyone in? Just wait until you see what we have for you back onboard! Okay, let's go!"

11

WATER SPORTS

Julie's onboard surprise consisted of as much alcohol as any of us could drink, consumed in hot toddies and Irish coffee and mulled wine and as many other ways the crew could come up with to combine booze with warmth.

We spent the afternoon slightly buzzed, being interviewed and fielding astonished questions from the six contestants who'd filled their ten bags and gotten out of there.

"You're a sucker, Big Eyes," Theo told me at dinner. "Jane-Alice and I were the first ones out of there. While you guys fought this blizzard, we had a great time in the sauna in our suite."

Next to him, Jane-Alice wore a cat-who-ate-the-cream smile. Sex for the adults-only program, captured on tape for all to see?

"She's not a sucker!" Rose, the smallest of us, leapt to defend me from the largest of us. "She's a hero! She's my hero. All four of them are, and I told the cameras that all afternoon!"

"Thank you, Rose," I said.

Theo shook his head at me dismissively and laughed, but he let it go.

"It was a good idea, though." Of all people, it was Jane-Alice who said it. I relished this brief moment of support from an unexpected quarter, but her next words dashed my innocence. "I bet that'll play well on the program tonight. Going for the sympathy vote, Joss? America's own darling?"

I sputtered and tried to explain that I hadn't considered that at all, but the words got tangled in my mouth, and I flapped my lips like a fish jerked from its pleasant, watery life.

Jane-Alice laughed in contempt. "Who, me?" She fluttered her hand, drawing the eye to her generous breasts. "Why, no, I never thought of such a thing!" She dropped her mimicry and nudged Theo. "We'll have to watch out for her."

Theo nodded back, looking at me like he was trying to solve for X. "Mm-hmm," he said.

"Jesus," Knox said, pushing back from the table. "Come on, Joss. Let's skip dessert. Cocktail in the lounge?"

I followed him from the table, inspiring a general exodus. (Though Mason did grab a slice of the chocolate cake on the way out, looking mournfully at the ice cream as we passed.)

Knox had a kind instinct. He wanted to get me away from Theo and Jane-Alice and the cameras that caught our every expression of dismay or excitement. But we'd signed away the right to privacy. The lounge was full of obvious cameras, too, and probably some hidden ones as well, and our cabin offered no more sanctuary.

We lost ourselves in the last refuge we had: beer for Knox, a glass of red for me. Soon, the entire cast was together again, although now grouped in definite clusters across the lounge.

"Can we sit with you?" It was Euphoria, the artist, whose braided hair was all the colors of the rainbow. "It's kind of like those are the Mean Girls over there, and we don't quite fit in, you know?" She nodded to the bar, where Theo and Jane-Alice had their heads together, plotting with handsome Alaric and Olivia, the high-intensity farmer.

"You bet," Rose said with a smile, shifting to make room.

I had a chance to meet Euphoria's partner, whose name I never could remember. He was Paul, and he was a facilities manager at a nonprofit arts center, which meant, "I do whatever the artists or performers can't handle. Unclog toilets, put out signs, change the ballast in the lighting. Whatever."

I looked at him with a new appreciation. A man who would snake a drain? Could I get one of those?

By the time the Watch Now Network's programming began, a warm lassitude had washed over me. I was tired from my morning's labors but pleased with the friends I'd made. The wine cast a kindly glow over my mood, and the sofa beneath me had molded itself to my body. I accepted another glass of wine.

School Daisy, the first show, was engaging and funny. I'd gotten used to the characters after the two previous episodes, and I enjoyed seeing the results of America's vote on what happened next. Just before the end of the program, I thought to look at the number of subscribers watching at the bottom of the screen. It looked as if it had gone up. Kids were telling their friends to tune in.

The sports show that followed was particularly entertaining; it included a long segment on dog teams training to run the Iditarod.

'I'd totally put all my HonorBucks on Jet's team winning," Paul said over a glass of something brown—whiskey, bourbon, whatever.

"We should subscribe," Val said. "We could win Honor-Bucks too."

"Are we allowed?" Euphoria asked.

"Why not?" Knox answered. "I've got my phone here, and I can spare the $9.99 subscription fee. I'm signing up right now!"

As we watched, the tiny number at the bottom of the screen went up by six as we all became subscribers, logged into the show, and placed our bets with our fully theoretical Honor-Bucks." I bet on Jet's team too.

And then it was time for the third episode of *Cupid's Quest*, which prominently began with twelve otherwise-rational humans stripping down to bathing suits while standing on an ice floe in the middle of Antarctica.

It was mesmerizing, I couldn't look away. And I'd been there. Were these people *crazy*?

Shout had made the decision to let the viewers see the cameras. (No hard choice there; with twelve contestants and twelve camerapeople, it would have been impossible to hide Luke and his brothers and sisters.) It went against most reality-show stereotypes, but it worked out well. Most of the field-producers-slash-camera-operators were handsome or lovely, and they might have been hired because they seemed as comfortable in front of the camera as behind it.

Luke, for example, was a natural as he talked about working with me and how I was doing. "That's smart," Knox said, squished in next to me on the sofa and leaning his head down to murmur to me. "If this show works and they come back for a second season, they'll have continuity with the camera teams. Like returning stars."

"Cool," I said, resting my head on his shoulder. He took my hand absently.

It was fascinating to see what the other teams did while Knox and I were hacking garbage out of the ice with our heels. Alaric and O spent the entire time squabbling, and Theo was caught on camera not retrieving trash but burying it. He hustled the camera away once it found him. His large, bald head filled the TV screen as he warned his camerawoman away: "Leave that there. Don't mention it to anyone. It'll pay off day after tomorrow. Promise."

In the lounge, we all shouted. Several cocktail peanuts were thrown at Theo, who ignored us all and refused to explain what he meant.

The show got to the moment where I asked Knox to give one of our bags to Rose and Mason. The shouts in the lounge were less vigorous, but the contestants did react. Theo and Jane-Alice both turned to look at me smugly, and Rose, on my other side, took my hand in solidarity.

"Thank you, Joss!" she shouted to the room.

The unseen editors, undoubtedly locked in a windowless room somewhere in the bowels of the Watch Now Network headquarters in Los Angeles, had opted to show every step of our collaboration to get Rose and Mason back onto the boat... including Luke's impromptu decision to offer me his jacket.

"The kid's gonna be a star," Alaric called out. We all laughed, but I realized anew how handsome Luke was—and how his kindness left the entire program with a rosy, hopeful air. He *was* going to be a star, or he should be.

The show ended with Theo calling me a sucker at dinner, and a teaser at the end told America to watch what happened when twelve amateurs took to the waters of Antarctica on kayaks.

"Amateurs?" Jane-Alice scoffed. "I've been kayaking since I was nine. You all can learn from me."

Her confidence was intimidating.

"You want to watch the last program? The half hour about heroes?" Knox didn't wait for my answer. He stood and offered me a hand to pull me out of the sofa. "I'm for bed, myself. It's going to be a long day tomorrow, learning how to kayak from Indiana Janes."

We departed on a wave of laughter, and several others followed us out. Perhaps they were going back to their cabins to have the sex of pretty people for the delight of the after-midnight viewer, but I was too buzzed and too relaxed to get nervous about it.

Knox gave off the same vibe. Despite holding my hand on our way back to the cabin, he knew I wasn't interested in more. He kissed my cheek like a brother, climbed into bed, and fell asleep quickly.

Fabulous. I did the same, and all was peace and rest at last—until that damned loudspeaker in the ceiling.

"It's quarter of seven in Antarctica and time to get up because breakfast is in forty-five minutes! And then we'll load you into the kayaks, and I hope you tried on your waterproof, windproof pants because the weather's not cooperating at the moment, although it turns on a dime down here, and just because the sleet is coming in almost horizontally at the moment doesn't mean it won't be blissful sun in an hour! If you have sun block, be sure to use it, and if you don't, I have some, so wear your bathing suit and your new pants, and you might want a hat—what? Oh, sorry. No, you can't wear a hat, so put sun block on the part in your hair—don't forget, Theo, put sun block on all of your head and—what? Okay. Breakfast in forty-five minutes, so get up, get up, get up!"

"Julie," Knox said as he rolled out of bed.

"Exactly." I wiggled my toes in comfort. "You can have the bathroom first."

That was the last moment of peace in the day. The morning went poorly from the moment we were loaded into our kayaks. Among the day's challenges:

1. It was hard to use an oversized pool skimmer from a kayak; it made the kayak dangerously tippy. This was deemed to be a bad thing, given that we were skating across the surface and winding around actual floating ice sculptures.

2. The plan to hook two kayaks together was a disaster. Theoretically, the second kayak would be like an outrigger stopping us from tipping over, and the camera team would ride

in that second kayak, filming us. But with their cameras, they couldn't paddle, of course. And the two contestants could make almost no progress paddling with an inert outrigger to one side.

3. The fear of a contestant or a camera operator ending up in the freezing sea was bad, but the fear of a camera sinking into those black depths was what made Shout speak out loud. (He said, "This isn't working. We have to figure this out." It was momentous.)

4. The ship crew and the production crew nearly came to blows over the subject of life jackets. The ship's captain had to be called to the mudroom to verify we would, under no circumstances, be allowed to kayak in an Antarctica cove without the bulky, bright-orange safety vests. But once we had our vests on, our nudity was nowhere near provocative enough for the cameras. There went the ratings. Shout's frown got more severe.

So, there we stood. Twelve contestants, twelve camera operators, six production crew members (including Shout and Julie), and too many able-bodied seamen to count, since they never stood still, waiting to either load us into the kayaks or haul the kayaks back up to the top deck.

Every person in the place had at least one eyebrow raised, waiting to see what the solution would be, except Shout, who was thinking.

Evidently, the silence was too much for Theo. "This is a hardware problem," he announced. No one offered any objection to this statement, so he went on. "Contestants work in three teams of two couples. No one is allowed to fish any trash from the water until the kayaks are connected. The back pair holds a pool skimmer between them for stability while the front pair fish the trash from the water and bag it with the second pool skimmer. Agreed?"

Everyone looked from Theo to Shout, who did not shout.

"What do we do with the garbage bags when they're full?" Alaric called.

Theo didn't even draw a breath to think about it. "Hand it to your camera operators, who will be alongside in Zodiacs. Since contestant pairs will be together, we won't need two cameras for two contestants. One camera operator films, one drives the Zodiac. They can keep the filled garbage bags in the boats with them."

"And the life jackets?" Jane-Alice asked. She wanted to do her rowing around the cove in her gold bikini, and the life jacket was getting in her way.

"Well, we have to wear them, so all contestants should get sent back to their cabins to put on sweaters. Nudity won't help. And besides, that drizzle out there might do us some harm." He gestured out the marine door, where the windy snow had turned into a sleety mist. Yuck.

Theo turned and put his hands on his hips as he stared at Shout. Shout stared back. Then the director whispered into his headset, and Julie began her chirping.

"Okay, everyone, back to your cabins to put on sweaters! Go now and then come right back. Get into pairs—or quartets, I guess—and then you'll be able to—" She was still talking as I fled up the stairs, Knox on my heels, to layer as many shirts and sweaters onto my body as I could fit. Maybe we *wouldn't* die.

Mason and Rose grabbed us as soon as we returned to the mudroom. Knox looked regretfully at Nick's broad back (had he planned on partnering with the carpenter?) but smiled as we shook hands with Mason and Rose.

No surprise that Alaric had paired up with Theo and Jane-Alice. Alaric had clearly decided arguing every point with Olivia wasn't productive; he was now ignoring her, and she was glaring at him. Bunny Stanford thought *they* were ideal partners?

That left Nick and Val (a carpenter and a veteran) to pair with Euphoria and Paul (the artist with he-who-plunges-toilets). Temperamentally, it seemed we'd made good partnerships.

Our quartet was the last to win our parkas. We weren't the strongest contestants. On the other hand, Knox kept us all laughing so hard that Luke (who was filming) and Danika (who was driving the Zodiac) seemed pleased with us. I was proudest when we figured out how to back our paired kayaks into an inverted *V* at the base of the "showgirl's headdress" Knox had spotted the day before—the one with the canary-yellow plastic bag fluttering from one long spire—so we could back far enough into the ice for Mason to grab the bag and ease it off the iceberg.

This was mildly terrifying, since if the point of the spire had broken off, it would have fallen on or into their kayak and almost certainly swamped them. But he was careful and patient, and Rose and I braced the boat to give him a steady platform.

And then—victory!

By that time, we were surrounded by Zodiacs. Half of them were filled with camera operators and contestants who were finished with their own tasks. The other half of the boats were filled with able-bodied seamen, waiting to fish us out of the drink.

Not needed today, my good man!

That evening, the broadcast was so slanted toward Knox and me that I was embarrassed. All of America would love Knox, and rightly so; he was witty and charming. But everyone in the lounge was suddenly sure I was acting in a way that would endear me to the public—to those who would decide who won the first Cupid Cash symbol.

Ugh. I didn't do well with the scorn and contempt of others.

"It's not like I can throw the competition," I complained to Knox that night as we got ready for bed. We climbed in together; we'd already gotten so used to the cameras that we didn't think about it. I turned on my side to face him, and he faced me.

"Please don't throw it," he said sincerely. "I'd really like to win this thing."

"Well, me too. But I swear, I'm not trying to be—I don't know. Popular or something."

"I know." He smoothed a strand of my hair back from my forehead. "Do you want to—I mean, should we try—"

He looked uneasily at the large mirror over the desk at the foot of the bed. We both assumed there was a camera back there. "I don't really want . . ." I said. Knox was sweet and kind, but I didn't have to kiss anyone I didn't want to. Right?

He nodded. "That's okay. I get it. Do you think the others . . .?"

"Jane-Alice and Theo, definitely."

"Definitely."

"But Alaric and O are too busy fighting, and Euphoria is so —I don't know. Comfortable in her skin, I guess." It was challenging to sum up why I didn't think Euphoria would be making out with someone she wasn't interested in. "She has too much self-confidence, you know?"

Knox agreed. "Nick and Val, maybe?"

"Maybe. But if they did, it would totally be their idea. Too strong to be led into something they didn't want, you know?"

"Strong of mind and body," he agreed.

"So that leaves Mason and Rose, and she would have told me, I think." Maybe my friendship with Rose had been forged in an unnatural fire; under normal circumstances, we wouldn't have done any of these tasks within the first week of meeting each other. But even if it was unusual, I felt like she was a lifelong friend.

"And there's no heat there. He takes care of her, but he's a nurse. He takes care of everyone."

"You know, you're right. Another strange pairing from Bunny Stanford."

I lowered my voice under the (probably stupid) assumption that any microphones wouldn't pick up a whisper. Knox leaned in to hear me, and we shared a moment of pillow-talk intimacy while I told him about the *Cupid's Quest* casting director and her decision to choose candidates based on the Jungian archetypes.

Knox liked the theory so much, he sat up to focus. "Go over the archetypes again."

I reached for my phone—Mom and Claire were still maintaining an uncharacteristic silence—and found a list. "Sage, innocent, explorer, ruler—"

"Wait. Slow down. Who's who?"

We decided Knox was the jester, which made him beam. I knew I was the orphan. Some of the choices were obvious: Euphoria was the creator, Val was the hero, Theo was the ruler or magician, and Indiana Janes was the explorer.

We amused ourselves, discussing our fellow contestants, until fatigue overwhelmed me. Knox pulled the blankets up around us again. "Do the jester and the orphan end up together? Is that, like, a known thing?"

"I don't know," I said sleepily. "I'm not sure Jung's ever been used as a dating app."

"Well, at least I don't feel so bad about not trying to get with you," he said as he turned out the light. "Most of us aren't rutting like bunnies. Or I don't think we are."

"Good." I yawned. "I'm not rutting until I feel like it. Not with all these cameras around."

I was able to get a good night's sleep because I didn't realize how soon it would be before I didn't give a damn if a camera caught me "rutting" or not.

12

THE SCOOP

Theo's large hand pinned my arm above the elbow as soon as I entered the mudroom at the bottom of the ship.

"You're with me today," he said.

"Excuse me?" I looked at Theo and then at Knox, trying unsuccessfully to pull my arm from his grip without making a scene. "I'm with Knox. As you know."

"Yeah. Right. He can come too." Theo pushed through the crowd to the open marine door. "We need two Zodiacs here," he said grandly, as if no one else was waiting. Jane-Alice trotted after him, looking up questioningly. "Pool skimmer? Sure, why not. We'll take two. Here, Knox, make yourself useful."

Simply through the force of his personality, Theo got the four of us into two of the black inflatable Zodiacs. Rose and Mason stood mournfully at the sea door, and I shrugged in confusion as the ship's crew pushed us off, trailed by our faithful followers with their camera rigs.

"Here's what I see," Theo said as he told Jane-Alice where to go. (He sat; she stood in the back of the boat to drive.) "Keep up, Knox—I'm talking to Joss. So, this is my take." Theo spoke to me across our boats, as if we were sitting on adjacent park benches. "America loves you, so the producers love you. Camera time is going to depend on who stays near you." Theo waved casually to Luke, who was in a boat on the other side of us. *I know you're filming*, Theo was saying. *I don't care.*

"America doesn't love me," I protested.

Jane-Alice scoffed out loud, and when I turned, Knox, too, wore a smile.

"Are you kidding? Did you sleep through last night's episode? This is the Joss Show and we're just bit players," Jane-Alice said.

"That's not true," I protested, but Theo overrode me.

"So, you're sticking with me today. I need a second pair for this part of the quest, and Alaric and O argue so much, they pretty much guarantee no on-air time. Pull over there, Jane-Alice. I'm getting out. I'll be right back."

Jane-Alice bumped her Zodiac up against the ice shelf near where we'd picked up garbage. "Is he supposed to be getting out?" Knox asked no one, which was exactly who answered.

We waited as Theo strode forcefully across the ice. "He's going for whatever he buried two days ago." I looked at Knox. "Remember?"

Jane-Alice tried to look confident, but I got the feeling she didn't know what was going on either.

Theo reappeared, his arms full of blue rope.

"What is that?" I asked as he stepped gracefully back into his Zodiac.

"Fishing net. I found it the other day. Here, take this end. Tie it here."

Working together, Theo and I tied the heavy netting to our boats while Knox and Jane-Alice watched with interest, and Luke, Danika, and the other two camera operators did what they could to film it all from their boats.

"Okay, that should do it. How many bags do we need?

Forty? We'll be done in an hour. Okay, Knox, back out slowly. Don't pull too hard. Follow him out, Jane-Alice."

Theo was either the Jungian ruler or the magician. His system was brilliant. The two boats puttered slowly across the cove, the net scooping below the surface in the front and rising at the back of the boats. Every piece of floating trash washed right up the net.

"Bag it up," Theo said to me with a grin.

"You bag it up." The words were bold, but I was obediently dragging bags and other trash from the net. He was right; we'd be done in no time.

"You do your forty and then we'll do ours. Good plan, huh?"

I willingly admitted his plan was, in fact, brilliant.

But then his cleverness backfired. Our work to scoop trash was so simple and so effective that we weren't good TV. Our camera operators filmed for a while and then sat on the puffy sides of their Zodiac, content to drift along beside us in the fairyland of iceberg sculptures. Knox and I took turns driving and fishing trash from the net (the skimmers meant we didn't have to reach into the freezing water), and Theo lay back in the sun as Jane-Alice drove.

We'd soon bagged up enough trash for both teams, and the garbage that overflowed from our boats was offloaded to the camera operators' boats. Theo woke up to notice he'd lost America's attention, so he had us offload our garbage bags onto the ship and then insisted on going back out.

"Who needs help?" he shouted, his voice reverberating across the water. "Anyone need a helping hand?"

He slipped so easily into the role of the charming helper that Knox leaned over to me. "Do you think he's a sociopath?" he whispered.

"Maybe," I agreed. Theo certainly was determined, and the other contestants cheered when he helped them fill their own quotas.

"There!" he said when we helped the last pair finish. Theo stood at the bow of his boat, making sure his camera operator, Nessa, could see him. "Today we've pulled an amazing two hundred and forty bags of garbage from the water, thanks to our excellent sponsor, Hefty. Yesterday's haul was a hundred and twenty bags, and the first day was sixty plus the extra ten. All in, this one cove had four hundred and thirty bags of trash in it, and it's lucky our ship isn't fully booked, because no cruise ship has enough room to pack out that much trash if they have a full complement of guests. *Cupid's Quest* cares about the environment, and so do we, the contestants. America?" He turned to face Nessa. "Please think twice before you glibly accept that plastic bag at the grocery store. Bring your own tote bag. Save places like Paradise Cove. It matters."

He finished his confident, self-assured speech with a blinding smile and then turned smartly. He'd tied his side of the net with some kind of easy-release knot, and he detached his Zodiac from ours rapidly. "Home, Jeeves," he said cockily to Jane-Alice.

They puttered off, followed by Nessa and her fellow cameraman.

"I think we've been upstaged," Knox said as we hauled the dripping, icy net into our boat.

"I guess I don't care," I admitted. "He can have the glory. That was a great idea. And look at this place." I stood after we got the net in the boat and took a moment to see the cove with fresh eyes.

White ice sometimes dipping into fluorescent disco blue. Silver water doubling everything in its reflection. Black mountaintops. The sky, once again the deepest blue, and a sun too brilliant to look at. "It's so beautiful."

"And clean." Knox laid a companionable hand on my shoulder. "We did good here."

"We did." I beamed at him, only then noticing Luke and

Danika were both focused on us. I sat quickly, embarrassed by my innocence.

Which was—to Theo's absolute disgust—the overwhelming focus of that night's episode of *Cupid's Quest*. Theo's genius invention and generous offer to help others was glossed over, and his bold speech was a voice-over on top of beauty shots of all the contestants working together.

Theo looked back at me and glared. I could almost hear him growl.

Shit. Had I made a terrible enemy?

13

OUT OF THE FRYING PAN

The journey from Antarctica back to Argentina was rough, with wildly rolling seas and powerful winds. The ship's crew called it "The Drake Shake." Just about everyone had a seasickness patch behind their ears, and no one slept very well in beds that refused to stay still.

To my surprise, I wasn't too badly affected. My sleep was deep both nights of the thirty-six-hour transit, and I was one of the few who made it to the lounge to watch the Saturday broadcast, when Knox and I were revealed to have won America's vote for the first *Cupid's Quest* challenge, worth five thousand dollars.

I shook my head. I'd take it, but we hadn't won fairly. Someone in the editing department was following orders. America had been led to vote for Knox and me.

And now the other contestants would dislike us. We'd have an unseen target painted on our backs.

I told Knox we won when I got back to our cabin, but he didn't care. His green skin clashed with the red hair, and I got him a ginger ale and then cleared a path for him to the bathroom.

By the time we got to calmer waters in port, the cast and crew all looked pretty miserable. At least any lingering effects and fatigue meant no one threw any shade at us for winning the first Cupid Cash symbol.

We looked like a flock of zombies as we trudged across the tarmac to board the Arrow. Both Theo and Jane-Alice looked pretty healthy (of course Indiana Janes wouldn't show the ill effects of seasickness), and the lone working camera was in the hands of a grinning Luke. Everyone else probably would have sold their souls for a hot shower and twelve hours in a bed with no movement.

Right. Definitely time to get on a plane to unknown lands.

The camera operators all disappeared into the other cabin, so at least we had double the seats in the contestants' cabin. Knox kissed my cheek and pushed me away as he went straight for his original seat in the second row. He was asleep in minutes.

I went back to the seat in the fourth row I'd shared with Luke on the way out.

We weren't the only ones drawn to our original places. Theo ignored the seat belt directives once again and sat across his two seats, his back to where a window would have been, if we'd been given windows.

The cabin lights dimmed, and the plane took off with much less fuss this time. Wink was too haggard to want any camera time. I tried to read on my phone, but the sense of isolation weighed on me. Cupid Cash wasn't a prize. It was a weight on me, and until Knox woke up, it was a burden I carried alone.

Except for Theo.

When a bundle of paper struck me, I looked up. Theo had thrown the safety instructions at me. Startled, I looked to see that he was pointing at my seat-back pouch.

"Lemme see it," he called, his voice muted by the dull roar of the plane's engines.

I sighed and fished the little dollar shape out of the pouch. He made an impatient "gimme" gesture with his hand. Typical.

I unbuckled and moved to the aisle seat so I could hand it across to him. He took it and then, as an afterthought, swung his feet to the ground. He jerked his head to the side. *Join me*, he was saying.

Might as well face him.

I crossed the aisle to sit beside him as he turned the dollar sign in his fingers.

"Brass," he said. "I would have thought plastic. It's nice. Milled nicely." He made an experimental jabbing motion, the *S* of the symbol in his hand and the two bars protruding from his fist. "Good weapon. If you needed one."

I swallowed. Was Theo actually a sociopath, and should I have handed a weapon-ready symbol to him? "I didn't mean to win, Theo. I swear."

He turned his head to me. I felt like a bug being spotted by some predatory bird. "Are you under the impression that I'm mad at you?"

"Um, well . . . yeah. You're not?"

His mouth never cracked a smile, although he uttered a definite chuckle. "Not at you. I'm learning how to play the game, and you're the odds-on favorite at the moment. I'm not mad. I admire you. I'm going to learn from you."

Distantly, I had the presence of mind to consider that there was something worse than Theo wanting to stab me with a dollar sign. "I have no idea why they chose me to win. I can't teach you a thing."

He only raised one mobile eyebrow at me, but that motion expressed his amused contempt. "Really," he said. It wasn't a question.

"Really," I insisted. "You were brilliant on the challenge. You figured out to go out and turn around before picking up trash on the first day, and you found and hid the net. You made the scoop. You gave that excellent speech. There's no reason why you shouldn't have been voted the favorite. No reason at all."

I exhausted myself with the force of my words. He uttered another one of those smileless chuckles. "You have no idea, do you?"

My mouth gaped open. "W-well," I sputtered. "Obviously not."

Theo nodded. "Probably why it's so effective."

Annoyance came to the front of my brain. "Why *what* is so effective?"

He half shifted in his seat so he could look at me. "You are apparently the only actually kind person I've ever met."

My train of thought was derailed. No forward progress. I sat back in the seat and stared, unseeing, at the camera lens watching me from the back of the seat. It took a while until I could form a thought, and Theo let me think.

"You think people voted for me because I'm *kind*?" My skin was itchy with frustration. I scratched uselessly at my neck.

He snorted. "I think the editors cut the program so your kindness was the top story. I think the editors—or the producers—told America to vote for you because you're kind."

The concept of kindness dissolved as a point of issue. I was thrilled to hear Theo voice what I'd been thinking. "Right? Why'd they choose me? Why did I get all that airtime when there were plenty of better stories all around? I'm trying to figure it out. I'm so glad you said that."

This time, he smiled when he chuckled. "You're a surprising human, Joss. That's not the reaction I thought you'd have, but I suppose it fits with your character."

"My character?"

"You're like an orphan in a fairy tale." I startled at his words; did Theo know about the twelve Jungian archetypes and that I'd been cast as the orphan? "Birds ought to fly down and cover you in a soft blanket of leaves. It would never occur to you that your take on the challenges deserves attention, huh?"

"Mine? As opposed to everyone else's?"

Theo's smirk made me feel like he knew things I didn't. "Most people, Joss, think they're the center of the universe. I certainly do. Why *wouldn't* someone want to know what I was thinking, what I was doing, how I was plotting?"

His total confidence tweaked my spirit. "Well, you're a tremendous narcissist, Theo. Of course you'd say that."

His bark of laughter moved further than our bubble of sound inside the plane. I looked to see if he'd woken any of the sleepers, but they were all still out. "So," he said. "America doesn't like a narcissist. Okay. Call this the first lesson. What should I do instead of being confident?"

He actually waited for my answer, one eyebrow raised. It wasn't a rhetorical question, then.

I thought about it for a moment and then gestured to the camera in front of his seat. "Maybe try being a little human? Theo, why don't you tell America why you want to win. Let's humanize the big bald guy."

Both eyebrows went up. "Why I want to win?" He bit his lip in thought and swatted the ball back to me. "Show me how it's done, Joss. You tell America first. Why do *you* want to win?"

Oh. My entire history loomed before me, private and personal and susceptible to the scorn of Theo and the rest of America. "I guess it's because my family could use the money."

"You guess?"

"All right. I know they can."

"Brother need a Porsche? Mom and Dad want a beach house? Maybe mink to the floor for Joss of the minklike hair?"

He thought my hair was minklike. It wasn't even a word I'd heard before Theo, but I liked it. "No brother. One sister. And Dad and Mom divorced many, many years ago."

"So what's the money for?"

I sighed. Sorry, Claire. "My sister has crippling asthma. She can't work. My mother's alimony ended years ago, and when Claire turns twenty-one next year, the child support agreement ends too. If we're going to keep the house, I need to find some money."

Theo's focused curiosity made me reveal more than I'd cared to, but he wasn't done yet.

"Mom doesn't work?"

"She hasn't since before she married my father. She's been out of the workforce too long. It happens to lots of women."

"Well, it used to. She could get a job if she wanted."

I shook my head. "You don't know her."

"Right. Maybe *you* don't know her."

His certainty was irritating. I squirmed in my seat. "Your turn. Why does Theo want to win? Tell us all."

He rubbed his hand along his face, where faint black stubble shadowed his jaw. "Yeah. Okay."

I gave him the "go on" eyebrow, and he gathered his thoughts.

"All right. I'm a developer. Software, you know?" I nodded. "I came up with a program that would circumvent just about any phone tree."

"I'm sorry—what does it do?"

His face relaxed as he explained. "You call your insurance company or your bank or Social Security—any large, faceless organization. You want the answer to one damn question, but it takes fifteen minutes of 'press two' to get to a human. Right?"

"I hate that." The thought of wasting time on my insurance company's phone system made me tense up.

"Everyone hates that. And I figured out how to go from intro panel to actual person. What would you pay for that? $1.99 a month? Five bucks for a one-time use when you needed it?"

Trapped in a phone maze and someone offered to get me to

a human if I handed them a five? "I'd pay it in a minute," I said stoutly.

"Right. That's what I think too. And I have two frie— colleagues." He edited himself to avoid saying *friends*. Interesting. "They went into business with me to find the backers to make the app."

He ran out of things to say, so I nudged him. "Yeah? Then what?"

He wrinkled his nose, which made him look about ten years old. "I'm a narcissist, as has been so recently pointed out to me. I pissed them off. I was right, of course." He made sure I understood and went on. "But they didn't care. They dissolved the company I started and took their backers with them."

His anger was surfacing. An angry Theo was an intimidating thing. "But do they have your program?"

"They do not." His arrogance was on high beam until he added, "But they say they're going to find someone to create something different enough to avoid an intellectual property challenge."

"Can they do that?"

He shrugged and looked down at his hands, gripping the brass dollar sign he held. "It's actually not that complicated. Yeah, they probably can. Might take them a while."

"That absolutely sucks."

"Yeah." He lifted his head, his eyes blazing. "So, I'm going to win *Cupid's Quest* and use the money to back myself. I'll get there first. Make a killing. Put them both in the fucking poorhouse."

There were no such things as poorhouses anymore, but I got his point. "So, your motivation is revenge, as opposed to fulfilling your creative enterprise."

"Huh?" He looked at me, startled. "Motivated by revenge? Well, fucking obviously. Why the hell not?"

It was heartless of me to be amused by him after that story, but I couldn't help it. "There's a good chance that on this plane full of sound-asleep zombies, this conversation will get aired, you know. What else are they going to show? More shots of Jane-Alice stripping to her bikini?" Theo grinned at the thought. Jane-Alice hadn't gotten much speaking time on the show so far, but the camera had followed her pert little ass and bouncing breasts across Antarctica with devoted lust. "My point is, you might want to lay off the swearing," I added.

His laughter rang out again. "I'm telling America I'm entirely motivated by the blackest, most fearful revenge, and you're worried about the bleeping the editors will have to add? You're hysterical!"

When he put it that way, I got to laughing, too, and ended up snorting in an attempt to let my neighbors continue to sleep.

"That snort!" he chortled. "I want them to use that snort on the air again and again." which made me snort all the louder. I ended up putting my hand over the camera lens, and then he did the same for his camera, and we were lost in helpless giggles.

Val, who was in the seat behind him, reached out and swatted Theo's head. "Shut the fuck up," she muttered, which made us laugh harder.

"Bleep," Theo gasped. "Got to bleep Val now."

I fanned my hand at him to get him to stop and finally had to move back to my seats across the aisle to calm down.

It took a few minutes before I had the courage to peek across the aisle at him. Theo was smiling at me, and I felt a slippery *zing* of lust.

Whoa—dial that back. Knox was my guy. And god knew I couldn't compete with Jane-Alice. No sense fanning any crushes, Joss.

I needed him to stop smiling at me, so I fished around for something to change his focus. "Have you done your trick with the cork yet? Do you know where we're going?"

He moved to his aisle seat to lean across the aisle, and I drew back against the bulkhead to stop myself from leaning into him. "No cork necessary—the plane has Wi-Fi and I have my phone again. See?"

He held up his screen so I could see a compass application. I squinted. "What's it say?"

"Northeast. I'm betting we're heading for somewhere in Africa, although I suppose we might be flying over trouble spots in the Middle East and ending up in Kazakhstan or something." I must have looked alarmed because he added, "But probably not. Biggest city in our path is Cairo. Ever been to Egypt?"

14

AND INTO THE FIRE

Wink and the production crew waited for us on the other side of customs. The Cairo International Airport was a madhouse, thick with tourists and travelers. And *Cupid's Quest* wasn't given the same VIP treatment we'd gotten at LAX.

The twelve contestants filtered into the arrival hall over a long two hours to meet Shout and his team as the camera operators guarded their equipment from the attention of interested travelers.

Knox and I had stuck together. He felt much better after his sleep, and while neither of us spoke any Arabic, the airport was used to English speakers, and we made our way without too much trouble.

"Over here!" Julie called. "Look, it's Knox and Joss—hi, come on over. Danika and Luke were looking for you, and you both look really good for Cairo—I had to send Jane-Alice to the ladies' and both Nick and Paul to the gents' to change because no shorts, you know, covered from shoulder to knee, that's the plan—and if you go into a mosque, then a headscarf and no shins! I mean, sure, shins, but no shin skin showing—that's funny, shin skin, I love it. Do you guys want a little sun block? It's really sunny out there! Let's get you fitted with a microphone pack."

At last, we were all present, our suitcases and backpacks on a pile to be taken to the hotel. Shout gave up trying to find a quiet corner to film a welcome and Wink raised his voice, to the fascination of all the other people crossing through the hall.

"Welcome to Cairo, in mysterious Egypt! We're now in the international airport in Heliopolis, ancient city of the sun!"

Theo shook his head. He'd been Googling Cairo, so he probably longed to correct Wink, but he saw me looking and smothered a grin. *I'll be good*, he sent with his expression.

Good. America could come to appreciate Theo if he'd dial back the know-it-all.

"We're going to start the True Love or Double Dud challenge right now—exciting, right?" Wink looked at us hopefully.

We were interested, but no one was so foolish as to cheer at the thought. The last one had put us inside a tornado on an icy balcony. No one believed this one would be much better.

"We're about to head for the most luxurious hotel in Cairo —the Nile Ritz-Carlton. They're sponsoring this segment of *Cupid's Quest*, and when you see the opulence and beauty waiting for you, you'll know why I'm so happy about that! Every traveler to Cairo knows the Nile Ritz-Carlton."

Wink continued with a little impromptu commercial for a hotel chain that probably didn't need help selling rooms, but never mind. I dialed back in as Wink returned to the details.

"To get there, your luggage is going by truck. Oh, see? It's already gone! So efficient, the Nile Ritz-Carlton! But you twelve? Afraid not. You've got to get there under your own power."

"We're walking?" Rose squeaked.

Wink nodded to her. "And it's a hair over thirteen miles, so you'll want to pace yourself."

Thirteen miles. Wow. That would take me—well, three miles an hour was comfortable. Could I keep it up for four hours? Thank god I was wearing my walking shoes.

"Can we run it?" Jane-Alice, as usual. She'd shouted her question to Wink, her head at a cocky angle. "Do we have to walk?"

"Shit," Knox whispered beside me. "Run it. I'm so sure."

Wink smiled like an indulgent father. "How you get there is your own affair—but each pair must go together, and each pair must arrive together. And keep in mind that while November in Cairo rarely gets into the high eighties, the pollution will surprise you. *And* you'll be running your half-marathon through a literal desert. It's dry out there, which brings me to these." He held up an oddly swollen backpack. "Think of this as your camel. Each one is filled with precisely two liters of water. You need to stay hydrated on your trek to the hotel, but be aware that the team who arrives with the lightest hydro packs will win the Double Dud, which is a week-long stay at a one-star rooming house near the Nile Ritz-Carlton."

He glared at us to emphasize how serious this was, and we all took note. Ritz-Carlton: good. Rooming house: bad. Got it.

"The pair who arrives with the most water will be staying in the royal suite for the week." He went on to detail the vast glories of the royal suite, including the offices, library, vast living room, big soaking tub . . . got it.

Let's get a move on.

"You don't have to, but we recommend that pairs travel in groups. You'll be passing through prosperous neighborhoods, but you're strangers in a new land and need to exercise reasonable caution."

Rose's hand crept into mine. "I can't run that far," she whispered. "Stay with us?"

I nodded. Of course.

"Your camera teams will be on motorcycles. One will drive, the other will film. Please remain in sight of the cameras as much as you can. Now, come and collect your water packs, your printed directions, and one thousand Egyptian pounds per couple—that's about forty dollars for emergencies. Everyone have a charged cell phone? Everyone have all the important numbers? Right—off you go!"

We were collecting our supplies as Jane-Alice and Theo moved to the doors, followed by Nick and Val.

Jane-Alice turned to them. "You're going to run with us? Well, don't slow me down. I have salt tabs and moleskin if you get blisters." She pulled a hat out of the many pockets of her vest and handed Theo a small towel, which he draped around his shoulders.

"Do we need salt tablets?" I asked Knox uneasily.

"I don't know." He took the cash from Wink. "Should we buy some?"

"Where?" We looked together around the arrivals hall, which—remarkably—did not feature a kiosk advertising salt tablets.

"We won't need it," Mason said as he and Rose came up. "We're walking, right?" We nodded, and Paul and Euphoria joined us. "Then we should be okay. If we sweat too much, we'll stop and buy a sports drink or something."

"Good to have a medical professional along." Knox chucked Mason on the shoulder, and Mason looked pleased.

I looked around the hall. "Alaric and O? Did they go with the runners?"

We couldn't see them. "Must have," Rose said. "Shall we get going?"

Luke and Danika were outside, Luke with his camera on his shoulder and Danika at the wheel. "Ready when you are!" he called with his white-toothed grin. Two other motorcycles, each with their own camera team, fell in alongside us as we opened the map and followed the directions.

I was grateful I'd pulled my sunglasses from my backpack before I'd surrendered it to the Ritz-Carlton luggage guys, and then I forgot about how fortunate I was because the walk turned out to be far less horrible than I thought it would be.

"I was assuming blistering heat," Euphoria said. We were walking side-by-side along a footpath which wasn't entirely smooth but certainly no obstacle to walking.

"I know. It's not even eighty degrees," I agreed. "I was expecting black-sky pollution too."

"Don't kid yourself. This is like breathing the air in Brooklyn." She took a big, comical breath and sighed. "Ahh. Just like home!"

We chuckled together, and I asked her about her art. She was a painter with occasional forays into clay sculpting, and her passion and enthusiasm made her a delight to talk with. She pulled up a few photos from her website on her phone, and I was impressed.

"You're not kidding—you really are an artist. Like, you make a living doing this."

"Yep," she said with satisfaction. "After twelve years as a waitress and an artist, I'm finally just an artist. Two good shows last year, and I cut the cord on the waitress job."

"Good for you! I'm still a waitress."

"Not a hyphen? Waitress-slash-artist? Waitress-slash-actress?"

I huffed a laugh. "Supposed to be waitress-slash-journalist, but you know how it goes. Now I'm just waitress-slash-waitress."

"It's a good living," she said. "Hard on the feet, though."

"Tell me about it." We swapped customer, chef, and head-of-house stories as we walked along. Knox and Mason brought up the rear, making sure everyone remembered to stay hydrated (but not too hydrated), and Paul the Lightbulb-Changing Toilet Plunger escorted Rose at the front of the pack. He was the one who watched the map and kept us going in the right direction.

We stopped a few times. We found a public toilet—about which the least said, the better—and Mason negotiated sports drinks for all of us.

"Hey," I said, something occurring to me. "Wink never said we couldn't buy all the water we wanted with our forty dollars. We could get back to the hotel with full water packs and win."

"Holy shit," Euphoria breathed. "Is that fair?"

The six of us looked at each other and then rounded as one on the camera operators, idling at the curb as they waited for us to keep going.

Luke shrugged. "*We* don't know," he said.

The camera operator who'd been shadowing Paul spoke: "But America will know."

"That's a good point." Knox finished his sports drink and disposed of the bottle in a wastebin. "Look, America! We not only care about playing fair but we've also learned our lesson about disposing of plastics! One sports-drink bottle in a recycling bin in Cairo means one less bottle washing up in Antarctica!"

He inspired laughter and smiles wherever he went. We finished our drinks and headed out.

"I keep waiting for something to jump out and go, 'Boo!'" Paul admitted as we followed the road during our third hour.

"Me too," Mason agreed. "Like, this is a little too easy."

"Well, stop sipping that pack, then, honey!" Rose dimpled at her partner, and he grinned at her. They seemed to be good friends. That made me feel better—not just because I wanted Rose to be happy but also because I hated the thought that I wasn't making out with Knox and thus falling farther and farther behind others who might be getting attention for the "love" part of our "love and adventure" quest. My friend Rose wasn't burning up the sheets either. At least we were sexually unadventurous together.

Euphoria was the one who scored servings of falafel from a sidewalk vendor, so we had lunch as we strolled along. We weren't going very fast, but we weren't sweating much, either, and the goal wasn't to get to the hotel first—it was to get to the hotel with as much water still available in our packs.

We walked smart. We chatted. We laughed. We enjoyed stretching our legs and looking at the Egyptian neighborhoods we walked through. The rapid Arabic we heard all around us was exotic and fascinating when we were in our own cluster. I felt none of the anxiety I often had when traveling.

The challenge turned out to be a wonderful experience.

The whole walk took us almost five hours, but our water bags sloshed deliciously as we turned into the shady, beautifully groomed landscaping of the Nile Ritz-Carlton.

"I don't think I'm clean enough to go in there," Knox said doubtfully. "How did I get covered with all this red grit?"

"Desert, man." He and Mason had bonded. "You've probably got the dust of the pyramids in your sweaty butt crack."

The idea tickled Knox, and he and Mason kept us in stitches as we approached the pristine lobby. The air conditioning was a blessing as we walked in. A group of people was gathered around a TV on the wall, watching—oh. They were watching *School Daisy*.

Time zones. It was past 3:00 p.m. local time, which was 8:00 p.m. at home. Time for *School Daisy*, which apparently had fans in Cairo.

We all paused in the lobby to consider the international crowd watching the show, which was dubbed in Arabic. Was Theo here? I caught myself scanning the crowd of strangers for his tall form and stopped myself. This wasn't high school. Get a grip.

But I did spot Julie, who was jumping up and down in excitement at a table against the far wall. Wink stood next to her, wearing his weatherman grin. Since he liked to be the one talking, Julie had apparently been sworn to silence.

"Here they come!" Wink said for the cameras. "Our final six contestants. Come on over—let's weigh those bags!"

"Who came in first?" Rose asked as she handed over her backpack.

"Well, we won't know for sure until we weigh your packs, but it'll be hard to beat Alaric and O," Wink said. "They got here with exactly two liters each in their bags."

"What?" Euphoria spoke our confusion for the group. "They didn't drink anything? Did they buy sports drinks along the way? Because we thought of that and decided it was cheating!"

"That's not what they bought," Wink said. "Alaric has an international car service for his business. He called a limo. He was here at the hotel before we were."

I was struck silent. The walk had been enjoyable, but there was no doubt that my feet hurt and my body was grimy. I was tired.

"That's legal?" Rose gasped.

Wink weighed our packs and Julie jotted down the totals. "We played back the description of the challenge from the airport. That's the benefit of having everything on film. There's nothing to say participants had to walk. In fact, after Jane-Alice asked if they could run, I clarified that, 'how you get there is your own affair,' so Shout and the team ruled the limo was legal under the parameters. Sorry."

He didn't seem sorry at all. Nor was he sorry when he insisted Knox and I had drunk the most water.

"It's the rooming house for you two, I'm afraid. Here's the

address. Now, let me show the other four of you to your luxurious rooms here at the Nile Ritz-Carlton. I know you'll want a nice, cool shower." He sent a pitying glance at me and Knox. "We'll meet back here in ninety minutes to watch *Cupid's Quest* together, as always. Off you go!"

Then we were abandoned in the lobby.

15

LOST IN TRANSLATION

Danika and Luke both had their cameras on their shoulders, making sure the *Cupid's Quest* show caught every moment of our confusion and despair—but it wasn't long before they got drawn into the conversation.

"Well," Knox said, "how are we supposed to get to this place?" He looked uncertainly at the address in his hand. "Can we walk to the rooming house from here?"

We used the maps on our phones and then spoke with a Ritz-Carlton concierge who did his best to overlook our sweaty, dusty appearance. No, he confirmed, we couldn't walk—the hotel was surrounded by high-speed roads, and that route lacked the pedestrian overpasses we'd traveled on to get here. We'd risk our lives to cross highways to walk to the neighborhood. And no, we didn't have enough money between us for a taxi.

Knox gave Danika the puppy-dog eyes. She caved before Luke did. He kept filming while she sighed and called someone on her phone. I could hear Julie's excited voice even with the phone pressed to Danika's ear.

We waited while Julie consulted others. The crowd around the TV had noticed the camera Luke was holding and they were edging closer to see if we were worth staring at. The concierge was clearly torn between hiding us from view and helping us. Danika shrugged at us as she waited for a ruling.

"They forgot about how we would get there," Knox said.

I was careful to guard my words, but Danika spoke them for me anyway. "They should find that guy, Theo. He seems to be pretty good at solving these—what? Really? Okay. Okay. I guess. I'll ask. Can either of you drive a motorcycle?"

Knox and I both shrugged. Not one of my skills.

"Nope. You want me and Luke to—yeah. Okay. It means the contestants will have to hold the cameras. You're good with that? I don't want our liability—yeah. Okay. If you're sure." She hung up and turned to us. "Luke and I are going to get two of those motorcycles back. We'll drive you to the rooming house. One of you will be the navigator on your phone, and one will film us."

"No way," Luke protested. "We'll lose our union status."

Danika shrugged. "You want to call Shout?"

"Jesus." He looked at me. "You filming? Or navigating?"

I ended up with the camera. It was surprisingly heavy. No wonder Danika and Luke both had such good shoulders.

Filming while on the back of a motorcycle turned out to have a surprising advantage: it gave me something to focus on so I could ignore the traffic hurtling around us, inches from my vulnerable knees. My vulnerable everything.

Danika went first, her camera strapped to her chest, while Knox called out directions from his phone—and off we went. As the crow flies, the rooming house was close to the hotel, less than a mile by GPS. But the journey took us much longer than it should have. Once we left the major highways, all the street signs were in Arabic. Knox developed a system of pointing firmly in one direction and then watching to see if he'd chosen correctly on the GPS. The "short" journey included several encounters with mortality (not to mention the time I lost control of the camera because of a massive pothole; thank god Luke had made me strap on his rig), but we finally pulled up to a bare stucco building with a wooden gate set across the lone entry. A house number written over the gate was the only part I could actually read.

We banged on the door, hoping we were in the right place. After an eternity, an Egyptian woman in a headscarf peered through a crack in the gate.

"Ah!" she called when she saw us, and then turned to shriek back into the depths of the shadows from whence she came. Although her words were incomprehensible, I did catch that she said, *"Cupid's Quest."* She knew Luke and Knox—although she called him *Ka-nox*—and peered in confusion at me.

I lowered the camera. It was clear she recognized me. "Joss?" she finally said. She gestured at the camera, and a flood of words came out of her.

Google Translate would help, but typing in, "Luke had to drive the bike so I became the cameraman, don't tell the union," and trying to say the results in Arabic was more than I could bear. I shrugged, and she unleashed an enormous smile.

"Ahlan bik," she said, opening the gate to allow us into a dark passage leading to a sunny courtyard behind. Although we didn't understand her, she continued to narrate steadily while indicating that Luke and Danika should wheel the bikes inside. She closed the gate behind her as a flood of women and children poured through the courtyard and up to us.

"Ka-nox! Joss! *Cupid's Quest!*" Their excitement and happiness was overwhelming.

"I guess we've got some fans," Ka-nox said as small, gentle hands reached out to touch his red curls.

We were ushered through the courtyard and into the dimness of a building beyond, where glasses of tea and small cookies were pressed into our hands. "Thank you," I said. "Um—*shukran lak*."

I spoke Arabic tentatively, my phone clutched in my hand, and the women were thrilled. The volume rose and questions peppered us from every side.

"Does anyone speak English?" I asked. "Wait—let me see—ohh boy. *Hal tatahadath alianjilizia*?" I sounded the words out carefully, and the first woman held up a finger.

"*Daqiqatan faqat*," she said and dialed her own cell phone. We all held our breaths until her call went through. She spoke again, whole paragraphs of words without pausing for a breath. This woman was Julie's alter ego. She handed the phone to me and nodded happily. *Go ahead—talk.*

"Hello?"

"Is this really Joss from *Cupid's Quest*? That's wild." The woman on the other end of the phone spoke with a British accent. "My mother told me someone from the show had taken a room, but I thought she must have misunderstood."

"Oh, this is great. Yes, I'm Joss. I can't believe you know me."

"Are you kidding? Everything at university shuts down while *Cupid's Quest* is on. That Alaric—he's smokin' hot, huh? Don't tell my mom I said so."

I blinked at the fear I'd let something slip to a woman with whom I shared exactly zero words in common. "Will you thank your mother for her hospitality?"

We passed the phone between us for a surprisingly long time. The daughter, Zara, was studying medicine in London. Her mother, Fatima, ran the Goddess Hathor Rooming House and Tea Room, and was delighted to have us stay with her.

We answered many of the questions from the aunts and sisters and friends clustered around us, and then Fatima demanded the phone and had Zara explain a problem.

"Joss? You there? Okay, she says the *Cupid's Quest* people came to set up cameras in the room for you guys, right? But she tried to explain you guys would be crazy to sleep there, see? You guys are going to want to sleep on the roof with everyone else. It's nice up there and not hot at all. Tell Luke and the blonde babe—right, Danika, thanks—that the cameras in the room are going to be useless. My mother says all four of you should plan on the roof while you're there. So, are you and Knox going to hook up? People are cool about it on the roofs. Everyone ignores it if the couple is married, but you're Americans, so the rules are different, anyway—"

Zara and Fatima and Julie. Double-hinged tongues. She was still talking as I explained the situation to Luke and Danika.

"I called last time," she said to him. "Your turn."

Luke stepped back into the courtyard to call a problem-solver like Shout or Julie or someone (Theo, I thought but did not say), but as he was followed by about fifteen children who wanted to touch his camera (now back on his own athletic body), he didn't find peace.

Knox and I were still fielding questions from our admiring public when Luke returned. "We're staying on the roof too. One of us sleeps, the other films."

"Oh, perfect. Like you and I don't get time off. Honestly."

I apologized to them both, and they assured me I wasn't the cause of this confusion. Luke had Zara tell Fatima the production company needed to rent two more rooms; she was wreathed in smiles. "And can we wash up somewhere?" he asked. He hadn't even walked thirteen miles and he wanted a shower. Poor delicate flower.

However, he'd said the magic words because Fatima's hospitality came on full force. She showed Knox and me to our (tiny, airless) room where our luggage waited and pointed out the bathing facilities down the hall.

It wasn't the Ritz-Carlton, but the water was cool and delicious. Unlike Luke and Danika, I had clean clothes to change into. Knox and I ended up sitting in the shade of a woven awning on the roof while Luke and Danika had to settle for washing their faces and keeping their sweaty clothes on, the stripes from the camera's chest harnesses cutting across the dust.

The pause on the roof was a balm to my overworked senses. We didn't have long; we were expected back at the Ritz-Carlton to watch the show. But for a while, the air was soft, the excitement of the family around us had died back to gentle murmurs, the tea was delicious, and the cushions, while plain, felt like heaven under my tired bones.

"I'm pretty happy here," I confessed to Knox. He was kicked back on a low sofa in a white button-down shirt and loose chinos. He looked adorable, and I thought I might be getting closer to wanting to . . . get close to him.

"It's pretty nice." He stretched, and all the aunties giggled. He giggled back at them, and they exchanged happy vibes.

In this relaxed atmosphere, I tried trusting to Google and had the phone speak the Arabic phrases I was sure to butcher. With great hilarity and mirth, we determined Knox and I would return after dinner, at which point Fatima's uncle, Ahmed, would join us to translate. If we liked, he would tell us more about Cairo and the busy, cheerful neighborhood we'd found ourselves in.

We were delighted, and Luke and Danika were pleased they'd have something more interesting to shoot than the inside of a hotel room that might be found in any major city around the world.

In a quiet moment, Knox asked me if I thought we'd really drunk more of the water in our hydro packs than the other two couples.

"No," I admitted as Luke focused on my face. "I think someone has their finger on the scale, if you're with me. We won the first challenge—it wouldn't do for us to have all the advantages."

"I agree." Knox looked around us and sighed in satisfaction. "I don't think they knew how nice this would be. If you only went by that bedroom downstairs, this place would be—um—less fun."

He was guarding his words, even though no one who might be insulted could understand him. On the other hand, they were all clearly fans of the show, so just because they didn't understand us now didn't mean they wouldn't understand us once the show was dubbed or subtitled into Arabic. He was right to be considerate.

Very like Ka-nox.

"You're right," I agreed. "I'm guessing the production crew didn't count on how sincerely hospitable Fatima and her family are. And I bet they didn't see this lovely rooftop."

We had no view of pyramids, none of the glass and chrome of the fancy hotel, but the cushions set up on the roof behind low screens looked comfortable. I was looking forward to sleeping up here.

"We've landed on our feet." Knox high-fived me and then had to high-five about ten children who wanted to slap palms with him too.

By the time we braved the motorcycles again to get back to the Ritz, I knew our loss in True Love or Double Dud was very much to my liking.

And when we learned about the *Cupid's Quest* challenge to start the next day, I was pretty sure we had an ace in the hole in Fatima.

16

MAKE IT AN EVENT

"Let's show America this glorious Egyptian culture!" Wink stood in the opening of a poolside cabana. We'd watched the most recent episode of *Cupid's Quest* in a meeting room, but the hotel wanted to showcase its most luxurious features, so we were spending our late afternoon against the backdrop of a Hollywood-ready sun deck.

"Hang on," Julie said, holding up her finger. Twenty feet away, Shout muttered into his microphone, and Julie nodded. "Let's show the *world* this glorious Egyptian culture," she corrected Wink. "Because people across the globe are watching, and it's only been a little more than a week and you're all big stars, so you can show Egypt to America, sure—America would like that—but that's not the only place the Watch Now subscribers are, and we're being translated into how many? Oh, fourteen languages, and that's pretty good, and the editors working back in Los Angeles are either going to quit to get some sleep or maybe they're taking over the planet, you know, so the Watch Now Network is happy with all of us, so we're supposed to keep going—and can there be more skin, please?"

Wink waited patiently until Julie expelled the last bit of air in her lungs. She smiled at him brightly, and he turned back to us.

"Let's show the world this glorious Egyptian culture! For the *Cupid's Quest* competition, you'll be grouped into quartets—two couples will work together. Like a double date!"

Rose grabbed my hand and I grabbed back, but Wink saw the movement and shook his head at us.

"Couples will be grouped randomly, except for one pair: our True Love or Double Dud winners and losers will go on this double date together. That means victors Alaric and O will be paired with the defeated Joss and Knox."

He beamed, but he was the only one. I resented being called "defeated" and the "losers," and of all the other couples, the argumentative duo of Alaric and O was by far my least favorite. Knox was frowning, and Alaric looked like he'd smelled something nasty. Only O was indifferent. She sat on a plush, white armchair and exuded boredom.

"Let's pick the other two quartets now." He reached into a fez turned upside-down on the table in front of him and drew out two cards. One said ROSE AND MASON and the other said NICK AND VAL. At least Rose would be with nice people.

"And that leaves the final pair of couples." Those cards read PAUL AND EUHPORIA and THEO AND JANE-ALICE. Euphoria shrugged and stood, crossing to push onto the sofa next to Jane-Alice, who raised an eyebrow but made room. Paul followed, standing behind the sofa.

Matching this example, Rose and Mason moved to sit with Nick and Val, which made it necessary for Knox and me to sit physically with Alaric and O. Alas, they'd both opted for armchairs and made no move to share their space. Knox and I stood awkwardly behind them like the help.

"So, what are we supposed to accomplish in our quartets?" Theo was wearing a forest-green shirt that looked old and supple and soft. It draped across his torso like—nope. No it didn't.

Wink turned to Theo. "I told you," he said. "You're to showcase the Egyptian culture. Each quartet will pick a portion of the day—morning, afternoon, or evening. You'll work together to design activities that bring us all closer to Egypt. You'll need to include a meal for all the contestants, as well as an event."

"What kind of event?" Rose asked.

"That's up to you, but it should engage the imagination and delight the participants . . . and the viewers!"

"Do we have to wear our bathing suits?" O asked contemptuously.

"Well, we'd be grateful if you would, but it's not a requirement!" Wink thought that was funny. No one else laughed. "First pick of time goes to the winners. Alaric and O? Do you want morning, afternoon, or evening?"

Not only did Alaric not consult Knox or me, he didn't so much as glance at O. "We'll take evening, of course."

"Evening. All right. So, which team wants morning?"

After a pause, Rose raised a tentative hand.

"Excellent. That means you people are afternoon. You'll have tomorrow, Tuesday, and Wednesday to do your planning, and all three events will happen on Thursday, so make sure your timing is tight."

"I need a budget," Alaric called. "How much can I spend?"

"How much did you bring with you?" Wink laughed. "If you can rent your own limo, why should the show provide funds?" He turned to the rest of us, hands held out soothingly. "*Cupid's Quest* believes in luxury. We'll give each team twelve hundred dollars. That's a hundred dollars per participant. That should make it a nice event, indeed. What other questions do you have?"

I resented the fact that Alaric had asked how much *he* could spend—not how much *we* could spend—but the delicious solution to our event planning was sparkling inside me, and I couldn't wait to tell Knox, Alaric, and O.

But once Wink dismissed us, Alaric did the same.

He held up a hand as I tried to explain my idea. "No. I need to think. You two come to the royal suite tomorrow at 9:00 a.m. sharp. We'll talk then. I don't want to hear from you either." He held up a hand to O, who looked furious at this treatment. "Not until nine. I'll tell security to let you up tomorrow. No, not you. You have your key. I mean them—the rooming-house rats."

He gave us a scornful look and strode away. The other two groups were already in full conversation, but my group was chilled to silence.

"I'm thinking of shaving off his eyebrows in his sleep," O said conversationally. "What do you think?" She gave us a saucy grin. "Think I can get through both brows before he wakes up?"

She didn't seem to need an answer and moved to the always-present bar. Knox shrugged and took my hand. "Let's go eavesdrop. At least we can hear what the others are thinking."

It was a good idea, but it didn't pan out very well. No one knew Egypt well enough to be able to define an event worth holding, unless people wanted to walk through Heliopolis from the airport to the Nile.

"Clearly, we need more information," Theo summed up as all the remaining couples coalesced into one large group. He smiled at me. (I ignored the butterflies that caused.) "I say we spend tomorrow reconnoitering—and drinking heavily this evening. Who's in?"

"Me," Nick said. "If not heavily, at least somewhat. Can I get you anything, Val?"

The gathering deteriorated into idle speculation and increasingly strange ideas for events. Knox, a beer in his hand, leaned over to whisper to me. "It's not that I don't like these people, it's just—" We were both wearing microphone packs; I knew the cameras were recording every word, but I was still drawn into his warm intimacy. "I think I'd rather listen to Uncle Ahmed tell stories on the roof. What about you?"

I looked around the impressive cabana, with its luxurious poolside furniture and its staff of white-coated waiters, and assessed the stress and tension the competition raised in my stomach. I saw Rose giggling happily between Mason and Paul. My friend was happy and safe. I could leave. "Let's get out of here."

I waved to Luke and Danika, and they looked up from their cameras. "Leaving?" she asked. "Already?"

I smiled at her. "I know you want us to get drunk and have catfights with other contestants. But wouldn't you rather go back to Fatima's? You could film Uncle Ahmed telling stories. Even take an actual shower."

Luke looked at Danika and then over to Shout's table. "The hotel said they'd get our luggage to the rooming house. It's probably there now."

"And we can't stay here if our contestants are leaving," Danika reasoned. "Let's get the hell out of here."

I thought Luke suppressed a whoop of delight. I explained to Julie where we were going (she was only interested in making sure Luke and Danika were going with us), and we left the cabana with no fanfare at all.

Back to the roof. To peace and kindness. To mint tea and soft air. Yay!

Once we were at the rooming house, I tried to explain my idea for the event to Knox, but Luke asked me to wait until Danika got back from her shower. "With dialogue, it's better to have both cameras rolling. Okay?"

He'd been so decent and friendly that we acquiesced. Once all four of us were in good camera angles and good camera light (what a fussy world I lived in now), I told Knox I wanted to invite all the contestants (and the crew and production teams) to Fatima's porch for the evening. Let them experience some actual Egyptian culture.

"We could hire Fatima to cater a for-real dinner," I said. "And if she can't manage to spend a hundred dollars a head"—the idea of spending that much on a meal made me laugh—"we could give her the rest."

Knox was nodding. "I love it. But we need an event, too, though. What do you think? Ask Uncle Ahmed to tell more stories?"

"Yeah—that would be good. But what would you think about doing a version of that old show, *The Dating Game*? Something to get the couples to know each other better. It could be silly and fun, and I bet the network would love it."

"Forget the network—*I* love it! I'm going to brainstorm some questions. Can I be the emcee?"

"You and I are hosting. Go for it."

"This is brilliant." We spent the rest of the evening embroidering our plan and ignoring the fact that we had two other cohosts we'd need to persuade.

As it happened, we didn't even get to try.

17

PHARAOHS IN BLACK TIE

"No," Alaric said the next morning.

"No?" Knox was more assertive than I was, although we were both outmatched by Alaric.

"No. We're not doing that." Alaric's certainty was as thick as his beautiful, black hair. "We're not going slumming on some roof."

"It's not a slum," I said, my anger overcoming my sense.

"No. Don't be stupid. Look around you. We have an asset no other couple has right here. Come with me."

Alaric walked us through the royal suite at the Ritz as though he owned the hotel. We were, of course, trailed by our camera operators—Roberta for Alaric, and Faisal for O joined Luke and Danika in recording our every reaction to the suite.

And it was worth the tour, I must say. The entry foyer alone was larger than our airless room at Fatima's. And then there were the two side offices. The full library. The guest bathroom. The dining room for eight people, and enough of a nod to a kitchen to make it clear no one staying in this suite would ever sully their hands cooking. The staff could use a kitchenlike space, but the food would be prepared in the hotel's five-star restaurants.

The bed in the lone bedroom was the size of a barge, and the bathtub in the vast acreage of the adjoining bathroom could hold Nefertiti and her retinue.

"Look at this living room," Alaric said, gesturing with a sweeping arm. "It's designed for elegant entertaining. Six sofas. As many armchairs. An unparalleled view over the Nile, across the city, and to the pyramids—and I can assure you, at night, the sound and light shows are amply visible from right here. So, tell me." He glared at us from his plush, posh kingdom. I gulped. "Under what circumstances would we possibly turn away from this to squat on a roof somewhere?"

Knox raised his eyebrow at me, and I frowned. When he put it that way...

I turned to O, who was sitting sideways in a cream-colored chair, her jeans-clad leg thrown over the arm. "Do you have an opinion here?"

"Oh." She made a big deal about sitting up. "Someone wants my opinion. Did you see that, Alaric? It didn't even look hard to ask."

He dismissed her with the smallest toss of his head. "Please."

"Please? Well, thank you. And thank *you*, Joss. My opinion is—let the guy spend his money if that's what he wants to do."

Her words confused me. I turned to Alaric. "Spend your money? What's that mean? We already have a hundred dollars per person for this event."

He flapped a hand at me and cracked open a chilled bottle of water. "Twelve hundred dollars for an event? Don't insult me. I listened to those words carefully last night. There is no provision stating we can't augment the budget ourselves."

Knox was as flabbergasted as I was. "Do you want to spend more? Do you *need* to?"

"For a black-tie event? I should hope so."

I squeaked. "Do we have to have a black-tie event? I mean, I wedged a skirt into my suitcase, but I don't have a gown. In fact, I don't even own a gown." Alaric's event was making me nervous.

"Obviously," he said. "I'll have my tuxedo flown in, but we'll rent for everyone else. O, you're on apparel. You'll need to get measurements for everyone. Julie should be able to provide that. Then pick gowns for all the women. I'll give you a budget."

O perked up at the thought. "Really?"

"Everyone will look nice," he said sternly. "This party will be beautiful. No putting your enemy in a flannel gown."

"The only enemy I have," she said pertly, "is you, and I doubt I could talk you into flannel."

"You could not. Joss, you'll take care of food. Do not go anywhere other than right here at the Ritz-Carlton, understand? They want to get value for their sponsorship, and I'm sure we're the only ones who will think to provide it."

We were being railroaded, but Alaric's command was irresistible. "How much of the hundred dollars a person can I have for food?"

Alaric scoffed. "Stop it. Don't go over three thousand. That doesn't include the wine, of course. That's what I'll take on."

He was going to spend three thousand dollars on a single dinner, not including the wine. Wow. We ran in different circles.

"And what do you want me to do?" Knox asked meekly.

Alaric toasted Knox with his water bottle. "The event, of course. You're in entertainment, right?"

"I'm a comic. Want me to get local Egyptian comics?" Knox straightened. "I could do some searching, find the best agents around here—"

"Comics. Obviously." Alaric's voice dripped with scorn. "No. Get me an Egyptologist."

Knox's eyebrows reached into his hairline. He looked his astonished question to Alaric but couldn't form the words. What, now?

"This event is supposed to be about Egypt, remember?" Alaric sniffed at us. "Do I need to handle all of this? Get me a professor or something. Someone who can give us a lecture on ancient Egypt. You know—pharaohs and pyramids and flooding along the Nile. Crocodiles. Like that."

"Like that," Knox echoed woodenly.

"Get me a list of the good ones and I'll make the final choice. Make sure their English is excellent."

"Hang on," I said. "You want to dress everyone in rented formalwear and feed them an enormous meal. Then you're going to prop them on soft sofas and make them listen to a lecture?"

"Our big Egyptian event will end in snores," Knox chimed in.

"God. You people don't understand at all. I am going to educate America. I'm going to educate the world, as I have been asked to do. We will make it delightful and informational and elegant. What part of this do you not understand?"

To fight? Or not to fight? That was the question.

In the end, it was O's reaction that made me back down. "I'm going to put you in silver sequins, Joss. With a headpiece. And Alaric will get one of those King Tut helmets, striped in blue and gold. It'll look great with his tux." It was the first genuine smile I'd seen out of her since the show began. "Come on," she said. "It'll be fun."

Knox and I exchanged a look. Alaric was never going to see the charm of Fatima's roof. We surrendered.

"We're in," he said.

"Let's get started!" Alaric was pleased.

"We shouldn't have let him be in charge," Knox murmured unnecessarily as we stood in the back of the living room while the Egyptologist bored the contestants. By unspoken accord, we were slowly edging our way into the foyer, where we could sneak off to slump at last in one of the private offices.

"Three days," I agreed. "Three days of listening to that man bully us and everyone else, and this is what we get."

"You do look gorgeous, though." Knox's admiration was heartfelt. By that time, I knew he and I were not fated to be together forevermore; Knox was like a brother to me, and his lack of all but pro forma pressure on me was proof he felt the same. We'd friendzoned each other.

I smoothed the skirt of my flowing gown. O hadn't found silver for me, but she'd put me in a daring white silk I thought I couldn't carry off. Turns out she was right, and I was wrong. "Thank you. You look very handsome in your tux."

He bowed. All the participants looked nice. O had done a good job with finding dresses to rent. Even the production staff and camera teams had been put into dark, simple suits and looked quite presentable.

Unfortunately, they were bored too. They kept sneaking away to the library to work their way through the buffet dinner I'd added to the evening. Alaric neither knew nor cared that the Ritz chef and I had created a lovely meal for the contestants and still had enough left over to feed the crew—for which the crew was grateful.

But no one else was. The Egyptologist, upon learning he was to be recorded for American television, had boosted his price considerably, which Alaric had paid. Then the man had set up a large screen for his PowerPoint presentation—a screen that, amazingly, blocked the view of the actual pyramids rising in the distance.

Disaster.

"How are Mom and Claire?" Knox caught me texting my

family. I showed him the latest message, in which my mother had opined that I definitely wasn't going to get any Cupid Cash this time.

"She's right, of course," I said.

"No question who the winners will be," Knox whispered.

I nodded. The morning team of Rose, Mason, Nick, and Val had hosted a breakfast of thick, dark coffee and light-as-air pastries and then held a charming scavenger hunt in the market, in which the participants not only got to keep the treasures they bought with the remainder of the hundred-dollars-a-person budget but also got to box everything up and ship it home. Nothing added to the suitcase. It was a glorious event and did a wonderful job of showcasing an aspect of Egypt.

The afternoon crew's disaster had been almost as bad as ours. Jane-Alice had experienced Middle Eastern baths in the past and persuaded her team to create a spa day at a popular hammam.

Sadly for Jane-Alice, she'd forgotten thermal baths are all segregated by gender, so our participants had to separate, which annoyed Shout and his team.

And then, obviously, the people at the hammam had definitively refused to let any cameras into the baths. Even if the camerawomen switched to female contestants and the men filmed men, cameras were prohibited without exception. This was also not popular with Shout. (Although the camera teams apparently enjoyed their afternoon off.)

Except for the lunch Paul and Euphoria had put together, which was nice and held in the shady courtyard of a small restaurant, none of their event even made it to film.

Now that we'd dressed our event in the same giddy excitement you get from the tranquilizing hum of fluorescent lights, it was clear one team was the obvious and justified winner. We just needed to give America (and the world) the chance to vote on it.

"We leave on Saturday," Knox said to me. We'd backed up enough to have removed ourselves from the speaker's sight, and we ducked into an office and sprawled in two chairs. "That means an entire day without a chore. We could spend it on the roof!"

"Fatima said she'd take me grocery shopping," I said.

"In the bazaar?"

"Regular old grocery store. She says the bazaar is mostly for tourists."

"Well, don't tell Rose and Mason—or Nick and Val. They did such a good job getting us into that aspect of 'traditional' Egyptian culture." We laughed.

"Thank god someone did well. Where do you think we're going next? We've been freezing and in the desert. What's next? Mountain peaks? Underground?"

"There's a whole wide world out there," Knox said happily. "And most of it, I've never been to. I say bring it on!"

Of course, that was before the axe fell, and I learned the much bigger question wasn't where we were going.

It was who were we going with.

18

HEART OF THE ARROW

Green-haired Julie popped out of the door from the mysterious areas at the front of the plane. Her arrival was so sudden after the "Fasten Seat Belts" light went off that that she had to have been waiting for the signal.

"Hi," she called, not bothering with the microphone. "It's going to be a long flight, I know, but don't get too comfortable just yet, okay? Because you're wanted in a meeting now, so come up front and join us in the conference room—it's through here, so no, you can leave your stuff, you won't need it, yes, right through here, come on now, Shout's waiting."

"My god." Val was next to me as we edged slowly toward the door. "Behind the veil. I never thought we'd get back here. And in our third week too!"

"I know. Should we bow or put on head coverings or something?"

Val snorted. "Approach on bended knee, perhaps."

We giggled, but our casual attitude didn't stop us from staring, wide-eyed, as we went through the door.

Offices lined either side of the central corridor. One door

was open, and every one of us peeked in to see a desk, screens, a madness of papers, and a full bunk on the bulkhead wall. Where you could lie down flat and put your head on a pillow.

"Hey!" I called in involuntary annoyance.

"Hey!" Paul the Lightbulb Changer was behind me. "How come they get to lie down?"

Ahead of us, tall Theo turned back with a smirk. "Because they have a union. This plane is lousy with bunks. Look."

We followed him into a large, open space with a comfortable sofa and a few armchairs grouped in front of a large screen. To one side, a big conference table ate up most of the space. And down the hall toward the cockpit was a series of curtains, hanging across the opening to what I knew were comfortable beds.

"Damn," I whispered, jealous. "Is there a contestants' union I can join?"

Euphoria heard me. "If there isn't, let's form one. Starting now. Bunks for me and my brothers and sisters!"

"Right on!" O joined with us to cheer the idea, but Julie overrode our impromptu protest by using up all the cabin's oxygen.

"Okay now, this is the meeting space, and you can't believe how many decisions get made here, so you're welcome, and you should sit at the table, but before you do, please get into the groups you were in for the last challenge. That means you"—she grabbed Knox's arm—"should sit—oh, you guys go on this side of the table with you and you, and oh, there you are—okay, you four here, right. Oh, you're doing it yourselves! That's good. You're in your groups, and that will make things easier for sure, and let me just count, and yes, three groups of four, morning event and afternoon event and evening—okay, I'll go get Shout, just wait here a minute and we'll be right with you—and you're good, right, you have what you need? I'll be right back." I sat with Knox, Alaric, and O and watched Julie be totally surprised when Wink and Shout appeared behind her. "Oh, you're here already! So you guys go here, and then you can—"

They both ignored her. Wink sat at the open end of the table and Shout nudged Julie to sit next to him. Then the showrunner turned his back on us and went to sit in one of the armchairs.

Again with the no talking.

Julie, queen of the Shout headset, took her place and opened her mouth, but Wink held up his hand and she subsided. Too bad. I liked hearing how long she could go on without needing to inhale.

"Welcome to what we like to call the heart of the Arrow." Wink chuckled as he gestured to the table. "As you can see, we have the tabletop cameras set up, so feel free to express yourselves freely. Now." His paternal gaze became stern. "Let's talk about that last challenge."

Oh dear.

America had awarded the Cupid Cash to Rose, who had come up with the idea of the scavenger hunt in the bazaar, and Nick, who had negotiated a pleasant breakfast; ironically for Knox and me, he'd done it on a rooftop in the bazaar, and it was hugely popular. This was the first time we realized the Cupid Cash wasn't awarded to a couple, but to individuals.

The other two teams—Jane-Alice's spa day and Alaric's tedious Egyptology lecture—hadn't provided much competition. I'd watched the episodes along with the rest of the world; our work had been played as humorously boring. But boring didn't put butts in chairs.

Network execs were probably pissed.

"The morning team's work was exemplary. You're all to be congratulated."

"No kidding," O said. "I found the coolest dagger for my 'sharp and pointy' thing. I can't wait to get home and unpack it!"

I'd found a luminous, sunset-orange scarf for my "colorful and floaty" thing; I, too, was glad it would be waiting for me when I got home. If Claire hadn't absconded with it by then.

"So, morning team, who do you think your MVP was?" Wink's question got the team gabbing, but I saw the writing on the wall. When he eventually turned our attention to us, he'd expect three of us to throw the fourth under the bus for the benefit of TV drama.

I would have to point to someone and assign blame, and the obvious person was Alaric. And as much of a bastard as he'd been on the challenge, he'd also been the leader. That was a tough roll.

Yuck.

Eventually, Rose accepted her team's praises as their Most Valuable Player, and Wink turned to us.

Wait—afternoon comes before evening! Don't look here. Look over there!

With the instinct of a natural predator, Wink went after the weakest member. "Joss," he said, and all my muscles seized up, "who's to blame for your loss?"

God. Not even any warm-ups. He went straight for the jugular.

"Well," I said in a panic, "I think O was our MVP. The dresses and tuxedos were spot-on."

Thankfully, others chimed in with how much they liked the outfits O had found for each of them. In the general hubbub of praise and appreciation, I felt like I'd sunk below the surface of visibility again.

But Wink was not to be denied.

"That's fine," he said, "but let's get back to you, Joss. If O was the best team member, then who was the worst?"

Damn it. The fisherman hadn't wandered off, after all. I was still in danger.

"I think we all did a good job, really. We worked together as a team."

My answer was lame. The episode had been edited to make it obvious that Alaric was the mastermind in what they'd coyly named the "Desert Oasis of Boredom." Wink wanted me to say it out loud. He waited me out, and I couldn't bear the silence any longer.

"Me, I guess. I suppose I was the weakest."

O and Knox both protested. To my surprise, even Alaric shook his head, but Wink ignored them. "I think you're wrong. And I know the camera teams would agree with me. They told me they were grateful for the buffet you arranged for them."

Alaric wheeled around to face me. "I paid for the *crew* to eat?"

I held out a hand to him. "Same price. The hotel chef and I made a few substitutions so the crew could have a meal too. No one even noticed. Dinner was delicious, anyway, right?" I looked my pleading to the rest of the table, and they didn't let me down. Praise provided that appealing hubbub again. Would Wink move on now?

"So, Alaric," Wink said. Reprieve! He'd focused on someone else, praises be. "If Joss wasn't the weakest member and you were the leader of the failing team, then who would you say was the weakest? Who gets the blame for your loss?"

Alaric was square-shouldered and ready. "Knox," he said with perfect confidence.

I gasped. "Knox? No way!"

I should have shut up. Wink came right back to me.

"You say no way, Joss. Why do you think that?"

"Knox was great! He did everything he was supposed to."

"Thanks," Knox said, reaching for my hand. "I tried."

"Not at all." Alaric was brisk and cold. "I told him to find us an engaging, entertaining speaker. He selected Professor Sound Asleep, who could not have been duller. Knox is why we lost."

"Now, hang on," Knox protested.

Wink turned to him. "What do you have to say, Knox?"

My adorable partner swallowed, his forehead wrinkled. He uttered a huff of unhappiness. "You asked me to give you a list of five speakers and said you'd make the final choice."

"I chose from the list you recommended." Alaric knew no fear.

"I told you one of them was a great comic and I thought we should go with him. You didn't want anything as lowbrow as *fun* at your fancy event."

I tightened my hand on Knox, and he took a deep breath and sat back.

"You gave me a list. I chose. I think that's all that needs to be said about that."

Wink had bloodlust in his eyes. He was trying to inspire a fight, and Alaric, at least, was willing. "What about you, O? Where do you stand on this question? Who is to blame for your team lost?"

O didn't have my fear of being mean, of being disliked. "Alaric, obviously. He screwed this thing up from the get-go."

"God. You are such a bitch. I have no idea why we were partnered together. If I never see you again, it'll be too soon. If you were on my staff, I'd fire you and ruin you in the industry."

"If I was on your staff, I'd kill myself."

Wink was enjoying himself too much. I stood and got behind O's chair. "Sit there," I said, pointing at my seat. She protested, but I gave her the same treatment I used on Claire when she wouldn't follow doctors' orders—the raised eyebrow, the implacable determination. "Move. Now."

She huffed in annoyance but shifted to sit next to Knox. I put myself between Alaric and O and put my hand on his arm. "Behave yourself, please."

He pulled his arm away as if my touch had offended him and turned his shoulder to me.

Fine. As long as they weren't fighting so America could have a cheap thrill.

"Our little peacemaker," Wink said. Julie, at his side, was wide-eyed. Since the people on either side of me were still seething, I thought he'd spoken stupidly. There was no peace here. But I'd said enough, so I gave him a sweet smile and refused to be baited.

No one else on our team was willing to break the silence, so Wink turned to fresher meat—the afternoon team.

Hoping for a fight between the two strongest personalities on the team, Wink skipped over Paul and Euphoria and went straight to the man who never bothered to filter his thoughts.

"So, Theo. The spa afternoon was a complete disaster. We didn't get any film footage at all. Whose idea was it to spend a few hours soaking in thermal baths separated by sex?"

Theo looked at Wink as if the host was a problem he could solve. His silence created an awkward pause.

Then Theo looked at me and smiled.

"We worked as a team, Wink. We all decided together. I had a very enjoyable soak myself, followed by the best massage I've ever had. It was amazing. I'm sorry you missed it."

Even Jane-Alice was astonished. She'd clearly expected Theo to lay the blame for the entire event at her feet. Instead of bundling up all her energy to rebut his abuse, she was left open-mouthed and flat-footed.

Wink was frowning. Julie was grinning. Behind us on the armchair, Shout was muttering.

"Ask Jane-Alice!" Julie shouted.

Wink jumped at the assault of sound at his side but gamely went on with his mission. "Jane-Alice, you rallied your team around this idea, and yet it went poorly. Who would you say was the cause of this disaster?"

Jane-Alice blinked at Wink and tucked her head back two or three times in a convulsive gesture, as if she were rebounding from an unexpected slap. She turned back to Theo, who was beaming like a large, impressively benevolent, totally bald angel.

He nodded to her with a smile. *Go ahead*, his attitude said. *Say your truth. Honesty is always the best policy.*

Jane-Alice read the room and changed her tactics. "We worked as a team, Wink. Absolutely. And we did our best to make sure everyone had an enjoyable afternoon. Of course, the modesty of the Egyptian culture is commendable, don't you think? Did you get a chance to enjoy a soak?"

Wink, finding himself facing an interrogation, lost some of his usual on-camera grace. "Well, yes, I did, but—"

Shout muttered into his headset. Julie put her hand on Wink's arm. "And now maybe we talk about what comes next, Wink. Like, you know, what we planned? Bunny's idea, right? Okay?"

Wink inhaled deeply, and then his Charming Weatherman face was back in place.

"We found the quartets to be an interesting concept," he said. "Our double dates were fascinating, don't you think?" He beamed at us. "It was nice for our couples to get to know other people. In fact, why don't you each shake hands now with the other couple you worked with? Boys shake with girls. Girls shake with boys."

Awkwardly, I held my hand out to Alaric, who gave me the least personal handshake in the history of handshakes. Grab, pump, drop. How charming.

"In fact," Wink said with a gleam in his eye, "why don't you all hold that hand once again. Everyone holding hands?"

Alaric's palm was smooth and cool against my sweaty one. We held each other reluctantly.

"That's nice," Wink said. "By the way, you're now holding hands with your new partner."

19

THE LAND DOWN UNDER

I tried to drop Alaric's hand, but he wouldn't let go. "Explain," he barked. "I'm no longer partnered with O?"

"That's right," Wink said happily. "Your new partner is Joss. O, you're now partnered with Knox."

Around the table, connections were being made and broken. Most people were confused and unhappy. A few were delighted.

I was alarmed.

"B-but—" I stammered and was unlucky enough that there was a gap in the noise level, so my voice was clearly audible.

Wink turned to me expectantly. "Yes?" he said encouragingly.

"But—all the personality tests we took. I thought we were all matched to someone who could be our—" I couldn't say something as stupid and syrupy as "our one true love" like this was a Disney plot, but Wink didn't need me to clarify.

"Ah, but what makes you think the first person you were paired with is the one you're fated to be with? How do you know it's not the person you're with now?"

He was enjoying my unhappiness. To swap sweet, funny Knox for arrogant, icy Alaric? No.

No, there had to be something I could do about this.

"Can we refuse the new pairing?" I asked in desperation.

"Certainly," Wink responded, but his glee was obvious in his sharklike smile, and I knew he was about to make me miserable. "When we get to Brisbane, we can let you go in the airport and call in an alternate if you wish. You'll have to get yourself home, I'm afraid. Still want to refuse?"

Asshole. I shook my head, hoping my grimace would read as a smile on the camera.

Alaric looked as pleased as I'd ever seen him. He watched me with an assessing smile. I gulped and turned away. New couples met my eye everywhere I looked.

Jane-Alice would eat sweet Paul alive.

Theo, still exuding his benevolent-angel vibe, chatted cozily with Euphoria. They seemed happy.

Rose and Nick—now both Cupid Cash winners—were conversing politely. He'd take care of her; I was satisfied.

And Val the warrior was a stronger personality than Mason the nurse, but they'd be perfectly pleasant to each other.

I was turning to check in with Knox when O's arms landed around my neck in a squeezing hug. "Oh, I'm so sorry for you! Don't let him have his way. You stand up to him, you hear me? Tell me if you need me to back you up!"

Alaric snorted. "She won't need backup. There will be no need for me to argue with Joss. She won't anger me the way you did."

O laughed in his face. "You are not my problem any longer." She turned to Knox and clung to his arm happily. Knox telegraphed his alarm to me, and I shrugged. What could we do?

Wink clapped his hands to get our attention. "Go back to your cabin now. I suggest you get to know your new partner.

We'll be landing in Australia in eighteen hours, so you'll have plenty of time."

Jane-Alice hung on Mason. "And if two of us want to make use of one of those lovely bunks? You know, pull the curtain and just . . . get some sleep?" She pressed her breasts to the back of Mason's arm. He looked shocked.

Wink didn't even blink. "Those bunks aren't wired for cameras. You'll have to wait until we get to our destination. Go on now. Get to know your partner. Please avoid conversation in the passageways until you're back in your seats."

So they could be sure to hear everything we said. Great.

Alaric made an "after you" gesture to me, which would have seemed courtly and polite if I didn't suspect he'd done it to judge the quality of my ass. Worse, I was perfectly aware of my lack of graceful curves. He may have hated O, but she had a much better figure than I did.

We sat, of course, in what I'd come to think of as Alaric's seats, not mine. I'd have to be careful not to be a doormat with this man.

"All right," he said once we were settled. "What are your assets?"

"My assets?"

"Your plan. How were you going to win this game?"

This was not a man who would understand. I hadn't planned to win the game. The eighty thousand dollars for participating was all I expected to walk away with.

Alaric, on the other hand, was a mover and shaker. A master of the universe. He had a plan and strategy and philosophy and treatise and I-don't-know-what-else.

"I guess—try my hardest?" He wasn't satisfied, so I tried again. "Be true to myself? Um, don't do anything too stupid?"

Alaric scoffed. "You have no plan. We'll need to make one. Occupation?"

"What?"

"Occupation. What do you do to earn a living?" He spoke slowly, as if I couldn't understand him. His attitude was so condescending, I burst out laughing, which startled him.

"I'm a waitress. And sometimes a writer-for-hire. How about you?"

"Waitress. Mm-hmm. I'm a financial planner." He saw my look and clarified. "Wealth manager."

"Uh-huh. So, in the real world, you and I would literally never meet, since I have no wealth to manage."

I got him laughing a little, and we spent the next hour or so letting the conversation wind where it would . . . which was nowhere near what my "strategy" for winning was. Alaric was Hawaiian, which accounted for the luxurious head of hair, but had grown up in Chicago. He was overly fond of Italian shoes, Italian cars, and German watches. Alaric was an acquirer, but he took such pleasure in his acquisitions that it was hard to hate him for it.

He unbent enough to grab us boxed lunches from the galley. When he sat again, he'd been thinking.

"This is your asset," he said.

"What? This sandwich?" I held up my lunch: delicious, cold lamb on pita.

He grinned, the look taking years off his face. "You're likable. People like you, Joss." He bit into his own offering, which looked like turkey in a whole-wheat roll-up.

"Thanks." If I could keep him relaxed and easy, sooner or later he'd let me run my fingers through that silken hair.

"People don't generally like me," he said. I choked on my mouthful as I offered the pro forma objection, but he shook his head. "No, they don't. They like me to manage their money. I'm good at that. But I've never been—you know. Popular."

I got past my mouthful. "I'm not popular either," I protested.

He dismissed my comment with a huff. "I'm sure. But

anyway, that's what you've got going for you. A generalized, likable appeal. How do you do it?"

Theo wasn't the only one, then. I'd found a second man who wanted to weaponize polite behavior. "How do I—I mean, how am I . . . likable?"

"Yeah. America likes you. The *Cupid's Quest* editors like you. Knox thinks you walk on water. Everyone likes you. Give me some of that."

I thought he was referring to the dish of cucumber and tomatoes, but he was grinning as he said it. "Give you some of my likability?"

"Yeah. Can I buy some? Like I'm going to buy my way into one of those bunks?"

I laughed. "Those bunks look great. Are you really going to bribe someone to swap with you? Force a cameraperson to sit back here while you snore in a real bed?"

"Why not? I bet I can get Roberta to do it. Everyone has a price."

"Who's Roberta?"

"My camera lady. Who's yours?"

"Oh. Luke."

"Right."

"Like, how much? How will you know how much to offer? How do you do that?"

We discussed the high-stakes game of bribery for a while as I cleared away our lunch. We sat back together in a companionable silence. It was so easy to forget the camera in the seat back in front of me.

And maybe that was a good thing.

"Alaric," I asked him. "What are you doing here?"

"Hmm?"

"I mean, you clearly have money." He chuckled in appreciation. Yeah, he had money. "So why are you doing this? What does *Cupid's Quest* have that you want or need?"

He chewed on the inside of his cheek for a minute and then reclined his seat. Turning to me, he drew me in with a confiding air. "Frankly, I lost a bet."

That made me laugh. "You're kidding."

He shook his head. "I have partners in my firm, and we play golf. We were playing one day, and they bet me I couldn't beat the market with underperforming stocks."

Alaric gave me all the details, which I pretended to understand.

"So, in the end," I summed up, "you lost the bet and you had to complete their task. Like truth or dare for stockbrokers."

"We're not stockbrokers, but okay. And Danny chose applying to be on *Cupid's Quest*, which I did, and the producers were thrilled to have a successful businessman on the show. And who can blame them?"

He gave me a dazzling grin, and I was persuaded. Maybe America would be too.

"Okay, then. I want to touch your head."

"Excuse me?"

"You have the thickest hair I've ever seen. Can I feel it?"

He laughed but leaned his head over. It was wonderful on my fingers. "Fabulous. Better than a teddy bear."

He sat up, feigning offense. "A teddy bear? That's not the image I want to project, madam."

"Okay. A shark. With teddy-bear fur."

"Jesus."

Later, when the whole cabin was trapped in the nightmare of trying to sleep in an airplane seat, I found Knox in the galley, and we had a moment to commiserate.

I hugged him when I found him. "I'm so confused," I said. "I feel like I'm cheating on you."

He laughed and let go of me to fish a bottle of water from the fridge. "I know. Do you think we were ever supposed to be together?"

I thought of Bunny Stanford, the casting director I'd met in LA, and her insistence that my one-and-only would be a contestant. "Well, I thought we were. And that there was something wrong with me for liking you so much without—you know—"

I'd backed myself into an awkward corner, but Knox understood. "I know—without wanting me. I get it. You're fabulous, Joss. I adore you. But I'm pretty sure you and I aren't going to fall madly in love."

"Then we're idiots, because you're awesome."

"That's true. On the other hand, am I supposed to fall madly in love with O? She doesn't even have a whole name."

As usual, Knox made me giggle. "It's Olivia and you know it. And you falling for her is a little more likely than me falling for Alaric."

"I don't know—you looked pretty chummy there this afternoon."

I shrugged. "Just talking. We're from different worlds. He wants to be more likable, so I thought I'd help him out a little. Maybe he'll pay me back by helping me with my millions."

"Oh—do you have millions? Maybe I'm in love with you more now."

"No, silly. Not until I develop the strategy that will let me win." Knox chuckled. "Do you know he asked me what my assets were?"

Knox leered comically at my chest. "He had to ask?"

I swatted at him. "Right. Like anyone would list these as assets!" He made a politely lustful face, which I ignored. "How are you doing with O?"

Knox leaned a hip against the counter. "Okay, I guess. She's not much of a rule follower. I keep thinking she should be with Theo or something."

"That would be a good pairing. Did you know he refuses to wear his seat belt on the plane?"

"Well, that seems self-defeating."

We giggled and chortled in the galley until someone called for us to hush up; it was the middle of the night.

"Australia tomorrow," Knox whispered as we gathered ourselves to go back to the prisons of our seats.

"What are we going to face, do you think?"

"Poisonous snakes?" he opined, making me shiver. "Crocs? Shrimp on the barbie?"

I went back to my seat, still amused and horrified by what was to come (and took cruel pleasure in having to crawl across Alaric, who, despite his assurances, had not figured out how to bribe his way into an actual bed).

As it turned out, Knox's list of possible challenges was missing a few key elements.

20

SOLAR RADIATION

Maggie worked at the resort, and she was a mermaid. There was no questioning that fact.

"So, keep your center of gravity low," she called in her endearing Australian accent, "and your stomach muscles tight. Ready to try it again?"

Twelve contestants sat on surfboards, our feet dangling into delicious water so clear, I could see the fish swimming below us. This was the only thing stopping me from constantly wheeling around on my shockingly orange surfboard, sure a shark was creeping up on me to remove my foot at the ankle. The group had pledged that we'd shriek if we saw fins.

God save my adrenaline if dolphins showed up.

A dozen Jet Skis ringed our sunny "classroom." Each camera operator rode behind a grinning Australian surf pro. Shout, Julie, and Wink stood on the deck of the gently rocking boat that had taken us from Shute Harbour in Queensland to the tiny, private paradise of the Whitsunday Islands.

"When the wave comes, you paddle, paddle, paddle, right?" *Roight?* "The water will carry you." *Wadda. Yew.* Her accent was so tasty. "Get your feet up and your weight centered. Hands and knees first." *Fust.* "Let the water move you along."

Maggie went through the how-to-surf instructions again. Each time, I got a bit closer to standing on my feet. Each time, the surfboard shot out from under me, throwing me hard into the water. If the sharks didn't bite my foot off at the ankle, the tether to the surfboard would. Who knew a fiberglass board could jerk that hard?

"All right, "Alaric ground out in his Masters of the Universe voice. "This time we'll do it." It killed him that he was a terrible surfer. Hawaiian heritage and couldn't stand on a slick board on fast-moving water? What kind of a man was he?

It made me giggle. I was sore all over from so frequently hitting the water (since when was water hard?), but this was our chance to learn. Wink was waiting for Maggie to give him the nod, and then it would be up to us to surf about a thousand feet, all the way from this sandbar to the island, while standing. First pair back would win the lighthouse suite at the gorgeous private resort.

Last ones back would get the servants' quarters.

Alaric was not a servants' quarters kind of guy, he assured me. We needed to win.

Or at least not come in last.

Finally, Maggie—her tight, athletic T-shirt insultingly dry, since she never fell in—signaled to Shout in the boat. "They probably won't die if we let them go now. My guys will pace them on the Jet Skis, but I think we're good to go!"

Wink had us form as much of a line as we could in the ocean. Knox thought to call out a question.

"If I fall and O doesn't, she doesn't have to stop for me, right? She keeps going? We don't have to arrive together?"

Wink and Shout put their heads together and then called Maggie over. A rendering was issued.

"Pairs do not have to arrive together. And if one person is

having trouble, the other can make it to shore and then come back by Jet Ski to try tandem surfing, to see if that will help."

Cheers greeted this entirely confusing concept. If I couldn't stand on a wave with only my center of gravity to contend with, how would I manage it if Alaric was on the board with me?

Never mind. Face that mess when we get to it.

"Cameras ready? Okay ... go!"

Wink's voice rang over the water thrillingly, but it was a bit of an anticlimax, since we all had to wait for the wave that would carry us.

We'd learned a surfer had to catch a wave at the right point. Two people twenty feet apart would find themselves on two very different waves. One could catch the power while the other couldn't.

And the first wave after Wink's shout was just right for three of us—Nick, Alaric, and me.

I set my jaw and took a deep breath. Paddle, paddle, paddle.

The water lifted under my board. I'd caught the wave!

"That's it, Joss! You've got it, Alaric!" Maggie the Mermaid had learned our names effortlessly. Where was Nick? "To your knees now! You can do it!"

I got my knees under me and pushed forward until my ass felt dangerously exposed, but when I straightened my knees, I could maintain a strange, hands-down crouch.

And then my hands came off the board.

I was hardly standing, but my weight was balanced on both feet, and I wasn't falling. "I'm kind of—I'm doing it!"

I heard cheers behind me and dared to turn my head in time to see Alaric hit the water.

I had an epiphany about balance, so I jumped into the water too (which hurt significantly less than losing my footing and falling over).

"What the hell are you doing?" Alaric shouted angrily as I

dragged my surfboard back to him. "You were doing it. You don't stop for me, remember?"

He clung to his board, and our camera operators circled to capture this interesting encounter.

"I figured something out," I said. My hair covered my eyes, and I ducked my head backward to clear it. "Listen."

"Don't stop for me. For Christ's sake, Joss, we want to win!" Alaric looked like an angry seal bobbing in the waves.

I ignored him and went on, "Listen to me. You're too stiff. I just got it—you have to loosen up."

He had great hair, which was shiny with water, and broad shoulders that all but gleamed in the golden sunshine. "Core strength. That's what she said." He hooked a thumb back at Maggie, who was surfing next to Knox and coaching him. Jane-Alice and O, both of whom had surfed before, were halfway to shore.

"No, I mean—here. Get up on your board and let me explain."

The trick was to slide onto the board belly first and use our legs to kick us around to point the nose to the beach. Then we sat up.

Brilliant sun. Cool water. Paradise.

"Okay. What could you possibly have to teach me about surfing that that woman couldn't?" Alaric was testy. He didn't take to failure well, but who did?

"Here's the thing. You're a golfer, right?" Alaric shrugged impatiently at me. "And when you golf, you're supposed to—" I held my hands out in front of me as if I held a golf club. I swung awkwardly.

"What are you doing?" Alaric asked, surprised out of his temper by my ineptitude. Luke caught my laughter.

"I'm swinging a club. Like, you rotate your body around one axis, right? Your ribs spin around your spine, sort of?"

"Abdominals," he said in haughty fashion. "That's what core strength means, Joss."

"Yeah, but we're on the water."

"Thank you for that fascinating point. I hadn't noticed."

"Calm down. I mean, there isn't just one point of rotation. You see?" He telegraphed his confusion, and I clarified by sawing my hand through the air. "The wave can do like this"—I dipped my fingers down from the wrist and back up—"or this"—I sawed my thumb higher than my pinkie and then back down again—"or this." I panned my hand flat over the surface of the water. "Three different planes. Not just one. Do you see what I mean?"

My demonstration was pathetic, but light was dawning for Alaric.

"So," he said thoughtfully, "I need to be able to—what? Twist? Rotate?"

"Or relax into it, you know? In all directions at once."

"Uh." He sawed his hand across the space in front of his impressive chest. "So—like, how?"

"Relax. Stop holding yourself so stiffly."

"I need strength to get up, though."

"Believe me, I know. But maybe instead of all your muscles at 100 percent, keep them at 40. On but loose."

He nodded and then grinned, white teeth flashing. "Okay. Let's give this a try."

Easier said than done. We had to wait for the wave. Meanwhile, Jane-Alice reached sand and held on to a towrope to have a Jet Ski drag her back to Paul. O was close to the beach. The lighthouse suite was looking less and less likely to us.

On the other hand, Euphoria and Theo apparently weren't even trying. They sat on their surfboards behind us, bobbing in the waves and giggling. Their camera operators were grinning. They'd be on tonight's show for sure.

"This looks good. Try for this one," Alaric called. "Come on—come on—come on—"

We paddled with as much strength as we could muster. Alaric was ahead of me when we both felt the power of the wave rise under us. We'd caught the ripple of energy and were being carried across the surface of the water.

"Knees!" Alaric called. I didn't need him narrating when I was concentrating so hard, but it was nice to have a partner.

I tried my previous technique of pushing my ass to the back of the board—I should have told Alaric to try it—and found myself again in a cautious crouch. My hands floated ahead of me and to the side, struggling to keep my balance.

But—40 percent power. Relax a little, Joss. Feel the wave. Be ready to react to a shift.

I shrieked as my speed picked up. I was doing it!

"Fuck!" Alaric, ahead of me, bobbled but caught his balance again. He was standing too. "Keep going, Joss, I've got it this time! Keep going!" The splash when he fell was epic, and I jerked to one side as his board sheered away and into my path.

Astonishingly, my body responded to the surfboard under me. My shift in weight caused the board to curl away from Alaric's board, and I passed it safely.

Holy shit. I was still standing.

Off to the side, I heard Luke shout a victory cry. Alaric's voice came from behind me: "Keep going! I'm right behind you!"

He'd have to catch the next wave, so he wouldn't be right behind me. But he'd made it to his feet once; he'd do it again.

I had a few minutes of blissful movement in which I got slowly straighter, but I forgot to stay relaxed. The board shifted under me, and I wasn't able to respond. Down I went again.

But this time, when my head broke the surface, I was grinning.

This was fun.

I'd gotten a fair way ahead of Alaric, but he was sitting on his board, waiting for a wave. He was fine.

Jane-Alice was balanced on the back of Paul's board, but she was shouting at him, and he was a wooden block of tension. That pairing wasn't going well.

O and Knox were on his board. Unlike the other tandem pair, they were grinning. Of course Knox was laughing. It wasn't in him to not enjoy himself.

And Theo and Euphoria were still gabbing at the sandbar.

"Wave, Joss!" Alaric called to me, and I caught what I'd almost missed—a wave that carried me perfectly.

It took me one more wave after that one, but I finally felt sand beneath my feet and laughed as I caught the surfboard under my arm. I made it!

The idea of attempting to help Alaric was ridiculous. I wouldn't be any help to him at maintaining his balance—rather, we'd double our chances of falling in. I sat on the beach to watch the others.

Knox and O were the first couple to make it to the beach. They balanced well together, and I tried not to feel jealous. That's *my* Knox, I thought, and then shook it off.

Seeing that the lighthouse suite was lost to her, Jane-Alice pushed away from Paul's surfboard in a pout and grabbed onto the towrope from her cameraman's Jet Ski . . . after which Paul did a great deal better.

Alaric made it to shore next. We'd come in second, and his mood had improved dramatically. I met him at the shoreline. "That's actually kind of fun," he said. "I'd do that again."

"Me too!" We stood with our ankles sinking slowly into the sand and watched the others make progress at wildly different rates. "Why don't we?"

"What?"

"We're just waiting for them. Hey, Luke!" My cameraman lurked offshore on the Jet Ski, behind the

Australian driver. "Can you tow us back out for another try?"

Luke laughed, and the Aussie waved his hand at us in a "Come on!" gesture.

Alaric and I both made it back to shore twice, getting more and more confident, before the final couple made it back. Theo and Euphoria paddled on their boards without ever trying to stand. They seemed extremely content with their servants' quarters billet. Theo was unusually relaxed and happy, which made me suspicious.

The resort was luscious—a beachside Eden with open walls and billowing panels of white sunshades. My room with Alaric was simple and spare. The large bed was dressed in white, and the bathroom had an open-air shower that rinsed salt and tension from my skin.

"Not bad," Alaric declared, hands on his hips. Was he referring to the room? Or to me? "Are you finished cleaning up? Let's go see where we should have been living."

We gathered a group of interested contestants (and their camera operators) as we went.

The lighthouse suite was on a breezy, rocky promontory. Knox and O invited everyone to climb the lighthouse and look at the world around us from their exclusive view.

It was truly breathtaking. Islands dotted the ocean, and the shadows of clouds raced across the sandy bottom—here, the palest blue of sandbars; there, the turquoise of reef waters; and over there, the navy of deep sea. Our island stretched to either side, empty white beaches reaching to a fringe of palms that rose gently to a far point before dropping away into water.

The gentle breeze smelled of salt and wood heated by sunlight, and birds wheeled across the sky with echoing, exotic cries. Alaric rested a warm hand against my back, and I leaned lightly into his shoulder, together in the crowd gathered at the rail. Was Alaric my One True Love?

Really?

I'd try. I'd be open to it. But I had my doubts. And my suspicions only deepened when Alaric spoke to the group. "Now let's check out the losers' quarters."

Did he have to? Was the tone of mockery necessary?

Theo and Euphoria had an airless room away from the ocean breezes, but somehow, Theo had scored a hammock, and the two of them lay in a shady spot, feet to head, still giggling and chortling over something, both of them at peace and happy. Their camera team had pulled over plastic lawn chairs and were kicked back where they could relax while keeping their cameras on Knox and Euphoria.

They both waved in contentment.

It was confusing. Where had Theo's brashness gone? Alaric was visibly annoyed that they weren't suffering.

His annoyance annoyed me. It would be hard to reach the One True Love stage with Alaric. Still, I was glad he was my partner when we heard about the next day's *Cupid's Quest* challenge at dinner.

21

DOWN UNDER'S DOWN UNDER

Alaric didn't snore. He would never do something as pedestrian as that.

But he did whistle in his sleep.

At least, his nose did. Upright and awake, his nose was fine. But tip him over and get him to relax, and air came through his nostrils with a peculiar, high-pitched wheeze that made me think of things like deviated septums and the corrosive effects of too much cocaine in one's youth.

At first, it made me giggle. He'd been decent about not pressuring me at bedtime, and I was feeling charitable toward him.

But as the hours of darkness went on—and as his shifting from side to side didn't affect the whistle in the slightest—I began to lose my sanity very slowly.

All sorts of options occurred to me, none of which were suitable to perform while being recorded by night-vision cameras. I could smother him, I thought. I could shake him awake and scream *STOP THAT!* I could sleep on the beach with the sand fleas.

In desperation, I packed pillows around my head, leaving a

tiny air hole for breathing, and lay still, determinedly focusing on relaxing every muscle in my body.

Sleep, come find me. Please. I knew what lay ahead, and I needed sleep. I'd never been scuba diving, and an hour-long instructional period in the shallows didn't seem like it would be enough. Didn't people's legs get stuck in giant clamshells all the time, unable to regain the surface? I'd die a horrible, watery death. Omigawd.

On the other hand, I wouldn't have to listen to the whistling anymore.

At last, I fell asleep—for about forty-five minutes, until Alaric shook me awake.

"God, girl, you sleep like the dead. Get up, will you? We've got a competition to win today."

He smacked my rump as he bounded out of bed. Tonight I'd make my way to Theo's hammock. No more sleeping with the demon whistler.

Coffee helped, and my fatigue at least spared me from the same panic Rose was clearly feeling. She grabbed my hand as we got to the beach at last.

"Have you ever done anything like this?" She eyed the long row of scuba tanks, fins, and assorted additional equipment.

"No," I yawned, "but I've cleaned up an iceberg in my underwear, so how hard can this be?"

It startled a surprised laugh out of her. "Another experience!"

"Absolutely."

She drew me aside. "How are you doing with Alaric? You're so sleepy. Did you guys, you know—"

I huffed a laugh through my nose, which didn't whistle. "Hardly. No spark there at all." Luke was around, of course, filming me as Rose's guy filmed her. (Nice guy named Collier.) But it was so common that the cameras were part of the scenery; it was too easy to forget we were being recorded. "How about you and Nick? He's cute."

"He is." She smiled. "And sweet. A truly nice guy. But he's not the one I'm interested in." She turned away with a sparkle, and both cameramen closed in.

I needed no prompting to follow up. "Who? Rose, who do you like? Tell me! Is it Mason?"

She blushed. "Not Mason. Stop." She gestured at the staring lens of the camera. "Come on. I'm sorry I said anything."

Oooh, so interesting. But then Wink summoned us to the pile of equipment and a small army of Aussies standing knee-deep in the surf, grinning at us. Rose's love life would have to wait.

"Welcome to the beautiful Cara-Sun Resort in the Whitsunday Islands of Australia! Are you ready for your *Cupid's Quest* competition?" The place was so beautiful and the water looked so inviting, we managed an out-loud cheer, and Wink was pleased. "Well," he said. "We've got a great challenge for you! You can see the beach has been divided into six sections." He gestured and I turned, along with all the contestants.

Huh. I hadn't noticed. Colored ropes ran from the fringe of trees down the mild slope and into the water. I followed the nearest rope, which was red, and saw it extended into the water, held up by floats every ten or fifteen feet. I squinted in the sun. Yes, all six colored ropes did the same.

"That's about fifty feet of beach from the trees to the shoreline," Wink said. "And the ropes mark off territory that goes about a hundred feet into the water. Each section is a rectangle, roughly fifty feet wide and a hundred and fifty feet long."

We nodded.

"Each section has a flagpole near the tree line. See them there? Here's what you're going to do." Wink turned and pointed at the water. "Somewhere on the reef is a flag in your color. Knox, you and O were the first back to the beach yesterday, so you get section one. Your flag is red. Alaric and Joss, you were second back—and the most enthusiastic surfers too! You get section two. Your flag color is orange."

He went down the line, assigning teams to sections of beach and water and doling out colors of the rainbow. Theo and Euphoria were in the last section. Their flag was purple.

"You're going to scuba around your part of the reef until you find your flag. It's weighted to stay on the ocean floor, but it's not too heavy. Bring the flag to shore with you because you'll find instructions on it."

"How long will it take to find the flag?" Paul asked, to the evident disgust of his partner.

"We'll figure it out," Jane-Alice told him sharply. He ducked his head and didn't repeat his question. That was a bad pairing.

"It doesn't matter how long. Remember, you've got three days for this challenge."

Wink's words just raised more questions.

"It's going to take us three days to quarter and search a section of reef that's only a hundred and fifty by fifty feet?" Val had her feet planted in her warrior stance, her confidence evident in every line.

"I hope not," Wink said with a smirk, "because that's just the first part. You find your flag out there, then you use the directions on the flag to dig there." He threw his hand grandly up the beach. "Buried treasure. There's a box hiding in the sand in each section. They're all about two feet down. It'll probably take a little digging."

Wink was exuding satisfaction. Alaric groaned. "Manual labor? I don't mind learning to dive—I've been meaning to do that anyway. But I don't think we should have to dig."

I bit my tongue to curtail my comment, which was, *Afraid of ruining your manicure, you prima donna?* But the example of Paul with Jane-Alice was still lively in my mind. I didn't want to be branded a "bad couple." After all, America was watching.

"Then you'll be dooming Joss to do a lot of digging by herself, if that's your choice." Wink beamed at Alaric and gestured to the cameras.

Alaric huffed his annoyance but remained silent.

"Once you find the box, you'll see there's a puzzle inside. Solve the puzzle. That will give you the combination to the banner locker at the foot of your flagpole. First team to raise their banner ends the competition for everyone. Then America can decide who they think the winner is. Good, no?"

It looked good to him. He wasn't going to need to dig up a beach while Alaric rested in the shade.

"Let's talk safety. You'll see that your camera teams have waterproof cameras. Your camera operator will always stay with you, and five of our twelve camera operators are certified divers. Two of them are certified in search and rescue, so you're in good hands."

"What about the seven of us whose camera operators aren't certified?" Rose's question came out as a squeak. She was still nervous.

"Ah, well, that's where these fellows come into it!" He gestured to the Aussies standing in the surf. "Meet your dive captains. Twelve experienced divers for twelve contestants! These guys are your instructors and guides. You listen to what they tell you. If one of them tells me you're not listening, we reserve the right to pull you from the competition." Wink seemed to want to glare at someone, but Theo had given up his rebel ways, and once O and Alaric had separated, a lot of the fight had gone out of them both.

"Okay! An hour of scuba instruction here in the shallows, and I'll fire my starter pistol when we're ready! Gentlemen, take it away!"

My dive instructor's name was Gareth. He managed to combine a great sense of humor with a no-nonsense style of teaching that filled me with confidence.

I got a weight belt (which was embarrassing; I had to tell him how much I weighed while Luke was right in my face, filming. Hello, America—yes, I'm underweight for my height, and I wish all the extra was stuffed into my bra) and swim fins, which Gareth wouldn't let me put on until I was in the water. The tank was annoyingly heavy.

"Won't be for long," Gareth said. "Once you're in the wadda, it'll be loit as ayah."

He was right—and it was far easier to put the flippers on once I was in the water. We crouched down in chest-deep water as our classroom and went over safety features. Far sooner than I was ready, I had the regulator in my mouth and sank slowly to sit on the sand, water closing over my head.

The first inhale was terrifying—but Gareth had impressed upon me that the worst thing I could do was to stop breathing, so I took that bold breath.

It worked! I was doing it!

Gareth motioned me back up, and we went through how to read the gauges to know how much air I had left and how deep I was. He taught me to use the air vest until I could hang weightless in the water, and we discussed the hand symbols we'd need to dive safely. Clearing fog from my mask while underwater was horrifying and very, very cool. I was James Bond.

"What about you now, mate?" Gareth said to Luke.

"Naval diver," Luke replied. "I'm good."

"Good on ya! You got a good one here, Joss!"

I smiled. Luke *was* a good one.

Alaric was farther out (chest-deep for him was deeper than it was for me) with a dive master who looked a bit like Luke—probably an Islander. The dive master was handling Alaric's arrogance by completely ignoring it. It was driving Alaric up the wall and giving camerawoman Roberta huge grins.

The time flew, and Wink gathered our attention from the shore before I expected it.

"Come in closer—closer—closer!" There were twelve contestants, twelve camera operators, and twelve dive masters. The thirty-six of us drew closer to shore, but everyone wanted to keep their heavy tanks in the water, so we ended up duck-walking until we were close enough to satisfy Wink.

"We've got five minutes to go, and it's a bit of a hike to get to that last section. Theo and Euphoria, you'd better head west!" He pointed up the beach.

"We'll swim it, if you don't mind," Theo called back "We'll go under the ropes."

Wink consulted with Julie, who consulted with Shout, who nodded to Julie, who nodded to Shout. "That's acceptable," the host said magnanimously. "Head out. Nick and Rose, your team is next. When you get there, stay between the blue ropes."

Each contestant pair peeled off the group in teams of six, so the waters quickly got less crowded. Jane-Alice and Paul and then Mason and Rose swam to their rectangles.

Once the crowd had thinned, I saw O's dive master was the mermaid herself, Maggie the surfing goddess. O looked particularly tense as Alaric and I slipped under the ropes to get to our segment.

There was enough of a pause before the competition started that I waved Knox over. We met at the pair of ropes—orange on my side, red on his. "Is O doing all right?" I asked.

"Claustrophobia," he said. "She doesn't like the mask and regulator, but Maggie's taking care of her. She'll be fine." He tried to speak with confidence, but I knew my Knox. He was worried.

"Maybe it won't be too long." I tried to reassure him.

He nodded, his camerawoman capturing his bravado.

"Joss!" Alaric called to me. "Stop fraternizing with the enemy! Get back here, huh?"

I made a face at Knox, who laughed, and we parted. Alaric drew us all the way to the yellow ropes, as far as he could get us from "the enemy." Paranoid much?

Once Wink fired his starter pistol and Gareth helped me sink below the surface, I sort of forgot about the competition. I mean, I knew I was scanning the ocean floor for an orange flag, but that was a faint background concern.

Instead, I was mesmerized by the world around me. Sunlight through the ripples overhead sent wonderful patterns across the sandy floor in endless, mesmerizing shapes, which hypnotized me until I saw a shell on the sand.

A moving shell!

I grabbed for Gareth and pointed. He nodded and gestured me forward. We were heading for low grasses rippling in the water. Thin silverfish darted through the blades, and more conchs made their way across their watery kingdom. I was the diver in the aquarium, only this aquarium was the entire ocean.

We came to our first outcropping of coral, which looked like a huge, stone brain standing in the grass. Branches in gold and green and red grew off the brain, and the fish here were hallucinogenic, in all colors and a million shapes. I discovered I could grin and hold a regulator in my mouth.

Alaric swam in front of us, his camera operator on one side and his dive master on the other. We'd been told not to separate, so my trio followed his into water that gradually got deeper. The reef became more ornate. I realized the coral had grown into endless little rooms, where sandy floors were walled in by the coral stone. Finding a single flag in this labyrinth would take forever.

I tried to be unhappy about that.

The world was so vivid. All those TV shows that made me think the underwater world was all tinted blue must have had something to do with the cameras. The world I was in was lush with sunlight and filled with a rainbow of colors. If I looked across the reef, I could certainly see blue water in front of us, but it wasn't impenetrable. The cluster of people that surrounded Mason and Val were clearly visible to my right.

This was beautiful. Breathtaking—that is, if it hadn't been repeatedly impressed on me that I must let nothing take my breath. The secret to safe diving was to keep inhaling and exhaling to avoid brain embolisms. Important safety tip. Thank you, Gareth.

When we reached the furthest anchor for our dividing rope, which lay across the surface some twenty feet over our heads, Alaric took a left and swam parallel to the beach. Ah—he was going to make increasingly smaller squares as we swam along, counting on a steady and consistent pattern to make sure we didn't miss the flag.

The fins were awesome. Just a flick of my foot and I jetted ahead. It was as close to flying as I'd ever felt. It was dreamlike, except for the surprisingly loud sound of the regulator. I sounded like Darth Vader with every inhale and was blasted by the noise of bubbles with every exhale.

Cool.

Alaric reached the second corner, where the float was anchored to mark the division between our segment and the segment where Knox and O were making their slow way.

They hadn't gotten very far; I was sure Alaric was feeling smug about that. He picked up his pace. I rolled my eyes and kept up.

And then I saw it. A flag.

But not an orange flag—not one on my side of the rope. I was seeing a small red triangle attached to a cement brick.

Knox! It was Knox's flag—and if he found it, he could get O out of her fear of scuba diving.

I came to a halt in the water. Luke swam past me and then doubled back. Gareth was right beside me. He gave me the "Are you okay?" sign and I let him know I was—but then I pointed at

Knox and O, drifting slowly through the water. I waved to him, but he didn't see me.

How could I get his attention? I looked to Gareth and then to Luke. I pointed to the flag, and then to Knox.

Luke, Gareth, and I had a silent conversation. Did I want to point out a competitor's flag to them?

Yes—yes, I did!

Was I sure?

I was sure. *Help me get their attention!*

Luke and Gareth consulted each other, and then Luke shrugged. He pulled a large knife out of the holster he wore on his calf (ooh, now *he* was James Bond!) and reached out to my arm. He turned me so I faced Knox and away from Luke. He must have used the handle of the knife to bang on my tank, for I felt the movement at my back and heard a sharp series of clicks spreading through the water.

Would Knox hear?

Again! I flapped my hand at Luke and imagined him laughing at me. He banged again.

This time, Knox looked around. I waved my hands. And he saw me!

Alaric must have heard the clicks, too, because he swam back to me. And he was coming fast.

Frantic, I pointed to Knox and then pointed to the flag, which was on the far side of a large clump of brain coral. *Here! Look here!*

Knox held his arms out in a shrug. *What?*

Here! Look here! I was pointing with my entire body when Alaric got to me. He saw what I was doing and groaned audibly. His hand on my arm was rougher than Luke's touch, and he pulled me away from the flag.

We were going up. Time for a chat at the surface, huh?

Gareth was messing with my air vest, and Alaric's guy was trying to get him to slow down, but Alaric wasn't having it. We made it to the surface, and he spit out his regulator and pulled up his mask.

"What the hell do you think you're doing?"

We had a brief argument that Luke and Roberta tried to film. The water this far out was rougher on the surface and their cameras kept getting slapped, but they seemed to be enjoying themselves anyway. At least someone was.

Alaric forbade me to help Mason and Val on our other side, if I happened to spot their flag.

"This time, you three swim inside my three. We'll cover twice the landscape that way. Let's get going. We're wasting time. Damn it!"

Life sure was argumentative on the surface. I couldn't wait to get back to the underwater world, where I could be Darth Vader without anyone yelling at me.

It took us almost two hours to find our flag and we had to swap out our tanks once—but finally, Alaric spotted the orange flag, pretty much dead center in our space.

Hurry! His gesture was crystal clear. *We've got to get to the beach!*

Off we swam, trailing our pilot fish behind us.

22

IN THE SANDBOX

"That was amazing!" Once I could stand in the waters off the beach, I turned to thank Gareth. "This has been the most incredible experience. I want to go again!"

He laughed and helped me get the tank off my back. "Anytime you're ready, darling," he said.

"I didn't even think to worry about sharks either."

"Ah, love, it's not the sharks you have to worry about out there." *Aught thayah.* I grinned at the implied threat of all the things that could kill me on the Great Barrier Reef, but Gareth was nodding up ahead of us.

At Alaric.

Who was attempting to kill me with the piercing gaze of his black, black eyes.

"Good luck with that one, princess," Gareth said. "If you need me to step in and give him a little love tap"—he made a big fist to show me what he meant—"just give a call."

"Ugh," I replied intelligently, my bubble of scuba bliss popping in the cold reality of being Alaric's partner.

"I'll take the belt and the fins from ya. Right. Well, I'll be voting for you, Joss. Good luck!"

Gareth walked away like having a scuba tank on his back in the open air was just another day. He was carrying my tank in one hand, Luke's in the other.

Bye, Gareth. Thank you.

Time to take my medicine.

I made it to the beach, where Alaric was waiting, and attempted to forestall his explosion. "Maybe you didn't hear that O has claustrophobia. Scuba diving was hell for her."

"That is O's problem. Her disability was our advantage, Joss. Jesus!"

I shook my head. "No. That's not—how can you—that's cruel."

"Cruel? *Cruel*? You're calling me cruel when you cost us this game?"

There were three other couples on the beach; two were still searching for their flag in the ocean. No one was digging yet. "Look around you, Alaric. We haven't lost yet. Calm down."

"Don't tell me to calm down! I can't believe you!" His rant was getting louder. Luke and Roberta were loving the fight, working together to get the best camera angles. I grabbed Alaric by the elbow, and he was so surprised I'd touched him, he let me turn him back toward the ocean for a private moment.

It did no good; Roberta squirted around us and returned to her close-up view of his face, red and tense with anger.

"What?" Alaric ground out. "What do you want with me?"

My frustration tightened my throat. No words could fit through the ring of tension in my neck, so I served my hands to the cameras. *See? Look.*

"What? What are you telling me? That Roberta is right there? I know. She's always right there. How does that matter?"

He was still spitting out words like watermelon seeds, trying to hit me with them. I dropped his elbow and turned away. "I'm crossing this rope!" I called to no one and to everyone as I stepped from our section to the first square.

Knox met me when I was a few feet in. "You okay?" His concern was soothing to me.

"Just a temper tantrum for all of America to enjoy," I sighed. Luke, still at my side, huffed a laugh. "How's O?"

"She's better. Thank you. She was having a bad time out there."

His words were unnecessary because O had reached us by that point. She wrapped her arms around my neck and tried to smother me with her gratitude. Laughing, I hugged her back.

"Thank you! Oh, how can I ever thank you enough?" O had tears in her eyes as we both laughed. I set her from me gently.

"My sister has terrible asthma. I know what it does to her. Feeling like you can't breathe—it has to be the worst thing ever."

O inhaled deeply, probably proving to herself she could. "It really is. You're the best. And I'm so sorry Alaric is giving you a boatload of shit. He's the worst, isn't he?" She looked from me to Knox, and guilt flashed across her face.

"He's the worst," I agreed, "but that's not your fault. And it's not mine. That's the game. It's okay. I'm going to go back and help him with the clue now. I just wanted to make sure—you know. You're good."

"I am! Thank you!"

I knocked knuckles with Knox and turned back to Alaric, who still faced the water. Roberta's camera was no longer in his face, so he must have calmed down.

He turned to me as I walked cautiously up to him. "I apologize," he said formally. "I lost my temper. That was poor form."

"Thanks. Apology accepted."

"How is O?" He tried to sound like he cared. I gave him credit for trying.

"She's okay. Have you looked at the flag yet?"

"Right. The flag." It was still clenched in his hand. When he unfurled it, the writing was easy to read:

FROM THE STARTING POINT:
9 PACES SOUTH
18 PACES WEST

"That's it?" I asked. "Is there anything on the other side?" There wasn't. I looked behind us to the swath of beach between the two orange ropes. It hadn't looked so big before I read the directions. Now it was enormous. "How do we know where the starting point is?"

"And how big is a pace? My stride? Yours? Little Rose's pace? How are we supposed to solve this?" He looked up, annoyed. It was clear why no one else was digging yet. "Christ. Do we even know which way is south?"

We both turned in a circle, looking for a compass that was clearly nowhere to be found. Theo would probably know, but he was one of the two couples still in the water. And would he share his information if he knew?

"Well, the sun wasn't coming in our room this morning when we woke up," I said. Months and months ago, back when my biggest problem was Alaric's sleepy-time whistling concerto. "I think sunset was . . . sort of there." I pointed out across the ocean. "So, let's figure that way is west."

"That's insane. But I can't come up with a better idea."

We're all lost here, honey.

"Let's take a closer look at our section. Maybe there's a pin somewhere that says 'starting point.' We haven't even looked at the flagpole yet, or the banner box."

"That must be it!" Alaric's eyes brightened, and he went running up the beach, Roberta pacing him with her camera.

Luke and I came up more slowly. I scanned the ground before me and found nothing.

"No joy in Mudville," Alaric snarled. "It's a pole in concrete.

The box isn't even fastened on. It's just sitting here." He picked up the black box and shook it at me. "No clues. A combination lock. Looks like eight numbers, zero through nine. We'll never stumble on the right answer to that."

"All right. Let's think about this." I sat on the beach, and Alaric reluctantly did the same. "There are only a few places that could be a measurable starting point, right?"

"Right. This pole! Set in concrete! This must be the starting point!"

"Hang on. The ropes are pinned down at the corners. They might be starting points. Or, given how crazy the *Cupid's Quest* people are, I suppose we shouldn't rule out the idea that the starting point is behind us, in those trees."

We both looked behind us and Alaric groaned. "Oh, fuck."

"Plus, maybe our starting point is wherever we came out of the water for this part of the quest. That's where we started." Alaric wheeled around to stare at the water, open-mouthed, but I saw the mistake immediately. "No, hang on, that can't be it. If we're right about assuming that way is west, then we'd be digging in the water, and they wouldn't do that to us."

"How do you know?" he said morosely.

"Scuba tanks are gone. Luke here seems to have switched back to his regular camera. Right, Luke?"

Luke refused to say anything, but he did grin at me.

"So—where does that leave us?" Alaric was now despondent. Handsome, evil, and despondent.

"I dunno. I'm going to see if there's anything interesting in those trees back there. You go look at wherever the ropes are pinned down. If you see something that would make a good shovel, grab it."

"Like what? You think I'm going to come across a backhoe on this beach?"

Attitude, buddy. We're all in this together.

I poked my fingers at the corners of my mouth in the

international unspoken symbol for "Smile, you asshole," and left him to his evilness.

"We're going to end up digging this whole beach down to a depth of two feet," he muttered as he stalked away.

There was nothing in the fringe of trees that screamed "starting point" at me, but I did find a fairly straight and sturdy branch. Once I broke the smaller twigs off it, it had digging potential.

I took it back to find Alaric by the flagpole again. He gave me his report: "The ropes are spiked into the sand. One spike only, but it's a big one. Nothing more until the floats that hold the rope up in the water."

"Okay. Then we've got two possible starting points."

"Two? You mean three. Both ropes are spiked." He pointed at the divider between us and the segment where Mason and Val were shaking their flagpole, and then to the rope that separated us from Knox and O.

"Just two. If that spiked rope was the starting point over there, then the directions would be sending us into the Knox-and-O enclosure. I'm pretty sure we wouldn't be allowed to dig over there."

"Fuck no. Bad enough we gave them their flag." I bristled at the words, but Alaric had spoken thoughtlessly and with no intent to hurt me. He was caught up in the puzzle. The fact that Knox and O hadn't started digging either must have eased his sting a little.

"Let's do some pacing," I suggested. "We do one dig based on that rope pin and one dig based on the flagpole. Good?"

Alaric shrugged. "Sure. But we're not going to be very accurate, given how obscure the directions are. What the hell is a pace, anyway?"

I took his elbow and led him to the pin. "You do one and I'll do one. We'll make a square between where we end up, and that's where we'll dig."

He shrugged. "As good as any plan, I guess."

Alaric started out boldly, taking long steps and counting out loud. Once he did his nine paces along the upper border of our section, he turned sharply to the water and counted again as he strode down to the water.

"Sixteen, seventeen, eighteen—here. This is where it is," he called. Stupid. All the other contestants (and Theo and Euphoria were now up on the beach, too, leaving just Nick and Rose still in the water) were watching.

I shook my head at him, and he looked abashed. He was taller than average and had been taking long steps; I felt sure his final stomp in the sand was too far from the actual buried treasure, so I tried to walk normally as I did my count.

I made my final stomp and used my handy stick to draw a box in the sand, using our two stomps as our outliers. The final square was about three and a half feet wide and probably twice that in length. I gulped as I looked at it. That was a big box.

"Let's get started," Alaric said.

"Hang on—let's do it again from the flagpole. See how far apart we get."

We ended up with two large squares drawn on the beach. "Piece of cake," he said when we were done. "Let's get to digging."

"Want to split up? I'll do this one and you do that one?"

"Nah," he said. "I'd better do the one from the flagpole. I'm pretty sure that's the right starting point."

It never occurred to him that, if right, he was dooming me to useless digging. That was the way it ought to be to him. *He should be the one to find the buried treasure.*

Whatever. I thought both starting points were equally possible, so I shrugged and took the first plot.

"Why are you starting down there?" Alaric demanded. "Start at the top of the box, like me."

"Well, I thought I could fill in the hole with the next strip of sand I dug up, and I wouldn't have to throw it uphill this way."

"Huh." He thought about it and moved down to my side. I hid my smile. *Not always right, are you, big guy?*

The first few handfuls of sand were soft and felt good in my hands. At about the twentieth dig, the sand got grittier, and the skin of my hands started to feel tight. Some forty or fifty scoopfuls along, I was glad for my digging stick.

"I need sun block," Alaric announced as he stood. "Where's that Julie?"

Shout and his team must have been monitoring the cameras because Julie came leaping down the beach like a sand gazelle.

"Do you need sun block? Oh, you're so smart. Here you go. I have plenty. Take some more. This sun is so bright, huh? I mean, it's glorious—this is like a vacation, really, I'm sitting over there and watching you guys and you're doing really well, and the scuba footage is incredible—did you see that Jane-Alice and Paul saw a shark? It's okay, it was a nurse shark, no danger there, but so scary, like, a huge gray torpedo in the water, and you just know it has so many teeth, and I guess I would have freaked out myself. We're going to call a mandatory lunch break in about fifteen minutes. I bet you guys are hungry, huh? Joss, sun block? Luke? Roberta?"

Julie shone her own version of happy sunshine on us, and Alaric sunscreened my back without me even asking him. I did his back in turn, glad for the feel of the lotion on my hands. And I wasn't ashamed to admit it: Alaric might have been a jerk, but his back was a work of art. Protecting that skin wasn't a chore; it was a pleasure.

Once she'd begun on her sun block quest, Julie flitted up and down the beach, ensuring all contestants and camera operators were safeguarded from the sun and that they knew the lunch break was coming. Alaric and I got back to digging.

"Where'd you get that stick?" he asked.

I nodded up the beach. "When I checked out the trees."

"That's a good idea. Can you break it in half?"

The stick was too sturdy, which secretly pleased me. "Sorry."

"I'll go find something of my own."

I was sort of surprised he didn't tell me to go get him a stick so he could keep up with his important digging. Where was that lunch break?

23

MY, HOW PUZZLING

Alaric caught up to me as I stepped over the picnic table's bench to settle in across from Rose and Nick, my plate filled with a shrimp salad that was calling my name. It had been a long, long time since breakfast.

"Joss, hi! Did you love scuba diving? Wasn't it amazing?" Rose was as thrilled by the experience as I was, and we were gushing about it when Alaric loomed over me.

"Not a word," he said to me sternly.

I smiled at him sweetly and turned back to Rose. "It was incredible. I can't believe the colors—"

"Didn't you hear me? Not a word." Alaric held up an imperious hand. "Pretty soon *he's* going to ask you how we knew where to start digging." He thrust an arrogant finger at Nick, who looked startled.

"Well, I was sort of wondering—" Nick said.

"See?" Alaric interrupted. "See? And you'd tell him, wouldn't you? Not a word. Not. A. Word."

I had a moment of calm in which I wondered whether I was going to take this behavior.

Why, no.

No, I wasn't.

"Can I speak with you privately, please?" I said to Alaric, rising from the bench.

He stood, too, but we were both halted by green-haired Julie, who rushed over with both hands outstretched as if to grab us both.

"Nope. Nope. Back to the table. The camera team gets their lunch and a break now, so you guys have to stay at the table with the tripod cameras. I'm sure you want to have a chat—after all, Alaric certainly thinks he's the boss, I can see why you'd want to walk him away from the group—but there's no getting away from the group on this show, remember? You need to sit and wait until your camera team is finished with their break, so have a seat and, you know, just talk about whatever you need to talk about. Right here. In front of the cameras. Okay, Joss? Okay, Alaric? Like, sit down now, right? And feel free to talk. What? Oh, right, okay, I'm going now. Enjoy your lunch, and do speak freely— no, I'm *coming*. Jeez."

We sat again, an uneasy silence falling over our quartet. The camera's eye, which I'd grown so used to I usually didn't see it anymore, was suddenly a huge, dark, beckoning abyss.

"This silence is perfect," Alaric said smugly. "Let's eat our food and not say a thing." When I opened my mouth to answer, he threw down another command. "Not. A. Word. Am I clear?"

I ground my teeth together and nodded vigorously. Let him think I was agreeing with him. He'd soon find out I had reached the "that's it, now you're going to get it" moment.

"Alaric, I am not your employee. I am not your slave. And thank god I'm not your wife. You're not the boss here. Do you understand? We work together, or you'll find out what happens when your partner decides to go on strike."

He threw back his handsome head and roared with laughter. "Oh, right. Like that's supposed to scare me. Get over yourself, Joss."

Being with Alaric was like biting into a lemon. A big, juicy, bitter bite. "On strike. No more digging. No more figuring out clues. No more working to help you succeed."

"Pfft. Like I need you. All you do is help other people. You never help me." His arrogant voice slipped into a whining tone at the end, like a child who didn't want to go to bed yet.

And how did we deal with whiny children?

We ignored them.

Fine.

I turned to Rose. "The scuba diving was an astonishing experience. I'm thinking maybe I'll ask Gareth to take me out again this afternoon while you're all digging."

Rose's eyebrows went into her hairline, but she came along gamely for the ride. "That would be more fun than shoveling wet sand around. Did you see a shark? I heard Paul swam right over one. Could you die? I'd be terrified, but he said it was fine. Just scary, that's all."

We talked about the dive and the Whitsunday Islands and the Great Barrier Reef. Alaric looked condescendingly amused and then bored. After an hour, when the camera teams were ready, we were allowed to leave the tables, and ten of the twelve contestants hurried back to their square of sand.

Alaric held out his hand to me in the "after you" gesture, but I refused to budge. Luke and Roberta had already started walking to our patch of beach, but he grabbed her elbow when he saw we weren't following. They doubled back.

"Joss. Let's go. Everyone else is going to get ahead."

I crossed my arms.

"Oh, ha-ha. Very funny. Come on, let's get going."

I looked out to the ocean. So blue. So tranquil. Sunlight rippled across the waves in sparkling diamonds, and the salt-scented air was fresh and quiet and warm. Lunch had given me new energy, but I was content to sit solidly and determinedly on the wooden picnic bench.

Alaric growled, ran his fingers through his glorious, silky hair, and then decided to grab me. Probably in a fireman's carry. I stopped him with a glare.

"You're really going on strike? Come on, Joss. We've got a quest to win."

"Sit. Luke, you and Roberta can sit too. I'm not going anywhere until Alaric and I have a chat."

"Christ on a cracker." No one in history had ever been more put-upon than Alaric. What a martyr. He sat, affecting the noble patience that would allow me to have *my* little temper tantrum.

"If you don't want me to share information with other contestants, just say so. In English. As a request. That would be legitimate. You could say, 'Joss, I want to win this, so please don't tell Rose or Nick what we're doing or why.' Do you see?"

"I have to treat you with kid gloves now?"

The arrogance of this man. "You have to treat me like a partner. Like someone who will work *with* you, not *for* you. Can you do that? Possibly?"

He stared over the beach, where the others were back to their digging duties. "You're being unreasonable."

"Do you keep employees at your business?"

"What?"

"What's your turnover rate? Do your employees find new jobs quickly?"

"That's the nature of our business. It's fast turnover. Happens everywhere."

"That may be, but it might also be because you think everyone is supposed to serve you. That you don't need to show them any respect."

"I pay them. That's respect enough."

"Do you like having to continually find new workers?"

He huffed his annoyance. "It's the worst part of the job."

"Then try being decent to people. Just try. See if I'm right."

He rolled his eyes. Astronauts in space could see his contempt. "Can we get to work now?"

"Sure. After an apology."

"You want to apologize to me? Go ahead." I gave him the fisheye, and he heaved another martyr sigh. "Joss, darling, my sweet. Honey. Lover. Please tell me you'll forgive me for trying to protect our chances in this. I apologize for thinking you wanted to win too."

My annoyance vented over into laughter. "Seriously?" I turned to Luke. "Want to go diving again this afternoon? Can we find Gareth?"

Alaric leaned forward. "No—come on. All right, I'm sorry. I'm sorry, Joss. I'll let you talk to people. Okay? Is that okay?"

"You'll *let* me? How gracious of you." I sighed. His panicked apology was probably about the best I would get. "Let's get going."

We didn't find the next clue that afternoon. (In fact, we had a vigorous disagreement about how deep two feet was, since Alaric was only digging down about a foot before getting impatient and moving on.)

I was so tired by the end of the day, I fell asleep before Alaric did and slept through any whistling. That alone was cause for jubilant celebration the next morning.

And then it was back out to the beach.

The morning sand was cool under my feet. Alaric looked over our tiny kingdom with calculation. "Now what? Where do we dig next? I think I'm going to dig a line from my square to the back border. Maybe I'll get lucky."

"Fine," I said. The fresh morning and my good night's sleep had strengthened my resolve. "I'm going to redig your square down to two feet."

"Don't waste your time. It's not there."

"Fine. You ignore me, and I'll ignore you."

It took me over an hour until I banged my badly frayed digging stick into something hollow in the sand.

"Got it!" I cried.

The small plastic box was bright red and not much larger than my hand. I looked up as Alaric skidded onto his knees beside me, reaching for the box. I let him take it.

"We're the first!" he crowed. "No one else has their box yet! Outstanding!"

Up and down the beach, contestants had stopped and turned to look. I smiled and waved. Alaric glared at me. "What? I'm not telling anyone anything."

"And you're not going to. Jeez. Okay, let's open this thing."

He fussed with the clasp until I showed him how to open it. Hunched over so no one could peek, he cracked open the box.

There was nothing inside but a sandwich baggie, sealed over a piece of white notebook paper.

"What's it say?" I asked.

He stared at it and then shook his head. "Um—"

"Can I?"

He leaned over so I could see it. The writing was simple—and puzzling.

1
1 1
2 1
1 1 1 2
3 1 1 2
2 1 1 2 1 3
3 1 2 2 1 3
2 1 2 2 2 3
1 1 4 2 1 3

"That's it? There's nothing more? Look on the back." He

showed me the back was blank. "Open it, maybe? You're sure there's nothing inside?"

There wasn't. Just a strange string of numbers.

We sat still for so long, all the other contestants went back to their digging.

"Let's try entering these numbers into the banner box."

My idea was a good one, but it was a fail. There were eight numbers on the banner box, and our strange series only went up to six numbers.

We sat in the sand, trying everything we could think of. Was it a code? Did the numbers represent letters?

1 would be *A*. That, at least, was easy.

1 1 could be *A A*, or it could be an eleven. The eleventh letter in the alphabet was a *K*.

2 1 was either *B A*, or... Alaric and I whispered the alphabet as we counted on our fingers. "*U*?" I asked. "Did you get *U*?"

"I got *T*. Hang on—no, it's *U*. Is this spelling anything?"

I was writing letters in the sand, which made Alaric look around suspiciously to make sure no one was spying on us. Just Luke, Roberta, and viewers around the world. We were good.

"I like the letter idea," he said. "None of these are over twenty-six."

"Yeah, but look at the next series. *1 1 1 2*. That could be *1, 11, 2* or *1, 1, 12*, or *11, 1, 2*, or *11, 12*."

"Does any of that spell anything?" he asked.

"Hang on, I'm working it out. Um... *kab*?"

"Well, that could mean *kabobs*. Or *hail a cab and get the hell out of here*."

"I don't think this is it." We sat glumly. "Maybe it's a cipher?"

"Huh?"

"We need a code key. Uh—hey. Where's the flag? From the ocean? Let's look at that again."

Alaric turned in circles until he spotted it, forgotten by the back corner. But it did us no good either. We were still fighting through confusion when we heard a shout. Down the beach, Jane-Alice was dancing on the sand, a red box held over her head.

"Shit," Alaric swore. "I need to solve this now."

"I guess we could try—"

"Be quiet, Joss. Let me think."

At it again, are you? You pig. "I think I've been pretty helpful so far."

"This is what I do. I solve problems. Just sit there."

"I solve problems too."

"You're a waitress." He wasn't even insulting me; he was dismissing me.

You got it, bud. "I'm going for a swim."

"Fine."

"Rot in hell, Alaric."

"Sure. Go along now."

I'd stalked almost to the shoreline when Luke caught up to me. "Don't go in too far, 'kay? I don't have the waterproof camera today."

I was in no mood to be compliant. "What? You mean there's a place I can go where the camera can't follow me? Hey, Knox!" I shouted up the beach to where Knox was using the serving spoon from the shrimp salad to dig. Smart. "Camera can't follow us into the water! Let's go out thirty feet and plot and plan!"

He waved at me with a grin.

"And make out!" I added loudly. "Let's have sex in the water where no cameras can follow!"

Just then, O let out a yip. She'd found their box. I sighed and spoke to Luke and his camera. "No sex in the surf for me. Guess I'll have to swim."

"Watch out for the sharks," Luke said hopefully.

"Meh. Nurse sharks. How can anyone be afraid of a shark with the word *nurse* in its name? Nothing to it."

Still, I didn't go very far out. I lay on my back in about three feet of water, floating in the crystal sunlight and letting the ripples wash away my ire.

Wouldn't it be awesome, I thought, if I could float out here and solve the puzzle? I squinted back up the beach. Alaric hadn't moved. His hung head created a picture of dejection.

All alone, huh? Shithead.

Two teams found their boxes at almost the same time. Theo and Euphoria did a dance on the beach to celebrate, which looked like a strange version of the Hustle with lots of John Travolta finger-pointing, and Rose and Nick slapped each other a high five, which sifted more sand down onto their scalps.

Only Mason and Val were still digging.

I had begun looking at the puzzle in a new way. It couldn't be a letter code; the combination lock on the banner box was in numbers. The answer was a series of eight numbers; trying to figure out letters was a dead end.

When I heard a *whoosh*ing sound, followed by a *thunk*, I opened my eyes.

A purple banner waved over the last segment of sand—Theo and Euphoria.

Holy crap. That was fast.

24

LIVING WITH DISAPPOINTMENT

Theo refused to tell us how he solved the puzzle.
The more we objected, the broader his grin got.
Alaric was particularly annoyed by this refusal.
"It won't make a difference now, damn it. Just tell us what the answer was."

Mason interrupted. We were gathered around the flagpole in Theo and Euphoria's space, and Mason held up the banner box. "I can see the answer right here. The code that unlocked the box was 3-1-1-2-1-3-1-4."

He looked up, and we all looked back. O spoke for all of us. "Well, what the hell sense does that make?"

"*Why?*" Alaric attempted to use his height and size to intimidate Theo when he asked the question, but Theo was taller and broader. He just laughed.

I turned to Euphoria. "Do you know why that's the code?"

She shook her head, her grin uncertain but clearly happy. "Not a clue. He stared at it for about five minutes. Then he walked to the box and keyed in the numbers, and boom. The box was open. I have no idea how he did it."

A laugh bubbled up in me. I was left confused but also

getting my mental hands around a growing sense of awe, and it tickled my sense of humor. It was like watching the work of a really good close-up magician.

Magician, I thought distantly, in the calm and rational part of my brain. Theo definitely fits that Jungian archetype.

We weren't the only ones left wondering what we were supposed to do now. The *Cupid's Quest* team had planned on the challenge taking us at least three days. Theo had slashed that schedule, and now we had time to spare.

After the cameras had their fill of Alaric and others attempting to browbeat, persuade, or bribe Theo into explaining his logic, we were summoned to an impromptu meeting on the terrace of the hotel.

The glory of the summer sunset had begun to paint the sky in ribbons of blush and apricot when Shout nudged Julie to stand. I was happy to settle in for a little of Julie's stream-of-consciousness. I'd had a shower and was wearing my blue sundress (appropriate to the weather at last). Plus, my "partner" was still steaming with unfulfilled frustration, and that knowledge was a warm ember glowing in my chest, where the meanest part of me chortled over his discomfort.

"Okay," Julie said, holding out her hands to hold back any conversation. (Unnecessary. We were poised to catch every word she said.) "So, that challenge went faster than anyone expected—so, like, applause to Theo and Euphoria, don't you think so?"

She clapped her hands together, and I joined in with a glad heart. Foxed Alaric, didn't you, Theo? Thank you for that.

Others joined in—with sincerity or with sarcasm, it didn't matter. We applauded, and each camera caught its intended victim's reactions.

I beamed in pleasure at the group. When I caught Theo's eye, he tipped me a quiet wink. A quiet, unspoken, secret communication from inside a thick crowd of people.

Now, what was that about?

And that little burst of excitement deep in my belly—what was *that* about?

"Right, well, it was a great challenge, and you all did really, really well—I mean, all that sand! And everyone found something to help them dig with—and Jane-Alice, the cook wants that frying pan back, thanks, so that was really interesting, and you did a great job. What? Right. So anyway, we don't travel until Sunday, right? Like, Sundays are our travel days, you know. Monday is the True Love or Double Dud, and then three days for the *Cupid's Quest* challenge, and then America votes on Friday, and we announce the winner on Saturday, and you guys get a rest day on Saturday because of the recap—and of course, to the next stop on Sunday, like, on Cupid's Arrow, which is the greatest name for a plane, don't you think? Sorry?"

She held her hand to her headset. Ten feet behind her, Shout muttered into his microphone. Why couldn't he tell her himself? Or tell *us* himself?

Julie whirled to face him and nodded, then whirled back to us. "So, it's only Wednesday, and that's a lot of free time for you guys, so here's what we figured. This would be a really good time to get to know your partner better. Like, you know? The 'love' part of the quest for love and treasure?"

"Finally!" Jane-Alice shouted. We laughed, but I thought it was nervous laughter.

Not on my part, though. I would have been nervous about being told to cuddle up with my partner if I was still with Knox because he was a sweetie. But with Alaric as a partner? Not a prayer in hell. You'd have to pay me more than five million dollars to kiss that snake.

Jane-Alice grabbed her partner's hand. Paul looked more than startled—he looked alarmed.

Next to me on the sofa, Rose whispered under her breath, "You leave him alone." When I turned to look at her, she realized she'd spoken aloud. "Nothing," she said. "I didn't say anything."

Sure you didn't. Maybe I knew who Rose was interested in—and it wasn't her current partner, Nick.

I caught myself. This was exactly why the *Cupid's Quest* team was asking us to get closer—to make this "empty" span of time more interesting. It was addictive, watching the relationships develop between the contestants.

Well, not me. I'd be dull as mud for the next few days. Fine with me.

"Now, no one is asking you to hook up with someone you're not interested in, of course. Don't do anything you don't want to do, and that's on camera, right? So you know and all the viewers know, and really, isn't that critical? I mean, we teach our daughters about consent and how important that is, but shouldn't we also be teaching our sons? Because that's really where the trouble—what now? Oh, sorry. Right. So, for the next three days, you guys are on vacation here at the gorgeous Cara-Sun Island Resort. You can go scuba diving, you can borrow a surfboard, there will be parasailing tomorrow if you want to try, and there'll be a big bonfire on the beach on Friday night with local musicians, and it's going to be a blast. All we ask is that you don't do anything alone, of course—not alone, because your camera will be with you always, of course, but you know what I mean. Stick with the other people and hopefully with your partner, right, because that's what this is about, and you're going to have a blast, and make sure you use plenty of sun block because I'm telling you, this sun, right? Do you have sun block? Because I have some if you need it—I mean, I have, like, a suitcase of it, but I can give you some whenever—what? Fine. Dinner's ready. Go on ahead!"

We stood, our silence turning to murmurs and questions and observations, until Theo, who had been in quick consultation with Euphoria, called out, "Hey, Roberta! Got a good camera angle? Great. Dig this!"

He turned like a ballroom dancer and spun Euphoria out to the end of his arm. She went with a natural flair, one arm held out dramatically at the end.

With a quick snap, he pulled her back in, reeling her up against his chest, where he dipped her until her braids brushed the deck. He leaned his bald head down and kissed her laughing mouth.

Euphoria flung her arm around his neck and pointed her outstretched toes while we all broke into spontaneous applause and catcalls.

He pulled her upright, and they performed a dramatic bow, as if they'd rehearsed it. "Now that," he called, "is a good first kiss. Stick around for more!"

Show-off. His action lit a fire under the other contestants. Knox and O shared a public kiss while waiting for their turn at parasailing the next morning. Jane-Alice cornered poor Paul after he'd fallen from his surfboard that afternoon. (Her expression of distaste after the kiss clearly expressed that Paul was not up to the bombshell's usual standards.) Val and Mason succumbed to peer pressure and exchanged an unhappy, wooden kiss at the bonfire on Friday night.

Alaric leaned down to me as we watched dolphins leap from the waters on Saturday. I held up my hand. "Don't even try," I said shortly. "Not after the way you've behaved."

We were all upstaged by Theo and Euphoria again, who managed to have an almost-natural kiss thirty feet below the surface when they both took out their scuba regulators to suck a little face. Like everyone else, I laughed when I saw it on that day's episode. (We watched the show after lunch. Time zones were so confusing.) Theo had managed to angle his head so their face masks didn't bump, and when they kissed, he pushed down the valve on the regulator in his hand, sending a jet of bubbles in front of their faces. It was a brilliant piece of stagecraft.

But to my astonishment, theirs was not the most noteworthy kiss on that day's episode.

That honor was reserved for a secret clinch caught on a night-vision camera, when Paul and Rose snuck away from the bonfire and wrapped themselves around each other.

Rose watched with her face in her hands. The small patch of skin I could see was red with embarrassment, but both she and Paul laughed when the hooting and commentary started up from the contestants.

"Well, really!" Nick was Rose's partner, but he wasn't mad. He was simply too good a guy to stand in the way of something so hot. "He treats you right or he answers to me," he said stoutly to Rose, wrapping his arm around her shoulder in a fatherly way.

Good guy.

I snuck a glance at Jane-Alice's face. She looked thoughtful. Maybe Jane-Alice was realizing it wasn't Paul who was the problem with her determined love connection.

To Luke's delight (and I assume, Shout's, too), I got Rose alone later and pressed her for all the details. She admitted that Paul made her toes curl, and she wore her happiness like the crown jewels. I didn't even bother trying to hide my smile.

But Alaric wasn't having as good a vacation. I didn't realize how poorly he'd taken the situation until we were boarding the plane on Sunday for destinations unknown.

He nodded to Theo and Euphoria, who were sitting in her seats and admiring their Cupid Cash dollar signs. "Go find out the answer to that damn puzzle," Alaric said to me. All I had to do was tilt my head at him, and he realized he'd been issuing orders again. "I mean," he said, "will you ask Theo about that puzzle? It's driving me crazy, and he likes you."

"No more than anyone else," I protested, but Alaric gave me a dismissing *tch* of contempt.

"It's not like you want to sit with me, anyway," he said.

He was right. What I wanted, after so many nights lying sleepless next to his whistling self, was a long nap in a cramped airplane seat. But okay. I surrendered with one raised eyebrow. "I'll see what I can do."

We took off. Once the seat belt light was turned off, I stood and moved across the aisle to Theo's two empty seats. I turned to see him looking at me. I gestured to his seats in the unspoken "Join me?" gesture.

I was flattered by how quickly he made his excuses to Euphoria, who waved her Cupid Cash to me happily. I waved back and moved to sit against the bulkhead, giving Theo the seat on the aisle.

"What's up?" he asked as he folded his long frame into the seat.

"I'm here on a mission. Alaric wants to know how to solve that puzzle."

Theo laughed. "And he sent you. And you're too honest to lie about it. Good for you, Joss. I have no intention of satisfying his curiosity. I'd tell you, but you'd just tell him."

"I would?"

"You would. You're devoted to helping others."

I snorted. "Not everyone."

Theo looked over the seat backs to where Alaric's dark head was bent over his phone. "He's driving you up the wall, huh?" I nodded. "Well, at least you're not taking it. You've got quite a lot of spine when you want to use it, don't you, Big Eyes?"

"I'm tough," I asserted, but Theo thought that was funny.

"You're only tough when you sense injustice. Otherwise, you're a total pushover. Nice, remember? *Honestly* nice."

"Why do you say that like it's a bad thing? Isn't *nice* supposed to be good?"

He shifted into his seat, turning slightly to give me his full attention, those dark eyes looking too deeply into mine. "Sometimes *nice* is associated with *naïve*, but I'm glad to see you're not a pushover. Keep annoying him. It's giving me a wicked boner."

The mild obscenity startled a chuckle out of me. "My pleasure."

He waggled his eyebrows at me. Had I implied his boner was my pleasure? The silence was awkward and also darkly exciting. I rushed to fill the pause with words. "Have you figured out where we're going yet?"

He gave me a half wink but let me change the subject. "Well, I've figured out which way we're going," he said, pulling out his phone. "But deciding where we're going? That's a little harder. There are lots of possible landing places on this tangent." I leaned over to look at the phone he held in his hands. His scent was warm and male, with a touch of pine. "Well, Singapore for one."

"Wow. That would be interesting!"

"I'm not done. How about Sri Lanka? Kuwait City? Athens? The southernmost tip of Ireland? Ever been to Greenland? Want to go?"

I shook my head, overwhelmed. "Would it be easier to decide where we're *not* going?"

"Probably." He put the phone away and then looked at me curiously. "From the past episodes, it looked to me like you were doing most of the thinking for your team, Joss."

"No," I said uneasily. "We were both thinking."

His hand made a convulsive gesture, from curled to flat, to dismiss my comment. "You were both thinking, but only you were thinking usefully. And personally, I was glad you helped Knox find their flag. O was struggling."

The heat in my face told me I was blushing. "Thank you." Watching that episode of *Cupid's Quest* had been particularly eye-opening; it was astonishing that O had the courage to get in the water at all. She was one tough lady. I was glad to have given her a boost. But compliments made me uneasy, so I threw the conversational ball back to him. "You've been doing well too. Got that Cupid Cash, didn't you?"

He shrugged. "Thanks to you. You taught me how to play."

"You always knew how to play."

"Nope," he said with perfect assurance. "I'm a good student. You told me I should be more human and not to swear so much. Now you see me—human and rated a strong R."

Fizzes of carbonation in my spirit popped out as laughter. "You've been very charming," I agreed. "Well done! And your kisses with Euphoria—absolutely wonderful."

He tilted toward me, and I leaned toward him. The cabin lights had dimmed, and we were in our own intimate bubble of space. "I'm glad you liked them," he said with a smile. "*Did* you like them?"

"Um . . . well, yeah." There was no need to express the little cocktail toothpicks of jealousy, after all.

"Good. Those were definitely Euphoria kisses. Custom-designed for her."

"Custom-designed?" I smiled. "Are you a kissing artisan?"

"I'm a good student, I told you. And kissing women is a subject I find deeply fascinating."

I willfully ignored the cameras in our faces. Nothing would stop me from pursuing such an intriguing subject. "So, you consider yourself an expert, then?"

"Not an expert. Never that. But a very, very good student."

"Lots of homework?"

"Not as much as I'd like." He leered at me, and I giggled like a high schooler in front of the captain of the football team.

"What have you learned in all this research, then?"

"Well." He leaned in a little closer and dropped his voice. "Just as no two women are alike, no two kisses should be either.

I mean, the Euphoria kiss would definitely be all wrong for you, for example."

I was leaning in too. "Really?"

"Really. I'd design an entirely different first Joss kiss."

"You would?" My voice was breathy, my pulse slamming me in strange places, like the backs of my knees.

"Entirely." His hand had made it across the endless gap between our bodies, and his fingertips slid along my jaw until they brushed against my earlobe.

A tiny "Oh!" slipped out of my mouth—you couldn't call it a whimper, could you? But then he leaned back a bit.

Disappointment.

"You know, Joss," he said. "We teach our daughters about consent, but we should teach our sons, too, don't you think?"

He was quoting Julie from a few days ago, and it made me laugh in surprise. The act of smiling eased something tight in my chest.

Consent. Theo was making sure I was okay with this.

I tried to come up with something witty. Some banter. Something worthy of Theo's big, mesmerizing brain. No luck.

"I consent," I said simply.

He leaned back in, and my smile widened. He was going to kiss me. And I wanted it like—like—

Like a sauna in Antarctica.

Like a rooftop retreat in Cairo.

Like sunset over the Great Barrier Reef.

His fingers teased my earlobe again and slipped over my cheek. "Your skin is velvet," he murmured.

My sound was definitely a whimper this time.

He continued his crooning. "The first kiss for Joss would be . . . soft." My eyes closed as the distance between us vanished. His lips, warm and firm and smooth, found mine. He made no attempt to go any further. He simply caught the edge of my lip between his.

Dry. Soft. Magnetic.

He was unhurried, as if caressing my lips with his was all he wanted in the world. "A Joss kiss would be gentle," he murmured against my mouth, and my hands were filled with the softness of his shirt.

He leaned in fractionally, the pressure on my mouth nowhere near as firm as I wanted. But I felt the faintest brush of his tongue against the skin of my lip.

He drew back just enough to continue his siren song. "A first kiss with Joss. Soft. Gentle. Slow. And with a tiny edge to hint at the steel you put in my cock."

I gasped at his words, my eyes flying open. He wore a dangerous smile and watched me carefully.

"Not too much," he decided. And he was right. He hadn't gone too far.

I wanted more.

I wanted to taste that tongue.

I wanted the privacy to see if he'd made up the steel part of his kiss description.

And he read that in my eyes. His smile turned into a grin.

"Ahem." Alaric stood in the aisle, staring at us. "Are you done making out with *my* partner?"

25

BONJOUR À PARIS

"Allow me," Theo said with a mean grin. He unfolded from the seat beside me and crowded Alaric back as he stood. "Do you have a problem, my guy?"

Alaric proved his lethal negotiating skills at that point, coming up with possibly the only thing that would have pulled me out of Theo's second seat.

"I don't have a problem," Alaric said with an icy stare. "But how do you think Euphoria is going to feel about you licking on Joss like she's ice cream? Where does that leave Euphoria in the competition? Are you really that cruel? Joss? How about you?"

The warmth of Theo's kisses was splashed away by a cold slap of guilt. Theo and I both looked back to Euphoria, now asleep across her two chairs.

I looked around in a panic. Even Rose sat with Nick, her partner.

Because Paul was with Jane-Alice.

Two by two. Partners.

"God," I said as I stood. "I didn't think—"

"Me either." Theo's voice was mournful, and he and I exchanged a glance filled with longing and humiliation and awkwardness. I pushed past him, and because he and Alaric were both blocking access to my two seats, I went to the front row to Alaric's seats and turned my back on the world.

Shamed.

Alaric, having defeated the dragon, sat beside me with an air of infuriating satisfaction. "All right, then," he said.

"Maybe I should go apologize to Euphoria."

He held out a hand as if to restrain me. "She slept through that semipornographic display you and Theo put on. Leave her in peace. Don't unload your guilt on her just to make yourself feel better."

I hated Alaric. My rage was black ooze bleeding out between my ribs. But there was no denying the truth of his words. I pressed back into my seat, wishing it would absorb me into some foam rubber world where sound was deadened and no one could judge my flaming face or my amputated lust.

I had plenty of time for my overwrought emotions to settle because our flight was—as usual—apparently endless. More of Dante's *Purgatorio*. Fourteen hours went by, during which time we watched the twenty-first episode of *Cupid's Quest*, in which Theo dipping Euphoria in a blistering kiss made heat fly off the back of my neck in distress. We had boxed lunches and then boxed dinners. We did not land.

Another seven hours went by, during which the concept of sleep was like a giggling fairy playing hide-and-seek in the woods. After five hours of strange twilight sleep, I gave up and crawled over Alaric to use the tiny bathroom. By the galley, warm and beautiful Theo stood amid a cluster of women. Of course. Did he never sleep?

Euphoria stood at his side, looking up at him adoringly.

I nodded in their direction with my head down and scurried for the tiny folding door. "We're well past the Middle East by now," he said. "I think we're looking at Europe. Maybe Greenland."

He overshot it, though. We landed in the international bedlam of Orly Airport, outside of Paris.

"We're in France," Rose breathed as she grabbed my hand. "I can't believe it! I've always wanted to see Paris, and now we're here!"

I had too. I just didn't think I'd be visiting the City of Lights as a scarlet woman—or one with smug, arrogant Alaric at my elbow.

"Stick with me," he said, pulling me away from Rose. "You don't want to make this situation any worse."

I was tired enough to let him get away with this, but not so tired I'd surrender to a temper tantrum on the jetway to the terminal.

The drive into the city was through far-from-romantic scenery, but the signs were all in French, and that seemed delicious. I began to perk up. On the bus, Theo was four seats behind me and to the left. I could feel him but didn't turn around to check. Or wave. Or catch his eye to run my fingers suggestively over my lips. He sat next to Euphoria, and I was good.

"Now maybe you'll listen to me," Alaric said. I was against the window with him on the aisle. His attempt to control me physically. "Don't talk to anyone else. Stick with me. I'm telling you, we could pour on the romance, Joss. You're good-looking enough."

The bus that took us into Paris was set up like all the buses we went on, with microphones between the seats and a cameraman who stood at the front, focusing on whoever sounded interesting. My reply to Alaric would definitely be recorded.

I bit my tongue and crammed my anger back down into the cave from whence it had stomped. "Ah," I said to Alaric as neutrally as possible.

He took it for assent and continued with his directions for

me, including how I should wear my hair and how many buttons on my shirt I should undo.

By the time we reached our destination—a baldly plain building on the outskirts of Paris—I had a tic in my eye, and Alaric believed I was being subservient at last. Wink stood to capture our attention.

"Bienvenue à Paris, mes chers! Welcome to the most romantic city in the world! You couples are going to have the date of a lifetime here—you simply won't believe it! But before we get to that, it's time for our True Love or Double Dud challenge. Are you excited?"

I was something. Not excited. More like a stick of dynamite with a one-inch fuse.

"Good! Follow me inside, where we'll get you set up with your microphone packs, and I'll explain!"

I moved away from Alaric as soon as we got off the bus, but he tucked right back against my side as if I were a magnet. The building was bland and institutional. We went through a front lobby and ended up in a large room, devoid of anything but cheap wall-to-wall and the staring lenses of our camera operator shadows.

Wink stood before a blank wall. "Now, for this challenge, we're going to test your poker face. Sound easy? You know it! The first people to react—and that means laughing, crying, smiling, frowning—will be staying in an unheated artist's rooftop atelier near our hotel."

The idea of staying away from the group was tempting—I had visions of Fatima's rooftop in Cairo—but it was late November, and the skies were dark with rain over Paris. Just the word *unheated* was enough to change my mind.

"The winners will find themselves in the bridal suite at the beautiful Hotel de Parfait Champs-Elysees, just one of the stunning options for your vacation destination here in magnificent France! All this and so much more has been made possible by the French Ministry of Tourism, sponsors of this week's challenges. We're going to explore culture and fashion and history and all the things that make France amazing—and Paris the most popular tourist destination in the world!"

I liked Wink. He was a cheerful presence, and he seemed to honestly enjoy his work. But if he didn't get on with it, I might step out of my shoes, lie down on the floor, and go to sleep. Either that or erupt into senseless fury.

"I want that bridal suite," Alaric hissed at me. "It's where I belong. Don't ruin this for me, Joss." I glared at him, but he was stupid enough to keep pushing. "Who am I kidding? You'll blow this just to spite me. All of America watching, and you're going to tank the competition, aren't you? Joss? Joss, can you hear me?"

My options were to lose my temper at last and discover for myself the color of his blood when I raked my nails across his face. Or I could wall off every emotion and get through the challenge without resorting to violence.

I slammed a lock on every possible reaction. Alaric didn't know it, but I was saving his pretty face.

"This wall is going to break into two and open. By the time you see what's on the other side, your cameras will be watching. We'll be able to tell who breaks first."

What the hell was back there? Was someone about to be guillotined?

"Ready? Here we go!"

Alaric's fingers dug into my biceps, but I refused to give him the satisfaction of shrugging him away. The wall rolled back, flooding our room with warm, golden light.

There, on the floor before us, behind a knee-high barricade, were—

"Oh! Puppies!"

It was Nick. The big, silent carpenter was helpless before the fluff balls that rolled across the floor or tugged on rope or stood in their water bowls, looking around alertly. Beaming men and women stood nearby to keep everything safe and happy.

"Well, we have our unheated atelier residents!" Wink cried happily. "That was fast! Nick and Rose, enjoy this lovely November weather."

Others had now broken from their silence. The rest of us were assured warm hotel rooms, so most of the contestants had stepped over the wall and were sitting on the floor, cuddling the puppies that yipped in excitement.

My hands itched to snuggle a puppy. There was one in the shape of a husky that was mostly smoke-gray fur and two button eyes above a clever little snout.

But Alaric. Damn him. I wasn't going to be the one to break.

I scanned the room impassively. Jane-Alice had a death grip on Paul, whose only emotion appeared to be pain. Alaric and I were like wooden statues. Everyone else (even Julie) was on their knees, cooing and playing.

But. Not. Me.

Wink approached us, preceded by his massive grin and trailed by our camera operators. "Well done, the four of you. Please come in and find a place to sit with the puppies. No reactions, please. And don't pet the dogs. The bridal suite is on the line, my friends."

I grabbed Alaric's hand and pulled him along behind me. I stepped over the fence and pushed through the cluster of puppies, cameras, attendants, and contestants until I found a place against the wall. I sat. Grim. Unlovable. Luke knelt in front of me, the camera never wavering even as one of his hands reached out to fluff the fur on a spotted puppy, who immediately rolled over to give Luke access to its belly.

Theo lay on his back, holding a basset hound puppy up to the sky. He crooned to the dog with love as a terrier licked his bare head. Theo's big hands and the basset puppy's big feet—hard to tell which were more adorable.

Alaric sat next to me, pushing away a chocolate-brown cocker spaniel who came to sniff him.

"Be gentle," I said woodenly.

"Shut up," Alaric replied.

I turned to him. "If you hurt one of these dogs, I will cut off your testicles in the middle of the night. Do not doubt I can do this."

My robotic delivery shocked him. He almost raised his eyebrows at me but caught himself at the last moment.

"You're a fierce bitch, Joss," he said evenly.

"That's true," I replied. "It's good you know that now."

I could have kept it up for a while. My determination to withhold all emotion was illogical and counterproductive—I certainly didn't want to spend any time in the bridal suite with the Arrogant Whistler—but I'd be damned if I'd break before he did.

In the end, it was Paul who decided the contest. "Cut it out, Jane-Alice. Jeez. Look at this puppy!"

"And we have our winners!" Wink was holding a Dalmatian puppy as he cheered us. No one else so much as looked up. And why would they?

"We won," Alaric said woodenly.

"I'm aware."

"We can stop now."

"I can't seem to stop. I'll be damned if I'll let you have your way."

"Um . . . Wink? Julie? Can someone help me over here?" Alaric looked around nervously, but it was Luke who duck-walked over to me and put the spotty puppy in my lap.

"Take a breath, Joss," he said. "Hold a dog. It'll help."

He was right. I scooped up the fuzzy body and hid my face

in its wiggling side. If the dog's coat was a few tears damper than before, no one mentioned it.

We played with the puppies until the attendants told us that was enough—the babies needed to rest. They gave a speech to one of the cameras, but as it was in French, I could only assume it was a plea for dog adoption.

"Are you okay?" Alaric asked as we walked back to the bus, covered in puppy fur and a few washable puppy fluids.

"Don't pretend you care," I said, overwhelmed by my fatigue. "In fact, don't talk to me. When we get to the hotel, I'm taking a nap. Alone. I don't care what you do."

"You don't get to decide what I—"

I held up a hand. "Don't sit with me. Go away."

One nap later, and that guy was going to get a powerful piece of my mind.

26

IN THE COURT OF THE SUN KING

My nap lasted for seventeen hours. I woke up with an urgent need for the bathroom and a realization that I'd slept through the night.

I blinked when I opened the bedroom door. The bridal suite was opulent and considerably warmer and more appealing than the heavily air-conditioned suite in Cairo. No modern furniture—this place was decorated with cozy sofas and chairs grouped around a working fireplace. Fancy molding a foot deep topped the walls, and sunlight shone through tall windows with a view of treetops, bare branches waving gently against a slate-gray sky.

Alaric was asleep on one of the sofas. I gave him points for that. As dead to the world as I'd been all night, he could have slept in the large bed beside me, but perhaps he thought my venom was too powerful for him. Safer on the couch.

Good thinking.

But this was a new morning. I was well-rested for the first time in a week. And I was hungry.

Once awoken, Alaric took pleasure in informing me I'd missed the most recent episode of *Cupid's Quest,* which featured

Theo thoroughly kissing me. "You should have seen Euphoria's face. What had happened while she slept? I could tell she felt betrayed, Joss. Betrayed by you."

"Oh, please," I said stoutly. "They're not married." But the question of breakfast became less important to me as I hid my wince. "I'll talk to her today."

He snorted as he sat up. "Like that'll help." He ran his fingers through his luxurious head of hair. "Are you done in the bathroom? I'd like a shower."

"Go ahead." I waved him away to contemplate my situation . . . and to wonder who might have recorded yesterday's episode so I could examine that kiss in close detail.

Euphoria wasn't at breakfast, although Theo was. He sat with Jane-Alice and Paul and only nodded at me as Alaric steered me to an empty table.

French bread. Butter. Jam. Pots of hot tea or coffee. It wasn't enough. I ate all of mine and then whatever Alaric had left over and then begged the waitress for more. Her smug smile said, *Of course you want more. This food is exquisite.*

Euphoria appeared as Wink was ushering us from the breakfast room. I couldn't grab her to apologize and couldn't read anything from her expression, either, other than she'd only recently woken up.

We ended up in a large conference room that was already filled with people. Our dozens fit in at the table and around the edges.

"I want to introduce you to the deputy director of the French Ministry of Tourism, Mademoiselle Marie-Thérèse Maitresse. Marie-Thérèse, we thank you for sponsoring this week's *Cupid's Quest*. Will you tell us something about the French Tourism Bureau?"

Marie-Thérèse was elegant. Her hair seemed to have been cut by a razor mere seconds before we arrived; not a strand was out of place. Her outfit was a soft, faded blue so beautifully tailored, it took me a moment to realize she was dressed entirely in denim. Marie-Thérèse was wearing jeans. Just not, you know, American jeans.

Her English was flawless and had a hint of a French accent to add a touch of the exotic. I feared and loved her immediately.

She had a great deal to say about France as the ultimate vacation destination for its fashion, food, nightlife, and culture. But none of us felt the need to pay a great deal of attention to what was undeniably the commercial she'd bought and paid for—that is, until her spine straightened, and she stopped looking at the cameras. She eyed the contestants, and we sat up.

"And our history," she said. "The amazing history of France —which is exactly where we place you in your next challenge!"

History of France? I cast my mind back frantically. *A Tale of Two Cities*, the French Revolution, Lafayette pulling the American bacon out of the fire during the Revolutionary War . . . what did I know about French history?

Wink recaptured our attention. "You met in Antarctica. You went on a double date in Cairo. You had a beach date on the Great Barrier Reef. What's next in your romance?"

He looked at us as if we should know. We looked back at him blankly, undone by the intersection of our dating progression with French history.

"Dinner and dancing, of course!" Wink was gleeful in his announcement. The idea did sound quite nice—if only I could switch partners.

"What's the catch?" O called from her seat down the table.

"No catch!" Wink was jovial. "Just a wonderful opportunity that everyone watching would love to have! Marie-Thérèse?"

She smiled as she folded her hands at her waist. "You are all invited to a ball in the court of the Sun King!"

There was a pause until Nick broke the silence. "The Sun King's dead, isn't he?"

The various Frenchmen and women rippled with discreet laughter.

"In 1715," Marie-Thérèse agreed. "But his palaces live on, as does the Baroque style he made popular!"

We were given a lecture on King Louis XIV that I mostly tuned out, except for the fact that he met his second wife because she was the nanny to the children he'd had with his lover, which must have come as some scandalous shock to his lover. Nice play, Lou.

Then Marie-Thérèse introduced the people she'd brought with her, which included:

—a historical chef who would make us a feast worthy of the Sun King. (Some of the stuff they ate back then was nasty; I hoped he would update a few things, like entrails and canary beaks and the like.)

—a costumer from the historical society, who would customize period costumes for us. (They weren't fooling me. They were talking about rib-crushing corsets and hoop skirts too wide to go through the doorway. If viewers in America and around the world wished for this opportunity, they could stand in for me.)

—a genderless being who was represented to us as our wigmaker. (Wigs. Because corsets, hoop skirts, and entrails weren't exciting enough.)

—our dancing master, who would teach us an eighteenth-century ballet as performed in the Court of Louis XIV. (Could I clean up an iceberg in my bathing suit instead?)

Wink thanked Marie-Thérèse and told us he'd learned his lesson in Australia; this challenge was so complicated, it would be a four-day and not a three-day challenge. We'd have costume fittings immediately, two days for dancing school and etiquette, and on Friday, which was *Cupid's Quest* voting day around the world, we'd have final fittings, a dress rehearsal, and then the ball itself.

"It's a big job you're doing, for in the Court of the Sun King, a single misstep and it was off with your head!" Marie-Thérèse tried to correct him, but Wink was immune to her little coughs and hand gestures. "Sharpen your wits, contestants! America and the world will be voting on who is most regal at the ball. Don't lose your chance to win Cupid Cash!"

He produced a dollar sign with a flourish like a magician. Ta-da. Great. Let's get to it.

"All right," he sighed. "We'll divide into groups now. Men, go with François here for costuming. Women, you're with Spike for the wig discussion. Then we'll switch when you're done. Go on now. Let's get going!"

We were shepherded down the hall to our next stop, and I took the opportunity to squeeze past Val to reach Euphoria.

"Hi!" she said brightly when I reached her side. "This is crazy, right? I'll bet they didn't have too many faces as dark as mine in the Court of the Sun King."

One of our sheepdogs, an assistant whose name I didn't remember if I'd ever been told, overheard her. "Well, actually," she started.

Nope. Sorry. I needed to interrupt. "Euphoria, I'm so sorry about kissing your partner."

We were led into a room set up as a salon, with chairs in front of lighted mirrors. "What? Why?" Her tone wasn't coy. She wasn't playing with me. She was honestly curious.

"Well, he's your partner. I didn't mean to—"

Euphoria cut me off by laughing out loud. "Honey. Really? Why would you assume I had any claims on Theo?"

"Oh. Um. You had some pretty good kisses—"

Her cheeks popped from the width of her smile. "Joss. He never kissed me like he kissed you. And I wouldn't want him to. He's my partner for the challenges, but if you want to pursue a love connection, don't let me stand in the way. He's a great guy. You look good together. Very hot."

We were seated in adjoining chairs, and on my other side, Jane-Alice overheard. "I'll say. That was a smoking-hot kiss." She sounded annoyed.

"Oh, well. I guess I'm sorry I slept through the episode." I was blushing but relieved. Euphoria didn't feel betrayed. Alaric, of course, had lied to me. What else did I expect?

And I could now eye Theo with a clear conscience.

I bit my lip to hold in my smile of satisfaction, but I didn't need to. Now all five women around me were providing an intensive critique of the kiss they'd seen on the last episode, and it was decided that they'd rate it as hotter than the secret, stolen kiss between Rose and Paul. Rose pretended to pout, but she winked at me, too, so I knew we were good.

"I am in crisis!" Spike, the wigmaker, broke into our chatter. "I don't know what to do!" His accent was thicker than Marie-Thérèse's, but he was perfectly intelligible.

Val, our warrior, took the lead. "What's wrong, Spike?"

"Ah. Ahh! You would not think of such a thing from an assistant deputy!"

"Explain." Val's voice was warm but firm. I'd follow her into battle.

"I am asked to create the ornate wigs of the late 1700s. You have seen them, I'm sure. The ladies who love the Navy show it by putting a full-rigged, three-masted sailing ship in her coiffeur. The aficionado of sport who wears a carriage in her hair. The madame or mademoiselle with a love of the garden who adorns her head with flowers or waxed fruit. Yes?"

I'd seen such things in movies—towering creations that wobbled over the actress walking so carefully and primly across a ballroom. We all agreed we'd heard of such things.

Spike wailed, a long and pale hand across the brow. "But mes cheres, those styles are from the late 1700s! And the Sun King died in 1715! It cannot be done! The costumers have prepared your gowns from 1688. Ah, what am I to do? My name is associated with this disaster! I shall never be able to show my head again!"

The wail disintegrated into French, and we had to leave all consolations to the assistants, who grouped around their leader in commiseration. Marie-Thérèse was summoned, and she read Spike the riot act until order was restored and hysteria averted.

"If I must, I must," Spike groaned. "Dear creature, what would you like to have in your hair?" Val was the first in line.

"What do you mean?"

"Ah. I am a fool. The book, the book!" A notebook was produced, and we all leaned in as Val paged through examples of ornate hairdos. Ships, harps, fountains—the collection was startling and absurd and entirely amusing.

"It should tell us about *you*," Spike said. "What do you want to say with your coiffeur?"

Val was in deep thought. "Anything?"

"Of course." Spike's honor had been offended. "I can do anything."

"Then I want an American flag. A big one. I'm an Army veteran. It's important to me."

"A flag? Just a flag? But . . . we could do that in mere moments." Spike was affronted by the simplicity. The forecast called for hysterics again.

I said, "What about if you did the American and French flags in honor of Lafayette and the combining of the armies to create America?"

Val looked at Spike, who stared into the distance and then clapped. "It is a theme worthy of the late 1700s. Yes, this I can do. A victory wreath with olive branches, and our tricolor with your Stars and Stripes. Mon cahier! Give it here, quickly!"

A battered notebook was proffered, and Spike was lost in a flurry of sketches. Then the next contestant was up.

Rose wanted roses, of course.

Euphoria asked for an artist's palette and a paintbrush.

Jane-Alice envisioned a lit candelabra that made Spike's eyes light up with delight.

O wanted a songbird in a cage, so halfway through the ball, she could open the cage and free the bird. "That's me!" she said fiercely. "I won't be caged!"

Spike loved the idea until he was told by an assistant that they couldn't knowingly free a live songbird in an historic palace. I opined that she could get a similar effect if she had a fake bird perched on top of a cage with an open door.

O was willing to accept the idea. "Can it be a falcon or something? Like a bird of prey?"

We had a moment of confusion when we needed to translate *bird of prey* into French, but Spike patted her shoulder at last. "I shall make you proud. And you, my dear?"

It was my turn. "I'm so happy no one else is doing it. Can I have Cupid firing an arrow?"

Again, translations were necessary, but Spike understood quickly. "Ah! We shall make you into the goddess of love!"

Jane-Alice huffed in annoyance, and I rushed to explain. "No, for the show, I mean—"

"Honey. Own it." That was Euphoria. "You've had the hottest kiss. You can be the goddess of love. We're okay with it." The others nodded, and I had a moment of gratitude for the unity we were forging.

I was in a pretty good mood by the time we got to the costumers. It only got better when we learned that although we'd be laced into corsets, this wasn't a period when ribs were crushed into submission.

"Yes," said the costumer assistant I was working with. "The ladies are always expecting corsets. Ready for them. Your gentlemen were not so accepting."

Jane-Alice overheard her. "What? You mean the guys are going to be in corsets too? That's wonderful!" She went off into gales of laughter and had to explain to the others what was so funny.

"But of course," the costumer said. "The gentlemens want to present a lovely line, too, don't they? In the Court of the Sun King, the gentlemens are more important than the ladies, even."

Alaric in a corset. Could I bribe the costumers to pull him even tighter than needed? This day was getting better and better.

The fittings themselves went on for hours because none of the assistants would work alone. Everyone had to consult with each other.

Euphoria went first. The costumers loved her dark skin and pulled out several gowns in cream and ivory. When they learned she would have an artist's palette in her wig, they decided on a pale gown with places along the neckline to weave colored ribbons.

Val's gown was dark blue with red and white to go with her patriotic theme, and Rose was, of course, shown a gown in a dusty pink that would go wonderfully with her coloring.

Jane-Alice asked for black to go with her midnight-tryst candelabra, but that was ignored by the Frenchwomen. "Not at all. The colors at the Court of the Sun King—always bright. Always joyous. To look young and vigorous, compared to the Spanish and the Dutch. They wore dull black. Not you. You, we shall put in this rapturous aubergine."

The offered gown was an intense purple. "Passion!" Jane-Alice crooned. "I love it!"

I was to wear red, of course, as the goddess of love. When told that O would have an uncaged bird on her head, the costumers put their heads together, and a rapid conversation in French ensued. Then they pulled out a sky-blue gown that would look ideal on her tanned skin.

We were all sent behind a screen to strip (the cameramen

teased us about finding the best angle to shoot behind the screens) and given kimonos to put on.

Lunch arrived. This was the first sign that the day would be a long one with the costume department.

First, shifts for all. Long, white, knee-length shirts edged in lace. They had necklines so big, mine draped open to below my breastbone. "Not to worry," my dresser said. "You'll see."

Then the socks—or rather, the stockings, but really, they were like knee socks. Mine were white. There was no elastic, of course, and no garters to my waist. Instead, they were tied below my knee, and the sock was folded down over the ribbon.

Fail. Those were sure to come down as I was doing my ballet moves, whatever they were, and I'd trip and fall on my ass. Maybe I could take Alaric down with me.

A long petticoat—white, again, after which I was laced into the corset. It wasn't brutally tight, but it wasn't effortless to breathe either.

"Man," Rose said as her stays were tightened. "No chance of bad posture in this thing, huh?"

She was right. We were standing quite tall. The corset came to below my waist, except in the front, where it dipped down as if I expected spears to be thrown at my lower abdomen.

Once the corset was in place, the dresser tugged my shift around until my shoulders were bare and the lace edge peeped over the top of the stays. "You see?" she said. "This neckline is not too big. Yes?"

Yes. I saw. I saw my boobs were pressed up by the stays, and the tops were exposed by the chemise. I was on display. For a small-chested woman like me, the effect was impressive. Maybe I'd dress like this forever.

"Look at me!" Rose's more generous chest swelled over the top of her corset. "Oh, Mama! Who needs a boob job?"

We all laughed and admitted we were rethinking our reluctance about this challenge.

Then, of course, the other layers descended. Huge wicker frames were tied to our waists to hold the skirts out like a ship in full sail. Pockets. Pockets on a ribbon, tied to my waist. Huge pockets.

"You could hide a little gun in here, easy," Val said happily.

"Or a dagger," Jane-Alice agreed. We were a bloodthirsty group.

Next: another petticoat, this one with slits in it so we could access the weaponry we'd thoughtfully secreted in our pockets. My dresser held up a gossamer-thin square she doubled into a large triangle, which went around my shoulders and got tucked into my busty bust like an illusion.

Then—and only then—came the dress. Despite being made of a thin brocade, it still settled on my shoulders with an impressive weight. "Oof," I said once I was in it. "Heavy."

"Heavy," the dresser agreed. "So it moves like . . . qu'est-ce que le mot? Gracieus? Graceful. You are graceful."

"It's a little big," I noted hopefully. "Maybe the corset doesn't have to be so tight?"

She *tch*ed at me. "Am I so clumsy? Non, we fit this dress for you. Why, then, do we need three full days? And I will be sewing my fingers off to make you the goddess of love, and so you shall be. Too big. Hmph. Stand still. I pin it now."

I stood, watching in the floor mirror as she worked and as the other costumers fitted the other women. "How will you hem this huge skirt in so short a time?" I asked meekly.

"I do not hem from here," she said, tugging at the fabric pooled around my feet. She touched my waist. "I shorten it from here."

I was impressed. I couldn't sew; the idea of hemming a huge skirt from the waist sounded as complex as brain surgery. She was an artist.

"But we don't measure how long until you get your shoes, of course, for we are not newborns."

"Shoes? What are the shoes going to be like?"

She smiled. "You won't like them."

Oh dear.

That's when we learned that historically accurate shoes had heels (mine were easily three inches tall) closer to the arch of the foot, instead of sitting under the heel.

"These are impossible!" Euphoria giggled as she tried walking. Her dress wasn't too long for her, so she was allowed to move about the room in her gorgeous cream gown. "We're supposed to dance a ballet in these?"

"Forget the shoes," O said. "Let's talk about the ballet. I can't dance, you know."

"Ah!" her dresser said. "No, not a ballet as we know it today. This will be a court ballet. A dance. You can learn it."

"Like a waltz?" Jane-Alice was luscious in purple, her spectacular bosom on generous display.

"A waltz? Nothing so scandalous! You will touch your partner's hand and only his hand, as is appropriate. You might even hold a handkerchief, so you aren't skin to skin. Amélie! We must have handkerchiefs!"

Wonderful. More costume to keep track of.

"Could I have lower heels?" I asked. "I'll be the same height as my partner in these."

"Non, bien sûr. Your partner has also the shoes so high. All do, you see? It is la mode. The fashion."

Alaric would learn to dance in high heels. And a corset. I couldn't help the chuckles that bubbled out of me. I didn't need to see anything more of Paris to know it was one of the greatest places on the earth.

Not that I would have minded getting out of this room to see the world a little. Which, ultimately, is what the six of us did.

27

MAY I HAVE THIS DANCE?

Rose had bonded with her dresser, Amélie, who told Rose about a nearby nightclub she was going to that evening. Wide-eyed, Rose turned to me and the others. "Let's blow off this show for an evening. What do you say?"

It would be hard to sneak out when each of us had a camera operator assigned to us, but the concept was cheered by all.

I turned to Luke, the plea in my eyes. He sighed and thumbed his radio's mic. "I need Julie in the costume department, please."

Julie arrived in a bundle of energy. "Hi. What's going on? Is everything okay? You guys look great—look at those shoes, I mean, wow, can I try some on too? What? Sorry. Do you need me?"

We all looked at Rose, who gulped and then put the idea forward.

"But you can't go to a club," Julie said as if we'd decided to not breathe for an evening. "You're touring the basement exhibition at the Ministry of Tourism. It's a private tour with a knowledgeable guide. It's going to be highly educational."

Hmm. Let's see. A stuffy lecture? Or a night of dancing with my girls? Which one should I choose?

"We'll take our camera guys with us," I said. "They can film us experiencing modern French culture. That will be the perfect balance to the ball on Friday night. And we'll be good as gold for the rest of the time in Paris."

I gave her the pleading eyes—we all did—and she bit her lip in indecision.

"And you should come, too, Julie. To watch us and make sure we don't do anything stupid."

"Yeah," Jane-Alice said. "So we don't, you know, drink too much or pick up guys."

"Oh, well," Julie said. "Yes. I'd better go with you. Hang on." When she came back, she was grinning. "The guys will go to the lecture, and we'll go clubbing. But the Ministry wants us to go to the best spots, so they're going to get us in to all kinds of places. And we're supposed to tell the costumers to help us with outfits!"

The costumers all shrieked and announced they'd be going with us too. After rapid-fire French uttered over a cell phone, a truck full of club apparel arrived—including suits for the cameramen.

We were going out.

This time, the three-inch heels were centered below my actual heels, and I didn't care who I towered over. I wasn't going out with a guy. I was going out with women—with my friends.

With my sisters.

It made me think: When had I ever had such a good all-female experience? Did my sister go clubbing with me? Did my mother weigh in on which dress looked best? Had I been denying them opportunities for joy while taking care with them?

We had a large table in a posh restaurant's private dining room. This was necessary because there were now two people from the Ministry of Tourism and nine dressers to accompany us, plus two wig guys who'd snuck in, too, in addition to Julie, six contestants, and six cameramen. More than two dozen people—and yet we were ushered into crowded clubs like we were royalty. Or celebrities.

And once on the dance floor, we discovered Fatima wasn't the only international viewer of *Cupid's Quest*. France apparently loved us too. Strangers shouted our names. Champagne was bought for us. DJs played songs for us. When we left one club for another—each filled with gorgeous people, thumping beats, absolutely no inhibitions, and always a bit more room left on the dance floor—people protested our departure.

But we contestants linked arms with Julie and stuck together, grinning at the world's disappointment. Our cameramen guarded us as they filmed the scene, and the dressers professed endless love for us. Somehow, as the evening wore on, we began to understand French. Might have had something to do with the champagne.

Someone must have stayed sober because we all ended up where we were supposed to be. Alaric was already whistling in the bed, so I headed for the sofa, still buzzed and giggly. A banging on the door stopped me.

"Here," Julie said, still slightly lopsided. "Two aspirins and two bottles of water. Get them down before you go to sleep. Dance lessons begin at nine sharp, and that's just six hours away, so really, try to get to sleep fast because you'll need it, but don't oversleep, you know?"

"I'll set my alarm. I love you, Julie."

"I love you, Joss. Good night, sweetie!"

Of course I forgot the alarm part. Alaric kicked the leg of the sofa until I woke up, groaning. He studied the wisps of silk I'd let fall to the floor when I went to sleep. I peered nervously under the blanket. Strapless bra and panties. At least I wasn't nude.

"Get up. Breakfast."

My stomach rolled at the thought. My head was too small for the brain inside. "Go away."

"Pfft. Right. Get up. Do you know what I had to sit through last night while you were out sucking down booze?"

"Please go away."

"Even if you miss breakfast, you're going to need at least half an hour to chisel that makeup off your face. You should get up right now. If you go back to sleep, you'll be late for dancing, and I don't intend to lose this. Shall I drag you off that sofa?"

Not in my bra and panties. Well, not in the costume department's bra and panties. "I'll get up. You go to breakfast. I'll be down as soon as I can."

"If I don't see you down there by 8:45, I'm coming back up to get you. Sick or dead, you're coming with me."

"Please. Please go away."

The shower was a gift from the gods. I managed to get downstairs while breakfast was still being served, and while I had no appetite for food, I was grateful for a large mug of hot tea. The waitress from the day before sniggered at my untouched plate. "Le Club Noir," she said knowingly. Guess she didn't have to watch the upcoming episode to know where we'd been the night before.

Some of us looked a little worse for wear, I saw Luke wince when the camera lights came on. But we were all on deck and conscious at the stroke of nine, when our dancing master returned to put us through hell.

Actually, he put us through two days of hell. *Point your toe, lift your head, back straight, smaller steps—Joss, you are not a farmer.*

Alaric, at the other end of my fingertips, was smug.

"Of course I'm an accomplished ballroom dancer," he told me. "My company has regular galas, and naturally it's useful to be able to dance with the wives of my clients at weddings and other formal events. I've had lessons before."

It couldn't have been any more different from the free-spirited club scene, where movement was expression and laughter. This "ballet" was about formality and a sense of place and couldn't have been more tiresome.

Plus, it was disturbingly long. This wasn't "learn one step and then repeat it over and over again." We had to remember when we crossed, when we promenaded, when we turned, when we acknowledged the people around us. And once we were done with that dance, there were four more to learn.

Five dances. In two days. Even Alaric was concentrating too hard to be smug, and we fell asleep as soon as we lay down. (I found the sofa was as comfortable when I was sober as when I was tipsy.)

Theo and Euphoria moved through the ballet with us, of course. Occasionally, our paths would cross, and he would look at me with his dark-eyed focus, and I would miss my footing—but we would be rapped back to attention. If the *Cupid's Quest* producers wanted to show the burgeoning of true love, they were doing a piss-poor job of enabling it.

On the other hand, if they wanted to show how much we sweated and tried and cursed and complained, then they were getting exactly what they asked for.

On Friday morning, it got worse—because we had to do all five movements in our period-appropriate shoes. The women had it bad; those high heels at the wrong part of the foot were precarious.

But the men, who I assumed had never been in heels before, were far worse. Within minutes, they were massaging their shins and complaining about their lower backs. Alaric found he wasn't as accomplished a dancer as he thought he was when expected to do it in heels. If I hadn't been so tired, I would have sneered at him.

Theo, I noticed, was now about six and a half feet tall. I tried not to purr when I saw him.

The morning was impossible.

The afternoon was worse.

After dress fittings, we ran through the dances one more time. Suddenly, there was no need for the dance master to tell me to stand straight; in the corset, there was no alternative.

"You must move graciously," he barked at us again. "Tonight, you will be wearing the wigs. They will be two feet taller than you. Every movement must be like a swan. I care not what your feet do, paddling below those great skirts. But your head, your neck, they must be still and serene! Olivia, serene!"

O, who was making horrible faces at him, uttered a brief curse and then tried again. We all tried again.

Dressed in our gowns, we could barely fit on the bus to take us to the ball. "Some Cinderella's coach," Euphoria muttered as we clomped up the stairs to figure out how to wedge ourselves into the seats without harming the gowns. There was no hope of sitting with a partner or a friend; each lady took up two seats and part of the aisle, and we couldn't move to the door unless we crab-walked sideways.

Maria-Thérèse used the microphone to address us as the bus drove through Paris and onto a highway.

"Not even for *Cupid's Quest* could the Ministry tie up the Sun King's most famous palace, Versailles. But we will be holding our ball at a palace just slightly less magnificent, the stunning Vaux-le-Vicomte." She told us about the architect, the artist, and the garden designer who made this ancient marvel, and then terrified us by telling us who else would attend the ball, including the wife of the president of France and every French celebrity anyone had ever heard of. "A ticket to this event is in high demand, so I know you're pleased you worked so hard on your dancing. And you look lovely. You'll look even more impressive with your wigs! We'll be there soon, so let me tell you more about Fouquet, who had this chateau built—"

I tuned her out and concentrated on breathing calmly and riding a bus without being able to fully lean back into the seat.

The chateau was, as advertised, achingly beautiful. Lines of guests wandered through the forecourt to the grand front door of a perfectly symmetrical palace, honey-colored stone walls rising to charcoal-colored slate roofs.

"I feel like a princess," Rose said. We couldn't walk side by side; our skirts were too wide. But she walked slightly ahead of me and to the side, so we could whisper as we minced in our strange shoes along the gravel.

"I feel like a princess in a fishbowl." The camera operators were dressed in dark, conservative suits, all of them walking backward to film our reactions as we saw Vaux-le-Vicomte.

I'll tell you my reaction: Awed. Overwhelmed. Slightly breathless, but that might have been the corset.

We were led away from the crowds to a slightly less-grand grand salon that had been converted for our use. Spike, the wigmaker, stood with a phalanx of helpers to tease our hair up into the creations they'd made from wicker, straw, wishes, and dreams.

The color and texture of my hair had been perfectly matched, so it looked like I had yards of hair swept up into a huge heart that rose over my skull. A perfect Cupid, pulling back on his bow to launch a dart, was fastened in the crest of the heart.

"I am most proud of this," Spike said upon my arrival. "The cherub is fine china from 1753. Too old for your hairstyle and too young for your dress style, but we must hope no one notices."

"Spike," I gasped. "This Cupid is older than the nation of the United States? I can't wear it in a wig!"

"Oh, you'll be fine. Just don't trip. You'll be divine, our

goddess of love. Here—stop that! The roses are supposed to cascade down the side. I'll be back!"

Spike was too busy to reassure me. Instead, I had to take a first cautious step and then another one, unassisted, as I learned to walk across the room carrying a priceless antique several feet above me on a wig that felt none too steady.

As a result, I decided my corset wasn't quite stiff enough and that I would quietly chop the heels from my shoes—if I could figure out a way to do it without looking down.

I sat between Alaric and Mason at the grand feast. The twelve of us were arranged down the long side of a table, facing the celebrities and beautiful people who had their dinner at normal round tables before us. They watched us eat course after course of bewildering foods. The chef told us what each course was, but I hadn't had enough champagne to translate his French. In fact, I'd had no champagne or wine of any kind. Julia had come along and collected all the wineglasses on our table, to the horror of the sommelier.

"Shout says," she said stubbornly and would not be budged.

I didn't eat much. It turned out to be challenging to load a fork if you could only look down without moving your head. I was giving my dinner the side-eye, but from above.

Alaric approved. "You look very queenly," he said. "A trifle wooden, I'd say, but beautiful."

I wanted to kick him with my elegant, torturous shoes. Especially since he, like all the men, wore a huge, curly wig of hair that flowed past his shoulders in a curtain. Alaric's visual appeal was confirmed; he had a great head of hair, and once that was hidden? Meh.

On the other hand...

Bald Theo wore his inky-black wig with panache. He liked to flip his hands through it to make a point, and his grin had physical force. It could stop me in my tracks.

Unlike the others, he was dressed largely in black. His

waistcoat was cream, to match Euphoria's gown, and his lace was snowy white. But his breeches and his frock coat were dark.

He looked stunning.

After dinner, we were taken back to our salon and allowed half an hour to practice the ballet with the wigs on. The dance master was jumping up and down in agitation. "The president of the Opéra National de Paris is out there! You must be perfect, do you hear? Perfect!"

Like I needed another reason to be any more stressed about this.

We stepped through the opening movement, now so worn down and fatigued, the actions had become automatic. The dance master wasn't pleased and turned to consult with his assistant. Alaric turned away to examine his reflection in a speckled, ancient mirror.

And a long arm snaked around my waist. I almost looked down at the hand but caught myself in time.

"Come with me," the voice murmured in my ear, and my pulse thumped against the confines of the stays. Theo.

He drew me backward and behind a column holding up the painted oval ceiling.

He leaned into me and ran his jaw along my cheek. His deep voice curled into my ear. "You are luscious, Joss. Radiant. The heart in your wig—I know it's wrong, but it reminds me of the curves of your gorgeous ass."

I melted against the column, grateful for his strong arms around me. "Theo," I sighed.

And then I kissed him. Or he kissed me. And this time, there was no question of tongues being involved. He tasted and licked me, and I did the same to him. I was panting, and he moaned.

And then I couldn't tip my head back to fit myself more closely to him.

Shit.

The wig.

I gasped and let go of his biceps, reaching up to make sure my wig was safe—that the Cupid was still where he was supposed to be.

"Stop," he said. "Let me. No, it's okay. Still on there tight. Hi, Nessa." His camera operator had found him. Luke wouldn't be far behind.

"Your wig is on crooked," she said with a grin. "You know I'm supposed to film these moments. You agreed when you signed the contract."

"I agreed to let you *try* to film them," he corrected. "Believe me, I read it closely. Hi, Luke."

Theo made sure I was steady on my feet before moving away. Luke grinned. "You've smudged her lipstick and gotten some on yourself. Spike's going to be annoyed."

"Oh no." Theo was clearly unconcerned. "What a disaster. We'll go get that fixed. Shall we?" He gave me his arm and a lascivious grin that made my adrenaline race.

"Yes. Let's."

By the time I got back to Alaric, I'd gotten my breathing under control, but I could feel two high, hot patches on my cheeks that told me I was still flushed. And I couldn't stop smiling.

"Where'd you go? You look better. Did you score some wine? I could use a glass."

When it was time for our ballet, I felt the change. My spine was straight but supple. My neck was long. My feet, taking mincing little steps, were sure. I knew I would dance our ballet perfectly.

And that's exactly what happened. The applause from the live audience was a reward, but it was the musicians in the balcony, who tapped their bows against their instruments in appreciation, that told us we'd done well.

The rest of the evening passed in a haze. We surrendered our wigs to Spike, sidled down the aisle of the bus in gowns totally inappropriate to the vehicle, and, once back at the hotel, were unstitched from our dresses by our new best friends, the costume team. Back in deliciously flat shoes and regular clothes, we met briefly in the conference room, where Wink told us the next day needed to be a rest day. Because the camera operators deserved a day off, too, we were asked not to leave our rooms until the evening.

Fine with me. I had some dreaming I needed to do.

Of course, Alaric had other plans.

28

RULES AND REVEALS

Theo was standing by his seats on the airplane, letting others board around him until I got there. Then he smiled at me and gestured with his hand. *Sit with me?* Pleasure crashed through me. *Don't mind if I do.*

I turned to take his inner seat in time to see Alaric waggling his Cupid Cash tauntingly in Theo's face. "Who's the most regal? That's right. The whole world agrees. I am. I'm the king."

Theo fished in the backpack at his feet and flourished the dollar sign he'd won in Australia. He said nothing, but perhaps the look in his eye (and the fact that he held the figurine in his fist again like a knife he wanted to plunge into someone's heart) made the arrogance melt off Alaric's face.

"Christ," Alaric said, attempting to sound scornful.

"Run along, little king. I've got an empress to greet."

Theo sat next to me and captured my hand, pressing a warm kiss to the back and then a second one to my palm. Every muscle in me sighed *ahhh* and went slack. When I looked up, Alaric was gone. Good riddance.

"Congratulations," Theo said. "Your second win. You're the leader on the tally board."

"We have a tally board?"

"In my head. Where I store all kinds of fascinating facts."

"Like what?"

"Like how your gorgeous eyes get shiny and dark when I kiss you. Shall I demonstrate?"

"Yes, please."

He was kissing me and my toes were curling in my shoes when Julie arrived in the contestant cabin.

"Sit down quickly, please. Get your stuff stowed—we've got a long flight ahead of us, and the tower told the pilot there's a window for us to cut the line to take off if we can get out of here in ten minutes, so get your stuff stowed, and anyway, it's the camera teams who take the longest, but do your best anyway, because I'm supposed to get you in your seats as soon as possible—want me to help you with that?"

Julie wasn't much taller than Rose, but it was Nick to the rescue. He helped Rose get her tote bag full of Parisian treasures into the overhead compartment, and Julie was satisfied.

"Okay, good for you—I have to go sit down myself, but then we'll be underway if the camera teams have their cameras secured. You can't believe what they want to go through every single time, it's like the cameras are eggs and the boxes have to be tied to the plane and it's a whole process and—what? Right. Once we take off, I'll come get you because we need to have another meeting. There are some new rules to discuss and—what, Shout? You're right, you're right. Anyone need anything? No? Okay, sit tight. I'll be back once we're up in the air, bye."

I wasn't the only one smiling in the silence left by Julie's departure. She'd been a wonderful addition to the girls' clubbing team and was a constant delight in our often-chaotic lives.

I turned to Theo. "If I am your empress—"

"You most certainly are."

"Then I want a love token from you."

The smile grew across his face. "I have a love token to give you," he assured me.

He was making me blush. "I get to choose this one."

"Name it, Big Eyes. It's yours."

"I want you to fasten your seat belt."

His grin dropped. "Oh, for god's sake. Really?"

"Really. Will you do it for me?"

He sighed. "It seems I can deny you nothing." He clicked the belt around his waist and then looked at me with one expressive eyebrow lifted. "Enough?"

I flushed with a mix of emotions: Happiness that he was a little safer. Pleasure that he would accede to my wishes. Lust for a man who would listen to what I wanted. "Enough." I reached over to pull his face to me and caressed his clever mouth with mine. Then I looked into the camera on the seat in front of me. "As empress," I said grandly, "I declare that Theo is my *Cupid's Quest* boyfriend. No more kissing other women, do you understand?"

I turned back to him, expecting him to match my teasing, but his smile was softer than I expected. He turned to his camera. "I declare that Joss is my real-life girlfriend. No more kissing other men. Okay?"

I inhaled sharply at his announcement, shocked and dazzled. "Really?"

One side of his mouth lifted. "If you don't mind." He took my hand and laced his fingers through mine.

"I don't mind. You think that would work?"

He shrugged. "A Pennsylvania/New Jersey relationship? Yeah, I think we can do that. You're in Reading, right? That's, what, two hours away from Perth Amboy? Match made in heaven, Empress."

He was crazy. And I was happy. "I'd like that," I said. "I'd like that a lot."

"Good. Show me."

I kissed him again, knowing it was crazy to feel possessive of a man I'd known for so little time but unable to keep even a fingertip on rational thought. He smelled so *good*.

We had an all-too-short bubble of whispers and cuddles (he told me my hair was like a mink coat on a celebrity; I said a mink coat would look better on the mink; he said he was in favor of removing my coat and all other layers; I asked him if he really was bald; he casually tossed out that his hair had been getting in his eyes and annoying him one day, so he shaved his head, liked the easiness of it, and shaved it every morning since —unless I wanted him to grow it out, in which case he would and forevermore wear a seat belt too; I cooed from within my primitive puddle of This Is Good emotions), and then Wink appeared.

"Ladies and gentlemen, if you please? We need you at the conference table."

"No matter where that asshole sits," Theo said, "I'm on your other side, right?"

"With Euphoria next to you," I agreed. "Thank you."

He winked at me and gestured for me to precede him down the aisle.

Once we were settled around the "heart of the Arrow" conference table, Wink wasted no time. "Alaric, it's come to our attention that even though you were told to stay in your room —or, in your case, your entirely generous suite—you opted to sneak out of the hotel for most of the day yesterday."

I was as surprised as everyone else. Rose turned to me. "Did you know he left? Did you go? Did you go shopping? Why didn't you take me?"

I held up a hand in protest. "I had no idea. It was my turn in the bed. He slept on the sofa, and I mostly napped and read yesterday. I didn't even know he left."

"Well, I did." Alaric was smug as always. "Something you

want to do about it now?" He addressed Wink like an underling. An underling who had done wrong.

"We'd like to know what you were up to." Wink's tone was stern. Alaric might be a corporate badass, but he wasn't as big as the consortium backing the Watch Now Network, and Wink knew the power was on his side.

"I have clients in Paris. I took them to lunch. Can I ask how you found out?"

The sound from the other side of the plane was startling; I'd never heard such a noise before. It took a minute to realize it was the silent showrunner, Shout, who hadn't bothered to muffle his laughter.

Wink ignored the boss. "Alaric, you were recognized. Repeatedly. There's so much camera footage of you sneaking out of the hotel, Roberta might as well be out of a job."

Alaric shrugged. "So, what's the problem? I was under surveillance the whole time."

"But not by us." Wink's exasperation turned the last word into a yell, and he took a deep breath to calm down. "We've talked with the network. We're going to dock your pay for this week. That's ten thousand dollars."

I would have burst into tears, but Alaric shrugged. "Like I care. Small price to pay to ensure the financial security of my customers."

Wink inhaled and settled his shoulders. "You must have wealthy clients indeed, if you can so easily shrug off the loss of so much money. No, never mind." He overrode Alaric's attempt to boast and bluster. "From now on, all contestants are informed that if you leave the hotel without your camera operator—and without permission—you will forfeit that week's payment. You'll all sign this document to prove you've been informed of this."

Julie passed pages and pens around, and we all signed, eyeing Alaric suspiciously. An exotic species in our midst.

"Good thing we got Julie involved when we went dancing," Val muttered, but Wink heard her.

"Yes, it was a good thing. We can be flexible. We want you all to experience the cultures we visit, and we want our cameras to capture your adventures." His voice took on an impressively low note, and he spoke with significance when he said, "We want to make great TV. That is our goal." His thunder rumbled through the conference area, and we were all suitably cowed. He let that go on for an awkward moment and then favored us with a warming smile. "And that's why we're going to make another change. Because we know good TV when we see it. From now on, our two pairs of lovebirds will be partnered together. That's Rose with Paul, and Joss with Theo."

I uttered an inelegant yip of delight, and Rose stood immediately and went to Paul. There were no chairs next to him, of course, so she sat on his lap. He looked like he'd died and gone to heaven.

Theo won for pure theatrics, of course. He turned to Euphoria and kissed her hand. "There's only one woman who could draw me from your side, my muse. You let me know if there's anything you need."

She laughed in reply and pushed his shoulder toward me. He obliged, turning in his chair so he could wrap me in a kiss.

A long kiss.

A kiss with skillful tongue work and my purrs and sighs.

"Perhaps you'd like to come up for air so I can redistribute the partnerships?" Wink was laughing. He did like good TV, and Theo was born to give it to him. I sat back, my nerve endings sizzling and relief in my soul.

"Thank you. Feel free to keep that up—but not just yet. Alaric, your past two partners have expressed a certain dissatisfaction with you." Alaric crossed his arms over his chest and looked down his nose at Wink, who went on, "So, we're putting you with the only woman we believe can handle you. We're putting you with our warrior. Val, it will take all your training as a soldier to endure and triumph, but we know you can do it."

Val's jaw had a stubborn tightness to it. "Yessir," she said smartly. Then she gave Alaric a tight grin. He gulped and looked away. Already she was asserting dominance. I loved it.

"You got this, Army Girl!" Theo cheered her.

"Euphoria, your new partner is Mason. O, you'll be with Nick. And that puts Jane-Alice with Knox."

Jane-Alice grinned. She probably thought happy-go-lucky Knox would be a pushover, but I had my doubts. Knox had a spine and a clever brain. She might have met her match.

"You'll notice we've evened out the couples a little. Each pair has at least one Cupid Cash symbol between them. The only exception is the pairing of Theo, with one dollar sign, and Joss, who, as of this last competition, has two. If their partnership lasts to the end, they'll have an extra fifteen thousand dollars for the finale."

Across the table, the eyes of my friends narrowed in concern. They regarded us with distaste, and I felt a chilly wave of regard that was unlike the friendships we'd developed up to that point.

"Yes," Wink said in satisfaction. "I see you've all remembered this is a competition. Well, then. We have three more places to visit before the end. Do your best. You can still catch up if you put your back into it. And your brain, of course. Possibly even your lips. Not that we're suggesting anything." Wink winked with a grin.

Nobody grinned back.

Theo and I had targets on our backs now. Perhaps the day had its ups and downs after all.

We'd need to be watching our backs.

"What can you tell us about the next competitions?" Theo asked.

29

A PULL TO THE EAST

Surprisingly, Wink answered a direct question. He looked back at Shout for confirmation and got a nod. "Okay. It'll be easier to discuss this here anyway. We're going to Tokyo."

Excited murmurs greeted this announcement. Alaric reached behind me to tag Theo on the shoulder. "Big guys like you and me are going to stand out over there like sore thumbs."

His "we're all buddies now" attitude didn't work on Theo. "Please. You think anyone in Tokyo will care that we're *tall*?"

Wink cut off the chatter. "We'll stay in a Tokyo hotel tonight. Yes, everyone in the same kind of room. Tomorrow, for the True Love or Double Dud competition, you'll all be fitted with GoPro cameras on headbands and mic packs. I'll explain why then. Enough for you, Theo?"

Theo eyed Wink like he was lunch meat and showed his teeth. "Enough. For now. Thanks for not making me figure out our destination on my own."

"That's enough. Get out of here, all of you. Enjoy your flight."

We were sent back to our far-more-cramped cabin. For

once, it felt like enough space to me, since I was cozied up to Theo. We took care of each other throughout the flight: napped together, ate our boxed meals together, talked and laughed and kissed. In the back of my mind, I knew we were being almost sickeningly cute, but I couldn't help it. If only I could casually throw my sweater over the seat back to block the camera.

By the time we were shown to our hotel room—my hotel room with Theo and one large bed—I was developing a split personality.

One half of me wanted to wrap myself around him and put an end to the maddening itch.

The other half was tormented by the cameras and the idea of the Watch Now late-night program.

Theo closed the room door behind him and pulled me into his arms.

We were—at last—body to body. Chest to chest. Groin to groin. I groaned as he kissed me. But the melting didn't happen. We were being filmed.

I pulled back and whispered, "I'm sorry. I don't want our first time to be filmed. Can you forgive me? I swear, I don't mean to be a tease."

"I hear you. Give me twenty-four hours to figure something out, okay?"

He was the magician, after all. "Okay. I can last that long."

His grin was decidedly lascivious. "A full day of anticipation." He leaned down to whisper in my ear, "You're going to scream so hard when I make you come."

Yeah—there was the melt. I cooed in reply and closed my eyes to contain my surge of desire.

He chuckled and nibbled at my ear. "Back up, then, Empress. Give me enough room to be a gentleman, please."

"And me to be a lady."

"An empress," he corrected. "Empress Big Eyes of the House of Mink."

We separated, and I wheeled my suitcase further into the room to assess the situation and let my skin cool. As always, the room was perfectly normal; there was a large glass mirror across from the foot of the bed. "Don't you think they put the cameras behind the mirror?"

Theo thumped his backpack to the floor. "My sweet innocent. You think they retrofit every hotel room with two-way mirrors? There's a nanny cam in the flowers. You never noticed?"

The silk flowers on the desk. I stared. Did they look familiar? Had I never looked before? The *Cupid's Quest* team was carting around hidden cameras in vases and setting them up in our hotel rooms minutes before we checked in? That seemed annoyingly low-tech. "I expected something a little more James Bond," I admitted. "Where is the camera in the bathroom?"

He laughed. "Like a child in a fairy tale. Did you think every hotel we went to stocked the same shampoo and conditioner in the dark bottles?"

I used my own supply; I'd never reached for the hotel stock. I'd been a fool, and Theo was more alert than I'd ever been. "We could cover the cameras," I realized. "I could throw my sweater over the flowers—"

"I tried it the first night on the ship in Antarctica. Roberta was banging on my door within twenty minutes. Even if our team is asleep, those cameras are broadcasting. There's someone back in LA who's watching all the time. It's a smart gig."

"Oh. Shit. Never mind."

"Twenty-four hours, Empress of Love. I'll figure something out."

I knew he would.

I slept that night with my head pillowed on his chest and his arms around me. It was hard to keep our fingers from wandering, but the vase of flowers was visible in the low light through the window. He'd find a way. I could wait.

Julie banged on our door far too early. "It's five thirty," she hissed through the door. "Are you up? You have to be downstairs by six to get mic'd up. Do you hear me? I can't call any louder because I'm not allowed to wake the other guests, but I have to—yipe!"

She gasped when Theo pulled the door open. Her nose came about halfway up his bare and impressive chest. "We're up," he said. "Go wake someone else."

"Okay, I will—I have to do Jane-Alice and Knox, and then Val and—"

Theo closed the door in her face and turned to me. "She doesn't seem to need to breathe, ever."

"I know." I relaxed back into the bed, wiggling my toes in comfort. Theo looked good, standing there in soft navy boxer briefs. When he saw I was looking, his good looks grew before my eyes.

I laughed in pleasure, and he winced. "Sorry. Can't help it. I'd better take the first shower."

We were downstairs on time. Luke fitted me with a camera on a head strap and the mic pack was strapped to my waist. "Word from LA is that you're happy this morning, but not as happy as you could be. Bashful, huh?" He grinned as he said it.

I shook my head. "See? This is why nothing happened last night. I don't want everyone up in my business."

Luke shrugged and nodded. "Sounds right to me. LA's kind of annoyed, though. Turns out Rose and Paul are as shy as you guys. They're not getting the late-night lovefest they were hoping for."

"Poor babies," I said, not meaning it. "Can you give me any clue as to what we're doing this morning?"

Luke raised an eyebrow, and I watched, astonished, as he fit his own GoPro onto his head. "I can tell you it's going to be a challenge."

Luke without his huge camera? What was going on here? "Where's your real camera? We're not going caving, are we? We look like we're ready to go caving."

"Oh, you're going to wish you were caving!" He was laughing as he said it, so my alarm was only dialed up halfway.

When everyone was teched up, Wink walked us out the door and down the street. The sun was coming up, but there were more people on the street than I'd expected. We had to step quickly to keep up with our host.

He halted at the corner and beckoned us closer. "I'm giving you each a ticket for the train, which is right over there." Julie flickered through the group, passing out cards. "This is the JR Yamanote line, one of the most crowded trains in this extremely crowded city. It makes a twenty-mile loop around the city. When I tell you to go, you're to go down the stairs and get on the first train you can. Then ride it. The last ones on will be staying in a five-star hotel on the thirty-fourth floor of that building." He pointed to one of the impossibly tall towers dwarfing us. "The first people to get off will stay in what is called a capsule hotel, where you'll be given a tiny compartment not much bigger than a coffin. These are businessman hotels, designed for working people who miss the last train home. They're clean and safe, but they're designed to be frugal. That hotel is on the sixteenth floor. And everyone else will be in a three-star hotel on the twenty-third, twenty-fourth, or twenty-fifth floors."

"All we have to do is ride the train?" Euphoria's voice expressed her astonishment, but she yipped as a herd of people pushed past her to get to the station entrance.

"That's all." Wink grinned. "Don't lose your camera team, please. They're the ones who have radios to tell you when your competitors drop out. And they will get you back here whenever you're finished with your ride. Any questions?"

Dawn was filling the street slowly with light, which made it easier to see the rising tide of people now streaming toward the train station.

It would be crowded. This would be an endurance challenge. I took Theo's hand, and he gripped back with reassuring strength.

"All right, then. The True Love or Double Dud competition is officially on. Get going!"

"Let's move," Theo murmured as he pulled me after him through the crowd. "We're going to be in tight quarters down there. Keep up, Nessa, Luke. Let's go."

He led us through the growing numbers of people. We had a moment of confusion on how to use the tickets, but a kind woman helped us, and we were through to the platform.

Hundreds of people were waiting, neatly lined up in rows. We got in line.

Theo, taller than most of the people around him, told us there was apparently a car just for women. "That means there are gropers on this train. You prepared to have your pretty ass fondled, Empress?"

I groaned. "Well, I'm not looking forward to it."

"What if I was the one groping?" He leered at me, and my resulting laughter eased my tension.

I turned and peered past Luke. "Nessa, keep your back to the wall!"

She held up a hand and flared her fingers; she had beautiful nails. "They might try, but they'll only do it once. Best thing about the GoPros. My hands are free for once!"

She looked like she would rather enjoy the experience, and I felt a sudden bond between the four of us. Strength in numbers. My grip tightened on Theo's hand, and I gave him a smile. This was going to be okay.

Once we were on the train, it wasn't so bad. We had enough space around us that the four of us could still talk to each other.

That didn't last, though. As we got closer and closer to seven in the morning, the crowds picked up. By the time we'd been crammed together and people were still pushing into the car, I missed that sense of space we'd had in the beginning.

I turned and pressed my chest to Theo. He grinned and wrapped his arms around me. I hid my head in his chest, my GoPro now totally blocked. Too bad. Theo's still showed what was going on. Somewhere in the car, Nessa and Luke were still facing us.

At the next stop, the press of bodies got even tighter. I felt Theo laughing. Despite being walled in on every side by bodies, the car was quiet, so I heard him when he whispered, "There are train guys out there literally pushing bodies in the doors. Jeez, would you look at that?"

Nobody seemed to mind, so I linked my arms around Theo's waist more tightly and held on.

A sudden hiss from speakers—Luke to the left of me, Roberta behind me—and Wink's voice was audible to all. "O and Nick are out. They get the capsule hotel. Now we're waiting to see who gets the five-star rooms."

Poor O. Her claustrophobia.

"Nick will take care of her," Theo murmured.

A woman at my elbow peered at me and then up at Theo. "*Cupid's Quest?*" she asked politely. "Joss? Theo?"

I smiled and nodded. She seemed quite pleased and gave the closest possible approximation of a bow possible when hemmed in on all sides. I nodded back, to her delight. She whispered to the man next to her, "Joss *to* Theo. *Cupid's Quest.*"

Word rippled politely through the car, and people turned in their tiny allotment of space to smile and nod at us. We smiled back. Perhaps our newfound celebrity would accord us more room?

Not at all. The squeeze became tighter as people turned to get a better look. Two stops later, Theo began to laugh again.

"What?" I asked him.

He ducked his head to me. "You won't believe it. Someone is groping my ass!"

He was so amused, I had to laugh with him. "I can help. Excuse the liberty . . ." I slid my hands down from his waist and over the firm curve of his lovely buttocks until I encountered a squeezing hand.

I scratched the unknown groper with my nails and heard a polite little gasp. The hand was removed.

"Maybe I'd better keep my hands here. In case he comes back." I explored the landscape with sliding, gentle fingers and laughed when Theo tried to spread his legs wider. No room. No luck.

"I could protect you, too," he said—and then he cupped me, pulling me more closely into him. He was hard, and I was wet. The train ride developed into a new and different kind of torture.

Very sweet torture.

We rode for dozens of stops. We passed the station where we'd boarded and kept going. Passengers squeezed to get off at their stops and others squeezed to get on. I caressed Theo's ass. He caressed mine. And every time people moved, he edged us toward a corner, until at last, my back was to the wall, and he could put his arms up to either side to force a space for me.

I took the first deep breath in at least half an hour. "It was like being in that corset again," I said to him.

"Tell me about it. I had no idea men wore corsets too."

"I'll bet you looked good in it." I waggled my eyebrows at him, and he kissed me. Not too deeply—we already edged toward desperation.

Nessa and Luke were still nearby, filming our makeout session in this sardine can, and I heard Wink announce Val and

Alaric were out and that Val had broken someone's arm and was being questioned by the police.

"Warrior," I grinned. "Someone groped the wrong ass."

"Alaric is going to be pissed he's not in the five-star." Theo preened with satisfaction, and then I saw an idea cross his face. He grabbed my hand and tugged me toward the exit. "Come on. Nessa—Luke, let's go. We're done."

"What? Why?" We wouldn't be able to make much progress until the train stopped to let off its cattle, but Theo got us started in the right direction.

"Because I just realized—I don't want the five-star room."

"You don't? Why? I don't understand."

He turned to me with a smile. "You gave me twenty-four hours. The three-star will be better for me. For us."

What? "Um, okay."

We fought our way (our very polite way) out of the car and bowed to all those who called out to wish us well. Luke radioed Wink, who announced we were out. The four of us piled into a taxi and were at the new hotel and checked into our new room before the next couple gave up. It was Mason and Euphoria.

That left Knox and Jane-Alice to outlast Rose and Paul.

My money was on Rose. She had Paul to hang on to, after all, and I knew how enjoyable it was to be pressed up by necessity to someone you wanted to be with.

Theo turned Luke and Nessa away at the door to our room, telling them they had the afternoon off because we would have a nap with our floral arrangements.

"Okay," Luke protested as he tried to stop Theo from shutting the door on him, "but you both have to be in the dining room at seven tonight for dinner. Hey—wait. *Cupid's Quest* is on in an hour here. If you want to watch it, it'll be—"

"Fine, fine. Bye."

The door clicked shut, and Theo turned to me. The eagerness in his eyes was in direct contrast to his words. "You need to go take a nap. Now." He pointed to the bed.

I goggled at him. What, now?

"Yeah. You need to take a nap. Relax. I'm going to take a shower. Man, do I need a shower."

He nodded at me, so I rolled my eyes and stretched my arms overhead. "And I guess I could use a nap. Right?"

"Right."

I lay down on the bed, confused, and heard the bathroom door click closed. But then I didn't hear any water.

Had it been the bathroom door? Or was it the door to the hall?

It took half an hour. Specifically, thirty-two minutes by the clock on the bedside table. Thirty-two endless minutes. And then the door opened again.

Theo appeared, grinning. "Come on."

I sat up. "What?"

He nodded his head to the hallway. "Come with me. Will you?"

I met him in the hall. As the door to our room closed behind me, he held up a key card.

I looked my question to him and held up mine. "Yeah? So?"

"So, mine doesn't go to *this* room. Can we get out of this hallway, please?"

"I'm so confused."

"Come on. The fire stairs are this way." He led me down a corridor lined with doors anyone at all could pop out of at any minute.

I planted my feet. "Theo, I can't. I need the money. We can't leave."

He stopped and came back to me, cupping my face in his warm hand. "We can't leave the building. Those are *their* rules, the way *they* set them up. You and I aren't even going to leave the hotel. Now, come with me before someone spots us and calls Nessa and her camera."

"What did you do?" My feet were following behind him without me being aware I was surrendering.

"It's a hotel. I rented us a room. With no flowers this time." He pushed through the door to the stairs.

"You can do that?"

He led me up one flight and ushered me into an identical corridor. "If Alaric can buy a limo service, I don't see why I can't spend my own money to rent a hotel room. I just can't afford a five-star hotel room, and I'm sorry about that. You deserve it, Empress."

"That's fine. I don't care. Oh—oh, Theo."

The door he opened led to an identical room to the one we'd left, with one tiny difference.

No camera. After so long. The relief was exquisite.

I turned to Theo.

30

OFF-CAMERA

He crowded me back against the door, his arms caging me in, but he held himself barely away from me. I clutched at his shirt to draw him to me, but he resisted.

He lowered his head to my ear. The heat from his skin radiated against my cheek. "Housekeeping first," he said hoarsely. "I have condoms. You good with that?"

My nervous system was in overload. I was jumpy with the tension. "Good," I gasped. "And I have an IUD."

"Good. Very good." He lowered his head until he rested on my shoulder in concentration. "And do you give consent for what I'm about to do to you?"

I curled my hand around his neck and tilted to caress his skull with my cheek and jaw. "What am I consenting to?" I desperately hoped it wasn't more than I could handle, because I was close to exploding just from his voice. "What do you intend to do to me?"

Against my palm, his jaw tightened. Was he biting down? Controlling himself? The thought was maddeningly exciting.

"Worship you," he said. "With my mouth. My hands. My

cock. Say yes, Joss. Let me do what I want with you. No pain. No fear. If you don't like something, you say 'stop.' I'll do the same. Okay?"

Nothing this exciting had ever happened to me in the bedroom. Not even close. "Okay," I breathed. Then I pushed hard on my hand to bring his head up, and he let me.

Our kiss went through me like a fever. I felt him in my mouth, which woke up the place where my neck met my shoulder, at the small of my back, in my wristbones. The body inside my skin pulsed with wanting. And an emptiness grew at the center of me—an emptiness desperate to be filled. "Theo," I groaned.

I reached for his belt, but he wrapped his fingers around my wrists and pulled my hands away. "Not yet," he said. "I get one chance to discover you for the first time. I'm not going to take a single shortcut."

Oh, the frustration. I was ready for clothes to go flying, and he was interested in—oh—in the lobe of my ear.

In the hollow behind and below, at the joint of my jaw.

At the neck tendon, now taut from me pulling up to give him access. His hands cradled my rib cage, reaching almost to my spine, and I arched against him with a sigh.

"Glorious," he sighed against my skin. "How can you taste so good? Does the other side taste—ohhh, Joss. You taste good all over."

My pulse was throbbing, which I felt most strongly at my center, where I was swollen, wet, and greedy. I needed more, but his fascination with my neck was—

Oh yes, like *that*.

I felt his smile when I moaned, and he returned to my mouth to kiss my pleasure. He drank me in, and I flowed bonelessly into his arms.

"You're melting me," I admitted.

"Good. Melted Joss. My favorite thing." He punctuated his

words by dropping soft kisses on the tip of my nose, on my temples, at the center of my forehead, and then butterfly touches of his lips across my eyelids. He was worshiping me, and I wasn't sure I deserved it.

But I'd kill anyone who wanted him to stop.

"Arms around my neck now, Empress. I want to feel you against me. Feel those gorgeous breasts on me."

It felt so good in my shoulders, in my arms, along my skin to reach up and draw him to me. It felt so right. His kiss made me dizzy, which might've been why I didn't notice we were moving until my calves brushed against the bed.

"I have dreamed of you against me like this," he crooned. "Your nipples hard enough for me to feel them against my chest." His hand slid up from my waist to press my spine closer to him.

But old demons whispered in my ear just the same.

"I know I'm too small," I protested. "I wish I had bigger boobs."

His finger came across my lips. "How can you possibly look like this and still be insecure? Look at you." We both looked down as his hand slipped over my breastbone and molded to my breast, the thin cloth of the T-shirt doing nothing to mask that my nipples were, as he'd said, puckered to hard berries. "Perfect," he breathed. "Look at how you fill my hand. Look how gorgeous that is."

"It's—oh—yeah, that's gorgeous, all right."

"Yeah," he said in satisfaction. "Now you see it. And you should. You're stunning." He kissed me again, and I almost whimpered when his hands left my chest. But then he tugged slowly at the cloth, pulling the shirt from my jeans. "Naked skin," he said, his eyes closing as his hand slid under the fabric to slip along my waist. He stroked heat into me, and I arched again to encourage him to slide his hands upward.

He would not be hurried. "Hang on. Let me just . . ." His

fingers met at my spine and flexed. He'd opened my bra with graceful skill.

"You're pretty good at that," I smiled, sighing.

"I told you, I've been a very good student. All in service to my empress. Let's see, now—" He pulled back from me and at last used his two broad palms to sweep up my T-shirt and bra, leaving my breasts exposed. I felt a buzz of shame at how childishly small my breasts were, and he noticed. "No," he said. "Don't. You're perfect. See? Look what the sight of you does to me."

He took my hand and brought it to his crotch, pushing me urgently against the heat of his cock.

"Feel that? Hard like iron? That's because of you. Because of these luscious tits. Joss, rub me. Just a little. I need the pressure of—ah." A shiver rippled out from his groin as I did my best to hold a cock bound behind damnably tight jeans. "Yeah. Okay, stop. You'll make me come like a kid. Put that hand here." He pulled my arms around his neck again and bent me over his arm so he could kiss down my neck, my breastbone, and across the slope of my breast. After an eternity of torment, he finally closed his lips over my nipple, and I jumped at the electricity. "Sensitive, huh? Okay. I'll be careful." He licked me, his tongue flat and strong, pushing a wave of wetness and energy to my crotch.

"Theo," I groaned. "I need more. Can't we—"

"No, Empress. Not yet. I'm not done exploring you."

I shivered at how delicious his torture was. After he'd satisfied himself that both breasts tasted the same, he pulled my shirt and bra off. They hit the floor. About time.

He turned me and nudged me to lay on my stomach on the bed.

"No—you. I want your weight on me. Theo—"

"Patience, Empress. I just want to take a moment to worship this ass."

I moaned, and his shirt hit the floor. Bare-chested Theo. I wanted that.

He wanted more too. His hands came to either side of me, and he must have done some sort of strange push-up because his chest brushed against my back without letting any other part of his body touch me. My back, so naked and cool before, soaked in his heat.

"Skin to skin. I'm afraid I'm losing patience here, Big Eyes."

"Good." I tried to turn over, but he stopped me.

"No, wait. I have to unwrap my present." He moved off me, leaving me bare and chilled without him. He ran a hand down my leg—wrong direction!—and lifted my foot. "One shoe off—and the other—and no socks. Your feet are like you, Joss. Long and beautiful and slim. I'm crazy about your feet."

He pressed a kiss to the center of one arch and then the other. I shivered, giggling and hoping my feet didn't smell. He had no objections. As he lowered my shins, one foot brushed against something hard and hot, and he held me to his cock for a moment, rolling his hips against the sensation. A little foot fetish?

Then his hands slid up. Over my ankles. Up the calves. Pausing for a beat in the tender zone behind my knees. Slowly up my thighs.

And then he filled his hands with the curve of my ass.

"*There* you are," he breathed. "That's the ass that's been driving me mad. I've got you under my touch at last." He bit me through the seat of my jeans and I twitched. How could a bite on my rump go so powerfully to my clit?

I fumbled under my belly to undo my jeans.

"No, Empress, let me. Please. Don't move. Don't move, please."

His hands slid under me and nudged my fingers away. He undid the button, and then long fingers teased the zipper down. Down. Down. *Oh, please, touch there. Please.*

I groaned when his fingers slid away, and he laughed. "We're getting there. I promise. I can't wait much longer either. In fact—I should do the jeans and then the panties, but—"

The heat of his hands branded my hips as he slid inside the waistband. And then he collected the panties on the way down, stripping me naked as I lay facedown on the bed.

"Joss," he said reverently. "I'm going to take you like this one day. Because you're the most beautiful thing I've ever seen. But not today. Today, just let me kiss this—"

I felt his lips against my skin, and he planted a kiss and a lick over the place where he'd bitten me. I writhed under him. His hands shaped me, and then he ran a palm across my buttocks.

"You're fascinating. Here, warm as toast. Here, cool as a breeze. I could study you forever." His strokes across my ass were bliss.

But I didn't want slow and soft. I wanted fast and hard. "Theo," I begged.

"Yeah. Yeah, let's move on. Turn over for me, will you, Empress?"

His jeans were open but still on his hips. I pouted. "I want to touch you, too, you know."

He jerked a little and grinned. "Good. Yes. All you want. But not yet, not this time. This time, I'm going to be very, very selfish. This time is for me."

It seemed to me like the entire experience was all about me, and I would have protested, except he parted my knees and knelt on the floor, looking at me with shining eyes.

"Joss. My god. You're perfect. If you could see this . . ." His finger, so gentle, slid along my thigh and up my central seam. He parted me and heaved a sigh. "You're a deep, luscious pink. Like the secret heart of a shell. Pink and shining. I have to touch—" He slid his fingers along me until he reached the apex. I yipped, and he laid one strong forearm across my hip bones. "Easy, there. Take it easy. I want to see. Oh god, you smell so good. I just have to—"

His mouth came down on me, his heat startling me.

Theo licked me. Long, flat strokes like the ones he'd used on my nipples. I wanted him on my clit, but the full strokes were too dreamy to resist. I threw one hand over my eyes and used the other to stroke his gorgeous, bald head. "Oh, please . . ."

"More? I can't deny you. Hang on."

He brought his attention and his mouth to the quivering bud of nerve endings. A long finger nudged at me and then slipped inside.

"Can you take two fingers? I'm going to try. Let's see. God, you're like a furnace. Secret and hot and wet and dark . . . there. Good girl. You okay? What happens if I—"

I thought his gentleness would kill me—until his tongue flicked at my clitoris and his fingers, deep inside me, moved from underneath.

Caught in a two-pronged assault, I was helpless before the gasps, the shivers, the tension he pulled out of me. Theo hummed in encouragement, and his tongue got firmer. His fingers got faster. And without any conscious thought on my part, I was swept into pure sensation.

My orgasm unfolded like dropped ribbon, unspooling across the universe.

I screamed his name as he forced me higher.

And then I collapsed, without the strength to even inhale. I'd breathe later.

I felt Theo's fingers leave me, felt the loss of his heat as he stood, but that was all I knew for a count of pounding heartbeats.

When I opened my eyes, he was standing naked between my knees, smiling at me. "You're the most beautiful thing I've ever seen."

In answer, I held my arms out to him.

One corner of his mouth twitched up. He showed me the condom he held. "Is it time?"

"Oh god, it's so time. Please, Theo. I need you on top of me. In me."

"Empress," he said in reply. He pulled open the package and rolled it on. Then he put one knee on the bed and dragged me upward until my head was on the pillows. "Good?"

"So good. Come into me now."

"Yeah. I will. Hang on—let me tour a few of my favorite places first."

This man was maddeningly slow. He had to kiss me (which gave my arms enough strength to hold him to me). He had to suck lightly on my earlobe (which woke my breasts up again and beg for his attentions). He had to kiss down my neck (which made me arch against him).

By the time he licked my nipples, my clitoris had gotten greedy again. *Don't forget about me.*

His hand slid down my belly and stroked gently down my crotch. "Still too sensitive?" he asked against my chest.

That made me smile. "You *are* a good student, aren't you?"

He lifted his head to look at me, his face serious. "I think all my studies have been in service to this moment. I hope I don't blow it."

I was touched and turned on and amused, all at the same time. "I'll do the blowing. Next time."

His hand convulsed against me, and I jumped. "Don't say things like that if you want me to last," he protested.

"Well, don't last, then," I smiled. "I am more than ready. Stop teasing me, Theo. Fuck me."

"Oh, Empress. Such language." He liked it, though. I felt his cock twitch against my leg. I nudged until he let me open my legs and fit him into the cradle of my thighs.

"Please. I need you in me. I'm so empty."

"Okay," he said, lowering his head as he moved over me. "I can't resist you."

I pulled one thigh up and away to open myself to him, and he seated his cock at the entrance. I watched him and he watched us, where we were joining.

Slowly, inevitably, he pushed forward and slid his length into me.

"You're big," I gasped. "Go slow."

"Slow as I can," he ground out. "Tell me if you want me to stop."

"Don't stop. Don't stop—oh—"

It took time for me to encompass his girth, but at last his groin fit up against mine. "Okay?" He was panting but determined.

I nodded. "Okay. So good. Do it again."

His chuckle was an afterthought to the concentration on his face. "You're so tight. So hot. God, Joss, how can you feel so good?"

He stroked in me again, and then a third time. My brain began to separate from my body. The tickle in my belly was like just before going over the top on a roller coaster. "Yeah. More. Theo, more."

"Yeah?" He bit his lip. Was his control slipping? Did I make him so mad with lust? The thought lifted me even higher.

"Harder. Go harder."

"Harder," he echoed. His stroke increased. "I'll try. I don't want to—"

"Yes. Do. Give in, Theo. Fuck me hard. Do it. Oh god, do it now."

Theo's brow was creased in concentration. "I hope I don't hurt you."

"Go. Damn it, go!"

His control left on an exhale. He reared back on his knees and grabbed my hips, tugging me down the bed to tip up to meet his thrusts. And all the power in that handsome ass and broad back and determined brain poured into me. Theo lost control.

And that made me lose control.

I was coming almost before he started, and his attack was so fierce and powerful that my second orgasm ran into the third one. I was caught in high waves for impossible spans of fierce, silvery, electrical pleasure.

And then Theo was coming with a shout of primitive ferocity, his hands locked onto my hips hard enough to leave bruises. I didn't care.

He collapsed beside me while I was still caught in the paralysis of muscles. He held me while I relaxed into limpness. "Jesus God," I sighed.

"Exactly right," he murmured.

I don't know if he slept then, but I did and didn't wake until I felt him slip out of me. I protested. "Let me get this condom," he said, and then he was back at my side.

I turned with a groan to bury my face in his chest, and he wrapped his arms and tangled his legs with mine. "Ha," I said stupidly.

"Ha," he agreed. One hand came up to stroke my hair. "You screamed my name." I could hear the satisfaction in his voice.

"I did?"

"When you came. You said 'Theo.'"

"And you liked that."

"It made *me* come." I laughed, and he chuckled with me.

I stretched luxuriously, twisting away from him to feel the lassitude in my muscles. "Well, you said you would make me scream."

"I did." He was smug. "And you sure did."

I swatted at him. "Don't make me self-conscious."

He rose on one elbow to face me, his hand coming down on my breast. "I want you to scream every time. Louder, if you can manage it. Wake the hotel. It's easily the sexiest sound I've ever heard."

I shook my head as I smiled. "You make me feel—"

"What?"

"I don't know." I was suddenly shy. "Pretty, I guess."

"Empress." He sat up, crossing his legs as he fixed me with his dark eyes. "Hear me. Whoever told you you weren't pretty, or your breasts weren't big enough, or you weren't deserving of screaming orgasms—well, that guy was an idiot. And I'd like to go beat him up for making you think such a thing."

I smiled through my embarrassment. "It wasn't any one guy. Just a general—I don't know—disinterest, I guess."

"Well, this guy is interested. Plenty interested. They were fools. You know what I like best about you?"

The question made me feel vulnerable. I wasn't going to like what I heard, surely. I sat up, too, to be braced for the pain that was coming. "What? Perfect, tiny boobs?"

He huffed in annoyance as he shook his head. "I like it when you make people do the right thing."

I blanched. "What? What are you talking about? I don't make people do anything."

"Don't misunderstand me. You're not demanding anything of anyone. But you're so good and kind, you show people a better way. And that turns me on huge."

I was confused. "I do . . . what?"

"Oh yeah." He yanked pillows around to suit him so he could sit against the headboard. Then he dragged me across him so I ended up between his legs, my back to his chest. "You tried to help Alaric."

"I tried to geld Alaric," I corrected. "I can't stand that guy."

"And yet who kept trying to help him get along with other people? Don't forget, I watch *Cupid's Quest* like everyone else. I've heard those conversations you had with him."

I brushed the comment away. "They edit those things all to

pieces. You know none of it's true."

"You're wrong." His hands began to stroke my belly idly, painting me in warmth. "They can't fake the footage. You said those things. Maybe you said other things, *too*, but they can't make anything up. They can't put words in your mouth."

His hands had risen, as if without thought, to cup and mold my breasts. I tried to concentrate. "That's silly."

"You made friends with Rose. And Euphoria. Knox thinks you hung the moon. Olivia would give you a kidney for bailing her out on the scuba challenge. Everyone likes you. Even Julie wants to be your best friend. I have one conversation with you about how to win the game and I'm holding a dollar sign. Do you see?"

"Well," I spluttered. "That's just . . . being nice."

"That's what I'm saying. You're nice. It turns me on."

"My niceness? That's so . . . unsexy."

"Joss." Both hands were now filled with breasts, and he shook me lightly to make sure he had my attention. "You got me to wear a seat belt. Do you know how sexy that is? You're a goddess."

"Oh, please." But I felt the evidence of his arousal against my back. Theo was hard. And if I was determined to hold on to insecurities about the size of my tits, then it had to have been his recounting of my personality that did it.

And that turned *me* on.

I twisted around to face him. "My turn."

My thorough Theo investigation was conducted almost entirely by mouth, until he lost his patience, removed himself from between my lips, flipped me onto my back, and made me scream again.

Well, twice.

When we woke up, I saw the clock. "It's almost time to meet for dinner. What are we going to tell them when they ask where we've been?"

31

THE PROPOSAL

"At the cat café," Theo said calmly.

Every eye in our private dining room swiveled to him.

"The what?" Wink was not pleased. "You were gone for almost eight hours, and you were—where?"

"The cat café. Didn't you see it? It's on the third floor. Well, the third and fourth floor. It's two stories, so the cats have plenty of climbing room."

"What's a cat café?" Rose asked, interested.

"Never mind. I'll ask the questions, thank you!" Wink, at his place at the head of the table, sputtered in anger. "Now, Theo, what is a cat café?"

"It's a café that has cats." I could only sit back to admire his calm. "You go in, get something to eat, pet the cats, and hang out."

"You're kidding."

"No, really. Right, Joss?"

I was deeply grateful he'd taken me to the third floor before we went back up to the hotel's dining room. "There's a perfectly spotted cat there. Like a leopard, but little. He's sweet."

"I want to go there!" Rose burst out.

"Let's go right after dinner!" Nick was all-in on the cat café concept.

"Stop it!" Wink tried to curtail the enthusiasm. "And you didn't think our viewers would enjoy a little time spent in a cat café? Besides, now I have to dock the week's pay for both of you. My god, you people are running amuck!"

"Well, no," Theo said mildly. "We never actually left the building."

"But you knew what we meant."

"Did I? Hang on." Theo pulled out his phone, where he'd taken a photo of the statement we'd signed the day before. He read it back to Wink: "'I agree to not leave the building without permission and camera support.' Right here. See?" He held his camera up to Wink and then to the tripod camera on the table in front of us. "So, you won't be docking our money this week, right?"

Wink pushed back from the table and had a whispered consultation with Shout, who was sitting as usual in the corner with his headset on.

Theo was smug, and I was impressed. I never would have had the nerve to bluff my way through such a total fabrication. He sat back in his chair and smiled at me. His hand slid from the back of my chair and into my hair at the nape of my neck. He massaged me gently, and I closed my eyes in bliss. I could still feel him inside me.

There was a cry of outrage from the corner. My eyes flew open, and I watched, open-mouthed, as Shout stood. He stalked over and stared at the two of us. Then he spoke.

"Dude," he said to Theo in accusation. Then it was my turn. "Not cool, Joss."

He stomped away, and Wink returned. "Late-night Watch Now. We need good content, you know. The two of you should be ashamed of yourselves."

Theo still looked contented. "Yeah?"

Wink shook his head in disappointment. "Keep your money. We're rewriting that particular clause. We'll call it the Theo Clause from now on."

"I was in on it too," I said. My guy wasn't going to be shamed alone.

Wink wasn't impressed. "Everybody knows he talked you into it, Joss. You never would have done such a thing on your own. I'm disgusted. I need a moment. Eat your dinner. I'll be back later to tell you about tomorrow."

Wink stalked out, and Shout hurried to catch up to him. In the silence after his departure, Mason asked the first question.

"You guys—did you really have sex in a cat café? What did the kitties think?"

I laughed. "We did not have sex in a cat café."

"I'm so sure." Jane-Alice was irate. "It's pretty clear we're looking at postcoital bliss. They have those love hotels in Tokyo, don't they? You found one in this building, huh?"

"The only hotel we've been in is this one," I said, glad my voice could ring with truth. "What I want to know is how the capsule hotel is, O? I was worried the tiny sleeping space would trigger your claustrophobia."

"After that nightmare on the train? Believe me, the sleeping space is generously sized. And there's a fresh-air vent right there. There's absolutely no problem. Thanks for asking, though, Joss."

"And here's the crazy part," Nick added. "The rooms are segregated by gender. They couldn't force two of us in the same bed. We're sleeping alone! I like you, O, but it's really nice."

We all laughed at his delight, and O agreed. The dinner continued on a lighter note, and all was well. When Theo got up to use the toilet at one point, Rose slipped into his seat almost before he'd left.

"Did you?" she whispered, and I longed to tell her. But the cameras were rolling, and the microphones were listening.

I waggled my eyebrows at her and nodded to the tripod in front of us. "Certainly not. We went to a cat café."

Rose tried to suppress her smile and failed. "Oh, I see. And how was the cat café?"

I melted and grabbed her hand with a giggle. "Incredible. Amazing. I've never... been to a cat café that good before."

"I'm so happy for you!"

"You guys?" I asked her the unspoken question.

Rose blushed, her happiness coming off her in waves. "Not yet. Paul doesn't believe in . . . cat cafés before marriage. Isn't that sweet?"

I was still sore from the delicious workout I'd been given, so it was hard to agree that waiting was something to be desired. But everyone got to make their own choices. "That's wonderful."

"It really is. I'm just crazy about him! Do you think he could be the one?" She gazed across the table to Paul, who was smiling at her.

"I'd say all signs look good." I smiled to see my friend so happy.

"And for you, too, I hope!" Rose was a truly lovely person.

"We'll see." There was no way someone as exciting and smart and beautiful as Theo would want to stick with me after the competition. But I'd ride that pony (or that studly prize stallion) as long as it was willing to carry me.

After dinner, Wink returned, followed by Shout, who was followed by Julie, carrying copies of a new agreement for us to sign. Now we were not to leave our hotel rooms without notice and without a camera operator. Alaric objected, theorizing there might be an emergency, but Shout glared at him until Alaric sputtered to a stop.

Then Shout muttered into his microphone, talking to Julie,

who stood literally at his elbow, and she turned and went back out. Soon we had revised agreements, which Theo signed with a bold flourish.

How were we going to scream each other's names now? I wondered. But he was the magician, after all. He'd figure something out.

He winked at me as he signed. I could trust him on this one. I signed too.

"Fine." Wink collected the papers and handed them to Julie. "Let's put this behind us. Here's what will happen tomorrow."

"Yeah." Val sat forward. "Mama needs some Cupid Cash. Hit me with it, Van Winkler."

Wink winced at the use of his full name but went on. "You've been through the getting-to-know-you stage and the double date. You've had the beach date, as well as dinner and dancing. Now it's time to get serious. This next challenge will be The Proposal."

The way he said it, you could hear the capital letters. The concept made me nervous. Most of us were feigning partnerships for the purpose of the game, but two couples had formed a closer bond. And I was one of them.

Theo and I had been together for so little time. We weren't ready to think about marriage. Having to fake a proposal could definitely kill our romance.

Rose, on the other hand, had her hands clasped beneath her chin like a little girl at the pony rides. Paul wore an undeniable smile. They might have a real proposal.

It's too soon, I thought. Don't be crazy.

"America and viewers around the world will be judging you on how creative, romantic, joyous, or fun your marriage proposal will be. You've got Tuesday, Wednesday, and Thursday to plan it, and we'll film your proposals on Friday. You've got all of Tokyo to consider as your backdrop, so do your research.

Take your time. Discuss it with your partner. And do it on camera." He whirled to glare at Theo, who smiled blandly back at him.

"Of course, Wink. Wouldn't do it any other way."

"Hmph. Your camera operators will come with you as you travel the city, so don't lose them. That's part of the deal."

We all nodded seriously to show we understood.

"And thanks to our sponsors, when you propose, you'll be able to put a ring on it—a five-thousand-dollar white diamond on rose gold, compliments of Babette Jewelers. Where all of America longs to shop."

Would I get to keep the ring after the show? I could sell it for the cash.

Alaric snorted. "You think I'd offer a five-thousand-dollar ring to the woman I choose to marry? Please."

Wink glared at Alaric. "Our sponsor is providing us with six magnificent diamonds to brighten your lucky woman's finger—and win her heart. We're grateful to them for sponsoring us so we can show these stunning rings to the world."

"Do we get to keep it after the show? If we don't get married, I mean?" Euphoria asked the question I was thinking.

"Of course—with the compliments of Babette Jewelers. Where all of America longs to shop."

"What about my fiancé?" I asked, surprising myself with the force of my query. "I'd need to give him a ring, too, wouldn't I?" All the men in the room nodded in agreement. "I mean, it only seems fair. If the women get an extra five thousand dollars, the men should get something, too, right?"

Wink was having a bad night. He visibly relaxed the frown on his face. "Thank you, Joss. That would be fair. We'll discuss it with our sponsors. Now, if there are no further questions, will you all kindly go to your rooms—and, for god's sake, *stay there*?"

"What time do we meet for breakfast?" Knox asked.

"I could not care less. You are on your own until Friday, and I don't want to see any of you until then. Coordinate with your camera operators, please, and leave me the hell out of it. No, wait. I mean—" he paused, his fingers counting backward from five as if a director were cuing him. "You're free to travel around the city, moving at your own pace and time. Julie has a per diem for you for incidentals, meals, and travel expenses. Please coordinate with your camera teams so you're always with them. We'll be viewing the Watch Now slate of programs every day in this room starting at 9:00 a.m., and you're welcome to join us. Otherwise, we'll see you on Friday morning at nine for the proposals! Best of luck to you all." He gave us a patently fake smile and pulled his mic pack out of his pocket. Tossing it on the table, he turned to snarl at Shout, "I'm getting a drink. I'll be in the bar."

As he left, Rose called out, "Can we go to the cat café now?"

"No!" he snarled. Then the Wicked Witch was gone.

Julie stepped up in his place. "I guess I can take a group downstairs if you want to see the kitties. A leopard cat, you say, Joss? Let's go see. That is, if the camera operators are willing—oh? Yes? Good. Apparently, everyone wants to see a cat café. So, Shout, we'll be going downstairs now. Do you want to? No? Okay. Then I'll just—right, okay, come on, you guys, let's go see Joss's cats."

The cat café really was a hoot, and no one seemed to notice that neither Theo nor I knew any more about the procedures as anyone else. We fumbled to put on the provided slippers like everyone did. I'd seen the leopard cat when we peered in the door earlier, but that cat was asleep in a high perch and refused to come down. We had to make do with various Persians, Siameses, a magnificent Norwegian Forest cat, and a pair of fur ball Maine Coon cats. Even Alaric unbent enough to stroke a white Persian, although he made a beeline for the provided lint roller after.

Julie was delighted with the cats, and the camera teams spent as much time filming felines as contestants. We were all happy. And I was with Theo.

Everything was right.

That evening, we were all escorted sternly back to our rooms and told not to leave. We closed the door on the world and looked at each other.

"I still want you," I admitted.

"I want you." We stood on opposite sides of the room, as if coming any closer would burst a dam.

"What do we do?"

"Well . . . get ready for bed. Meet me here." He patted the bed and winked at me.

I was in and out of the bathroom in minutes. He did the same. He slid under the covers with me and gathered me to him for a kiss.

"But—the cameras—" My need was an ache, and yet I didn't want to be in an amateur porn video.

"They can only show R-rated stuff. So, let's give them some R to make them happy, and then you and I are going to be boring. At least, above the covers. Hands only, facing each other. What do you say?"

I say yes. Yes. And right now, yes.

After he showed me how tightly he wanted me to hold his glorious cock and we'd swallowed any screams of bliss in the pillows, we lay at peace, forehead to forehead as our breathing returned to normal.

"What are we going to do about tomorrow?" I asked.

He sighed and tugged on the strand of hair he'd been stroking. "I don't know. I feel like you and I could be, you know—"

"Real?"

"Yeah. Real. You make me want to be a better person, and I'm normally one huge dick."

"One huge dick," I agreed with a smile, giving him a lazy stroke. He jumped, still too sensitive, and pulled away from my greedy fingers.

"Cut that out! Anyway, I feel like a fake proposal at the start of what might be a real relationship... you know?"

"I know. I agree. So how about we agree to lose this one?"

His sleepy eyes widened. "Lose it? Really? Because between us, you and I could do a proposal that would knock people's socks off."

He made me smile. "I know, but let's not. How about we spend the next three days getting to know each other, instead of planning a fake proposal? Tour Tokyo. Talk. Make out in inappropriate places."

"Ride the train again," he said, groping my ass. I jumped, still a little sensitive.

"Am I crazy?" I asked him.

"A three-day-long date in Tokyo? Just you and me? And Nessa? And Luke? And America? And the world? I'm totally in. I would love that."

"And on Friday, I'll take the ring and get on one knee in front of you, instead of the guy doing the proposing. How about that? We'll know it's not real, and we'll just keep going."

His eyes crinkled in amusement. "Is that why you wanted me to get a ring too?"

"I wanted that because you should get something too. If they don't pony up, I'll split the value of the ring with you after the show."

He traced a finger down my nose and across my lips. "You'd do it, too, wouldn't you?"

"Well, why wouldn't I?"

"Because most people aren't kind like you. Most people don't play fair. But you do."

"Naïve, I know." I sighed.

"Not naïve. Wonderful. The world I want to live in from now on."

He kissed me, and it was lucky he'd given me so many orgasms in one day or that kiss would have ignited something more. As it was, we wrapped ourselves more tightly in each other and went back to drifting.

"Any idea of where we should go tomorrow?" I asked.

When he was silent, I nudged him. "There is one place I've always wanted to go. But you'll think it's stupid."

"I won't. I mean, I might, but I won't tease you about it. Probably. What is it?"

32

JAPANESE ANIME

We stood, the four of us, in front of a building blazing with screens and figures and color and movement.

"Radio Kaikan," Theo said with satisfaction. "Ten stories of anime."

"What?" Nessa said. "Like Pokémon?"

"Or *Sailor Moon*?" That was my experience with Japanese animation.

Luke snorted. He stood to my side, pointing his camera at our faces while Nessa stood behind us to get the madness of color past our heads. "*Sailor Moon*. You're old, Joss."

"Shut up, Luke." My demand had no real venom. I was too overwhelmed by the store.

"All of that and more." Theo had his hands on his hips, a king regarding his kingdom with approval. "And if there's any justice in the world, they'll have volume three of the *Parasyte* tankōban."

"Of the what?" I asked. Luke and Nessa were interested too.

"It's manga. Came out in 1988, and the collections were released in, like, 1990 or so. I have volumes one and two and four through ten. I've been looking for volume three, and I thought this might be a good place to start."

A quest during *Cupid's Quest*. I shrugged. "I've got nothing better to do. Let's go." We headed for the escalator leading in and up, Nessa getting in front of us and Luke riding behind.

"Do you think," Luke said, "if we come across Naruto figurines, I could get an Obito for my nephew?"

"Luke, my son," Theo said grandly. "I positively guarantee it."

The place was overwhelming. The utilitarian white walls, steel fixtures, and industrial lighting in the low ceilings had as much charm as any Walmart, but not one of the millions of shoppers moving down the endless aisles noticed or cared.

"I'm hoping I'll find vintage manga on the third floor, but we may have to go as high as eight."

We wove through the people crowded thickly around displays of color and violent figurines and big-eyed images of large-breasted girl-children and man-boys with vicious weaponry. I began to experience sensory overload.

Theo found a clerk on the third floor who listened to him politely and suggested he try the sixth floor. We lost Luke briefly on the fifth floor but promised to stay within sight of Nessa until he got back. "Don't tell Shout," he said, turning off his camera. When he caught up to us, he was clutching a shopping bag and grinning.

The sixth floor advised asking an expert on nine, who sent us to the fourth floor. Along the way, Theo got to explaining the *Parasyte* story to me—something about an alien who takes over a guy's hand and becomes his buddy.

I enjoyed the store, but I was glad when the expert on the fourth floor suggested we try a used bookstore about a mile away.

"Want to take a cab?" Theo asked me but also included

Luke and Nessa in the decision-making process. "Or we could try the train again."

Nessa shuddered, and I agreed. "It's not too cold outside. Let's walk. We can see more of Tokyo that way."

Theo pulled up a map and found our route. As we strolled down the busy, crowded street, he reached out easily and took my hand.

I laced my fingers with his and tried to suppress the high-school crush reaction I was having. He caught me smiling and grinned back.

As we walked across a bridge over the Kando River, I teased him. "All this for a kids' comic book?"

He came to a stop, tugging on my hand and almost running into Nessa, who swerved to protect her camera. "Comic book? Did you really just say that? Joss, love, did you not see the tower, the shrine, the holy nature of that place we were in? Is all that for a comic book?"

His drama was accompanied by sweeping gestures which, since he didn't let go of my hand, I also made. I laughed. "Comic book," I said distinctly.

"Oh. Fool." We got walking again. "What did you say you got your master's in?"

"English literature, and it's been very useful to me so far." I tried to keep the sarcasm from my voice.

"So what if I told you about a great novel by some white guy —we'll make him British, so an English major like you will feel comfortable—that covers these huge philosophical and psychological questions, like the meaning of humanity?"

"Yeah, but—"

"No, hang on." He dropped my hand and put his arm around my shoulder, drawing me to his side as we walked. Happily, I looped my arm around his waist. "What about mankind's relationship with the environment? Or other species? The role of instinct, of love, of sacrifice? We're talking the inherent anthropocentrism of morality, man. Can you hear what I'm saying?"

"Theo," I laughed. "You're so deep!"

He tugged on my hair and laughed with me. "Volume three. The *Parasyte* tankōban. That's *Parasyte* with a *y*. None of the reissues, either—we want the original. And in Japanese. Don't let anyone sell you an English version. We pay no more than fifty US dollars."

"Yessir. I understand. Your mission is now my mission."

Before we got to Kitazawa Bookstore, we came to the Toyodoshoyen Used Bookstore. "Look at that," I said. "Should we try here too?"

"Wait—right next door. What's Gyokueido Books?" Theo looked past me.

Luke, who'd been walking ahead of us and shooting backward, gestured behind him. "There's a bunch of bookstores this way. Like, I can see five . . . six . . . seven from here."

Theo's dark eyes widened in excitement as he turned to me. Before he even asked, I held up my hand. "English major, remember? You think I'm going to mind spending the day pawing through used bookstores? Let's go!"

That was the moment when we entered a sort of book lover's opium den. Theo and I were soon drunk on the scent of leather-bound volumes and pages of art prints and spills of novels and studies and children's stories and nature tales. We passed from bookstore to bookstore in a haze of delight.

I found a rainbow-bright book from my childhood I'd totally forgotten about. Theo fell into an entire section on the history of computer programming. We didn't find his manga, but Luke bought several graphic novels for his nephew, and Nessa came away with the prize of an entire book on Persian kittens for her mother. By the time we stopped in a café, we were grinning and dusty.

"Incredible," Theo said happily. "And it looks like we're not even halfway done yet. We still have Komiyama to go."

"And Isseido. And Kitazawa. I asked for you."

Theo leaned over and kissed me in thanks, a firm and hot and too-short caress.

I sat back happily and drank my tea. "If you had to pick one book as your all-time favorite, what would it be?"

Luke and Nessa took turns being "on." He had his camera up while she rested. Theo thought for minute. "*Algorithm Design* by Jon Kleinberg. I read it when I was twelve, and it rewrote my entire future."

I chuckled. It was such a Theo thing to say. I turned to Luke, who watched me through his lens. "How about you?"

"Me? I'm not part of this."

"Sure you are. What book changed your future when you read it?"

"Um." The lens drooped as he thought about the question, and Nessa yanked hers up to focus—not on us, for once, but on Luke. His face lit in a smile. "*The Last Navigator*. About Mau Piailug and others. So cool." When he looked at us smiling back at him, his smile dropped. He pulled his camera up.

But the camaraderie wasn't over. He turned to Nessa. "What about you, Ness? Got a favorite book?"

She chuckled. "Happiest day of my life was when I graduated and I could put books behind me. I have dyslexia, so I'm one of those 'I'll wait for the movie' kind of people."

"Movies are good," I agreed stupidly. The idea of being dyslexic was so sad, I had to hide my sympathy. Imagine not loving to read.

"What about you, Joss?" Nessa asked. "Have a favorite?"

I shook my head. "I have a favorite *bookcase*. They're the books I'm going to need to have with me if I get abducted by aliens and displayed in an Earth-themed zoo, like that Kurt Vonnegut story."

"I read that book!" Theo grinned. "It was awesome."

It was easy to forget the two large cameras at the table and imagine we were on a double date. The easy warmth persisted as we continued through our used-bookstore journey, which was extensive.

Theo had wandered to an upper floor, Nessa on his heels, when I saw it. "Luke," I said, "I'm asking you as a friend—turn your camera off for a minute. Please?"

He screwed up his mouth at me in unhappiness and I thought briefly of blackmailing him with the knowledge of the anime figurine in his backpack, purchased for his nephew while Luke was supposed to be on duty.

In the end, I didn't have to. Luke lowered his camera. "Go ahead," he said. "As long as you don't tell anyone."

Impulsively, I kissed his smooth cheek and had my acquisition stowed away in his backpack before he turned his camera back on, and we went to find Theo and Nessa. Theo had found an entire room of vintage magazines and was in a heated discussion with the clerk about something called *Morning Open Zōkun*, which was remarkable because neither of them spoke the other's language. Ah, the common love of manga—the great leveler.

"I came close!" he said happily. "This is the best day! Are you having fun?"

I grinned and wiped a smudge of dust off his arched cheekbone before pulling his head to me and kissing him. Nessa had the best angle, but I no longer cared. "The best day. Can we keep going?"

It was midafternoon before we came to the end of the used-book bonanza. All four of us had made purchases, and I was wishing I had my own backpack.

Theo cemented his place in my heart by taking my bag from me and hanging it on his arm. Carrying my books home from school? Swoon.

He consulted his phone. "We're about ten minutes from the grounds of the Imperial Palace. Want to walk through some gardens before we head back?"

Luke and Nessa loved the idea of getting footage of us holding hands against something other than row after row of books, so we continued our stroll in a greener direction.

"Couldn't come in March when the cherry blossoms were out, could we?" Luke grumbled, but he wasn't really annoyed.

Nessa and Luke leapfrogged us, one getting in front and the other staying behind to get the close-ups. We ignored them.

Theo told me about his family. His father was a classics professor at Rutgers and had taken it out on his three sons—Theophilus, Plutarch, and Seneca. "Or, as we prefer it, Theo, Tark, and Senny."

As far as I could tell, Theo and his brothers expressed their love for each other through wrestling. It sounded violent to me, but Theo was grinning when he told me about them.

"Are they bright like you?" I asked.

He shrugged. "They're bright."

"But not like you."

He cocked an arrogant brow. "No one's bright like me. But I'm a dick, and they're sort of not, so I guess it evens out. They can both keep friends for years, which I don't understand."

"You *were* a dick," I corrected. "You're learning a new way, huh?"

"Because of you." He wrapped me closer to his side, and then we stopped walking because the kiss was too intense. The warmth in my heart drifted downward to below my belly. *Want.*

"Shall we go find a love hotel?" Theo murmured against my mouth.

"Yes," I said, grinning. "But we'll have to get a room that can take Luke and Nessa, too, because of the paper we signed. How's that sound to you now?"

Theo groaned and put me from him. "You stay over there."

Nessa grinned, and I bit my lip in amused frustration. "Tell me about *your* family."

All right. Distraction. Good idea. "My mom is Frieda and my sister is Claire. I love them both more than I can say." I told Theo how we'd taken care of each other since the day my father left.

"What happened to him?"

"Oh, he's around. I see him. He paid for my education, which was amazing of him."

"And for your sister too?"

"Well, Claire didn't really want to go to college." I glossed over the part where my father never took to Claire, which went hand in hand with why Claire didn't much look like my father and why he divorced my mother after Claire was born. "It's hard for her to study with her asthma, you know."

"Uh-huh. Must be bad." His tone was studiously neutral, but I took a quick peek at him to see if he was being sarcastic.

"It is. She can't breathe. It's awful. I'd do anything to help her avoid an attack." He nodded, not meeting my eye. "She turns twenty-one in July, and my dad's child support payments will end then."

"He paid until she was twenty-one? Not eighteen?"

"Is eighteen normal?"

He shrugged. "I thought so."

Huh. "My dad's very generous."

"And yet you work all those jobs. You're on a reality TV show to earn money. For them."

"Well, yeah. They'd do the same for me."

"Would they?"

"What are you saying?"

"Nothing. Want to get a snack? Dinner's not until seven tonight at the hotel."

I was being distracted again. It left me feeling unsettled. What *did* Theo mean?

33

TOKYO PAGE BY PAGE

I knew I could rely on my magician to figure out a way. Theo discovered the closet in our hotel room was large enough for both of us to get into and still close the door. He used his phone to broadcast vigorous electronic dance music to foil the microphones, took me into the closet, and made me scream his name twice more.

(My foot banged the door open when I was, to my overheated delight, draped across his front while he totally held me up—but when he nudged me face first into the wall and took me from behind, the door stayed obediently shut.)

(He got me screaming in both positions.)

Such a magician.

We met the group for breakfast the next morning and were met, again, by Wink's irritation.

"That's it," he said. "There's been a change of rules."

Theo, who clearly believed there was one set of rules for himself and another for everyone else, grinned in rebellion, but his happiness was more sincere with Wink's next statement.

"From now on, your in-room cameras will be turned off at

midnight. If you're awake, we'll collect them. Apparently, the lack of privacy is driving some of you"—he glared at Theo and me—"to go to extreme lengths to circumvent our thorough right to film you."

Even those who (at least theoretically) weren't having sex in closets erupted into cheers—except for Theo.

He grabbed me and dragged me across his lap. "Let's reward them for this intelligent change, shall we?" Then he kissed me until I was dizzy. Once he knew I was fully off-balance, he ran his hand slowly up my rib cage until he cupped my breast—in full view of the cameras.

It felt so good—and yet—my mother would watch this—and my—yes—my—

"Theo!" I gasped.

He grinned against my mouth. As the roaring of my pulse in my ears subsided, I heard the others cheering and catcalling. "You're so pretty when you blush, Joss."

I squirmed to move. After enjoying my efforts for a bit, he let me go. *Woof. Mm.*

Once our little show was over, the conversation turned to what the others were planning for their proposals. I realized we'd still be spotlighted on Friday, even if we didn't want to win. We'd have to come up with something.

The others had been to all kinds of iconic Tokyo sites. None of them had spent a happy day in used bookstores, but I wouldn't give up our journey, even for another win.

"We need to figure something out," I said when the four of us were back on the sidewalk, ready for the day.

"I have it figured out. Two more bookstores. You up for it?"

I grinned. "You're ignoring the Cupid Cash, but let's see what you can find today!"

Unlike the day before, our quest took us to the high-rent district. The Maruzen Marunouchi main bookstore was slick and polished, filled with shiny new books and a section devoted to writing and stationery that would have bankrupted my checking account if I hadn't kept a stern hand on my credit card. Those pens, that creamy, rich paper ... sigh.

"When we win *Cupid's Quest*, I'll bring you back," Theo said confidently. "Now we'll take a stroll through some of the most high-priced real estate in the world to the next store. Need some Prada? Gucci? Hermès? This will be the route."

We stopped along the way for tea and people watching. This time, I asked my fellow quest seekers what real wealth looked like.

"Revenge," Theo answered promptly and then saw my face. "All right. Wealth. Real wealth. An apartment in Manhattan, way up high. And a guaranteed parking spot in the basement. For my—um—my Porsche."

"Which one?" Luke asked. They had a long and tedious discussion about various high-priced cars.

I looked to Nessa. She shrugged. "Paying every bill as soon as they come in," she said. "And a trip to Italy to meet my father's people. Maybe I'd bring them all gifts."

"What kind of gifts?" Theo was interested. "What do we have in the US that they don't have in Italy?"

We all thought about it. "Wide-open spaces?" Luke said after a bit. "Less obviously corrupt politicians?"

"Outstanding junk food. I've decided. Like Twinkies." Nessa looked pleased.

"So, you're going to meet your relatives and then kill them?" Luke laughed.

"All right, Luke, what's your answer?" she asked.

"I'm liking this car idea. How about a sports car *and* a big truck? Or a Jeep to hold my surfboard?"

"You surf?" Theo's eyebrows were up. "Why were you on that Jet Ski in Australia, then?"

"Camera, dude." Luke patted the camera still on his shoulder. "The waterproof ones are even heavier. They throw my balance off bad. What's your answer, Joss?"

"Wealth. Real wealth." I savored the concept. "It would buy me time."

"To do what?" Theo asked quietly.

"Read. Have a den or a nook or some quiet place where I could just curl up and read all the time." I came out of my daydream and saw they were smiling at me. "Let's go to the next bookstore so I can buy something for my nook."

And I found my nook—or at least, a new image of what a nook should be. At the Ginza Tsutaya Bookstore, a central well was lined with thousands of books and magazines far above human reach, soaring up to a central skylight that brought the sun pouring down.

"I'm moving in," I said.

"Okay with me. I'm going to anime. Find you later?"

I looked my happiness to him, and he chuckled as he wandered off.

But we came back together eventually to continue our day. And hours later, promptly at midnight, a knock came on our door.

"Evening, folks," Luke said with a smile. "I'm here to turn the red light on, if you get me."

"Come in," Theo said. "Can I help you move the cameras?"

"I got it. Nessa will be by at 6:00 a.m. to put them back in, so don't sleep too soundly. She's got a master key."

Theo turned to me. "We'll have to put our clothes back on before then."

I was scandalized and thrilled by his comment. Move a little faster, Luke.

I shut the door behind him when he left, and Theo grabbed my hand. Whirling me past him like a dancer, he spun me until I ended up on the bed, my legs hanging over the side.

"The closet was fun," he said as he stripped off my shoes. "But this is better."

It was. He took his time like the first time, driving me crazy with his patience. By the time he had my knees over his elbows and was working himself slowly into and out of me, my nerve endings were jumping.

"More, Theo," I moaned. "*Please* go faster."

"Umm ... not yet. Not yet. Not quite yet—"

I writhed before him, and finally his broad, heavy thumb landed on my clit. I jerked and felt the building cycle of pressure. "Yes—"

"Yes," he echoed, watching me carefully as he took me apart.

I cried out his name as I came.

After, our heads on the same pillow, he murmured, "I'm beginning to know what you like."

"You've always known what I like."

"No, I'm still learning you."

"And you're a very diligent student."

"Well, the subject fascinates me."

"I like being with you. Without the cameras."

"I don't know. I sort of like claiming you and showing everyone. I'd do bodily harm to anyone who tried to come between us."

"Sweet talker. There's nothing a girl likes more than gestures of bloody violence."

"You shut up." He goosed me, and I laughed and managed somehow to snuggle closer. "Remember, we have to wake up in time to put our clothes back on."

"Mm."

We didn't. But when Nessa knocked, she gave us time to dress before coming in to set up the damn cameras again. "At least do us the courtesy of showing us some after-sex hair," she said. "Well, not you, Theo. But Joss, leave it messy, please. Shout's request."

Creepy. The director wanted me to look like I'd had a lot of sex.

On the other hand, I could get back into bed and sleep some more. That would please everyone—and I was a people pleaser.

After breakfast (which, breaking the pattern, did not include Wink being angry), our quartet gathered again.

"Everyone else is working on proposals," I said. "Today we should come up with something."

"I have come up with something. I'm going to take you to one of the most beautiful bookstores in the world."

I took his hand, my happiness bubbling out of me. "Better than yesterday? I don't think you can do it. Where are we going? Do they have vintage manga?"

"They'll probably have it but not for sale. They have this huge library of periodicals. We can go look at it. Come on, you guys—we're springing for a cab."

Daikanyama T-Site was more like a stunning, tranquil museum set in a tree-lined park. "Look," I said. "That corridor goes through the building to the one beyond!"

"I read about it online. It goes through *three* buildings. Come on—let's find the magazine library."

Luke and Nessa were as interested in volume three of *Parasyte* as I was. We all poured over it, and Luke shot footage of the colorful, bizarre story where it lay on a display table. The helpful clerk stood by, ready to assist.

"I feel like I've been to church," I said as we left.

"That's my church," Theo agreed. "This is our sacrament. And our religious quest. Onward?"

"Indeed!"

"I've got one last place where we might be able to find volume three. It's about an hour by foot. Want to grab a cab?"

"I'm enjoying seeing Tokyo from the street. Everyone good to walk?"

Nessa shook her head at me. "You're not supposed to ask our opinions. We're not here, right?"

"You're here. I see you. I like you. And I have a new question for when we stop."

She grinned, and I grinned back. Luke and Theo were already starting out. One more day of books and easy conversation. I set off with a glad heart.

"All right," Nessa said once we found the sandwich shop and grabbed a table. "We've had favorite books and definitions of wealth. What's today's brain pick, Joss?"

I had it ready. "What's one goal you'd like to achieve?"

"Sitcom," Nessa said promptly. "To work on a popular one that films for years. I'd have steady work and could be at home, close to my mom. No more wondering whether the next job would show up in time to help her with her bills. That's my goal."

I understood her reasoning on a very primitive level. Help the family. Yes. "It's a good goal. The best goal. I hope it works out for you. Luke?" I looked at my first friend and smiled, but his usual grin didn't appear.

"Figure out some way to help my family, I guess. Although that's impossible."

"Why?" Theo was as interested in a suddenly serious Luke as I was. "What would you need to help them?"

Luke shrugged, his eyes darting to the side. "Just solve global warming, that's all." Luke was from the Cook Islands, I remembered. Maybe his home was in danger of flooding. That would be terrible. "It's not about me, though. It's about you two. What's your goal, Theo?"

This time, Theo caught my eye and did not speak of revenge. "Get my software idea off the ground. Make my own fortune, not dependent on brass dollar figures."

"Yeah?" Luke was curious. "Circumventing the phone tree? How would you do that?"

"Can't tell you on camera. Come on, dude—proprietary information. Joss, you're up. What's a goal you want to accomplish?"

Easy. "Keep my mother and sister in our house for years to come. Let them continue to live the way they're used to living. That's all I want."

"Nothing for yourself?" Theo asked.

"A book nook for me that looks like yesterday's bookstore. With an atrium and lots of sunlight."

"There you go!" Theo cheered for me. "How do you know the next bookstore won't be even better?"

"Let's go see."

The final bookstore on the list, called Book&Beer, encouraged its patrons to wander the store, shopping, while carrying a full cup of Japanese beer. It was a clever plan, but I was still dreaming of the light-filled atrium.

When we braved the train back to our hotel, I found I was ready to be done. Book saturation had been achieved.

And yet we still hadn't planned an engagement event.

I fell asleep on the bed while Theo showered. He woke me when he curled behind me, fitting himself to me. I sighed and stretched and felt him rise against my back.

"Theo...?" I asked him with a sigh.

He responded by kissing my shoulder.

I never moved from my position. He lifted my thigh over his leg and slid into me from behind, rocking against me as I curled my fingers and toes and arched against him.

Theo had a magic touch. I wasn't impressively experienced, having had four lovers before him, but no one had ever brought me to the same heights I reached with Theo.

And I was becoming addicted to the crashing, electrifying thrill of the orgasms he gave me.

To the fulfillment that came from his groans of pleasure, his shuddering when he came. His calling my name.

To sleeping in his arms, melted and spent and heavy.

None of which would help us on the following day, when the cameras turned to us for our proposal and the world was watching. What the hell were we going to do?

34

PUT A RING ON IT

"Anyone need to go first?" Wink asked at breakfast.

Knox's hand shot into the air. "I need to propose to Jane-Alice before 10:30. Can we go first?"

"Objections?"

"I'll need sunset," Alaric declared.

"What time?" Julie asked. She was holding a clipboard and making notes.

"We'll need to arrive at three this afternoon," Alaric stated.

Val held up a hand. "Four will be fine."

Alaric opened his mouth to protest, and she shot him a look. He closed his mouth.

I'll be damned. She trained the feral animal. It only took an experienced soldier.

"We'd like to be last, if that's good with you all," O said. She looked at Nick with a smile. They might not have been dating, but they got along.

Julie organized the schedule. "And Joss and Theo, what time is good for you?"

I looked at him and shook my head. He was calm. "The timing doesn't matter. We'll take whatever is left over."

"All right," she said eventually. "I've got it. Everyone ready? I've got the rings, and I'll give them to the guys when it's time, and the camera operators will have time, and we've allotted a full hour between proposals because have you ever seen traffic like this city? I mean, it's worse than LA at rush hour, and when all the people cross the street, I mean, look out! Why everyone isn't dead, I don't know, and—what? Sure. Out to the bus, everyone! Jane-Alice and Knox, give your location to the driver. Here we go! Aren't you excited? I really am, this is going to be—you look nice, Rose—okay, okay, okay."

Jane-Alice and Knox were up first, and they set a high bar. Somehow, they'd gained access to a sumo wrestling stable, and we sat in the empty stands while they disappeared.

When they came back, spotlights blazed on, and we laughed in delight to see Knox, his pale skin on full display, in the traditional loincloth. But the cheers were even louder when curvy little Jane-Alice also stepped into the ring in a very small "mawashi." It took a wide-eyed moment to realize she was also wearing a flesh-colored bodysuit.

They'd clearly spent their time working with wrestlers, one of whom observed and instructed as they engaged in an amateur but serious bout. The only element that wasn't in keeping with Japan's national sport was the ending, when Jane-Alice tripped Knox, who fell obligingly on his back. She landed across Knox's chest, wrenched the engagement ring from his hand, raised her arm in triumph, and cried out, "I do!" Our thunderous cheers filled the arena, and Knox and Jane-Alice bowed to their instructor and thanked him.

An impressive start to the day of proposals.

Rose and Paul were very sweet in a beautiful tea garden. The winter-bare trees were still lovely, and evergreen plants provided color next to the teak teahouse. Rose cried when Paul asked her to marry him, and I thought that perhaps this engagement would hold.

Mason and Euphoria weren't as touching at the Shinto shrine they'd located, although the setting was lovely and graceful.

And Val walked Alaric through a seriously shortened and not-at-all pompous proposal from the terrace of the Tokyo Skytree, high above the city. The sunset created an unbeatable backdrop.

"All right, Joss and Theo, you're up. Tell the bus driver where to take us next," Wink said once we were all back on the bus.

"No need," Theo said. He stood. "Can the camera see me okay? Can you hear me?"

Confused, Wink nodded. "You bet," Julie echoed.

"Good." He turned to me and knelt in the aisle of the bus.

To give him credit, he'd definitely surprised me.

"Joss, I hate everyone. I trust no one. And yet I trust you. I like you. Maybe more than that. I know it's too soon—you don't even know if I turn into a werewolf on the full moon or not. But I'm not kidding. I think maybe I want to marry you. For real. Not just for the show. I'd like to keep you with me forever. Not like a stalker. Will you? Will you marry me?"

He held out the ring to me, and I wasn't crying so hard that I couldn't see his hand was trembling.

Heat flashed across my skin as adrenaline raced through me. I stood and turned, gesturing to the back of the bus. "Luke? Please?"

Theo's brow creased at my reaction, and he watched as Luke made his way down the aisle, my package in his hand. He passed it over to the seat to me, and I sat again. My legs wouldn't hold me up anymore anyway.

"Theo, you're right. It's too soon. It's crazy. And yet I can't imagine going on with my life without you. I would love to marry you, as crazy as that sounds. And here—because you deserve something too."

He blinked and smiled. "Really?"

I smiled too. "Take it."

"What is it? You take the ring."

We swapped. The ring was beautiful. It sparkled, flashes of fire catching the light.

"Oh, Joss!" He'd ripped the wrapping off. "Volume three! Where—how'd you—oh, for god's sake."

He rose to his feet and pulled me up, and then I was crushed against him, and he was kissing me, and I was getting him wet with my tears, and he was getting me wet with his kisses and hands and body and proposal.

Yes.

Yes, I wanted this man.

Eventually, Wink had to stop us. "We've got to get the bus out of traffic. You can sit down now, please. Please. Hey—Theo. Put her down. Theo. Come on, man. Sit down. Thank you. All right. Now what?"

Julie stood, and she had tears in her eyes too. "Well, that only leaves O and Nick, but we've got time because they didn't want to—what? Okay? We go now? Okay. O, Nick, come on up and tell the bus driver where to go—although how you're going to beat that, I don't know, and maybe I should—yeah. Okay. I'm sitting."

Theo was wrapped around me and I was wrapped around him. "Really?" he whispered. "I wasn't kidding. Were you?"

"I'm not kidding either. I think maybe—" It was too soon. I couldn't say it. "I don't want to let you go."

"Me either. Are we swept up in the moment? We should have our heads examined. God, I think I might be having a heart attack. Feel my chest. Can you feel that? It's slamming in me."

My hand on his skin was a caress. I could feel his heartbeat. It matched mine. "This is insane."

"It is." He kissed me again. "We don't have to do anything.

Not get married right away. We'll be engaged for a while, right? Like, you have to meet my mom. Christ, she's going to love you."

"She will?"

"She'll think you've tamed me."

I laughed. "You can't be tamed."

"Joss." He rested his forehead against mine. "You got me to wear a seat belt."

"Which you think is sexy," I whispered.

"Yes, I do. So sexy," he agreed. Trusting that the camera angle was focused on faces, he pulled my hand to his crotch, where his cock grew under my touch. "So damn sexy." He stopped me when I tried to caress him. "Later. My fiancée isn't going to give me a hand job on a bus."

Fiancée! How could this possibly be?! What would Mom and Claire think of him?

Who cared?

Still, warning bells clanged along with peals of pure joy in my soul. I was determined to ignore my doubts. I longed for someone to love. Someone just for me.

O and Nick had rented a large private room at a karaoke bar, which included free drinks. All the engaged couples were toasted with champagne, and then Nick took the stage.

He proposed to O by singing a Bruno Mars song called "Marry Me." And he had a wonderful voice, rich and resonant and low.

"Jesus," Theo said, "I'd marry him."

"Me too." I proved the lie by kissing Theo again. We were pressed up tight to each other on a sofa, cozy in the darkness. His hands were wandering; mine were too. How soon before we could go back to the hotel?

"Have to wait for midnight anyway," he murmured in my ear. "Which is going to be torture."

"Tell me about it."

O had learned a song she said was by Colbie Caillat that I'd never heard before, but it was pretty; it was called, appropriately, "I Do." When she finished, Nick presented the ring to her with a smile, and she accepted with the same. We all applauded.

Nick turned to us all. "That's the end of the proposals, but we've got this room until eleven tonight. Is there any reason why we can't stay here and have a night out?"

Even the camera operators cheered that idea, and a whispered consultation between Wink, Shout, and Julie led to agreement.

"We're here for the night!" Julie shouted. "Can I go next? I want to sing some Stevie Nicks!"

Someone pulled out some tripods for two stationary cameras, and the operators took turns roving the room for reactions and interviews so they, too, could hoist a drink or two, get up onstage, and belt out their favorite songs.

"Do you sing?" Theo asked me.

"What, my fiancé doesn't know if I can sing? That's crazy." I kissed his nose.

"It is. Tell me. Do you sing? Are you a siren, destined to lure me onto the rocks?"

"You're the one doing the luring. I sing, but never in public. For the good of humanity. You?"

He shrugged. "I can carry a tune, but I'd rather sit here with you. Besides, I'm sporting a pretty big boner right now. It would be better if I didn't stand on a stage in a spotlight."

"I thought you liked the idea of those cameras."

"Only in respect to claiming you. Which, I think you'll agree, I've now done." He held up my hand and kissed the finger that held the ring.

"I need to text my mother and sister. They're going to freak out."

"Good freakout, or bad freakout?"

"Good, of course. Why would it be bad?"

"Well, I intend to monopolize a lot of your time and attention." I grinned at the declaration. "And those are commodities they're pretty accustomed to using."

"They don't use me. They'll be happy for us. And I can still take care of them. Can't I?"

He kissed the sudden frown on my face. "We've got nothing but time. Go ahead and text them. We'll figure it out."

35

MESSING WITH MY HEAD

"You were robbed."

Jane-Alice had become my new best friend. Every time I went to the plane's galley for food or to the bathroom, Jane-Alice popped up at my elbow.

"I feel really badly," she said, which I doubted. "There's no way Knox and I should have won that challenge. Everyone on the bus was sobbing when you and Theo got engaged. I mean, you guys are for real. You know?"

"Thanks." I pulled my tray of lasagna out of the microwave and put Theo's in. "But don't worry about it. We didn't put any effort at all into ours, and you guys really did study sumo."

"Yeah, for three days. And Knox never took it seriously. Me? I like to learn a sport from the best, but he was all about the joke. What a goofball."

I felt a spurt of annoyance at her tone. Knox's goofiness was part of his undeniable charm. Why couldn't Jane-Alice see that?

"Anyway," she went on, "I really think you should register a complaint. Like, I bet the total votes are tabulated somewhere. You should demand to see them."

Still one more minute on the lasagna. I wasn't enjoying this conversation. "Why do you care?"

"I don't know. It seems like you and Theo should complain or something. You know? And don't you worry? I mean, now Knox has two wins, like you. He's totally your competition now. You could take him out."

My spider senses were tingling strongly now. "Why would you want me to take wins away from Knox? And from you? Do you have Cupid Cash to spare, Jane-Alice?"

"Hey." She held up a hand. "I'm trying to be a friend. You know? Like you are. You'd help someone else, right?"

Her look was sly. I smiled at her and retrieved our dinners. "Thanks. I'll think about it."

"You really should." She followed me out of the galley until we came in view of the wide-angle camera at the front of the cabin. As soon as we weren't alone, she smiled happily at me and went back to Knox.

I put Theo's food down on his tray and sat. "My god, you're a good cook," he said happily.

Another thing my fiancé didn't know about me. I actually was a good cook, and I would be glad to prove it to him after the competition ended. But shouldn't the man I was engaged to know such a thing?

"Jane-Alice is up to something," I said to him.

"Yeah? Oh jeez—hot." He gulped his water. "What? What's she plotting now?"

"I don't know. She wants me to go to Wink and ask to see the vote count on the proposals. She's sure you and I won."

"Why would she do that? She'd lose her only dollar sign."

"I know. It's weird."

"Ah." Theo nodded and gestured with his fork. "She wants to ruin your sweet, innocent good-girl image."

"I don't have a good-girl image."

"No, because you are a good girl. Just a good girl who's now hanging out with the bad boy." He kissed me, leaving me with tingles and a hint of marinara. "Now, I could go in there and demand the vote totals and nobody would think a thing of it. In fact, I might do that."

I put my hand on his arm. "Can't we let it go?"

He smiled in satisfaction. "See? Such a good girl. And the only reason I'll let it go is because the win was far from the most important prize in that competition." He lifted my hand and kissed my engagement ring.

I melted. "Agreed. So I should—"

"—do nothing. Eat your lasagna. Wait on me hand and foot. Fan me. Feed me grapes and tell me what an incredible lover I am."

"Hang on. Only some of those things are likely to happen."

"Grapes?"

"Eat your dinner. Have you figured out where we're going yet?"

"Depends. If we land at around six tonight, it'll be Hawaii."

"Oh, that would be fun."

"I dunno. A lot like the Japanese culture, you know? Might be too close."

"Right. All that sunshine and beaches. So similar to Radio Kaikan."

"Don't sass me, young lady. I'm betting we're doing our South American challenge next."

"We've been to South America. We were in Argentina."

"But just long enough to get to Antarctica. No, I think we'll bypass Hawaii and end up in Brazil. Rio de Janeiro is my bet."

"Oh, Rio! That would be amazing!"

"And maybe I can take you to Hawaii one day."

"I would like that." Planes were such cuddly, cozy places. How had I not noticed before?

When six o'clock came and went and we didn't land, Theo was smug. Night came, the cabin lights dimmed, Theo draped me over his lap to sleep. We got cozy under the blanket of his sweater, and his hand began to wander.

I sighed. "Can you cover the camera? Just, you know, casually?"

"Give me your hoodie. Let's see how long it takes them to notice."

The other contestants were at least pretending to sleep. I turned more closely into Theo's chest and bent my knee to give his hand access.

But all too soon, he stopped. I opened my eyes. Nessa was standing in the aisle.

"Don't you know we're particularly watching you two? Take the hoodie down, please."

"Shit."

"Don't make me come back here. It's not my turn to monitor, and I was having a nice dream."

"Poor baby," he told her with smirk. She smirked back and left.

"Well, it was a nice try," I sighed. "Isn't there anyplace? Bathroom? Galley?"

"All wired with cameras. Haven't you noticed?"

I sat up. "The galley too? So Jane-Alice's little attempt to sabotage me was filmed?"

"Of course. Everything is filmed. The question is, will the producers opt to include it in the next episode? Do they want Jane-Alice to be the sexy beauty? Or the bad, bad, bad girl?"

I loved the way his brain worked. "Which do you think?"

"Well, my research indicates that every reality show needs an enemy. I thought it was Alaric, once I was sure it wasn't me. But I suppose we could have a male and a female enemy. Tomorrow's show will tell the tale."

"You're so smart." I kissed him, and his arms tightened around me.

"If I was so smart, I'd find a place where I could work my wicked ways on you."

"Hmm. How about where they stow the luggage?"

"Right," he said. "We'll carve a hole in the floor, drop down a portable heater and lots of blankets, make sure there's a good source of oxygen, and go at it. I'm pretty sure no one will notice." I felt his laughter through the hands caressing his ribs. "Go to sleep, Big Eyes. We'll be landing at nine tomorrow."

But when the announcement came, it was after five in the morning. "Fasten your seat belts. We're going to land soon."

"Land?" Theo was annoyed. "We can't land yet. Hang on . . ." He got out his phone for the compass and did calculations in his head. "Too far east for Lima. Where the hell—oh, man."

"What?"

"Cusco. I never even thought."

"What's Cusco?"

"Ancient city of the Inca kings. Actually, it's a brilliant place to have some challenges."

"How come? Will you fasten your seat belt, please?"

He grimaced and kissed my nose. "Yes. Here. The reason it's brilliant is because—oh, shit."

"What? Your face went white. What are you thinking?"

"I'm thinking—how good are you at high altitudes?"

"What? I don't know. Why?"

"Never been up high? Denver? Someplace like that?"

"Uh, no. I don't think so. You're kind of making me uneasy."

"Yeah. Well, we're going to find out. If I'm right, we're landing in Cusco, which is thirteen thousand feet in the air."

I shook my head. "I'm sorry. I have nothing to compare that to."

"Well, people have trouble in Denver, which is called the Mile High City for that reason. Cuzco is more than twice that high. But I bet we're not stopping in the city."

"We won't?"

He shook his head and took my hand. "The Inca built Cusco, but it's not their most famous place. Ever heard of Machu Picchu?"

I nodded but couldn't come up with much, except that it was in the mountains and was mostly gray stone ruins. "I guess."

"It's kind of a bucket-list place. The show would be smart to take us there. Armchair travelers will love it, and watching the twelve of us suffer from the altitude is going to keep everyone entertained."

"It's going to be bad?"

"Well, maybe. Hang on, let me look up the symptoms. Sure —it's a real party. Headache, nausea and vomiting, loss of appetite, inability to exercise, trouble sleeping, rapid breathing, shortness of breath. And who wouldn't want to sit in their sweatpants in bed and watch contestants york up their breakfast for fun?"

"Oh." And I thought "nearly naked on an ice shelf" was bad. "I'm beginning to suspect Shout is a bit of a sadist. Is there anything we can do about it?"

"Yeah. There's a medicine for high altitude."

"That's great!"

"You bet. We'll need a doctor to prescribe it, a pharmacist to fill it, and we'd have had to start taking it three days ago to do us any good. I'll bet the production crew is all on it. As for you and me, don't worry about it too much. Some people are more susceptible, and you don't know how bad you'll be until you get there. Stay calm. We'll know soon after we land."

After the plane thumped down and came to a halt, Wink stepped through the door to the production section.

"Welcome to Cusco, Peru! We're about to open the doors and depressurize the plane. Take a deep breath!"

36

SKY-HIGH HIJINX

I held Theo's arm as we stood in line for customs. "I can't tell if I'm dizzy, or I'm so sure I'm going to be dizzy that I've made it happen through force of will."

My sentence was too long; I halfway ran out of breath by the end of it.

"That's my effect on you." He smiled. "I have a headache, myself."

"Look at the crew. They're absolutely fine. How can we get some of that medicine?"

The production staff waited happily in line, Luke and the others still carrying their cameras with casual brio. The contestants sat weakly on their luggage. O had a hand on her stomach and had already doubled back to the bathrooms once.

"Not gonna happen. We'll adapt. It takes a few days."

"Days? We'll have our True Love or Double Dud challenge today and be halfway through whatever hell they've got for us before we adapt."

"Or die," he agreed. "We might die."

Knox was in line in front of us. He turned. "Your tone is disturbingly cheerful as you consider expiration."

"Yeah. Just thinking about all the other people who might go toe-up alongside me." Theo gestured with his chin at Alaric, who looked green. Good.

As it happened, we couldn't fit the first challenge in that day because we weren't done traveling yet. Six hours on a bus. Two hours on a train. Apparently, there was no other way into Machu Picchu Pueblo. Not a single paved road.

"Let's be clear," Wink said jovially from the front of the special train car carrying *Cupid's Quest* even deeper into the mountains. "The Inca had roads. Wonders of the world. And they're still in use to this day."

"Why aren't we on them?" Alaric's nausea had been enhanced by the rocking of the train as it ran along the Urubamba River, which was (as far as I could tell) nothing but twists and rapids.

"Because they went everywhere by foot. Actually, they ran a lot. Straight up the mountains and down the other side, on trails so beautifully engineered that the stone staircases are still perfect today, almost six hundred years later. Want to use the Inca highways instead of the train, Alaric?" He smirked at Alaric, who had no snappy reply for once. "Be careful. You might get your wish."

Uh-oh. "That doesn't sound good," I whispered to Rose. She and Paul had seats facing ours across a small table.

"No kidding. If I can get some aspirin, I'll be fine, though. I'm sure."

"I have some in my suitcase. As soon as they return our luggage, I've got your back."

She reached out and squeezed my hand. She lived in Florida, but we'd keep in touch when all this was over. She was a true friend.

By unspoken agreement, we told Luke not to bother retrieving our camera from the hotel room that night; Theo's headache had gotten worse, and I was short of breath. Our lust bowed before our altitude sickness, and we fell into the perfectly normal bed in our perfectly normal hotel room in exhaustion at the end of the day. He pulled me onto his chest, and we both dropped into a deep sleep.

It turned out we were the lucky ones. Both Val and Mason weren't able to sleep, and Alaric was up all night with nausea. Theo and I were among the more cheerful that morning when the bus let us out on the side of a nearly empty road.

"Let's come over here," Wink shouted. No problems with *his* breathing. "Come on. These buses go up and down the mountain pretty regularly, taking people up to Machu Picchu, and we don't want to get in their way. Everyone here? Everyone have your camel packs with water? Camera operators, do your contestants all have their GoPros on?" Luke and the others had fitted us with the same GoPro cameras on headbands we'd used on the Tokyo trains. That was ominous.

"Okay, here we are at the foot of the mountain. You can see the road right up there." A green bus was coming through the trees. It lumbered down the road, heading back to the town.

"Let's be clear," Nick called. "What's on top of that cliff?"

Wink nodded, pleased to have the opening. "The fabled lost city of the Inca, Machu Picchu." He gave us a history lesson that wasn't as complete as Theo's phone research. "And the only way up . . . is up." He threw a thumb dramatically to the sky.

"We have to bushwhack up a mountain?" Val looked haggard but determined. Warrior spirit.

"Not at all. I have three different options for you. First, you can flag down any one of these buses. They've all agreed to stop for you if that's your choice. But be aware they won't let you off until the top. And if you arrive by bus, you'll have two penalties. First, you'll get the Double-Dud accommodations—a rough cabin behind the hotel. It has an electric heater and a lot of drafts. Oh, and I'm told there's an outhouse."

A general murmur of discontent rippled through our group.

"That's for one lucky couple. Four pairs will get a nice hotel room at the only hotel at the entrance to Machu Picchu. And the first couple up who comes under their own power will get a suite. It's nice. A bedroom and a sitting area. A perfectly normal bathroom."

He paused dramatically. "Something's coming," Knox whispered. Theo nodded.

"And oh, by the way. The room is sealed and pumped with oxygen." Wink looked like someone had given him cupcakes, and rightly so. An oxygen-rich room. Oh, bliss.

"Hang on," Euphoria called. "You said there were two penalties for taking the bus."

"Right. I did, didn't I? The second penalty is that if you don't climb up on your own, it will take you longer to adapt to the altitude. And the *Cupid's Quest* challenge is going to be easier if you can breathe. Got me?"

"Christ." Alaric's arrogance had finally faded.

"Call on the gods of your choice," Wink said genially. "Now. Your second option is to *walk* the bus route up this mountain, across terrain so steep that you'll go through thirteen switchbacks. It'll be a hike. Challenge your breathing. But you can do it."

"Or?" Jane-Alice was wearing her many-pocketed vest. She looked disturbingly refreshed.

"Or you can do it the Inca way. Take the stairs."

Wink pointed at bushes growing at the foot of a steep embankment on the side of the road. We peered closer. A stone projected out of the side of the slope. About ten inches above it, a second stone *did* make a sort of staircase.

"Holy shit." That was Paul, whom I'd never heard swear before. "That's a staircase?"

"All the way up. And it's pretty much a straight line," Wink said. "A little wandering, but it's definitely the fastest route."

"How far up?" Val eyed the stones.

"Not bad. Only about thirteen hundred feet."

"Piece of cake," Jane-Alice said stoutly. "Just an ancient StairMaster."

"You can get to the top as fast as you like, but you can't win until your partner is with you. In this case, you're as strong as your weakest link."

Jane-Alice glared at Knox, who held his hands up. *Hey. I'll do my best.*

"I'll carry him if I have to," she said. She had balls; I had to give her credit. Knox pretended he was going to climb on her back, and we laughed.

"Any questions? Okay. See you at the top!"

Wink, the rat bastard, climbed onto the bus, followed by Julie, who waved hopefully to us, and every single camera operator, all of them grinning. Off they went in an assault of diesel.

We were on our own.

"Well, let's go," Val said. She headed for the stairs, but Jane-Alice pushed past her.

"Come on, Knox. At least try to keep up with me."

Val eyed Jane-Alice thoughtfully but let her go. Val's partner, Alaric, was on his feet, but every line of him drooped. He wasn't doing well.

Theo turned to me. "What do you think?"

A second bus was coming down the hill, traveling across where it looked like the stair went. "I'm betting that road is built around the route of the stairs. Can we try going up the stairs? If we come to the road, we'll know. And when the stairs get too hard, we can walk the road until it doubles back and comes to the stairs again?"

"Why do you sound like that's a question? Sounds like a plan to me." Theo held out his arm as if he was escorting me to a ball.

"Let's do that too," Rose said to Paul, who duplicated Theo's move. Rose and I both walked to the start of the Inca staircase, clinging to the elbows of our menfolk and giggling at the absurdity of it.

Wink was right about the stairs being in perfect shape, but he'd left out the part about the Inca not being much interested in regularity. One step might be three inches above the other; the next might be ten. There was no chance of falling into the mindless repetition of Jane-Alice's StairMaster.

And I was panting for air by the fifth step. Asthma, I thought. A little like this.

It came as a relief when the long length of Theo's thigh stopped in my face. "What's up?" I gasped.

"Hang on," he said. "Rose and Paul stopped. What? Oh. Alaric needs a rest. Mason is with him."

"I'll bet Val is too." I knew Val wouldn't outstrip her partner, even if he was a colossal asshole. I passed the word back to O and Nick, the last pair in our daisy chain.

The rest was nice—and then it was annoying. I was standing on an outstretched stone above a drop of some fifteen feet to the treetops growing on the steep slope. The staircase had survived for centuries. Surely it wouldn't collapse on me now?

We got moving at last. Slowly. I was surprised to realize I could have gone faster. A little faster. Theo had the same thought.

"We need to get past Alaric somehow," he murmured to me as I clung to a convenient tree trunk.

"Agreed."

That actually worked out because, as I'd hoped, we'd climbed up to the bus road, where Alaric now sat by the side of the road, his head hanging. Beside him, Mason was making him drink from his camel pack. Val and Euphoria stood beside the men. Val waved at us from across the road.

"Stairs continue there. Have fun." She smiled, and her

integrity shone out of her. I gave her an impulsive hug. She gave me a wink and a half smile.

"Ready?" I asked Theo.

"Onward."

We ended up ahead of Rose and Paul, both of whom were shorter than us. As challenging as the poorly spaced steps were for me, they were worse for Rose, whose legs weren't as long.

Nick and O were still behind us. That meant the only people ahead of us were Jane-Alice and Knox. That was encouraging.

My thinking shrank to two things: Breathe. Step up.

But Theo put his hand on my arm as I started to cross the road for the fourth time. "Hang on." Rose and Paul stopped to hear him too. O and Nick plodded on and disappeared up the next impossible stone stairs, their heads down.

"They're getting ahead of us," I complained. He'd disturbed my trance.

"Wait. Wink said there were thirteen switchbacks. We've been past three of them. It's a long way up. I say we pace ourselves. Let's walk the bus road and pick the stairs up at the next point."

"But—but they're—"

"They won't for long," he soothed me. "We're not even a third of the way up yet."

God. "Okay. Let's go." Rose and Paul came with us, which made me feel better. At least we had friends with us.

The bus road seemed flat after our ascent, but I was still breathing hard. "Water," Theo said. "Keep drinking."

I sipped from my water bag. I couldn't see that it was doing much good, but it wouldn't hurt.

We found the stairs and managed to make it up two flights before we had to walk again. Theo, king of pattern recognition, predicted our path from there.

"We came up three flights and walked one hairpin. Then we

did two flights and we're on the next hairpin. Next, we'll go up one flight and walk one loop. Then we'll be so worn out, we'll do one flight of stairs and walk two loops. And then the final staircase, and we'll be there."

"Shut up," I said, panting. "Drink some water."

For a while, Rose and Paul fell behind on the stairs and caught up to us on the road. Then they didn't catch up as quickly, and then they were lost somewhere behind us. We passed Nick, who sat with O's head in his lap, about two-thirds of the way up.

"You need help?" I called to them.

"We're good. Just resting."

"Fuck that," O said. "I'm waiting for a bus." But her voice had far too much spirit. I smiled. They were worn, but not out.

"No, you're not," Nick said affectionately.

"Well, maybe not on this stretch of road. But up there, definitely." Her arm shot straight up to the sky, pointing at the mountain above us.

I laughed. Theo reminded them to keep drinking. "Mind if we pass you?" he said, and I beamed at him through my gasping for air.

"On your way," Nick said. "Tell me if you come across Jane-Alice and Knox dead in a tree."

"What's that smile?" Theo asked me as we went on.

I shrugged. "I don't know. That was nice, you asking him if we could pass them."

He made a face. "Don't make a big deal. I'm still a badass."

"Uh-huh. Drink some water, badass."

At one point, I decided I had climbed my last Inca staircase. We could walk the bus road the rest of the way; I was done with this. Theo reached back and took my hand, helping me up a particularly steep rise. He looked to the side. "Huh," he said mildly.

"What?" I was keeping my head down, concentrating on not

falling, on my leaden thighs, on the gasping dryness of my lungs.

"We're there."

His tone was so calm, I didn't register the words at first. Then I looked up. There was a large structure up the hill, along the road, and past a long line of buses. A banner reading "Cupid's Quest" stretched over the walkway.

Sitting on the side of the road, just before the banner, were Jane-Alice and Knox.

"It's about fucking time," she said. "Could you hurry it up? I want to pee."

"What?" My brain was too foggy. I couldn't make sense of what I was seeing.

"What are you doing?" Theo asked. "Go check in. You win."

"Sure I do," Jane-Alice said sarcastically. "I win the worst possible reward in the history of the game."

Theo came to a halt next to them. He put his hands on his hips and stretched his spine. "You figured it out too?"

"What?" I said, still confused.

"Of course." Jane-Alice was contemptuous. "Like I'd ever get all this way in this altitude and then blow it by going into a room with extra oxygen. You'd have to be a damn fool."

"Oxygen," I said mournfully. "Oxygen?"

Theo put his arm around my shoulder. "Let's sit, shall we?"

"What? Now? But—right there—"

"I know. But we don't want to win. All we want is to not come in last. Come on, have a seat."

Nothing had ever felt as good as that pavement I sat on. Every muscle cried out in relief. I leaned my head on Theo's shoulder and sighed happily. He linked our fingers together as we waited.

Rose and Paul were next, coming up the road and talking as they gasped. We explained what we were doing, and they pulled over too.

Nick and O said they were fond of sitting on the shoulder of a road, and they plopped down next to Rose and Paul. We were strung out in a long line, and after a while, Wink and Julie came down the road to stare at us.

"What are you doing? You're about ten feet from the top."

"We know," Knox said. "We're waiting. What would you do if all twelve of us crossed the line at the exact same time?"

"Jesus. It's a rebellion." Wink scurried back up the hill, followed by a grinning Julie. She was talking nonstop into the headset. No breathing problems for her.

Almost a full hour later (Jane-Alice whining the whole time about having to pee), a bedraggled quartet appeared around the final corner. Mason had gotten under one of Alaric's arms, and Euphoria was under the other. They walked him slowly up the road with Val taking point.

When they reached us, Alaric squinted. "What the fuck is this," he said bravely.

"Welcoming reception," Knox said. "Anyone have any trouble if we have a winner?"

Theo shook his head. "As long as there's no loser."

"Okay," Knox said to Val. "Can you get him the last ten feet?"

Val looked strong. She eyed us each slowly and then nodded to Knox. "You never know who'll be affected by altitude sickness," he said.

Val replaced Euphoria, and Mason stepped back. "Thanks, you guys." Val spoke to Mason and Euphoria, but she swept her eyes along our row, and we knew what she meant.

"You're still an asshole, Alaric," Knox called cheerfully as the pair staggered up the hill.

"I know," Alaric groaned.

Val got him under the banner, and two of the camera guys came forward to get Alaric into the oxygenated room.

The ten remaining contestants stood and stretched and

adjusted their packs and GoPros and the seat of their trousers, unsure of what to do next.

"Hold hands?" I suggested. "All ten of us across the line together?"

There was a pause, and then hands found hands. We walked up the road in a line, one of the green tour buses forced to crawl along behind us at our pace.

"Hi," I said weakly to Wink as we paused at the banner and then all stepped forward together. "No losers today. Unless all ten of us have to go to the cabin."

Wink shook his head. "We got an extra room. No Double Dud today. You guys are ruining the strategy."

"It's great drama, though, huh?" Theo's grin was irrepressible, and even Wink had to agree.

"Go on," he said. "Julie has your room keys. We'll meet for dinner at six. Rest up. You're going to need it."

We were moving toward the hotel in a grateful huddle when Nick stopped, blocking our forward progress.

"Nick," Paul said. "Let's get going."

"Hold on," Nick said. "Look at that bus over there. What's that?"

"Huh?"

"What?"

"Which one?"

"That one. The one with the blacked-out windows. What's that all about?"

37

BREATH OF LIFE

We found out about the blacked-out bus the next morning, when we stood before Wink outside the gate to the Machu Picchu ruins.

"Thank you all for staying in your rooms until now. We needed time to set up the *Cupid's Quest* challenge."

"Nice to sleep late!" Alaric called. He looked better and had clearly decided to be as full of bluster as possible to make up for yesterday's weakness. Val, at his side, looked grim. Euphoria had whispered to me that Val had slept on the floor of Euphoria's room with Mason, so she wouldn't lose any adaptations her body had made to the altitude.

"Glad you enjoyed your morning lie-in," Wink called back. "All right. Here are your maps of Machu Picchu. Everyone have one? Good. You're going to want to study them because there are treasures within for each of you."

"Inca gold?" Rose called.

"Better! How about Florida gold, Rose?" She looked confused, as did we all. What was Florida gold? "How'd you like to come across gold named Eloise? And maybe Wendy?"

Rose screamed, her face lighting up. "My mom! And my

bestie! They're in there?" She darted forward, ready to run through the gate, but Wink held up a hand.

"Hang on."

A flicker of panic came to life in me—below my heart, above my stomach. I was able to think about it quite calmly in a distant, walled-off safe room in my skull. Family members? Hidden somewhere in Machu Picchu? At an extremely high altitude?

Wink was talking. "It's not just Rose's loved ones who came up the mountain last night. O, your sister and brother. Mason, your parents. Theo, two brothers who say they can't wait to wrestle you to the ground. And now they're hiding somewhere in there."

"Wink," I gasped. "My mother? My sister?"

"That's right, Joss. Frieda and Claire. They're—"

"My sister has crippling asthma, you asshole! No, let go—I have to find them!"

Luke had to join Theo in holding me. I fought them like I was being abducted. Wink tried to calm me, but I couldn't contain the horror I felt until Wink held up a small canister.

"Joss. Joss, listen to me. I have an oxygen canister for each of you. You can use it yourself, or you can share it with your loved ones. Joss, settle down!"

My face was wet. Apparently, I was crying. "Give me the air!"

Theo grabbed me around the waist. "Wait!" he roared in my ear, loud enough to break through my panic.

That was when Wink lost control of the gathering.

Theo turned, still with his arm wrapped around my waist. "Everyone! Lean in!"

Not only did every contestant turn to him, but so did every camera. A cluster of interested tourists who recognized us had built up behind us, and they leaned in to hear too.

"I'm going to let you go, Joss. Give me two minutes to plan. Stay here with me. Will you?"

He was so certain, so sure of himself. It calmed me. "I hear you."

"Okay." He unfolded his map and knelt, flattening it on the stones of the plaza. "Val and Alaric, Mason and Euphoria, and Paul and Rose take the lower area. Here." He made a circle with his finger on the map. "Joss and I are going up here with Jane-Alice and Knox and O and Nick. Spread out. Don't stay together. Look everywhere."

"What do we do if we find them?" Rose asked.

"We use these guys." Theo flung a thumb at Nessa, who was kneeling to get her camera in his face. "You find anyone's parents, you send them here to the main gate to wait for us. And you tell your camera operator."

Wink was listening and didn't like that. "Now, wait—"

Theo ignored him. He looked at Nessa, and then at Luke. "You'll help us, won't you? You've got radios."

Luke looked at Shout and Wink. He and Nessa exchanged raised eyebrows, and then Luke looked at me. He had to agree. He had to. Pleading poured out of me, too large for words.

"Yeah," he said. "We'll help."

Wink threw his hands into the air and turned away.

O interrupted. "Once we find them, my brother and sister will want to help in the search. Can they?"

Theo grinned at her. "They can, but if they find anyone, they have to tell a camera operator. Anyone in the crowd, you can do the same." The various tourists grinned, and some translated for the others. "You guys"—he turned to the cameras, most of whom were now grinning—"are going to be our communications relay. Right? Okay, we're working under emergency conditions here, so the first person to find Joss's sister gives her the oxygen, right? Anyone else in need, we'll stick them in Alaric's room when we get back, but right off the bat, it's oxygen for the sister. What's her name again?"

"Claire," I gasped, tightness in my chest overwhelming me. "She's only twenty. Long blonde hair. *She can't breathe.*"

"It's okay. We're going to find her. Anyone need anything? No? Move, Wink. We're leaving."

The flood of people threatened to overwhelm the gate attendants, who gave up any sense of normalcy and waved us through, at least two of them shouting our names in excitement as we passed. We had fans in Peru too. Not that I cared.

"Up, Joss. Turn here. We go up." Theo was still behind me. I flew up stairs no more regular than the ones I'd climbed yesterday, but this time, my panting for air was just background noise. Claire. I had to get to Claire. Could my mother take care of her before I got there with the oxygen?

At the top of the cliff, I turned in indecision. Right? Left? Ahead? Theo arrived behind me and pushed Luke aside to take a moment to pull me into his arms.

"When she can't breathe, Theo—oh god, it's horrible. And up here, I just don't—oh!" I was panting and crying, my eyes darting everywhere to find them.

He soothed me as Jane-Alice and Knox made it to the top with Danika and Jane-Alice's camera guy. In that still, calm safe room in my head, I had the time to remember that her camera man's name was Bingo. Funny name. How humorous names are. Was I going into shock?

"Go that way," Theo told them. "Nick, you and O go there. Joss and I are heading over here."

He took my hand, and we raced along a wall, terraces of grass stretching up on one side and stepping down the hill on the other.

Machu Picchu was built on a saddle of land between two mountain peaks. The earth fell away on all sides, down to the

Urubamba snaking its silver way along its course. The site was dazzling.

I couldn't have cared less.

A report crackled through Luke's radio. Paul found Alaric's golfing buddies in the Temple of the Sun. Both of them had agreed to join the search.

Good. That was good.

Theo and I raced along the terraces until we reached a straight drop to death in the river below. "Go left," he said. "Be careful. Take care of her, Luke. I'll go right."

I grabbed his hand briefly in grateful thanks and followed the path. I sobbed when my path dead-ended at a wall of rock.

"Joss," Luke said. "Calm down. They'll be okay, I'm sure."

"Did you see them?" I asked him. "When they came in last night? Was she okay?"

"I'm sorry, I didn't see anyone. But I'm sure she's fine. They wouldn't let her be—Joss, slow down."

"I have to find her!" I caught up with Theo, who was ruthlessly violating signs to not walk (or climb) around a building called the House of the Guardians. No one home.

Nick's parents were found outside the Royal Tomb, and Jane-Alice found her own parents sitting on a terrace with their feet dangling over the edge. Good, that's good, I thought abstractly. People are being found. It won't be long now.

One of Theo's brothers grabbed the radio and blew a Bronx cheer at his brother when Tark and Senny were found in the Prisoner's Area. Theo laughed and borrowed Nessa's radio long enough to return the salute.

Euphoria's mother and aunt. Rose's mother and best friend. Knox's parents. They were all being found, and I was glad.

And angry. Where was Claire? Why couldn't I find her? The event was taking on a nightmarish quality where I could run but get nowhere, scream yet make no sound.

"Hang on," Theo said. "We'll find them."

He hadn't gone to find his brothers, for which I was swamped with desperate gratitude.

Mason's parents. Paul's were found sitting on a bench in the sun at the Intihuatana, whatever that was. O's brother and sister were the final pair to be discovered.

Where were my mother and Claire?

We met Mason and Euphoria at the City Gate. The top part and the lower part had been searched. Where was Claire? The place was too large. I screamed her name in desperation, and the mountains absorbed the sound.

"It's okay," Theo said, but his forehead was wrinkled. "What have we missed? We've been everywhere. Even the tourists are helping. What am I not seeing? What's the pattern?"

Terraces stepped down the mountain to where they disappeared over the edge. Grass. Stone. Sky. Mountain. Everyone was now looking.

"What are those buildings over there?" I asked.

"Where?"

"Way over there. At the end of this terrace." A trio of stone buildings stepped down the mountain, perfect triangular roofs creating a geometric progression. "What are those?"

Theo looked. "I don't know. They're not on the map. And there's that fence—Joss! Wait!"

I was gone, flying along the terrace to the highest building. I heard the shout of the park guard, but he wasn't going to catch me before I got there.

The top one was empty—just a chill, dark place filled with shadow and time. I scrambled to half climb, half fall down the wall to the next terrace. That hut was empty too.

Claire and my mother were sitting on folding chairs in the third one, laughing and clapping their hands when I stumbled in the door and fell, my arms reaching around Claire's knees.

"You found us!" Claire laughed. "I knew you would! Here we are—in Peru! Isn't this a good hiding place?"

With his camera, Luke couldn't fall down the walls as I had, so I'd outpaced him. He arrived too late to see me collapse. But I was still on my knees, drying my tears on Claire's jeans, when he appeared in the doorway. Theo almost picked up Luke to get him out of the way so Theo could drop to the floor by me.

He wrapped an arm around me, and I transferred my hysterics to Theo's chest.

I heard him talking to my mother, Claire, and the uniformed man who had been waiting with them, unused oxygen canisters at his side.

"Joss," Claire said, "get a grip. Come on. I'm fine. We're both fine. Aren't we, Mom?"

By the time I got control of myself, the hut was full. Nessa was back to filming Theo, and Wink had arrived, Julie at his shoulder, narrating so Shout knew what was going on. A distant cheer went up from all over Machu Picchu when Luke used his radio to announce I'd found my family.

I came out of Theo's embrace with a huge smile to balance my tear-streaked, sweaty face. I hugged my sister and mother, and the mountain applauded when we came out of the hut. Mom and Claire waved excitedly to their adoring fans.

"This is really fun!" Claire cooed. "This is the best show!"

Theo looked at her oddly, but I had Claire in one hand and Mom in the other, and I wasn't letting go.

"We can put you in Alaric's room," I said. "He's got oxygen. Are you okay? Can you breathe? Mom, are you good? How do you feel?"

"We're fine, Jossie. Slow down. There's no need to hurry. Isn't this place incredible?"

"How are you doing so well? Claire, what about your asthma?"

"Well," she said, linking her arm with mine, "the show sent us this medicine. We've been taking it for days now. I feel really good."

"You do?" My heart swelled. "Should we get Dr. Milford to prescribe it all the time? If it helps?"

"Don't be silly, Jossie." My mother waved her hand. "It only works above about eight thousand feet. Do you want us to move to Machu Picchu?" She and Claire went off in gales of laughter.

"I'm so glad you're here! So glad you're happy. Oh! Mom!" I stopped, and the cluster of people behind me had to back up. "I want you to meet Theo! He's my—um—"

"I know," she said. "I watch the show. You're engaged. So, Theo, you know my daughter will need someone to take care of her. Can you do that?"

"Mom, I take care of myself."

"Let him answer."

Luke and Nessa had both squirmed past us to record this drama.

Theo bowed. "Yes, Mrs. Joss's Mother. It's my plan to take very good care of her."

Mom smiled. She'd always appreciated a handsome man. "It's Buckley," she said. "Frieda Buckley. The girls are O'Neils, but I took my maiden name back when I divorced their father."

Theo offered her his arm with a naughty wink, and she dimpled and took it. They led us back to the main ruins.

"You know, Theo, Joss does a lot for her family."

"I've heard," he said, and I realized I didn't want to listen to any more of this conversation if I could help it.

"How was your trip here?" I asked Claire. "Do you have enough inhalers? What did the doctor say when you told him you wanted to take a trip?"

"The trip, omigawd, it was so long. You can't imagine. We were on one of the planes for twelve hours!"

I had to smile. That was a quick hop for me these days. "I'm so glad you're here. I want you to meet Rose. She's going to be our best friend."

"I like Rose," Claire said. "But I really want to meet Alaric. He's so damn cute!"

"Come on—you've seen how annoying he is!"

"I don't want to marry him!" Claire giggled. "Just look at him."

"He is cute," I allowed. We walked back to the main entrance, where everyone had gathered with their families. I was filled with gratitude and relief. The crisis had been averted.

But—

I searched for the reason for my unease, and it came when we got back to the gate before lunchtime.

"Was that it?" O asked, her younger sister leaning on her. "Don't these challenges usually take three days?"

"Well, four," Knox corrected, standing between his parents. His mother's hair was as red as his. "Since Theo did the shortcut in Australia. But we took an extra day to travel here, so . . . is this challenge over?"

Wink strode up. "You're right to wonder. The challenge is far from over!"

38

TEMPLE OF THE MOON

"This is crazy," I said. "Are you okay?"

My mother was taking a breather on the steps. We were maybe a third of the way up Huayna Picchu, the pyramid-shaped mountaintop at the far end of Machu Picchu.

"We haven't even gotten to the good part yet," Mom said. "I'm just pacing myself."

"Smart thinking." Theo grinned. He and Frieda were getting along. I was afraid she was flirting with him too much, but he'd said not to worry about it.

"Are you coming?" Claire stuck her head over the wall from above. She'd made it to the next terrace, which had been carved into the side of the mountain by ancient peoples. Great engineers, but not so good when it came to fending off invading Spaniards and their diseases.

"Slow down, Claire. I grabbed the extra inhaler from your room. Do you need it?" I was concerned. Her cheeks were unnaturally flushed and red. She was getting overexcited.

"Yeah, no. I just took a puff. I'm fine."

"You're sure?"

"Get up here. Those guys are ahead of us. I need that wardrobe!"

The guys she was referring to were Theo's brothers. Neither was as tall as their big brother, but both were strong and bright-eyed. The altitude wasn't bothering them at all. That medicine must be great.

I wished I had some.

"Want a hand, Frieda?" Theo edged past me on the tiny stairs, and I pressed against the wall to let him by. The fall was only ten or fifteen feet to the next terrace, but it still wouldn't have felt good.

"I suppose you could boost me, Theo." She stuck her butt out at him with a giggle. Horrifying. I rolled my eyes and looked up in time to see that Luke had captured the whole exchange. Of course he was above me, looking down.

He, too, had the altitude medicine. Damn it.

Theo kept his hands off his theoretical future mother-in-law but got her going just the same. When I made it to the terrace, Claire was already at the other end, making her way up the next staircase. She turned and saw me looking. I sighed in relief when she waved her inhaler at me.

Don't drop it. It's a long way down, I thought.

My mother linked her arm with mine as we walked across the grass. "What's twenty-five thousand dollars divided by three, Jossie?"

"Um—" I was trying to do it, but why bother with the human calculator right behind us?

"That's $8,333.33. Planning your wardrobe, Frieda?"

"That's all?" She frowned. "Jossie, you don't like baby alpaca, do you?"

Wink had introduced the week's sponsor that morning before outlining the rest of the challenge. Kuna was a Peruvian company that specialized in luxurious fashions made of the softest baby alpaca ("Warmer, softer, and more exclusive than the finest cashmere"), and they were offering a twenty-five-thousand-dollar shopping spree to the family that completed the challenge first.

"That's the family—not the pair," Wink had clarified. "Theo, you can let go of Joss for a few minutes on this one."

Both my mother and sister had decided they wanted that shopping spree, and now Claire thought she was a mountain goat. She would have an asthma attack right there on the side of a cliff. Maybe they could land a helicopter around here. Somewhere.

Voices called from above us, and we looked up. Tark and Senny were leaning over a drop, a good forty or fifty feet above us. They were flying up the climb.

"Theo! Get your ass up here! I'm gonna get that long coat. I'd look good in that coat."

His brother hit him. "You'd look like a pimp in that coat. Theo, he wants the mustard-colored one!"

"Blue, you asshole. I want the blue."

"You're the asshole. No, Theo's the asshole. What are you doing down there, man? We need to win this. I can get one of those tight angora sweaters for Kitty."

"Angora's a rabbit, you moron. Alpaca—it's like a llama."

"Don't call me a moron."

Theo was uninterested. "Don't wrestle up there. Keep going. I'll catch up."

"Hurry up! Remember, we have to go up to the top and down the trail on the other side to the Temple of the Moon!"

"Grand Cavern, not Temple of the Moon. You really are simplistic."

"Knock it off. Which one, Theo?"

"Both, you potatoes. Temple of the Moon and then the

Grand Cavern and then keep following the trail until you get back to the start."

"All three of us have to cross the finish line before we win. Get your ass in gear. Two more teams are behind you, you know."

"Quit yelling at me. Get a move on. I'll meet you."

"Yeah, after you finish helping the ladies over the nasty old mountain. Sorry, Joss."

I already liked Joss's brothers, and they weren't wrong. Theo was voluntarily hanging back to help me with Mom and Claire, and I was grateful. "No prob," I called up to them. "Don't fall off the trail."

"Right. Like that'll happen. C'mon, Senny. Race you to the top."

Half an hour later, I demanded that Claire take a break. She was still flushed and eager. Her color didn't look good.

But she peered over the side to appraise us of what she saw.

"So, Theo's brothers are the only ones in front of us. You'll stay with us, won't you, Theo?" When she blinked at him soulfully, Theo laughed at her. "I really want those clothes, you know. And you and Joss are going to get married, and you'll be my brother-in-law. You want me to be happy, right? I need that new wardrobe."

Mom nudged her. "What about me? We're splitting the spree, right?"

Claire thought about it. "You can borrow some of my stuff. If you don't stretch it. Jane-Alice is still coming along. Her mother looks like she could cross the plains in a Conestoga wagon, but the mom's boyfriend—he's old. I'll bet he doesn't make it."

"Jane-Alice will give him a piggyback," Theo commented dryly.

"Maybe. I wouldn't. He smells like funky peppermint. I sat

across the aisle from him on the bus. Yuck. The only other group still trying is gorgeous Alaric and that hottie who met him is way out in front of them. What's the story there?"

"Alaric has altitude sickness," I said. "We can have compassion for him, can't we?"

"We can have compassion for that hair. But it looks like he's hanging out with the other buddy. He's not breathing hard or anything."

I stood from my boulder and peered over the edge with her. "Where?"

"Down there. See? Red jacket?"

"Huh. He looks better. The other guy doesn't look too happy, though."

The puzzle was solved when one of Alaric's business partners strolled past Jane-Alice and her family and caught up with us.

"I don't know what you did to Alaric," he said to me, "but he's helping Carson. Go figure. This is a good workout, huh? Mind if I pass you guys?"

"What's the matter with Carson?" I called as he went bounding up the mountain in Gore-Tex and other kinds of high-tech performance gear.

"Discovered he's afraid of heights. Wow. He's not going to make it past this turn. Well, see you at the end!"

We came around the turn and discovered the staircase had now left the terraces. Now it clung to the wall, curving out of sight around the living rock. On one side of the step was the carefully joined wall to the top.

On the other was emptiness. A fall from the stairs would end in a thousand-foot fall to the river far below.

"Oh, Christ," I said. "Claire, don't go any further."

"I'm fine," she insisted, already crawling out along the stones. "Come on. It's held up this long."

"Mom? You good?"

"Baby alpaca is absolutely the most luxurious fabric. Keep that in mind. I'm coming, Claire."

"Whatever," Claire called back. Mom hustled to catch up, leaving Theo and me alone at the foot of a "staircase" that was little more than a ladder.

Theo turned to me. "Just want to make sure you know—there's nothing wrong with your sister. Except greed, maybe."

"Stop. You don't know them."

"Big Eyes, come on. Are you serious? She doesn't even have asthma."

"She has terrible asthma." My frustration grew. "You should see her when she has an attack. It's horrifying. I need to catch up to her."

"Joss," he called, but I was already inching up the stairs. I refused to acknowledge him, so he came after me with a sigh. "Damn. This is high."

"Don't look."

The journey was alarming enough—until I realized the staircase was a two-way highway, and the tourists who had climbed to the top to see the sunrise had now decided to come down this way instead of making the loop. We had to pass on the stairs, clutching each other as we went up and they went down. My stomach fell into my crotch, nerves tingling in electric terror.

If only I could draw a full breath.

We crept through a cloud, and the stone got slippery. Then we climbed above the cloud, and I looked down at the fog Luke was rising from. He was doing the same thing we were, but with a large, heavy camera perched on his shoulder. What a very strange, very scary experience.

We made it to the top at last, where I collapsed, shivering slightly, on a low stone.

Claire was still standing, hands on her hips, surveying the

astonishing mountain range that spooled out all around us. She seemed so vibrant. So alive.

She *was* sick, wasn't she?

Of course she was. It was the altitude medication that was helping her. Back home, her attacks were so bad, she couldn't even go grocery shopping. Watching her endure suffocation was worse than living through it myself. I checked my pocket. Yes, I still had her inhaler. When she needed it, I'd be ready.

Mom was tired, but she was proud as she looked back down on Machu Picchu. "I think I can see where the others are. It's amazing to me that only four of the twelve contestants bothered to make the climb. What wimps."

"Well, Mom, most of them have elderly parents down there."

"I'm an elderly parent. I made it. For you. I did it for you."

"And for the sweaters," Claire added.

I laughed and put an arm around each of them. "Well, you're sturdier stock than them."

"Or you want the sweaters more," Theo said. I swatted lightly at his stomach, but neither Mom nor Claire seemed to mind.

"That woman from Kuna—her skirt was exquisite."

"I saw." Claire nodded at Mom's statement. "I'd look really good in that skirt."

"I would too. We'll get two."

"We'll see," Claire said, which made Theo laugh.

"Feeling an asthma attack coming on, Claire?"

She glared at him, which made two of us. "Stop it," I whispered. "Leave her alone."

He pulled me further up the path, followed by Nessa and Luke. "Why won't you see it? They're using you. I'm pretty sure they've been using you for years. Probably since your father left."

"Stop it! You don't know what you're talking about. They need me. I take care of them."

"And they like that, don't they? I'll bet."

I wasn't going to listen to this. I had not wasted my life caring for them. I had devoted myself to the care and comfort of people I loved. That was enough.

I turned from Theo and went back to Mom and Claire, and he didn't speak again.

"The path down the other side is over here," I said. "Ready?"

"Finally! Come on—let's go. Looks like Jane-Alice has reached the stairs." Claire was off like a shot.

It was the altitude medication.

Even Mom had a spring in her step.

There were no more terrifying stairs with drops to death below them, but I learned pretty quickly that as hard as it was to climb up, it was every bit as hard to climb down a steep slope. Even Luke and Nessa were panting by the time we got to the Temple of the Moon. (Without someone there to tell us what we were looking at, the name was the most interesting thing about it.)

The path wound down and around and to a second cave. We took another break here, and again, Claire was eager to go on.

Just the medicine.

She hadn't been using me.

Terrible, crushing asthma.

Theo watched me as I watched my mother and sister. He reached out to hold my hand, but I couldn't take it. I swatted him away. "Joss?" His concern turned to a frown.

"I'm fine." I wasn't fine.

"Can't hear the truth, huh?"

"Stop." I turned away.

He was silent, then he came up behind me. "You'd choose them over me, wouldn't you?"

I wheeled around, slightly dizzy. "That's my *sister*. My *mother*. I've known you for about a month, Theo. Who would *you* choose?"

He was frozen for a moment, and then the skin on his forehead tightened. He nodded with raised eyebrows. "Who, indeed?" He turned to my mother and sister. "The path seems to be okay from here on, so I'll be on my way. See you back at the hotel."

In three long strides, he passed out of the clearing, a surprised Nessa scurrying to keep up.

"Theo!" But the cry of desperation didn't come from my mouth. Not from my heart. It was my sister who called out. "Don't go without me! I have to be first! Wait—Theo!"

She raced out after him. Luke looked back at me, wondering what I would do.

I sighed and helped my mother up. "Ready?"

She let me lead her. "If Theo crosses to meet his brothers, we'll never win that wardrobe. You should call him back, Joss. He'd come if you called. Go ahead. Call him. Just shout. He's still close enough to hear you."

I shook my head. "Let's go. I'd like to get back to the hotel before Claire has an attack."

The final stretch of the trail wasn't that bad. We'd apparently descended lower than Machu Picchu, so the path went uphill. Ancient stone stairs made the climb easier when the path got steep, and when we made it back, the celebration was already over. Claire sat in a huff by the trailhead, angry with us for taking so long.

"I hope you know we lost," she said. "Now those beefcake boys are going to be wearing baby alpaca dusters to their ankles, like a trio of idiots. I swear, I don't even know why I came on this trip. Thanks a lot, Joss."

I bit my tongue and led them both back to the hotel, where I got them settled and went to my room. Theo had come and gone, so I took a shower in peace.

I would have to make it up to him.

If I even wanted to.

I twisted the ring on my finger. Was this really the guy I was supposed to be engaged to?

39

THE FAMILY CAR TRIP

At the end of a long day, Theo and I met back in our room. He closed the door behind him but wouldn't look at me. I stood by the window, my arms crossed over my stomach. Too tense to sit. "Are you still mad at me?" I asked him.

Emotions flitted over his face faster than I could read. "I'm not mad at you." He sat at the desk to unlace his boots.

The silence shrieked along my nerves. "Well, what, then?"

He shrugged, putting his boots under the desk. He looked at me as he sat back. "I can't be mad at you, Joss. Your kindness is what attracted me to you in the first place. How can I be mad now because you're kind to your family?"

The words were right, but the tone was . . . final. We weren't having a discussion. We were having an ending.

"Yeah?" I said, hoping he'd give me something more to work with.

He stretched back in the chair and rubbed his hands over his head. Ghosts of the soft bristles he was feeling prickled at my empty palms. "You are who you are, Joss, and that's wonderful. I've always done better as a lone actor. I'm not the partner type. Every time, something reminds me of why it's better for me to only rely on myself."

Roll the closing credits. Bring down the curtain. My romance had turned into a tragedy. Blood from my shoulders to my toes threatened to burst out of me from the pressure. "But this is a couples' show. A partners' thing. You can't go it alone, Theo."

He stood suddenly, startling me, and untucked his shirt. "Don't look so upset. We're still partners for the show. I'm going to grab a shower."

"But—wait. What about me? Um—us? Are we—" I looked at my hand, at the ring he'd put on it, and found the courage to ask the question. "Are we still engaged?"

"For the show? Definitely. For us? For you and me?" He paused in the doorway to the bathroom. "Why don't we just relax and see how this goes? That good with you?"

All my protests—all my determination to make him see how fragile Claire was and how frail my mother was—dried up. He looked unhappy but resolute. My Theo Fever had broken, and all the reasons why it would be insane to marry him flooded in. "I suppose that's best. We got into this pretty quickly, after all."

He swallowed, not looking at me, and then nodded. "Yeah. You want the bathroom first?"

"I'm good." Even though I wasn't.

We slept side by side that night, legs straight and not tangled together. Hands empty. Skin unstroked. By the time Luke came in at midnight for the camera, I could have told him it didn't matter.

We weren't going to need our privacy this time.

The next day, seven large passenger vans were parked outside the train station. "No buses back to Cusco?" Euphoria asked.

Wink explained, "We thought it would be fun for you all to have a little extra time with your families."

"And your cameras," Alaric said dryly. "Because no family has ever gotten into drama on a six-hour car trip."

Nervously, I looked to Theo, my support. My rock. My partner. He smiled at me as if we didn't know each other well. As if he didn't know what my inner thighs tasted like. As if I didn't know every muscle of his back.

Wink and the camera teams made sure everyone had a mic pack, and one camera operator sat in the front seat next to the driver while the other sat in the back row. Our loving family journey would be well-recorded.

Claire pushed Mom and me into the first row of seats so she could drag Theo's brother into the middle row with her. That left Luke, Theo, and the other brother to the back row. Theo was, I noticed, as physically far from me as he could get.

The long string of vans pulled out, driving us through the stone town of Ollantaytambo. Claire, however, wasn't interested.

"So, Senny," she said.

He interrupted. "I'm Tark. That's Senny."

"Oh gosh, I'm so sorry! So, Tark, who's going to help you wear all that alpaca you guys won? Is there a missus at home?"

"A girlfriend. How old are you?" His voice was suspicious but amused.

"I'll be twenty-one in a few months, and I would look great in that skirt in the Kuna catalog."

"I bet you would."

"My sister and your brother are engaged. That makes us practically family. Isn't that something?"

"I see." Tark sounded entertained. I felt the weight of the ring on my finger. *Was* I still engaged? "And I should want my sister to be well-dressed, is that it?"

"And your mother-in-law," Mom said from in front of him. "Well, your brother's mother-in-law."

"Sure. And my girlfriend wouldn't mind at all that I'm spending money on you guys?"

"Your girlfriend will love us. Besides, I can help you pick out something nice for her too. I've been studying that catalog..."

I tuned out Claire's attempt to get baby alpaca out of Tark. If she failed, she could always try Senny.

Under the cover of their banter, Mom turned to me. "Trouble in paradise, huh?"

I shrugged. "I dunno."

"Oh, come on. I saw the last episode, same as you. He asked you to choose him over us, and you stood with us. And now he doesn't love you anymore."

"That's not—"

"No, I watched carefully. It was sweet of you, honey, but stupid. He could be worth a lot of money one day. You'll want to hold on to that one. Unless you think someone else is going to win?"

It was easy to see Nessa's screen from her place in the front seat, so there was no denying the fact that she'd adjusted her focus. She was no longer filming Claire and Tark's banter; she was listening to Mom and me. "I don't want to talk about it," I said to Mom.

Even though I did want to talk about it. I wanted to sort through the puzzle that was Theo with someone. Shouldn't that be my mother?

"You can always try my way," Mom said.

I looked my question to her. She shrugged and made a quiet gesture, as if stroking a pregnant belly.

I was horrified. "Mom!" My god. Had she never loved my father? Had she only wanted to trap him in a marriage? Was she suggesting I trap Theo in the same way?

"I'm just saying," Mom said.

"Please remember you're on camera," I hissed.

"Oh, please. Anybody who hasn't thought the exact same thing is either an idiot or a liar." She was perfectly content to have a camera in her face and an embarrassed daughter at her side.

"I do not want to talk about it," I insisted. "I'm going to take a nap."

I closed my eyes, as far from sleep as possible. Adrenaline and sorrow and anger and depression were rocking my soul boat. How long was this damn ride?

Any pretense of sleeping was useless once Claire discovered all three brothers spoke ancient Greek, taught by their classics father.

"You do not," she said to Tark.

He responded with a slippery string of words that went on and on. Senny joined in from behind him, and they finished their demonstration together.

"What was that?" Claire asked, delighted.

"Plutarch. My namesake. That was my favorite of his."

"What did you say?"

Tark and Senny translated the quote together with the glee and unity that comes from long familiarity. "'I don't need a friend who changes when I change and who nods when I nod. My shadow does that much better.'"

"Oh, nice!" Claire clapped her hands and then turned in her seat to fix her eye on Senny. "Can you do it too?"

"What, you want some Seneca? Okay, here's my favorite quote." Again, the sounds were exotic and slippery. Tark joined in so the two brothers finished together.

"Okay. What's that mean?"

"'Life is very short and anxious for those who forget the past, neglect the present, and fear the future.'"

"Nice quote! I believe that too," Claire said (improbably, I thought; Claire spent little time worrying about her future, save for whether it would include an alpaca skirt). "What about you, Theo? Can you do it too? Theo? Hey, Theo!"

I heard a slap. She'd gotten his attention by swatting his knee. Why was Theo so distant from the conversation?

"What?" he asked.

"Are you listening?" Claire asked.

"To what?"

"To your brothers. They're telling us sayings in ancient Greek."

"My brothers don't speak ancient Greek," he responded immediately, which caused both brothers to round on him and start a flicking war with their fingers. The van driver objected to the sudden descent into violence.

Far from being chastened, all three brothers were now grinning.

"You do one, too, Theo," Claire said. "For your future sister-in-law." I wished she'd stop bringing it up. "From whoever you were named for."

"Can't do that," he said. "My dad never decided which Theophilus he'd named me after. There are too many. Instead, I'll give you my favorite quote from Aristophanes."

"Oh, here we go," Tark groaned.

"In which Theo proves his point about saying we don't speak ancient Greek," Senny agreed. Yet when Theo began his quote, all the brothers joined in—and when pressed, they all translated together.

"'Man is naturally deceitful ever,'" they shouted together, "'in every way!'"

Claire frowned. "Oh, well, that's cheery."

"True, though," Theo said.

"You're such a pessimist."

Theo paused. Perhaps he thought, as I did, that his pessimism had faded over the past few weeks, and that this bleak view of humanity was a throwback to an earlier version of the man. "Yes, I am," he said at last.

I blinked back sudden, hot tears and turned to look out the window, hoping the camera wouldn't catch my reaction.

Once we were all put into our hotel rooms in Cusco, Theo barely spoke to me. When I asked what he was thinking about, he said, "Pattern recognition," and left to meet his brothers in the hotel bar.

I took a nap.

He kissed me absently that night as we got ready for bed, then rolled on his side away from me and went to sleep. I lay awake for long hours, telling myself it was good to find out we weren't compatible now, before anything else happened between us.

The following day was spent filming interviews—all contestants and family members—for the fortieth episode. Theo kept his distance, so I did, too, and refused to answer any questions about my relationship with him. Shout seemed content to let me squirm and get away with not answering.

That evening, the families were flown to Lima for their flights home, to Claire's annoyance. "Obviously, you're going to North America for this leg. You've already been to every other continent. Why can't we fly with you guys?"

But Julie talked at Claire and Mom (and all the other family members) until they were successfully herded onto the bus for the airport.

Saturday was "rest day," in which the camera crews got to have a day off. Instead of sneaking off or renting another hotel room or making love to me in a closet, Theo sat in the room's armchair, lost in thought. He would answer a question if I asked directly but wouldn't speak otherwise.

I tried to reach him once more as we boarded the Arrow. "Theo, are you mad at me? Please tell me."

"I'm thinking, Joss. This is my process."

"But what are you thinking about? Talk to me. You're driving me crazy."

He raised an eyebrow as if just noticing I was there. "Don't worry about it. Give me some space, okay?"

Once he spoke, his eyes went distant again. He wasn't seeing me, even as he was looking at me.

I sat in my own two seats instead of with him. Before we took off, I leaned over and touched his shoulder. "Put on your seat belt, okay?"

His eyes cleared briefly, and he gave me a chilly smile. "Not this time, Big Eyes."

That was a death blow if I ever heard one. Or felt one. Whatever. I'd lost my connection to Theo. We were done.

The other contestants eyed us in confusion. It wasn't as if my estrangement from Theo was a surprise to them—or to anyone who watched the show. The entire debacle had been recorded and broadcast. The world was witness to the melting of my romance.

So, it was stupid of me to be surprised when Wink appeared at the front of the cabin once we were airborne.

"Contestants, can I have your attention? We're going to skip the meeting at the conference table this time in favor of one short announcement."

He eyed us to make sure we were all watching. Eleven of us were. Theo glanced up and then ignored Wink.

"For our final week of competition," Wink said, "we've decided to let you choose your own partners. Talk to each other and find mutually acceptable pairings. You'll give me your decision when we land. That's all."

He left.

We were frozen, poised on the brink of possibly hurting someone else, or increasing our own chances of success, or—in my case—having my heart broken.

Of course they'd put the choice in our hands at the moment

when we knew each other best and could hurt each other the most. It was good drama.

No one moved for a good five minutes. Then Val moved casually back to the galley. With Alaric as a partner, she was one of the ones sure to want a new pairing.

Mason stood and stretched. He and Euphoria had made a pretty good team; she looked startled when he stood. He smiled at her and shook his head reassuringly, but then he headed for the bathrooms.

Movement slowly crept through the cabin. I was still trapped in pained paralysis. Would Theo want to dump me for someone else? Did I want someone else? What was he thinking? Did he even know this was going on?

Not knowing eventually overcame me. I moved across the aisle to lean down to Theo. I touched his shoulder nervously, and he jumped when I interrupted his thinking. "What?" he said shortly.

"Did you hear? New partners?"

"I heard."

"Well... do you want a new partner?"

"Do I? No. Right? I'm working on something here."

I was dismissed.

I stood, my confusion burned away by the embers of anger. Yes, I'd chosen my family over him, but did that give him the right to be so disrespectful to me?

Knox had headed back to the galley. I turned to follow.

40

STRAIGHT TALK

"Are you kidding?" Knox goggled at me. "Joss, sweetie, I'd love to partner with you again. But if you think I'd willingly break up your partnership with Theo—if you think any of us would do it—"

"It's not much of a partnership anymore," I said mournfully. "And you don't want to be stuck with Jane-Alice again, do you?"

"She's not that bad. Anyway, no matter what you think, all of America—hell, the entire world—is rooting for the star-crossed lovers. I can't get in the way of that, Joss. People would throw rotten fruit at me in the streets."

Even in my misery, Knox made me smile. I chuckled. "No, they wouldn't. Besides, it doesn't matter now."

Knox wrapped a hand around me and gave me a one-armed hug. "Why doesn't it matter?"

I gagged up the bitter truth. "Because Theo doesn't want me anymore."

Knox frowned at me. "That's what you think?"

"I know it. He won't talk to me. He won't even look at me. He hates me, Knox."

He paused for a minute and then took my hand. "Come

with me." He walked me down the aisle until we got to Theo. Knox kicked at Theo's outflung foot until Theo looked up. Knox held his hand up, my fingers woven into his. "Joss and I are going to be partners for this last round. Thought you'd like to know."

Adrenaline raced through me, making my fight-or-flight responses kick in. Knox was giving me what I wanted. That was a good thing, right?

Theo didn't move, and yet somehow, he became a predator. His muscles got hard, and his attention focused on Knox with blistering intensity.

All he said was, "No."

But it was terrifying. Knox backed up an involuntary step and then looked at me in triumph. "I don't think he hates you, Joss. Want to grab some lunch?"

Theo flicked his eyes to me to see my reaction, which was to blink and then go with Knox back to the galley. Theo didn't want a new partner.

Well. That was something, at least.

In the end, there was little switching of partners. Val wanted to go back to her friend Nick, so Alaric was forced to be respectful to O. O put Alaric through the ringer before agreeing, and Alaric put up with it. He even apologized for treating her badly in the first challenges, and he sounded sincere.

We were all on our own developmental journeys.

I didn't bother to ask Theo where he thought we would land, but when Nick asked him, Theo got out his phone and worked out that we were probably going to New York City, which wasn't a surprise. It was either New York or Los Angeles.

The day passed in a blur. We were taken to the Brooklyn Bridge for a three-legged race across the pedestrian pathway; the winner would get a palatial suite at the show sponsor, the Waldorf-Astoria. Losers would get a cheap double in a hotel they didn't name.

"We'll be good at this," Theo said coolly. "I'm the tallest man and you're the tallest woman. We'll do fine."

But we didn't do fine. We couldn't get each other's rhythms. Val and Nick won the suite, with a laughing Rose and Paul right behind them. Theo and I came in fourth, and Alaric and O were last.

A cheap hotel for Alaric? Couldn't happen to a better person.

Theo's pessimism was rubbing off on me. Such an uncharitable thought showed how much the show had changed me.

For the final competition, we gathered in a meeting room off the Waldorf's gilded ballroom. Wink let us know that this week, they had a second sponsor—the Chapel of Love Wedding Chapels, "where America marries."

"And thank heavens they're around, because weddings are expensive!" Wink was everyone's jovial uncle as he explained the challenge. "You've got to plan a wedding—the location, invitations, music, food and drink for the reception, and what you're going to wear—on a budget of just five thousand dollars. And I don't think I have to tell you that New York City is one of the most expensive cities in the world! Exciting?"

There was a buzz of conversation as the pairs consulted with each other.

Wink overrode us. "Now you can see why you're fortunate to have some Cupid Cash in hand from previous wins. If you choose, you can turn a dollar-sign symbol in to me in exchange for an additional five thousand dollars for your wedding. And that is the only money you can use. No adding your own finances, Alaric." Wink tipped a waggish finger at Alaric, who shrugged. "Everyone understand? Sound good?"

"Or we can keep the Cupid Cash five thousand dollars for ourselves," Jane-Alice called.

"Yes, if that's your choice. Now, you've got through Thursday for your planning, and we'll have the mock weddings on Friday.

Unless, of course, you actually want to marry, in which case make sure you stop at the courthouse today to get your license. We want everything legal! Any questions?"

"Can we go to a Chapel of Love Wedding Chapel?" Euphoria asked.

"No, that's the one location that's off-limits. It would make the challenge far too easy on you. Let me explain why."

Wink gave us a commercial on the sponsor, which I ignored. What would Theo and I do to plan a mock wedding that wouldn't be a mockery of our once-real engagement?

When Wink finished, Theo spoke up. "If I take my camera operator with me, how far can I go?"

"Go? Well . . ." Wink looked at Shout, who shrugged and muttered into his headset. Julie whispered in Wink's ear. "If you take your camera operator, you're good to go. But any travel must be included in your budget, including the camera team's costs. And you must be back here each night to enjoy your luxurious room here at the world-famous Waldorf-Astoria."

Theo nodded. "Can we go?"

"Oh? Well, sure, I guess. Go!"

Theo stood and grabbed my hand. He gestured at Nessa and Luke. "Keep up," he said.

At least one of us had a plan.

Theo knew the confusion of the New York City subway system, and before long, we were buying train tickets for the New Jersey Transit. He herded us onto a train and found us seats where Nessa and Luke could film to their heart's content.

"Okay," I said. "Where are we going?"

"Yeah," Theo replied, working his phone. "That's right."

"The tickets say Perth Amboy," Luke said. "Should take about an hour to get there."

Luke nodded as if he was going to speak but then forgot to. I shrugged at him and Nessa, who shrugged back.

When we got to the train station, Theo already had a Lyft

waiting, big enough for the four of us plus the camera equipment. The ride wasn't long, and before long, we pulled up to a Victorian-style house in a pleasant neighborhood.

"C'mon in," Theo said, pulling keys from his jacket pocket.

"Theo, what—"

"My house. I live here."

"You brought us to—to your house?"

"I brought *you* to my house. These guys are just along for the ride."

I was off-balance, followed by cameras showing my every reaction to the world—and still somehow in Theo's house.

"No bathroom downstairs, sorry. House was built in 1919. One potty upstairs if you need it. Let me hang your coats."

Theo was acting as if this was a regular day while I walked around in a daze. I peered from the front hall into the living room, which was totally empty. Just polished wood floors and a large bay window to the street, filled with plants.

"Theo, where is your furniture? And how do you have living plants if you haven't been home in almost two months?"

Luke and Nessa were filming the house. The dining room was also empty.

"I never got around to getting anything. And the plants are my mom's. She thinks I need them. She probably came over while I was gone to water them and work her plant magic on them."

"She watered your plants?"

"Well, they're more her plants. Come on back. Anyone need the bathroom? No? Let me show you my study." He led us through a white-on-white kitchen filled with vintage appliances and through a door I assumed went to a back porch.

It didn't.

He'd converted the porch into paradise.

The room was lined in bookcases, except where tall windows let in the light from the winter-bare backyard.

The bookcases left the wall and came into the center of the room at the midpoint, turning the space into two bays. The first featured a large desk covered in computer screens. The second had two overstuffed armchairs in front of the fireplace that backed the dining room, along with a window seat, ideal for reading on a winter afternoon.

"It's a nook!" I cried. "You have a book nook!"

He smiled, and it was as if he'd seen me again for the first time in ages. "I do. I thought you'd like it. I'm going to put on coffee. Or would you like tea?"

I trailed my hands over the spines of Theo's books as if I were caressing his brain. They were organized by some system that was not apparent to me and ranged from technical manuals to adventure books for boys. Some history, some biography, a lot of textbooks, quite a few novels. "I want to stay here," I whispered.

"What was that?" Theo came back with cups for all of us. "Nessa, set up a tripod here, maybe?" He pointed out good camera angles, and Luke and Nessa did their jobs between sips of coffee. Then Theo sat me in one of the armchairs and faced me in the other. "Okay," he said.

I heaved a big breath. What was coming now? "Okay?"

He nodded. "To me, everything has a pattern. Patterns are what I understand. They're what I'm good at."

"Like the puzzle on the beach in Australia."

"Right. That was fun. But you're more complicated. It took me a while to figure out your pattern."

"I have a pattern?" I wasn't sure I liked where the conversation was going. No one would want to think they lived according to a pattern they didn't even recognize.

"A very complex pattern. And two things are important about your pattern."

"What are they?"

"Well, the first is that you think we went too fast when we got engaged."

Theo wasn't pulling any punches. We weren't just talking; we were having The Talk right now, ready or not. "Well, I do sort of think that," I said unhappily.

"I know, which is why I've brought you to my home. And we're going to have lunch with my parents, so you can meet them. Then I'll take you around my neighborhood and tell you stories about me so you can get to know me."

I gulped. "That's so—so—"

"I have a vested interest in hearing the end of that sentence, Joss. Good or bad?"

"Good," I whispered, my heart puffing up. "You want me to get to know you? You want to—to be together?"

He drew his head back as if I'd attacked him. "Well, obviously. Don't you?"

There was something in my throat. I had to cough to clear it and then took a sip of coffee that was far too hot to drink. I dribbled coffee down the front of my sweater—and on the day I was apparently meeting his mother, too—so my response took a while. But all the mopping up and fussing gave me a moment to clarify my thoughts.

"Are you aware you've been absolutely horrible to me since we were in Machu Picchu?"

"Horrible? No, I was thinking. I told you."

"Theo!" My anger suddenly boiled over. "You wouldn't even talk to me. I lay next to you each night in bed and we never—you didn't—" I looked at Nessa and Luke, side by side on the window seat and watching our discussion with great interest.

Luke let go of his mug long enough to gesture to me. *Keep going. Tell him what you think.*

I blinked for a moment, wondering if Luke was encouraging me because of the show or because he was my friend. I'd worry about that later.

"You wouldn't *touch* me. No kisses, no teasing, nothing. What was I supposed to think?"

"Oh." Theo deflated visibly. "I see. I'm not used to this. Being with someone long-term. You know—more than a hookup. What was I supposed to do? How should I have handled it?"

"Are you kidding? How about some reassurance? Tell me I shouldn't worry. Say you need some time to think and that I shouldn't—" I came to a halt, realizing he had pretty much said exactly that. I just hadn't listened. "Okay," I said at last. "Okay, maybe I overreacted."

He shook his head. "No, your mother overreacted when she suggested you get pregnant to trap me."

I shuddered. Theo had been in such deep thought, I'd been hoping he'd missed that particular scene on *Cupid's Quest*. "I'm sorry about that."

"But it does bring me to the second thing I figured out about you."

I groaned. There was more? "All right. Tell me." I braced for his words.

"It's that you'd do anything for your mother and sister, wouldn't you?"

My eyebrows met over my nose. I worked my hands against the worn velvet of the armchair. "Well, yeah. I told you. They need me."

He nodded. "I remember. Your dad left when you were twelve, and you knew you had to take care of Claire and Frieda. They are . . . I think you said fragile and frail."

"They are!" The protestations I'd wanted to make in the cave in Machu Picchu were still balled up in my throat, but if he gave me time, I'd make him understand.

But he didn't need my explanations. "I know. I know they are. And I know they need you."

His voice was sincere. He understood. Tears of relief

prickled at my eyes. "They do need me. And I need them."

"And you'd do anything for them."

"Anything."

Theo nodded. "That's what I figured out about you. It's part of who you are. Your kindness. Your need to be a peacemaker and help people."

"Those aren't bad things. Right?" My question was more tentative than I'd intended, but Theo didn't leave me hanging.

"They're the best things. They're what make you so unique and special. I wouldn't change them for the world." He smiled at me and I smiled back, embarrassed and shy and delighted. Then he shifted in his seat, and I knew he had more to say. "Tell me what you think of how your mother and sister handled that hike in Peru."

He wasn't challenging me. He wasn't making me defensive. He was asking my opinion, and I was able to answer without getting upset.

"Well, I'll admit that confuses me."

He inhaled deeply and sat forward. "I'm so glad to hear you say that. I'm so glad."

"Why?" My voice was meek, and I didn't want to consider why. Was I asking him to lead me to some unhappy truths I couldn't get to without his guidance?

"Because it means you're willing to see what *is*, not what you *want*."

I sat back, squirming in my chair. "I don't—want to—"

"—see what is," he finished for me. "I know. But Empress" —I had to swallow the lump in my throat at the return of the loving nickname—"I know you'd do anything for them."

This was leading somewhere, and it made me nervous. "As previously established," I said guardedly.

That made him grin. "What I'm thinking is, maybe your mother and your sister are confused about that hike too. Maybe they didn't realize how strong they were."

His logic was unexpected. I was pretty sure he would tell me they'd been using me, lying to me.

Instead, he was telling me they didn't realize what they were capable of either.

Theo let the thought percolate for me. He held his words while I considered.

And what he said . . . didn't make me defensive. It didn't make me angry. He was . . . perhaps . . . right.

"Maybe so," I said in a small voice.

Behind me, Nessa inhaled sharply. When I looked back, she was smiling, and Luke gave me the world's smallest thumbs-up. They were with me.

They were with us.

Theo wasn't smiling, for which I was glad. He was taking the discussion seriously. "After all these years of them believing they're frail and fragile, it's possible they could discover new strengths. New passions and interests and—and ways to live. You know?"

"Claire has terrible asthma," I began, and Theo held up a hand.

"I've done a little research. You know better than me, of course, but there are some people who have really bad asthma as a child. It's very dangerous—"

"It is! It's very dangerous!"

"I know. And I suspect the reason Claire survived is because her big sister took such good care of her." His eyes were warm and sincere. I felt seen in a fundamental way I didn't even know I'd been lacking.

The whimpers of a toddler who didn't have the air to cry. The panic in a little girl's eyes. The frantic reaching for the inhaler—and the terror when the inhaler hadn't been enough. I'd been with Claire through all of it.

"Thank you," I said quietly.

Theo nodded. "Some of those children have better control

of their asthma when they grow up—when their lungs are larger. Has Claire been tested as an adult?"

"She sees her doctor every three months."

"That's good. I'm sure that's good. She did so well on the mountain at high altitude, her doctor must be good."

I sat back, my lips pressed together in thought. "I see what you're doing."

"Do you?"

"I do. You want me to admit that Claire's asthma is better than it was."

"Well, do you think it is?"

I rubbed my hands across my face, wanting to deny what he was leading me to. Muffled by my palms, my voice was small. "I don't know."

Behind me, Luke huffed a sigh. This time, I wouldn't look to see what the peanut gallery thought. I had enough going on inside my own head.

"And you'd do anything for them. I know that." Theo's voice was calm. He'd said it so many times.

"Get to the point," I said woodenly.

"All right." I watched through my fingers and then lowered my hands as he sat forward. "It's possible your superb care has held them back."

"Held them—held them back?"

"Yeah. They think they're frail and fragile. What if they're not? If you would really do anything for them, then I think you have to let them find out."

"H-how?"

Theo looked down at his clasped hands. "Maybe back off. Let Claire get a job, perhaps."

The protests were automatic. "She can't—she couldn't—"

But she could. I knew now she could. Was I stopping her from living a full life?

"Maybe you could get your own place," Theo suggested.

"Not live at home? Bu—" I choked back the word *but*. My objections were only going to make my family weaker.

Theo watched me. My face, locked in an expression of confusion, developed aches between my eyebrows, at my jawline. When I spoke, I could only whisper. "How would I tell them?"

Nessa and Luke sighed, and Theo sat forward to take my icy hands into his warm ones.

"What if you weren't alone when you did it? Suppose you had someone who would help you with that?"

I gripped his hands in panic. "You'd do that with me?"

"If you wanted me to."

Someone to help me. And not just anyone.

Theo.

I burst into tears, and he pulled me onto his lap and held me while I cried.

Fifteen years of caregiving since my father had left. He'd wanted me to move in with him, but I couldn't leave Mom and Claire. For fifteen years, I'd been the one to make the decisions. Care for Claire. Pay Mom's bills. Make sure we had food and heat and the car had gas.

Just me.

For all that time.

And now Theo was offering to help.

I wasn't alone.

He let me cry, and Nessa got me napkins to blot my tears and (most unromantically) blow my nose. By the time my throat was painfully tight and my eyes were swollen, I was able to calm down.

I sat up and pawed uselessly at Theo's chest, where my tears had left a large damp spot. "Oh, wow."

Theo grinned. "Now that you look particularly lovely, want to go meet my mom and dad?"

41

MEET THE FAM

Xenia Fisher linked her arm with mine as soon as we got out of the car.

"Of course, I feel like I know you," Theo's mother said to me, "because I watch the show every night. Obviously. But you don't know us, so I'm going to introduce you." She looked nervously at Luke, who smiled at her from behind his camera.

Xenia set her shoulders with determination. "You boys take that out back," she called to her three sons, who were already wrestling on the lawn as if they hadn't seen each other in the Cusco airport four days ago. "People will think we're animals," Xenia sighed. She shook her head and led me up the steps to her tidy home in New Brunswick. "Well, never mind. The neighbors already think that. Herman, here's Joss. And Luke, the cameraman."

She knew Luke's name. When I grinned at him, and he shrugged. He was part of the *Cupid's Quest* story too.

Theo got his height from his father, and the dark hair and eyes from his Greek mother. (I was now in a position to confidently assert Theo's hair color, even though he continued to shave his skull every morning.) (She said coyly.)

Herman Fisher looked down at me with benign disinterest. "Oh?" he said politely.

Xenia swatted him lightly. "It's Joss!" she said. "I told you Theo was bringing her to lunch today. Have you already forgotten?"

He had one finger holding his place in a book and held it up as if to discuss it. Then he did a double take. "Why, you look like—who is it? Zenny, who does she look like?"

"Herman, you're too much. This is Joss. Theo is engaged to her, remember? From *Cupid's Quest*?"

His face cleared. "Ah, of course! My dear, how lovely that you're here. We're ardent followers of yours, I assure you. And this gentleman with the large camera? Is that thing on? Should you be filming?"

"I told him he could. Let's sit." She led me to the living room, confiding in me as we went. "I'm sorry about that. He's very intelligent, but once he gets to working on a problem, nothing else exists for him."

I laughed. "I know the type. Theo just did the same thing to me."

"I know he did!" Xenia sat me on the sofa and then plopped down next to me. "I watched on the show. I wanted to shake him—I could see how upset he was making you. I formally apologize for raising such a clueless man. Luke, make sure you get this. I apologize to Joss because Theo gets obsessed with a challenge and ignores everything in favor of resolution!" She gestured to a plate of cookies on the coffee table before us.

"I'm fine—no, thank you."

"Lunch will be ready in a few minutes. I just want the lasagna to heat up fully. Luke, I know you have to film, but could you just look into the backyard and tell me what those boys are doing? Please don't say they're wrestling in the mud."

"Um," Luke said, unsure if he should aim his camera at us or at the mayhem in the yard. "Tark is raking leaves, and Senny and Theo are throwing leaves at Nessa's camera."

"No bloodshed yet? That's good."

"No blood. They're all laughing."

"Very good. Well, things usually start peacefully, anyway. Joss, let me introduce the family."

"Well, I know the boys, of course."

"Surely. Well, I'm a nurse for a home health practice, and Herman here teaches classics at Rutgers."

He beamed at me, and I risked a stupid question. "What does it mean that you teach classics?"

"Oh, Lordy," his mother muttered. "Here we go."

But Herman's smile grew. "Well, Joss, I teach about the greatest civilizations on earth—ancient Greece and ancient Rome."

"Ah, so that's why your boys speak ancient Greek."

"I saw that!" Herman puffed with pride. "On that curious television program. They did quite well, don't you think? Of course, nobody really knows about the proper accent, but I thought they were quite intelligible."

Xenia leaned forward to recapture the conversation. "Tark is a lawyer in a family practice in West Trenton, and Senny works for the EPA in Philadelphia. All my boys are right nearby. Theo is the closest in Perth Amboy. You know Theo is our genius, of course. We had such a time with that boy, didn't we, Herman?"

"I almost became a grade-school principal," Theo's father joked. "It would have saved time instead of always having to come to the school to discuss Theo."

"He was bad?"

"Oh, Lordy." Xenia threw her hands into the air. "Fistfights every day. In nursery school! Can you imagine? The other kids were afraid of him!"

"And that's the way he liked it, the little hellion." Herman growled in memory.

"Really. What happened?"

"Well." Xenia's smile lit up the room. "His third-grade teacher pointed out that he wasn't bad—he was bored."

"He was bad *and* he was bored," Herman corrected.

"Hush, you. She advised we get him tested into the gifted and talented program, and the fighting dropped way off. Of course, around that time, Tark began to be able to punch back, so Theo began to calm down."

"He tested off the charts," his father said with a proud smile. "The hellion." He repeated his version of a curse; the word seemed to be associated with Theo in his mind.

"First it was math, and then any form of science, and then robotics! Remember the robotics days, dear?"

Herman chuckled. "The robot dog walker. It would have worked, too, if not for—"

"—the squirrel," Xenia finished with a smile, their married-forever shorthand making me envious of them and the boys they'd raised together. "And with robotics came computers, and then there was nothing that could distract him."

She smiled fondly until Herman interrupted her. "Girls. Girls could distract him. And women. Like that hootchie-mama who gave him the motorcycle."

"Hush, Herman!"

"Someone gave Theo a motorcycle?"

"Now, we don't need to discuss—"

"He was seventeen and she was, what, forty? Wildly inappropriate."

"Come with me, Joss. Let's go see if the lasagna is ready." Xenia hustled me from the room, and I muffled my laughter. We left Herman behind, muttering about older women in circulation-killing leather pants.

Lunch was served in a large, sunny kitchen. Xenia drew me

to one side and Nessa to the other. "Sit by me, girls. Those boys have never learned not to manspread. Don't you love that term? 'Manspread'?"

Theo claimed the seat to my other side and kissed my cheek. Xenia smiled with her eyes when she saw that.

"I've been hearing stories about you," I said.

His eyebrows went up. "Every word is a damn lie."

"About a motorcycle, among other things."

Tark and Senny threw down their forks and banged on each other's shoulders. "Arabella Di Giuseppi! Oh man, did I have the hots for her!"

"Get in line, you pathetic little man. I saw her first."

"She would have eaten you both alive." Theo had an evil grin.

"I would have been okay with that."

"Where is she now? How old would she be now? That was, what, twelve or thirteen years ago? She'd be—how old, Theo?"

"I dunno." Theo had gone back to his lasagna, disinterested. Below the table, he held my hand in a loose, warm grip.

"Yeah, maybe fifty? She's still hot, I'm sure. Bet she could teach you a thing or two, Shrimpy."

"Who you calling shrimpy, Mr. Zero Biceps?"

"Boys, stop that. We have guests."

"Guests with bigger biceps than Senny's."

The meal was silly and noisy and fun. The boys tormented and teased each other with glee, Xenia stayed above it all, and Herman would occasionally offer an incomprehensible statement in Greek (or maybe it was Latin), whereupon the boys would all laugh uproariously. Or hand him the salad.

It was a sharp contrast to eating at my house, where we'd grab our food and go to our separate corners. My fault, I knew. I'd started it when I was in high school and didn't have much time to study if I didn't have a book propped up in front of me as I ate.

And then college.

And then grad school.

I'd been leaving my family alone for a long time. They deserved better. We could at least eat together, instead of on trays in front of the television.

I resettled my hand in Theo's. Things were going to change. Somehow.

When lunch was over, Xenia caught Herman's eye and raised an eyebrow at him in expectation.

"Oh yes," he said. "We want to talk to you, Theo."

Theo blinked. "I thought we were talking."

"No, I mean about something important." Now everyone was looking at Theo, even his brothers, who had settled down and were waiting quietly.

"Is this an intervention or something?" Theo laughed nervously, clutching my hand.

"Sort of," Herman said. "Theo, we've enjoyed watching you on that silly show."

"It's not silly!" Xenia cried loyally.

He smiled absently at her before continuing, "We've enjoyed getting to know our son as an adult. You know, so much of a parent's view of their child is colored by their history. Marcus Aurelius said it best when—"

"Can we get on with this, dear?" Xenia asked.

"Yes, certainly. Well, we always knew you were extremely intelligent, Theo. We've always been proud of you."

Theo ducked his head. Was he blushing?

"But we didn't understand your heart. Well, your emotions. You seemed so . . . careless of others."

"A hellion?" I said sweetly. Theo growled at me, and Herman laughed.

"A hellion! Precisely. But we've had a new view of you lately. Thanks in part to your new friends." He smiled and inclined his head to me. Touched, I returned the gesture.

"A new view?" Theo was uncomfortable. Been there, done that. Just a few hours ago.

"Yes. One that tells us you *do* have a heart. You *can* care about people. Other than your own family, of course."

Theo groaned. "Is this going someplace?"

"Hush, dear. Your father is being sweet."

Theo grunted in acknowledgment.

"As I was saying, your mother and I have found that we quite like you. Don't misunderstand—we've always loved you, and we always will. But it comes as a pleasing discovery to find that we like you too."

Luke and Nessa had divided the *Cupid's Quest* gold they'd stumbled across: Luke filmed whoever was talking and Nessa never wavered from Theo's flaming-hot, ducked face.

"Gee, thanks, Dad," Theo said with overt sarcasm.

"You're welcome. And that's why we and your brothers have decided that we want to back your project."

Theo froze. "My—my project?"

"Your phone tree software thingy. We want to invest in it. You don't need those horrible partners who left you high and dry. We'll put our money into your whatever, and although we don't have quite enough to match those rapscallions, there are people we can ask."

"The partners at my law firm," Tark said.

"And there's a guy on my soccer team who's rolling in it," Senny added eagerly.

My eyes prickled. More unshed tears? What a day.

Theo studied the plate before him and then shook his head. "I can't let you do that."

"Why not?"

"We want to, sweetie." That was his mother.

"Fucking A, we do. Your big old brain and our money?" Senny said. "We're all going to be rolling in the Benjamins with your ideas, Thee."

"Just say yes," Tark advised. "I'll draw up the paperwork. We'll make it all aboveboard and legal."

Theo dropped my hand to scrub his hands across his face and then up and over his skull. He peered at his family with his hands on his head like a prisoner of war. "Thank you. Can I think about it?"

"What's to think about?" Senny asked, but Xenia shushed her youngest.

"This is a big change for him. Give him a minute. Theo, I'm going to send you home with the rest of the lasagna. You won't have to eat that nasty catered food. I'll send some to that Wink too. He's very attractive, don't you think?"

"Hey!" Herman sounded offended, and Xenia patted his cheek on her way to the counter.

Theo got us out of there at a speed I would have considered rude if it had been any other family. Xenia hugged me as Theo dragged me out the door. "Come back and visit me," she whispered. "No matter what happens with Theo. I could use a daughter in this household!"

With one visit, she'd shown me more maternal love than my mother had in a lifetime. I hugged her back, hating to leave.

By the time we got to the train, Theo's gaze had gone blank again. Unlike the ride down, Theo didn't commandeer one of the tables with four seats facing each other. This time, he nudged me into a seat and left Luke and Nessa to fend for themselves in the row ahead of us.

"Are you okay?" I asked him as the train pulled out.

He smiled at me as if we'd never met.

Oh no. Not this time.

42

NO MATTER WHAT

"Theo." I pinched the back of his hand hard, and his eyes cleared.

"Hey—ow. What?"

"You did this to me last week." Luke turned around in his seat and knelt so he could film more easily. "When you start in on this pattern recognition thing, I need to know what's going on. Please. Think out loud for a while, will you?"

He rubbed his head. "Yeah. Okay."

"So, what are you thinking about?"

"You had it right. Pattern recognition. And now I have new data, and it doesn't match the pattern, so how do I incorporate that?"

I hid my smile. "The new data is your parents offering to back your project?"

He nodded and threw his hands wide. "They don't have that kind of money. They're talking about their retirement, maybe a mortgage on their house. You don't gamble with that stuff. I can't take that money."

"They should be allowed to make that choice, shouldn't they?"

"Hell no. But that's not the point. The anomaly in the pattern is why they did it now. They've always been supportive, but they've never offered money before. So, what changed?"

He looked at me with new suspicion. "Hey, I didn't do anything."

Theo shook his head. "You're wrong. This is totally—I mean this is Joss territory from the ground up."

"What is?"

"All this." He gestured back and forth between us and then broadened it to include the whole train car. Maybe the whole world. "Being with people. Talking to them. Learning how to, I don't know, partner. Can you stop filming for five damn minutes, please?"

Luke shrugged. Nessa moved across the aisle to get the wider shot. "You didn't mind us filming when *she* went through her growing moment."

"Her growing moment," Theo repeated sarcastically. But then he shook his head in resignation. "Well, that's true."

"Ignore them," I said. "Keep explaining to me because I'm still confused."

He rolled his eyes but didn't shut down. "Look, you've kind of turned into my role model. How you work with other people, how you care about them, how you try to help everyone."

"I'm also naïve. People can take advantage of me." I wasn't saying who was taking advantage; I wasn't willing to admit that much yet. But progress comes in baby steps.

He waved my statement away. "My parents didn't offer me money until I watched your pattern—until I tried it myself. A little bit with Jane-Alice, a lot with Euphoria when we won the challenge, and then with you." He took my hand. "I thought I was a pretty good partner with you. I mean, most of the time."

"I agree," I said, admiring how hard he was working for this.

He looked to make sure I was serious and then nodded. "It

made my folks want to risk their retirement and call in favors from other people for me."

"That was nice of them."

"It was. It made me almost cry." He offered that confession casually and gripped his hand tighter with both of mine. "So what I'm trying to resolve is—" He paused. I waited, giving him time. "What I'm resolving is . . . if I hadn't been such a dick to my partners, would they have walked?"

This was such fragile territory, but he deserved the truth from me. "When you first told me about it, you said you'd been an asshole and that's why they withdrew. You seemed kind of proud of it." I hoped he could hear the apology in my voice for saying something so harsh.

But he nodded. "I was. It was—what I was supposed to—I don't know. It was just me, I guess." We sat in silence until he looked up at Luke hanging over the seat. "This isn't my fucking growth moment, is it, man?"

A corner of Luke's mouth turned up, but he didn't respond otherwise.

"Ugh," Theo groaned. "So now I'm supposed to reassess who I am in light of this new Joss world of emotion and cooperation, huh?" He lifted my hand and kissed it.

I blushed to the roots of my hair. "Is it so bad?"

"It fucking terrifies me."

I smiled. "I know. It *is* scary. When you let people in, you're giving them the potential to hurt you."

He sighed, his fingers tightening. "Like I hurt you. I'm so sorry."

"You've already learned how to not do that. We're good."

I basked in the admiration in his eyes. "You're so patient with me."

That made me chuckle. "I'd say you're the one who's been extraordinarily patient with me."

Luke laughed, and Theo glared at him.

"All right," he said. He turned in his seat to face me, tucking one foot under his leg. "Here's what I've learned. The people I let in can hurt me, but that doesn't mean they will. And I've got a better chance of not being hurt if I'm open to other people too. Is that making any sense?"

The sun was coming up in my chest. I glowed with warmth. "Makes sense to me."

"My family doesn't want to hurt me. Well, my brothers—but it's nothing I can't take." I laughed. He went on. "And I think you wouldn't want to hurt me."

"I wouldn't." My voice was hushed, but he heard me.

"That's not all, though. I mean, I also trust Knox, and Euphoria, and Roseandpaul." He slurred their names together and made me laugh again. "I like that Julie, and even Wink has his moments." His eyes looked across the aisle. "And Nessa. You're one tough lady, Ness."

Luke swung his camera to get Nessa's reaction. She was grinning.

"You're one tough lady, too, Theo."

"Thanks." He held a hand out to her, and she shook with him. Then he turned back to me. "This is what I have for you, Joss. I know you're worried that you and I fell in—" he paused, took a deep breath, and said it. "Fell in love with each other." He looked up and pinned me with his eyes. "I fell in love with you, Joss. I'm in love with you."

I inhaled so quickly, I made an undignified squeak of excitement, but he held up his hand for my silence.

"Hang on. Let me finish. I'm in love with you, but we don't know what will happen after the show is over. I want you to know that whatever happens, I'm going to be your friend."

One of my hands gripped his. The other had moved up until I clung to his wrist.

"When you're sad," he said, "I'm going to cheer you up. When you're scared, I'm going to beat people up." He ducked his head to hide a determined grin, and my hand came up to cradle his jaw. "When you're lonely, I'm going to tell you how amazing you are and how lucky I am to know you. And when you've got reasons to celebrate, I'm going to cheer for you. And with you."

Faintly, in the back of my mind, I was profoundly grateful Luke was recording the most glorious words I'd ever heard. I strained toward Theo.

He looked up at last, his dark eyes liquid and deep. "Is that something you'd like in your life? Does that sound, you know, good?"

I smiled. "It sounds like wedding vows." Clarity and rightness were ringing through me like bells. "And is that something I'd like in my life?" I paused to make sure he was listening. And I gave him his answer. "I do."

He gasped and kissed me. I craved the pressure of his mouth, the warmth of his body, but I needed to speak first. I pushed him back resolutely.

"I'm in love with you, too, Theophilus." He exhaled, his eyelashes fluttering. "So now hear me." I took a moment to gather my thoughts, and he waited, his hand trapping mine against his cheek. A grin seemed impolite under the circumstances, but I couldn't control the smile that slowly took over my expression. "I want to read in your book nook while you work on your programs. I want to hang out with your mother. I want you with me as I figure out my new relationship with my mother and sister. I want to work hard for you and me. And when it's time for bed, I want to curl up with you. Only you. Whether it's as cold and windy as Antarctica, or hot and gaspy like Egypt. As crazy as a ball for the Sun King in modern days or as fun as surfing on the Great Barrier Reef. I want to make you wear your seat belt. Because you are too precious to—"

My final words were cut off when his arms came around me

and his mouth covered mine. He inhaled me, and I filled my hands and my heart with Theo.

"Oh my god," he said when we broke apart with a shaky laugh. "How can you be so wonderful?"

I needed to verify that a nibble on his jaw would still make him shiver. "Does that sound like something you'd like in *your* life?"

The shiver did not disappoint, and there was a catch in his voice when he pulled back to look at me. "I do," he said.

I heard a slap; Luke and Nessa had exchanged a high five. I grinned at them and then leaned my forehead to Theo's. We breathed into our new closeness. He loved me. And I loved him back. How absolutely astonishing!

"Are you thinking—" I asked him, but I didn't need to finish the question. He'd picked up my thought.

"I am. Are you?"

"I am. Where could we?"

"Hang on. Let me get my phone."

We pulled reluctantly apart, and Luke shot me a question. *What?*

I shook my head. While I had his eye, I slashed my hand across my throat with a question.

"Oh, you're kidding," Luke said.

"Please?" I raised an eyebrow at Luke, my first *Cupid's Quest* boyfriend.

He heaved a huge sigh and then lowered the camera. The various lights and screens went dark. "Nessa. Shut it off. We're so going to get fired."

I stood in my seat impulsively and kissed his tanned skin.

"Hey!" Theo looked up from his phone. "I told you I loved you thirty seconds ago and you're already kissing other guys?"

"They're not filming," I explained.

Luke shook his head. "Consider it our wedding present to

you. Although if you let us film it, you'll win the competition hands down."

I looked at Theo, and we both shook our heads at the same time. "Nope. This is for us. Just for us. And you two. Luke, will you be my maid of honor?"

He laughed. "I would be delighted."

"That makes me the best man?" Nessa laughed. "Awesome! Let's do this! Where are we going?"

Theo's fingers flew. "Connecticut will allow a marriage on the same day as the license, and we can—yes, we can get a train as soon as we get to Penn Station if we run, which will get us to the Hall of Records before they close, and let me find us a justice of the—got it. The county clerk can do it." He looked up. "This could happen."

"Good," I said, sitting beside him again. "I can't wait."

"Me neither. But you don't want a big wedding? Family and dress and cake and all that?"

"Well . . ." Something was niggling at me. Then I realized what was missing. "I want your mom there. Call her."

"Now?"

"Call her," I insisted. "She can get your father and brothers, and they can meet us there. Okay? They'll keep our secret?"

Theo chuckled. "You may have saved me from an ass-whupping. She would kill me if she missed this. But if we invite my family, what about Frieda and Claire? Shouldn't we invite your family too?"

I thought about it. I thought about my mother advising me to get pregnant to "land" Theo. I thought about Claire's fanatical focus on winning a wardrobe for herself. In a micromoment, I saw exactly what would happen if I called them now.

My mother would be furious that we'd decided to marry away from the public eye; how could we win the show if we didn't put on a huge, fancy wedding for the cameras? And my sister would immediately alert the tabloids, purely for the money they'd pay.

There was no hiding from it.

They didn't care about me. About my happiness.

"We'll tell them later. They'd rather have the Cupid Cash."

Theo raised an eyebrow and sighed. "Life's lessons can be pretty cold, huh?"

I nodded. "And yet I feel like I'm protecting myself for the first time. I'm standing up for what *I* want, not what they want. And what I want is you."

Theo gathered me in a hug. "That's what I want too."

"If my mother complains," I decided, "then we'll renew our vows on our ten-year anniversary and do the whole formal thing. This time is just for us. If you're cool with that."

"Very cool. I love you, Joss."

"I love you back, Theo."

We pulled into the station. "If we're going to make that train, we've got to run. Everyone ready? Follow me!"

We were off again on another adventure.

The End

EPILOGUE

Week eight of *Cupid's Quest* was the recap week, in which America and the world were treated to the look back and asked to vote on all sorts of made-up importances. Fan Favorite. Worst Villain. Biggest Fail. Et cetera.

On the final evening, we sat in the original theater in Los Angeles, although this time, all the contestants were comfortable on chairs and sofas set up like a living room on the stage.

When Rose and Paul were announced as the first winners of *Cupid's Quest*, Theo and I were as thrilled as everyone else, but we weren't surprised. Just days after our secret real wedding in Connecticut, the impromptu (and entirely unauthorized) faux wedding we'd staged on a Manhattan street corner hadn't had anything like the love and style Rose and Paul had displayed when they pretended to get married in Nick and Val's spectacular Waldorf suite. The win was entirely justified, and I kissed Theo in quiet satisfaction for the outcome.

His clever tongue barely caressed my lip before he let me break away. No pornography on *Cupid's Quest* if we could help it. But then he frowned.

"What? What's the matter?"

He looked down at his watch. "We've still got twenty minutes to go in the show. They should have saved the final winner to the last minute. What's left?"

Alaric overheard Theo's comment and he mentioned it to O, who turned to Euphoria. Soon, all twelve contestants were buzzing to know what was going on.

Well, ten contestants. The winners were cuddled together, starry-eyed and shocked to be holding a huge commemorative check for ten million dollars.

Wink stepped back up to recapture the attention of the contestants and the audience. "Before we end, we have one more surprise to share with you, the *Cupid's Quest* audience. It seems you were all denied a peek at a very special wedding."

I froze. Theo's arm around my shoulder tightened. I kept a grin plastered awkwardly to my face, but I found Luke in the stands set up for the camera teams.

He shook his head and pointed to himself and Nessa. *Not from us*, he mouthed. But he also didn't look surprised.

Oh.

"Now, here's a member of the crew the audience might remember from the epic girls' night out in Paris—our own Julie! Come on up, Julie, and tell us what we're going to see!"

Julie, whose hair was now a remarkable shade of lavender, waved to us as she stood and joined Wink. Then she proceeded to prove inhaling was largely overrated.

"Well, Wink, as you know, the contestants have all become pretty good friends through all of this, which isn't so surprising with all they've been through, not to mention those really, really long plane trips without even a window to look out of, and—what? Right. I got to be friends with them, too, and I like them all, but Joss is, you know, she's like—everyone likes Joss, right? I mean, she's just so likable."

Theo grinned proudly at me, and I hid my head on his chest. Julie went on ... and on ... and on.

"And she and Theo, I mean, they just seem like the real thing, and my friend the casting director—there she is, hi, Bunny—she's the casting director, and she told me before we set out that there was at least one pairing she thought would be a slam dunk, and that was Joss and Theo, and it turns out she was right, you know, because, like, look at them! They could hardly be cuter together, and he's so handsome, and she's so pretty, and okay, I *am* getting to it. I was watching them during the fake weddings because they went through something pretty hard before that with Joss's family, right, and Theo not being used to not being a loner, you know, and I was worried for them, and all right, I'm getting to it. They just seemed so happy during the weddings and didn't care at all when their wedding was so small and I don't know, not like them, so okay! I'm telling it now! I went to look at really, really recent marriage licenses in New York, New Jersey, and Pennsylvania, but there was only one state nearby that allows weddings on the same day as the marriage license and that's Connecticut, and they still had the footage from the security cameras, so that's what. Okay?"

Wink, who had totally lost control of the situation, was startled when Julie suddenly stopped talking, but he rallied gamely. "They thought they'd keep their wedding a secret, but America, we've got the happy moment to show you now!"

The footage wasn't up to the *Cupid's Quest* standards, but it was enough to verify that both Theo and I had cried, his mother had clutched at my hand as she bawled, Luke and Nessa had held us up, and that the kiss when the clerk pronounced us married had been powerful and very, very loving.

"We could sue the show," I whispered to Theo as we watched our wedding like strangers.

"Nah," he replied. "We gave our consent to be filmed. Not worth it. It doesn't make it any less special for being seen by others."

"Okay," I said, my heart light. And then I was attacked by tiny Rose, who flew across the stage to wrap me in her arms.

"Why didn't you tell me?! I was going to be your bridesmaid! Did you really? Oh, I'm so happy for you!"

Paul followed her to shake Theo's hand, and that led to a spontaneous receiving line of hugs and laughter. Julie's embrace was wriggly and warm and lovely, and even Shout unbent long enough to kiss my cheek and whisper, "Congratulations."

The last person through the line was Wink. When Theo held out his hand for a shake, Wink put a comically large check in Theo's hand.

"As promised, five million for the first pair to marry. Don't spend it for a year if the marriage is fake and you're going to get divorced, because—"

"No need," Theo said, tugging me against his side. "We could spend it right now. Neither of us is going anywhere."

I joined in the happy cheer, warmed by the joy and care from those I'd come to love.

Wink turned away to face the camera and used his I'm the Host voice to quiet our excitement.

"And that's the end of the first season of *Cupid's Quest*. We hope you all enjoyed it. And as a sneak peek of season two . . ." The pause drew out, spinning our anticipation higher. Wink played it like a maestro. "The second season starts on Valentine's Day! And you'll be delighted to know that season one's fan favorites will be invited to compete again!"

Eyebrows went up across the stage. Had he announced who the Fan Favorites were?

Wink held up his hand, holding a creamy envelope with the

Cupid's Quest logo on it. "I have the result of the voting right here! We'll be glad to welcome back Fan Favorites..."

He opened the envelope and drew out the card inside. He eyed us all mischievously until Rose squeaked in annoyance.

"Knox and Euphoria! Make sure to tune into the Watch Now Network in just a few weeks!"

TEMPTING NOTE

Ever wonder how Theo solved the puzzle on the Great Barrier Reef? Happy to tell you . . . but you have to sign up for my newsletter to get the bonus scene! Isn't that manipulative of me?!

https://pruwarren.com

You can sign up, get the scene, and then unsubscribe—won't bother me at all. But stick around, why doncha? We'll have much giggles and fun!

BLISS & GIGGLES

Sign up for my newsletter, sweetpea! Go to https://pruwarren.com

My newsletter philosophy? Never take yourself too seriously. Skip the boring stuff. Amuse yourself; maybe others will be amused too.

There's generally a smoochy gift to thank you for signing up. As of this writing, I'm offering the surprise end to CUPID'S QUEST SEASON ONE—how Theo solved the puzzle on the beach.

But I swap up my newsletter lure from time to time. Go see what I'm dangling in front of you today; maybe you'll find it tasty!

ACKNOWLEDGMENTS

Kim Killion is the bomb. Not to use the parlance of the yung'uns, but seriously: This woman is astonishing. Kim is my cover designer, and how she pulls brilliance out of my vague notes is beyond me. If you want a cover designed (and for a VERY good price), you could do a lot worse than checking out the Killion Group at https://thekilliongroupinc.com/

My copy editor/proofreader is Larissa Pienkowski. She's got the sharpest eye in the business and seems to have a near-occult grasp of when to and when not to use a comma. Any mistakes in this book are very definitely my fault, not hers!

My beta readers were brilliant author Meg Napier, clever new author Glori Medina, and my sister Lexie...except Lexie never got around to giving me any notes, so I'm taking this opportunity to shame her out loud. It's what sisters do. Meg and Glori, thank you! Lexie, you're a big stugapoop. But I love you anyway.

ABOUT THE AUTHOR

Pru Warren (who is writing this in the third person as if simply too modest to toot her own horn) bores easily and thus has been a daydreamer since roughly the Bronze Age.

She is addicted to writing because in a novel, you can make things come out the *right* way. Life and karma really ought to take note. There are *better solutions* to these pesky daily annoyances!

Besides her in-the-laptop God complex, Pru laughs often and easily, loathes cooking, and plays way too much solitaire. She's plotting world domination even as you read this, as long as she doesn't have to wake up too early to accomplish it.

The Pru Warren website is an action-packed laff riot. (Well, it ought to be, anyway.) You can explore at https://www.pruwarren.com/

ALSO BY PRU WARREN

Cupid's Quest:

Cupid's Quest Season One

Cupid's Quest Season Two

Cupid's Question Season Three

The Muse Books (contemporary, not romcoms)

City Muse

Memory's Muse

Muse of the Open Road

The Ampersand Series:

Cyn & the Peanut Butter Cup

Dash & the Moonglow Mystic

Ellyn & the Would-Be Gigolo

Farrah & the Court-Appointed Boss

The Surprise Heiress Series:

Breath of Fresh Heiress

Full of Hot Heiress

Vanished Into Thin Heiress

You Decide Books:

Emma's Mission

A Spirit Guide for Anna Maria

Joan's Journal (Love Gone Viral) (out of print, alas, but available free in ebook form to newsletter subscribers) (hint, hint)

Made in the USA
Middletown, DE
22 September 2023

38811871R00215